I0670035

# THE MASTERS REIMAGINED

A Speculative Fiction Anthology

BLUE BEECH
PRESS

Front and back cover designs by Charles A Cornell

Cover images licensed from Shutterstock.com

**The Masters Reimagined/ A Speculative Fiction Anthology** -- 2nd Edition

(PB) ISBN-13: 9781734754483

(Ebk) ISBN-13: 9781393230359

(Ebk) ASIN: B08RD9GLFR

# ABOUT THE ALVARIUM
# EXPERIMENT

The Alvarium Experiment is a consortium of writers working "independently together" to create short stories based on a central premise. The name comes from the Latin *alvarium*, meaning beehive, a colony working towards a common goal for the benefit of all involved.

*The Masters Reimagined* is the third collection published by this Hive Mind of award-winning and bestselling authors. Stories from the first, *The Prometheus Saga*, collectively won seven literary awards including five prestigious Royal Palm Literary Awards from the Florida Writers Association. The second anthology, *Return to Earth*, has multiple stories that have received recognition for awards.

To follow The Alvarium Experiment's current and future projects online, please join the conversation at these websites:

Website:
AlvariumExperiment.wixsite.com/prometheussaga/alvarium
Blog:
TheAlvariumExperiment.wordpress.com
Facebook Page:
@alvariumbooks

# ABOUT THE MASTERS
# REIMAGINED

*The Masters Reimagined* is the third project of the Alvarium Experiment, a consortium of accomplished and award-winning authors. Each author was given a central premise of tackling a classic work of literature and reimagining it with the elements of speculative fiction, be they fantasy, science fiction, alternative history, or horror. The authors were allowed the freedom to interpret this premise and were unaware of the contents of each others' stories before they were individually published. The stories do not need to be read in any particular order as any story can become an entry point for the reader.

**"Shere Khan"** by Jade Kerrion. Jade Kerrion. Uncover the truth Rudyard Kipling conceals in his unforgettable masterpiece, *The Jungle Book. One-hundred rupees for the skin of Lungri...* A mysterious Chinese girl arrives in India, determined to claim the bounty on the man-eating tiger. Intrigued by her unrelenting purpose, Rudyard Kipling follows her into the jungle on a mystical adventure that will transform *Lungri—The Lame One*—into *Shere Khan—Tiger Lord*.
     Visit Jade at www.jadekerrion.com.

**"Thornfield's Ashes"** by E.J. Wenstrom. Jane finally found her happily ever after. But can she remain content as the ghost of Mr. Rochester's first wife haunts her? In this reimagining of *Jane Eyre*, Bertha has a dark secret she must share, leaving Jane to choose between her independent mind and her soul's yearning for love.

Visit E.J. at www.EJWenstrom.com.

**"Treasure In My Pocket"** by T.L. Woolsley. When Jaquie discovers the space coordinates to "treasure," she becomes the target of a mysterious one-armed stranger who is also seeking the prize. Forced to leave her father and everything familiar to her, Jaquie becomes an apprentice on a starship dispatched on a covert mission to discover what lies hidden at those coordinates.

Visit T.L. Woolsley at www.tlwoolsley.com.

**"When the Hurly-Burly's Done"** by Ken Pelham. A Depression-era theater troupe performs for Brigands Key, and the witches of Macbeth once again twist the futures of hungering souls. Sam Hawke, impatient with life, finds himself in a position to seize the moment and achieve more than he could ever have hoped. But what is the price of unbridled lust and ambition?

Visit Ken at www.kenpelham.com.

**"The Lottery"** by Kristin Durfee. As Earth is dying, Eve Line may have found a way to leave the doomed planet. The world's best and brightest have fled to Mars, but as the last ship is ready to depart, a lottery will be held for the remaining residents to have a chance at a new life. Eve thinks her plan can succeed, but at what cost to her family, and herself? This modern retelling of James Joyce's "Eveline" asks an age-old question: where should your loyalties lie?

Visit Kristin at www.kristindurfee.com.

**"Pupak and the Great Fish"** by John Hope. Forcefully taken from his Amazon rainforest home, Pupak is faced with helping the very Brazilian white men who slaughtered his village people. But the gods are angry that he's running from his destiny and after superstitious sailors toss him to the sea in order to calm a ranging storm, he is swallowed by a great, metal beast the white men call a submarine.

Visit John at www.johnhopewriting.com.

**"The Count of the Alician Apocalypse"** by Bria Burton. On a visit to Stonehenge, a handsome stranger offers Alice an escape from the man who has been following her by way of a magical portal in one of the monoliths.

Visit Bria at www.briaburton.com.

**"Annie Karenina"** by Veronica H. Hart. Elizabeth Killington, recently widowed at age twenty-seven, flies to England to claim her late husband, Lord Horace Killington's estate. She finds she not only owns a grand manor house in the country, but also the "crowds of people" who made Lord Killington avoid home for many years. As she meets and recognizes characters from her favorites books, and some she never heard of, she learns a wonderful secret from her lady's maid, Bridget. Is it possible that all stories can have a happy-ever-after ending?

Visit Veronica at www.veronicahhart.com.

**"The Brazilian Millionaire's Butler"** by Scott Michael Powers. Young, beautiful, and mysterious, Olívia arrives in Rio de Janeiro in 1944 too interested in keeping the party going to worry about the past she fled in America, the foreign world she entered, the true nature of the Brazilian millionaire she married, or the world war. When they drive her into depths of deception and treachery, Olívia is all but isolated. But she is not totally alone, for Brazil is a magical place. And because of that magic, the millionaire's butler knows he must become Olívia's champion, even at the risk of destroying himself.

Visit Scott at www.facebook.com/ScottMichaelPowers.

**"Regarding Mr. Bulkington"** by Elle Andrews Patt. As the *Pequod* plunges into the hunt for Moby Dick, Ishmael discovers the power behind Captain Ahab's mastery of the sea lies within the mysterious skills possessed by Mr. Bulkington. Are some secrets worth keeping to the grave?

Visit Elle at www.elleandrewspatt.com.

# Introduction

"*The ascendancy over men's minds of the ruins of the stupendous past, the past of history, legend and myth, at once factual and fantastic, stretching back and back into ages that can but be surmised, is half-mystical in basis. The intoxication, at once so heady and so devout, is not the romantic melancholy engendered by broken towers and moldered stones; it is the soaring of the imagination into the high empyrean where huge episodes are tangled with myths and dreams; it is the stunning impact of world history on its amazed heirs.*"
—Rose Macaulay, *The Pleasure of Ruins*

What makes a Master of Fiction? Who are they if not the ones who inspire entire generations? What are their works if not doors to living worlds they have created, to which everyone is invited? We all enter and come away with our own experiences, our own responses, and our own wonderment. And we sometimes ask ourselves after reading, what if? What then? What's next?

These questions bring life to these words decades, sometimes centuries, after they were written, giving wonder and adventure to millions of readers. The answers can lead to further exploration of the stories, revealing elements even the masters never envisioned.

Enter these familiar worlds with fresh eyes. Discover the speculative elements of science fiction, fantasy, and the supernatural that the masters might have only hinted at. What would Kipling's India be like if it were controlled by the more mystical forces of nature? How would a James Joyce story hold up in a future, dystopian setting? What if Alice's rabbit hole was a dimensional portal?

The Masters earned the title not only because their work exemplifies the best of a given time period, but because their stories inspire us all to open our hearts and explore.

—The Authors of *The Masters Reimagined*

# SHERE KHAN

### JADE KERRION

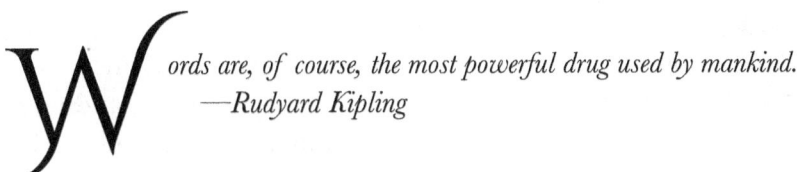 ords are, of course, the most powerful drug used by mankind.
—Rudyard Kipling

JULY 23, *1886*

"EXCUSE ME, MR. KIPLING?"

Her shadow fell over his leather-bound journal, blocking the glare of the mid-afternoon sun. Rudyard looked up; his instinctive smile conceded to a frown when he saw only a Chinese girl, scarcely older than a teenager.

She held a yellowed copy of the *Civil and Military Gazette.* "I have a few questions about your article." Although she wore the shapeless black tunic favored by Chinese coolies, her careful English hinted at a privileged education, or at least a great deal of exposure to Christian missionaries. Her snub nose and yellow tan stood out among the dark-skinned Indians and pale-skinned British in Simla, the summer capital of British India.

His mind still on the story he had been plotting, Rudyard grabbed the newspaper and glanced at the three-week-old article she had circled in red ink. *One-hundred rupees for the skin of Lungri.* "Article" was, in fact, too generous a term; the piece consisted of five lines in the classifieds section, detailing the bounty offered by the city. He had grabbed the snippet off the government archives to fill in an empty spot on the page. "What do you want to know?"

"Where can I find this tiger?"

He eyed her. "There are easier and safer ways to earn a hundred rupees. You're too small to be hunting man-eating tigers."

"Where has the tiger been seen?"

"I don't know." Unless the tiger ventured into the city, he had no reason to care, either. Two weeks into his month-long vacation, Rudyard had settled into the relaxed routine of early morning tea and long conversations with the British officers, gentlemen, and ladies who turned the hill station into the center of power and pleasure. He spent afternoons drowsing on rattan recliners, filling his journal with his stories.

Stories the girl had interrupted.

He slapped the newspaper into her extended hand.

Without saying thank you or goodbye, she walked away. Rudyard watched as her skinny figure cut through the crowds in an unwaveringly straight line, expecting all to give way to her—men and women, British and Indian—and they did, the furrows on their brows more puzzled than angry. She shunned conversation with the British in favor of brief exchanges with the Indian servants. Expansive hand gestures pointed in varying directions, but most of them directed her to the city's southern gate. The terror of Lungri—the Lame One—clearly ran rampant among the Indians who lived in the villages in south-eastern Rajputana. Her conversation with a white-clad Indian boy carrying a tray lasted longer; after which, she strode away, not speaking to anyone else.

The Indian boy continued on his way, coming up to Rudyard.

"Your tea, sahib." He spoke in deferential tones as he set the saucer and teacup on the small table next to Rudyard's chair.

"That girl. What did you tell her?"

"She asked about the hunting range of Lungri, the tiger. I told her he stalked the villages between the river and the mountains. I saw his paw prints not two mornings ago." Lines creased his brow. "Did I do wrong, sahib?"

"No, of course not." Rudyard's thoughts—his reporter's instinct, his storyteller's hunch—churned into a tangle. "Did she say why she wanted to know?"

"No, sahib." The Indian boy looked in the direction the girl had gone, but she had already vanished into the crowd, her course southbound.

THE GIRL WAS a head shorter than everyone around her, but she was not hard to follow as she hiked through the fields, stopping occasionally to speak to passing villagers. Gesticulating hands directed her to the foothills where grassland gave way to jungle. Without hesitation, she stepped over the boundary and passed into a different world.

Rudyard had tramped along the edges of civilization before, where the tangle of undergrowth thickened into impassable paths beneath a dense leaf canopy, where light melted into the speckled darkness of the Indian jungle.

He had never actually crossed the line.

He paused and glanced over his shoulder at the setting sun. Amber rays spread over the distant city of Simla, infusing it with a golden glow. The jungle in front of him seemed equally untouched by civilization and by light.

He grimaced so hard his jaw ached. Time to dispense with this nonsense and return to his inn, where his hot tea and warm dinner awaited him. He could spend the evening in lively conversation around a blazing hearth.

After all, what kind of person would chase down a tiger, alone, armed with nothing?

*A girl who asked question but gave no answers.*

Rudyard drew a deep shuddering breath. *Just a few steps.* He could turn around at any time. He would easily find his way out.

Head spinning, heart thumping, he ignored the churning knot in his stomach as he crept into the Indian jungle. The dense curtain of leaves swallowed the faint light of dusk. The scent of the earth, rich with rot, swarming with life, permeated his senses. Night sounds—the buzzing wings of insects and the rumble of a toad—rose in uncoordinated symphony.

Warm air brushed against the back of his neck. He jumped, spinning around so quickly he stumbled back.

"Why are you here?" The shadow of leaves slashed across her features like the distinctive markings of a tiger.

"You…startled me."

Her calm expression did not change. Her precise British accent entirely at odds with her Chinese peasant appearance, she said, "You are not safe here."

"And you are?" She was shorter, smaller, and younger than he—although he could not tell for certain. The youth of Asians seemed to last until well into middle age.

"You should go back, Mr. Kipling."

"Why are you hunting tigers?"

"I am not hunting a tiger. I am looking for…Lungri."

"Why?"

She shrugged and turned away.

She did not bother to lie or make something up.

His eyes narrowed against her back when she slipped into the jungle, the darkness swallowing her up as if she were part-*raaksha*. Rudyard scowled. His imagination was getting ahead of him. Half-demon, indeed. She was just a girl, albeit a rather odd one. "Wait, where are you—"

The jungle warbled around him; he could no longer hear her footsteps. He was the trespasser here, a gentleman in a realm ungoverned by British laws. Rudyard drew a deep breath but could not steady his racing pulse. He could turn back, retrace his steps. With luck, he would only be an hour or two late for dinner.

The jungle wove its insidious rhythm against the beat of Rudyard's heart.

Two hours later, he had to admit he was lost, befuddled by the maze of trees and bushes. He caught glimpses of the sky through the leaf cover, but could not see enough stars to point his way. Rudyard slumped against a tree trunk. Waiting until morning was his best bet. His friends clearly were not alarmed enough to look for him; he did not see the bright flare of torches or hear the shouts of men feigning lordship in a place that cared nothing for people.

Rudyard hugged his legs against his chest. He should have thought harder and planned better. A warmer coat would not have been amiss.

That, a great deal more common sense, and a better honed instinct for self-preservation.

*Only eight hours until dawn.*

He jolted at a flicker of motion and caught a glimpse of a long, furry tail disappearing under a bush. His skittering heartbeat steadied. A mongoose, or a really large rat. Nothing to worry about.

A low rasp, like the friction of scales against the rough bark of a tree, sashayed to the rhythmic beat of the jungle's night song.

Fear shuddered down his spine. Not snakes. Anything *but* snakes.

All his years in India should have inured him to snakes, but between the coldness of their scales and the sinuous glide of the movements—*death in motion. Lucifer.* Rudyard squeezed his eyes shut and willed the reptile, invisible in the darkness, away. If he did not move…if he tried not to breathe—

The grating sound slithered closer. He squeezed his hands into fists, his fingertips so cold he could scarcely feel them. His lungs burned from shortness of breath.

Several moments, perhaps even minutes, passed before he realized that silence surrounded him.

Absolute silence.

The skin on the back of his neck prickled.

Whatever it was, *it* was in front of him.

Did he want to die with his eyes open or closed?

Willpower forced his eyes open slowly, the crack widening to a slit.

Blackness melted into gray. The details of the surrounding jungle emerged.

*Nothing.* His shoulders sagged. Nothing out there.

Hot, humid air, infused with the metallic stench of blood and the rancid fumes of rotting flesh, wafted against his neck.

He swiveled slowly. White fur streaked through slashes of orange and black appeared in his peripheral vision.

Some part of his mind stuttered. *Tiger...*

His body seemed no longer under his control. Dread turned him until the only thing he could see—the only thing that filled his vision —were the unblinking amber eyes of a Bengal tiger.

He had never been this close to a tiger.

He, the writer, found the Lord of the Jungle beyond the realm of description, beyond the power of words. The expression in its golden eyes transcended time.

*Like a god...*

*No.*

*It can't be real.*

Rudyard's shuddering breath shattered the perfect reverence of that moment.

Animal instinct jolted into the tiger's eyes. Its snarl bared gleaming incisors.

The girl's quiet voice forestalled the tiger's leap. "*Zūnjìng de fùqīn.*"

The tiger's massive head—as large as a man's torso—snapped in her direction.

She was like a ghost—her black hair and clothes blending into the shadows, only her face and hands visible, unnaturally ashen in slivers of the moon's pale light.

Rudyard held his breath as the tiger stalked toward the girl, each paw soundless against the carpet of rotting leaves and crackling twigs. Only then did he notice the limp in the tiger's stride.

Tiger and girl stood four feet apart, less than half the length of the creature. Even lame, it could have covered the distance in a half-hearted pounce.

"*Zūnjìng de fùqīn.*" The girl repeated softly. She lowered herself to her knees and touched her forehead to the ground.

The tiger stood as still as a marble statue but for the swish of its tail. It did not move until the girl crawled forward to stand abreast of its head. She reached out so slowly that she seemed scarcely to move at all. The palm of her hand brushed against the thick fur. Something clinked—metal?

The tiger roared. The vast sound vibrated through Rudyard, rattling his skull.

The animal swiped out a heavy paw, knocking the girl onto her back. Its claws raked across the side of her face, from forehead to chin. Jaws clamped on her shoulder, lifting her off the ground with no more effort than a large dog toying with a rag doll.

"No!"

The stick Rudyard flung at the tiger bounced off the animal's hindquarters. The creature should scarcely have felt so tiny an impact, but it dropped the girl and twisted around. Its face tugged into a garish smile before expanding fully into a snarl.

Rudyard could not swallow through his clogged throat.

The tiger recoiled, the prelude to a pounce.

A sibilant hiss breathed from the darkness of the jungle. A blunt-nose rock python launched itself from shadow. Its heavy coils slammed into the tiger, knocking the animal off its feet.

The tiger roared. Faster than a thought, it scrambled upright and chased the massive snake into the undergrowth.

*What the*—Rudyard shook off the shock of the stillness following the battle. The girl! He hurried forward but before he could reach her, something glinted in the deep shades of the jungle. Large and curved, like elephant tusks—

The faint reflection of light suddenly vanished and something—someone—stepped out of the jungle.

The newcomer stared at him. "Who are ye?" he asked, his voice heavy with a Scottish accent.

"Rudyard—Rudyard Kipling…"

The man, in his late forties and crowned with a shock of red hair, smiled. "Daimh Faerrleah. Ye are a long way from safety, Mr. Kipling."

*So are you*, Rudyard would have retorted, except that the Scotsman looked quite at ease in the jungle. Daimh knelt by the unconscious girl and made a low sound of disapproval. "Fool of a tiger."

Rudyard looked over Daimh's shoulder. His stomach churned at the bright smear of blood over her face and arm. "Is she alive?"

"The lass needs tending, but she will live if all goes well." Daimh gathered the girl in his arms and carried her deeper into the jungle. He did not hesitate or look around. He seemed utterly certain of his direction and indifferent to the darkness around him.

The girl, Rudyard recalled, had walked like that too, with confidence that bordered on arrogance.

If Daimh traveled along a path, Rudyard could not see it, but he followed the man because he had little choice. Between tigers and snakes, he would rather take his chances with the odd Scotsman. He quickened his pace to keep up with Daimh. He cast an anxious glance at the girl's bloodied face. In Daimh's large arms, she looked even smaller and younger, but neither fragile nor vulnerable. The incongruity entangled his thoughts. "Do you know who she is?"

"No, but I have a guess. If I'm right, the moment of reckoning has finally come for Shere Khan."

Not Lungri—not the *Lame One*—but Shere Khan. *Tiger Lord.*


RUDYARD SAT by the girl's bedside, silent and watchful as several Indian women smeared finely ground leaves and herbs over her open wounds before covering them with strips of clean cotton. Ruddy coals beneath a pot-bellied stove warmed the large room and cast a gentle glow over the polished wood furniture. Wide-eyed Indian children, cheeks chubby and gazes alert, hovered near the open door, their lilting voices polished with the accents of the upper class.

In a tiny village in the middle of…*literally*…nowhere.

It did not make sense.

Rudyard squeezed his eyes shut against the disorientation, but opened them again when one of the women spoke in English. "Would you like some food and hot tea, sir?"

"Yes, please," he murmured, his confusion complete when they served a meal finer than any he had seen in Calcutta's best dining establishments. The aroma of the fragrant vegetable curries dazzled with the complexity of many exotic spices. The flatbread was freshly made from finely ground wheat, and perfectly baked over an open flame. He glanced up to find Daimh looking at him with an amused smile.

The Scotsman shrugged. "I have had no luck convincing them to add meat to their diet, but with meals like these, it is easy to forget what ye are missing."

Scales rasped against the ground.

Something—changed. Rudyard stiffened against the suddenly charged atmosphere. The children backed away from the door, their heads bowed in silent respect. The shadows shifted and reared. For an instant, the glow of the stove cast light on the blunt nose of a massive snake.

Rudyard's eyes narrowed, blinked, but saw only a young Indian woman in a copper-colored, gold-trimmed silk saree. Her braided hair coiled over her head like a crown.

"Nagarani." Daimh's voice was low and reverent.

Surprised to see the Scotsman standing straight with his right hand on his heart, Rudyard scrambled to his feet.

Nagarani's direct gaze pierced him. "Welcome to my home, Mr…"

"Kipling. Rudyard Kipling."

"What are you doing here, Mr. Kipling?"

He gestured at the unconscious Chinese girl. "She asked me about Lungri. I followed her into the jungle."

"What is her name?"

Rudyard blinked off the vertigo of his distorted reality. Nagarani possessed none of the deferential silence of Indian women in the presence of English men. *And the snake*—had he actually seen it? His mind stuttered; fear clenched his spine. "I don't know. Do you?"

Her brown-eyed gaze followed his. "I suspect she's the one I've been expecting for the past ten years."

Daimh's snorted. "They dinna move fast."

"She's hardly out of her teens," Nagarani said.

"Are ye suggesting that they have been waiting for her to grow up, to be old enough—" Daimh wore a ferocious scowl. "That is cold, even for them."

The Chinese girl's eyes flickered open.

Swift and silent, Nagarani was by the girl's bedside even before Kipling realized she had moved. "You are safe," the Indian woman said simply. "Among those who know."

Some—not much—of the hostility and suspicion faded from the girl's eyes. She sat up slowly, only wincing faintly. "I am Hu Jia."

"You are welcome here."

"You know why I am here."

"It is finally time for the Tiger to move on."

Hu Jia nodded.

"We've been expecting you for a long time."

"All these years, why did you do nothing?"

Nagarani's shrug was as graceful as the sinuous sway of a snake. "It was not our place to do so. We do not interfere with the business of the Yang. We would not take the life of Shere Khan lightly."

The girl straightened. Her chin lifted. "You have to."

Nagarani's brown eyes fixed on the girl, but unlike Rudyard, the girl did not flinch from the penetrating gaze. "We do not interfere with the business of the Yang," Nagarani repeated.

"You know the laws. I cannot raise my hand against the Tiger."

Daimh's huge presence loomed over Kipling. His shadow fell over the girl. "So ye would have us do ye evil work?"

Nagarani held up her hand. "Not evil. Necessary, but still, not our task."

Hu Jia's voice trembled. "The Tiger's lack of control, of aware-ness, is dangerous for all of us—and especially to *you*, so close to your sanctuary. There is already a government bounty on the

Tiger's head. How long before the English, perched high on their elephants, storm the jungle while their Indian minions wave flaming torches? And if—*when*—he is killed, can we risk—" She darted a glance, simultaneously suspicious and condemning, at Rudyard. "—knowledge falling into their hands?"

Daimh scowled. "It still dinna make it our business."

Nagarani waved his objection away. "She is right. We are at risk, all of us, and because of my proximity, I, most of all. If the true nature of Shere Khan is revealed…" She sighed softly. "We will help you."

Daimh's jaw dropped. "But kill Shere Khan?"

Rudyard's gaze flicked to the ruddy Scotsman who looked pale beneath his outrage.

Daimh shook his head. "We canna. We would start a war—"

"No," Hu Jia said emphatically. "The tigers stand with you, as do many of the other clans."

"The dragons?" Daimh asked pointedly.

Hu Jia dropped her gaze.

Daimh glared at Nagarani. "Ye canna defy Lord Yang."

"Cannot?" Nagarani's voice dropped to a silky hiss. "We do not direct our lives according to the pleasure of the Yang, let alone the Dragon Lord. Shere Khan's absence has allowed the dragons to grow strong, to imagine themselves unchallenged." She looked at Hu Jia. "Perhaps it is time for the tigers to return to their customary role as challengers for leadership of the Yang. A bit of infighting among the Yang would not be amiss for us here, living our quiet lives on the fringes of society."

Daimh snorted a reluctant chuckle. "Right ye may be. They will be too busy to interfere with us." He shot Hu Jia a grumpy look. "Seems wrong, though, that she help none, when this is *her* doing."

"Hu Jia…" The girl's name flowed from Nagarani's lips like the gentle fall of water from a brook. "*Beautiful tiger.* You are the tiger's child, are you not?"

The girl nodded, and for the first time, she looked stricken.

"Born in the year of the tiger. A contender for the animal spirit," Nagarani continued. "Ten years ago, you would have been too young to compete and win, but now, you can."

Hu Jia nodded.

Nagarani inclined her head. More than acknowledgement, it might even have been respect. "We will act where you cannot." She looked at Daimh. "We will kill Shere Khan."

Rudyard looked at the Scotsman, expecting him to disagree vehemently with the Indian woman more than ten years younger than he, but the older man lowered his head in submission. "As ye will, Nagarani. But how? Shere Khan is not who he was, but he is still wise, shrewd, and the greatest predator in the jungle."

Nagarani was silent for a moment, and when she spoke, her words rang with finality. "We lead him into a trap."

"He is too canny. Shere Khan canna fall for a trap."

"He will. Hate overpowers even his animal instincts."

"What do we use to bait the trap?"

A smile curved Nagarani's lips. "Mowgli."


RUDYARD JERKED AWAY from the hanging coils of a snake, then flushed when he realized it was only a loop of a thick vine draped from a low branch. He bit back an irritated curse as he followed Nagarani, Hu Jia, and Daimh through the thick undergrowth. "What or who is this Mowgli?" he asked.

"A twelve-year old boy orphaned by Shere Khan ten years ago." Nagarani said. "The boy fled when Shere Khan killed his parents. He found his way to a den of wolves. They raised him."

"A boy raised by wolves?" Rudyard's eyes widened. "That is an amazing thing."

"The boy is remarkable," Nagarani continued. "He possesses an uncanny understanding of the ways of the jungle, and a human's capacity for complex thought. If he does not lose either, he will be a force to be reckoned with, but for now, he's just a boy, with a boy's tendency to be both foolish and reckless."

"Are we going to the wolf den to retrieve him?"

"No." Nagarani looked up. A large bird wheeled overhead, its cry riding on the wind. Woman and bird seemed to regard each other, unspoken words carrying through the silence. The kite twisted sharply and soared toward the west. Nagarani continued speaking, "The Bandar-log—the monkeys—have taken him to Thand Thikaanon."

"The…" Rudyard sputtered. Indignation was easier than confusion. "Next, you'll be telling me the little birdie said so."

"The bird did indeed say so. Ran, however, would be insulted that you referred to her as a little birdie. She's large and inordinately proud of her feathers."

His jaw dropped, scarcely managing to keep his voice steady. "Who are you people?"

"Who said anything about people?" Nagarani walked ahead, gliding through the jungle with no more effort than in her home.

Daimh chuckled as he fell back to walk alongside Rudyard. "Dinna mind her. She is still a woman, and like most of them, enjoys toying with a man's mind."

*Still a woman?*

Rudyard's already shaky grip on reality wobbled.

The brisk pace did not allow him to pepper them with questions. Rudyard huffed, struggling to conceal his exertions, especially from Hu Jia who, despite her recent injuries, kept up easily. Infrequent stops made the day-long trek through the jungle marginally tolerable. On one such break, Rudyard staggered to the river and splashed water over his flushed, sweaty skin.

"Here."

Concealing his surprise at the first friendly gesture on her part, he accepted the cotton cloth Hu Jia held out and wiped his face. "Thank you." Fixing a smile on his lips, he asked, "What part of China are you from?"

"Tai Shan, a mountain in northeast China."

"You speak English well."

"My clan owns tea plantations. We trade with the European merchants. I speak English and French."

"I thought you might have learned it from the Christian missionaries."

Her nose twitched. "They are stooges, pawns of their imperial governments. They lull the people with talk of forgiveness and love while their agents lie and steal."

"That's…a harsh view."

"That's reality."

He scowled at her. "Trade is not theft."

"It is when you enslave the minds, wills, and bodies of a nation just so that your people can enjoy their afternoon tea." She spun sharply, her braid swinging out to slap him in the face, and stalked away.

Daimh grunted. "Let her go. Ye will never be able to convince her that the Opium Wars were fairly fought."

"The Opium Wars? But that was years ago."

"For some, the wounds are not healed. Her father—" His lips pursed, and he fell silent.

"What about her father?" Rudyard asked.

"It's why we're here today."

Rudyard's eyebrows drew together. "Looking for Mowgli?"

"The threads of life interweave, not often in ways we expect. It is the nature of the Yin and the Yang. Life always comes full circle— light balancing darkness, death balancing life."

"Over here," Nagarani called. She tugged back the leaves of an ashoka tree. In the distance, red towers rose like steps over the tree tops.

"What is that?" Rudyard asked.

"Thand Thikaanon."

Rudyard's rudimentary Hindi translated the words as *Cold Lairs.* "But it's a *city*, in the *jungle*."

"A maharaja's palace, abandoned several centuries ago."

"What's in there?"

"Mowgli." Nagarani shrugged. "And an army of bad-tempered monkeys led by Louie."

"Louie? There's another man in there?"

"Not quite." She straightened and turned. Her brown eyes searched the shadows that surrounded them, and she made a beckoning gesture with her fingers.

A pair of yellow eyes appeared first before the darkness peeled back from the form of a black panther. A grey bear shuffled forward.

Nagarani's voice was cool. "Bagherra. Baloo."

The panther sat and for a moment, lowered his head to his paws.

Rudyard frowned at the gesture of respect. Who was Nagarani that all living beings, even wild animals, deferred to her?

The bear's snorts blended with moans, the sounds emphasized by the waving of a long-clawed paw.

"These are Mowgli's companions," she said. "They set out to rescue him but were driven back by the monkeys."

Rudyard noticed the deep scratches and bleeding wounds on the panther and the bear.

"What do the monkeys want with Mowgli?" Rudyard asked, and immediately felt ridiculous for asking. What would any monkeys want with a human child?

"Louie thinks Mowgli knows the secret of fire," Nagarani said.

The last thing he had expected was a logical, coherent answer to what he had thought was an absurd question. "Does he?"

Nagarani shrugged, the motion impossibly graceful. "It doesn't matter." She flicked her wrist, and the panther and bear faded back into the jungle.

"Are we still going to find Mowgli?" Rudyard asked.

"Of course."

"Pardon my asking, but if a panther and a bear could not win against an army of vicious monkeys—despite claws, fangs, and outweighing us several times—how are *we* supposed to?"

Daimh roared with laughter. Nagarani smiled, and even Hu Jia chuckled softly. "Because…" Nagarani said. "Humans are notoriously incapable of admitting defeat, and in the final count, we are humans."


"YE SHOULD WAIT HERE."

Rudyard looked at Daimh askance. "It seems…ungentlemanly."

"Excuse me?"

He gestured at Hu Jia who was clambering up the stones with the grace of a monkey. Nagarani had chosen to scale the fortress from the north, and had already vanished into the surrounding jungle. "The two ladies aren't holding back."

"Nagarani is a queen, not a lady—the difference is profound—and Hu Jia would be offended if ye called her a lady. Fact is—" Daimh looked Rudyard over. "Ye should never have left Simla."

"You sound remarkably like the voice in my head." Rudyard managed a tight smile. "You, too, are a long way from home."

"It is customary for the heads of the clans to pay their respects to Nagarani. This year it was my turn." Daimh watched Hu Jia's progress up the cliff before starting his own climb up the southern face. "Stay close to me, and ye will be all right."

Rudyard drew a deep breath and followed Daimh, careful to use the same hand and footholds. Small rocks tumbled away beneath his grasp, but the sound of cascading sand and pebbles were swallowed by the cacophony of the jungle. "Quiet now," Daimh cautioned before he hauled himself over the ledge. Rudyard grabbed Daimh's proffered hand and scrambled over the edge.

For a moment, both men studied the vine-covered edifice. It was less colorful and more colossal than any of the Hindu temples Rudyard had seen in his travels around India. The white stone reflected the glow of the setting sun, alternately golden and crimson. The creeper vines curling around the columns choked them, squeezing until the pillars seemed engorged with blood.

Even from that distance, the abandoned palace was alive with movement. Monkeys—macaques, langurs, and gibbons—leapt across fallen columns and gamboled up the broken steps, like ants swarming over sugar crystals.

Rudyard's heartbeat skittered. "That's far more than I expected."

"They are not the problem. Their king, Louie is."

"They have a…king?"

"The ill-gotten half-animal offspring of an avatar."

Rudyard's mind tripped over a word he understood in principle, and yet did not understand in context. *Avatar.* "What…do you mean?"

Daimh did not take his gaze from the temple. "Many years ago, the monkey avatar visited India. It is rumored that he enjoyed some of the local flavors while in animal form."

"I'm not following."

Daimh turned to Rudyard. "The Yang avatars are reckless, irresponsible bastards, and the result—Louie—is a perversion of nature. It should never have been allowed to live."

*Still not following*—but Rudyard heard the snap of irritation in Daimh's voice. "So what do we do?"

"We follow the plan. We find Mowgli and get him out."

"And the monkeys? And their king?"

"Nagarani will handle them."

"But she's—"

"Hu Jia is approaching the palace." Daimh pointed to a slight shadow pressed close to the rocks. "Let's go."

They crept over the ruins of a stone wall and around the columns, some tumbled in pieces, others still standing tall, making their way into the inner courtyard. Steps led down to a square, like the sunken center of a pool, before rising again on all sides. The edifice of the ancient palace faced east to greet the first rays of dawn. Sprawled behind it was a vast complex of smaller, interconnected buildings.

Rudyard searched for glimpses of Hu Jia or Nagarani, but could not see either of them. "What do we do?"

"I am the diversion."

"And what do I do?"

"Stay here. If the sixteen *narakas*—"

"*Naraka?*"

"Hell."

"There are sixteen hells?"

"In Buddhism, yes. If the fight does not go our way—"

"Charge in?" Rudyard asked.

"No. Run. It is easier to save ourselves than to save ye too."

Rudyard was not certain if he was grateful for such consideration or insulted at having been told that he was a hindrance in the battle.

Daimh rose and strode toward the temple, not bothering to remain concealed. The chittering of monkeys fell briefly silent, before uniting in an outraged howl. They leapt off their perches and charged toward Daimh. The air around Daimh shimmered and for an instant, Rudyard caught a glimpse of sleek blue-black hide and upward sweeping horns, before the Scotsman vanished into the palace.

The screams of the monkeys morphed from anger to terror. Smaller monkeys cascaded from the palace, hooting and leaping for the safety of the rooftops. A thunderous bellow, more jarring than that of a full-grown bull elephant, rang out.

Something else shrieked, the resonance part-human, part-animal. The sound clutched Rudyard's shoulders and shook him until his spine rattled. The vast outcry of monkey screams and howls rose alongside, a symphony rising to a crescendo. Rudyard leapt to his feet and ran.

Not away from the sound but toward it.

Rudyard burst into a vast hall supported by columns on all sides. In the middle of the hall, Hu Jia, a boy crouched at her feet and matching daggers in her hands, slashed at the monkeys attacking her. Rudyard's stare, however, was drawn to the buffalo. Slate blue, almost black, it gleamed in the beams of light shafting through the broken roof. Man-tall at the withers, it was the largest swamp buffalo Rudyard had ever seen, and it was not a lazy eyed creature munching on wet grass. It snorted visible puffs of air. Its heavy hooves crushed the bones of monkeys and vibrated the stone floor. The tips of its sweeping horns dripped blood.

A part of Rudyard's stunned mind screamed in recognition. *Daimh?*

The ghastly part-animal, part-human cry shrieked again. Rudyard's gaze fixed on the far end of the room as something emerged from the back of the palace. Larger than an ape, it seemed deformed—its arms too short, its legs too long. Its face was equally misshapen—forehead protruding, snout flattened. *Almost…*

Rudyard's muscles tightened around his spine...*Almost human.* Fury further deformed the creature's features. The massive humanoid monkey threw its head back and howled.

Monkeys swarmed in through the holes in the roof, around the columns, from all sides, to surround Rudyard, Hu Jia, the buffalo, and the boy, Mowgli. The monkeys pushed and shoved, chittering impatiently, as if waiting for a single command to be unleashed.

A familiar, quiet voice dropped silence over the restless creatures. "You have interfered in the affairs of men for too long."

Rudyard's glance snapped toward the northern wall of the palace. Nagarani stood on the upper level of the palace, her brown skin golden in the shaft of sunlight.

He was staring at her when she transformed—skin mottling into the recognizable brown and golden stripes of the Indian python, her body lengthening to coil upon the terrace. The monkeys—and he—stared transfixed as the python lowered herself to the ground. If she were floating, she could not have been more graceful. The shifting coils seemed endless—at least forty feet long—heavily muscled, and flawlessly fluid as she wove, her blunt nose swaying.

No Indian goddess could have been more captivating, more enthralling.

The humanoid monkey's gaze remained fixed on her, his outrage silenced, his body submissive, as her coils looped around its body. The smaller monkeys did not leap to its defense. They were as hypnotized as their king.

Rudyard did not move either until someone grabbed his upper arm and shook him harshly. Rudyard blinked and found himself staring into Daimh's blue eyes. "This way," the Scotsman said. "Quietly. And do not look at her. The Nagarani's dance is often the last thing a living being sees."

"What is she?" Rudyard spun to face Daimh. "What are you?" His gaze flicked to Hu Jia. "And you...are you like them?"

Hu Jia shook her head, her eyes fixed on the magnificent snake. Her voice was a reverent whisper. "I am not an avatar."

Rudyard's mind stumbled over *that* word again. "Avatar?"

·  ·  ·

DAIMH TURNED the speared fish over the fire as sparks frittered over the surrounding stone pit. He leaned back against a tree and spoke, his voice as sonorous as a song. "When Buddha lay on his deathbed, he summoned the great animal spirits to him. Only twelve came, and these twelve he burdened with the eternal care of mankind. For centuries, the animal spirits have passed from generation to generation—sometimes easily, at other times not."

"And you?" Rudyard asked.

"I am the ox avatar."

"And Nagarani, the snake?" Why had he not realized it earlier? Nagarani, translated literally, meant Snake Queen.

Daimh nodded. "She is also Lady Yin."

"Lady Yin?"

"The avatars are divided in how their animal spirits should pass on. The Yin believe in guarding our traditions; the responsibility demanded of the avatar is cultivated through upbringing, not won at the edge of a blade. For the Yin, the animal spirit passes to the first eligible child of the avatar. The Yang, however, compete to be the next avatar." He cast a glance at Hu Jia. "And that is why she is here."

"But you said you're not an avatar…" Rudyard's heart stuttered as the tangle of conversations he had barely understood straightened into the truth. "And you're not…" he murmured. "*Shere Khan.* Shere Khan is the tiger avatar…"

HU JIA STARED down at her hands as she took up the tale. "The Tiger Lord left for India ten years ago, after China lost the second Opium war. The drug was destroying our society, our people. Even some within the tiger clan had succumbed to it. The Tiger Lord wanted to cut off opium production at its source, including India. He conspired with the Russians in the Great War to block the expansion of English power."

"And for that, the English poisoned the Tiger Lord," Nagarani spoke as she stepped out of the darkness, once again a perfectly poised, beautiful, young Indian woman. "His manservant had fallen ill on the journey, and when he arrived in India, he hired an Indian man to be his guide and servant. The man brought along his family —his wife and his young son." Nagarani sat across from Rudyard. The shadows cast by the flames flickering on her face made her seem otherworldly. "The Tiger Lord came to my village, seeking our help. We were not involved in the opium trade, and never intended to be. We did not want to draw the attention of the British to our quiet home, and we turned him away. He left, with his Indian manservant. A few days later, rumors whispered that a vicious, man-killing tiger had claimed new hunting grounds. It was Shere Khan. His manservant, bribed by the British, had attempted to poison Shere Khan. But Shere Khan is not a man—not entirely. The poison that would have killed a human damaged him, nonetheless—destroying his mind, sapping his will, trapping him in his animal form."

"And the Indian couple he killed…?"

"His treacherous manservant and his wife."

Rudyard's gaze darted to the sleeping Mowgli. "And the servant's young son?"

Nagarani, too, looked at young boy. "He fled when Shere Khan killed his parents, and was found by Bagherra, who brought him to the wolf pack to be raised among the cubs. Some might say Mowgli is an innocent, yet to Shere Khan, there are no innocents. There is only vengeance."

"But all this happened ten years ago. What happened in all that time?"

Nagarani shrugged. "Nothing happened. One does not lightly raise a hand against an avatar, even one who is no longer everything he could be. We watched him, hoping that time would heal, but it did not. We waited for the tiger clan to retrieve him—and finally, they have sent someone."

Rudyard's stricken gaze locked on Hu Jia. "But you came to kill him."

Stony faced, she said, "That is correct."

"But none—" Rudyard winced. "*Little* of this is his fault."

Hu Jia shot to her feet. "Do you think I do not know that?" She snarled. "The Tiger Lord was a great man who wanted only what was right for his people. For ten years, we braced against the meddling of the dragons, lost without our lord. We can wait no longer. We need our avatar."

"You haven't even tried to save the one you already have."

"I did." She glanced down at the bandages that still swathed her arm. "He is beyond salvation."

Rudyard drew a deep, shuddering breath. "He attacked you."

"He no longer recognizes his clan. All that remains is to retrieve his amulet of power so that the animal spirit can claim a new avatar."

"And you need the help of the other avatars because——"

"I am a contender for the new avatar, but I will be disqualified immediately if I kill the avatar."

Rudyard's hands curled into fists. "So you're getting others to do the dirty work for you? How are you different from the British who hired that Indian manservant to poison him in the first place?"

Hu Jia lunged at him, and Rudyard found himself slammed back against a tree, lights exploding in his brain. He felt her breath on his face.

"You know nothing about the choices I have made. I came at the behest of my clan. I would have given anything *not* to be here… not to be the one chosen to return the amulet to the tiger clan."

"The tigers would have sent none but their best," Daimh intervened. The regret in his eyes betrayed his distaste for the situation but his words, at least, seemed to calm the girl. "We have Mowgli now. Best we get to work. Just be sure we have thought this through —all the repercussions, the possible conflict with the Yang, even with the rest of the Yin."

Rudyard's eyes narrowed. "What do you mean, conflict?"

"The Yin and the Yang do not agree on many things…" Nagarani paused. "In fact, we do not agree on *anything*, except perhaps this one fact. It is time for the tiger spirit to return to its clan, and it falls to those closest—Yin or Yang—to make it happen." Her cool gaze rested on the boy. "Bring him. It's time."

.  .  .

RUDYARD PERCHED at the top of a gully at least thirty feet deep. Nagarani and Hu Jia sat beside him. Nagarani studied the ravine with a frown on her face. "I am not certain it is deep enough. Why wouldn't a tiger be able to leap thirty feet when driven by dire need?"

"Only the largest and strongest tigers will be able to leap thirty feet vertically," Hu Jia said.

"And is not Shere Khan among the largest and strongest tigers?"

"He is, but he is lame in his right hind leg. He will not be able to get out of the ravine."

Rudyard winced against the cold-blooded plotting. Shere Khan was not just a man-hunting tiger. He was a man…poisoned and trapped in the body of an animal…hunting those who had damaged and destroyed him. "How did he become lame?" he asked.

Hu Jia glanced at him. Her initially hostile gaze melted into suspicion, before giving way to grudging relief for the change in topic. "When a Yang avatar dies, the animal spirit is contained within the amulet until a new avatar is selected through a competition."

"What kind of competition?"

"Only those born in the year of that animal spirit may compete in the arena."

"It's a fight to the death?"

"No, of course not. It would be ridiculous to wipe out all the heirs and the spares. Deaths and maiming injuries, if any, are accidental. It takes more skill to win decisively without killing."

"But Shere Khan—"

"He was severely injured in the fight. The wound caused him to walk with a limp for the rest of his life, but he won anyway. I'm told it was one of the most spectacular rites of choosing."

Rudyard glanced at Nagarani who wore an amused smile. "You don't agree?"

Nagarani laughed softly. "I'm sure the battle was spectacular. I'm merely tickled, as always, by the Yang who assume that the ability to win a brawl is the sole qualification to be the avatar, and that the animal spirit quietly submits to whomever still happens to be standing after the dust settles. Surely, the rite of choosing is as much about the animal spirit choosing the avatar as it is the clan choosing the avatar."

Hu Jia frowned. The possibility of a willful animal spirit clearly had never occurred to her. "How is the way of the Yin any better?"

"Who's to say it is? However, I was raised to assume the mantle of the snake avatar, and it wasn't about being faster and stronger than everyone else on the field of battle. It takes more than skill with a sword to govern a clan and to fulfill our role in the universe."

"And what role is that?" Rudyard asked.

"To protect the eternal balance."

"Balance of what?"

Nagarani's eyes met his. "Everything." She straightened. "He's here."

Rudyard searched the area. "Where?"

She pointed to the other side of the gully. "There."

He followed the line of her finger but saw nothing. He felt something though, like a tremor in the silence.

Nagarani looked at him, an approving smile on her lips. "Finally, you sense it—the animal spirit. More than animal. More than human. It is an elemental force, and Shere Khan no longer has control over it. In him, the balance is lost."

He saw the tiger standing on a low rock. The creature's amber gaze fixed on the boy Mowgli huddling in the canyon. Shere Khan crouched and leapt, landing silently in the ravine. Even so, Rudyard thought he felt the earth tremble.

Mowgli shot to his feet and retreated slowly from the approaching tiger. The boy's jaw was slack, his mouth hanging open, eyes wide with alarm.

Rudyard's stomach twisted. They were using a *boy* as bait. A twelve-year old boy, stricken with terror, stared certain death in the face.

Mowgli spun around and ran, his arms and legs pumping furiously. With a roar, Shere Khan set off in pursuit.

Nagarani shot to her feet, her body blurring into the python.

The snake remained on the upper edge of the gully but effortlessly kept up with Mowgli.

In the distance, thunder rumbled.

Rudyard glanced up at the cloudless blue sky. Next to him, Hu Jia made a choked sound. Her hands clenched into fists, and her eyes were wide in her suddenly pale face.

Shere Khan closed the distance. A hundred feet. Fifty feet. Thirty.

Within a few seconds, he would be close enough to leap. Close enough to kill the boy he had hunted for so long.

Mowgli wailed as the coils of a python yanked him into the air, lifting him out of the gully.

Shere Khan skidded into a turn. He roared and lunged at the child dangling just above his reach. Golden eyes narrowed, the powerful body coiling into a living spring.

Nagarani pulled Mowgli up even higher as Shere Khan leapt. The tiger's claws swiped the air where Mowgli had been moments earlier.

Rudyard swallowed through the tightness in his throat. Even lame, the tiger had cleared almost twenty feet vertically with no difficulty.

The thunder rolled in, and with it a dust cloud several miles long. A massive herd of Indian buffalo, gleaming black and slate blue, sunlight glittering off their ridged horns, slid down the side of the ravine and charged through the gully. Leading them was a bull larger than any other. *Daimh.*

Shere Khan stared at the inevitable tide of death. Mowgli forgotten, the tiger leapt up the side of the ravine. His claws scrabbled for grip on the rain-slicked surface, but he slid all the way to the bottom of the gully. The distance between the buffalos and the tiger shrank.

Shere Khan fled. The muscular grace of the tiger should have allowed almost any tiger to stay ahead of the buffalo, at least for a few minutes, but Shere Khan was lame, and the distance diminished. Terror and panic drove Shere Khan's final leap. Unnaturally high, it almost cleared the ravine. His claws clamped down on the ground at the top of the ravine. Rudyard sucked in a breath. With little or no effort at all, Shere Khan would pull himself free of the trap.

The tiger looked in Rudyard's direction—not at him, but at the small-framed Chinese girl standing next to him.

Something transformed in the tiger's eyes. For a single instant, it was more than an animal, more than a human. It was once again, an avatar. The magnificent striped head inclined in a gesture of acknowledgement, and perhaps even of respect.

Shere Khan let go.

Claws retracted willingly, and the tiger tumbled off the cliff into the tossing horns and pounding hooves of a buffalo herd led by the ox avatar.

Hu Jia screamed and dropped to her knees.

The sound of wrenching pain and rending loss would wake Rudyard up in the middle of the night for the rest of his life.


WHEN THE BUFFALO herd once again grazed peacefully by a river, Rudyard, Daimh, Nagarani, and Hu Jia ventured into the canyon.

They found Shere Khan's battered, bloody body, the vivid orange and black stripes dusted brown and grey. While Rudyard, Daimh, and Nagarani stood a respectful distance away, Hu Jia walked up to the tiger and dropped to her knees. She touched her forehead to the ground in the reverent gesture she had assumed in her first meeting with Shere Khan. "*Zūnjìng de fùqīn.*"

Hu Jia reached around the tiger's neck. Something glinted gold beneath the heavy fur. She drew the chain out from around the tiger's head. In her hand, an amulet glittered in the sun.

The tiger's body shimmered before re-forming into that of a man, past his prime but with traces of strength and dignity in his now-still face. In his features, Rudyard saw glimpses of Hu Jia—the slash of the cheekbones, the shape of the nose and chin…

He inhaled shakily. "What did she say to him?"

Nagarani's cool brown eyes were oddly gentled by compassion. "Revered father."

"She's not…" Rudyard could not complete his question. Hu Jia crumpled against the dead man's chest.

Nagarani continued softly. "She was six when he left the tiger clan, never to return. It is fitting that she, the child of the tiger lord, return his amulet to the tigers."

"What will happen then?" Rudyard asked. "In the competition?"

"Does it matter? The tigers will have a new avatar. It may or may not be Hu Jia, but Shere Khan's story is told. It is over."


RUDYARD relaxed in his recliner as the courtyard of his Simla inn bustled with activity. Soon, the sun would set, and dinner would be served in the whitewashed dining room with a bright fire blazing in the hearth. He stared down at his leather journal, filled with scribbles of his notes—no more than a handful of words. His mind could not yet fully wrap around everything he had witnessed.

"Are ye enjoying ye return to the real world?"

He glanced up as Daimh sat down across from him. The Scotsman wore a broad smile that belied the concerned look in his eyes.

"How is Hu Jia?" Rudyard asked.

"On her way back to China, with her father's body. They will bury Shere Khan at Tai Shan, among the other tiger avatars."

"And you?"

"On to Bombay, and then on a ship back to Scotland. I should be home within a month. And ye, Rudyard. What story will ye tell?"

"None that anyone will believe."

Daimh chuckled. "Most people will believe anything. They will twist the story to mean what they want it to say."

"But avatars…people who shift into animal forms…animals that talk, that have will, that make decisions with repercussions that extend far beyond this so-called real world…"

"How about a story about a boy raised by wolves?"

"What about the ones who really mattered? Shere Khan? Nagarani? Hu Jia? You?"

"It is ye story." Daimh grinned as he rose to leave. "We would take it as a favor if ye keep the location vague. Nagarani dinna appreciate the publicity."

Rudyard glanced down at his journal, struck out the location *Rajputana* and after a moment's thought, replaced it with the name of a village his friends had visited and spoken highly of—*Seoni*.

"Oh, by the way." Daimh glanced over his shoulder. "Ye might give some thought to changing Nagarani's name and gender. No one in British India would ever believe that an Indian woman wields that kind of power."

*Probably not.* Rudyard scratched out Nagarani's name in his journal, and wrote down a single word. *Kaa.*

## AUTHOR'S NOTES – JADE KERRION

DID you know that in Rudyard Kipling's *The Jungle Book* (not the reimagined Disney version), Shere Khan was first called Lungri? Did you know that Kaa rescued Mowgli from the monkeys? And did you know that Shere Khan was killed by stampeding buffalo?

While researching my story, I stumbled upon an early draft of *The Jungle Book*. Rudyard Kipling had originally set the story in Rajputana. Later, he changed it to a location several hundred miles away, Seoni. It got me wondering…why?

The entire notion of a boy raised by wolves amidst talking animals was already fantastical. Everyone knew animals did not actually talk. Why did the location even matter? What was Kipling trying to hide?

What if the truth was actually stranger than fiction?

My short story, "Shere Khan," weaves around Kipling's story, to tell another story of the conflict between the east and the west, of clashes between cultures and countries, and of a mystical world that runs parallel to our own. It tells you why the man-eating tiger named *Lungri*—Lame One—was first and forever acknowledged as *Shere Khan*—Tiger Lord.

Download a copy of The Jungle Book at Project Gutenburg.

*—Jade*

# THORNFIELD'S ASHES

## E. J. Wenstrom

"*I am no bird, and no net ensnares me,*"
    *~Charlotte Brontë,* Jane Eyre
    *This one's for Jane.*
*It's also for Alice, and Elizabeth, and Emma, and Eloise, and Catherine, and Tess, and all the others who taught me to be strong and independent and smart with their example.*
    *—E. J.*

ONCE AGAIN, Mr. Rochester's bedroom is on fire.

A different home, a different time, but the same scene all over. And this time, it was I who set the flame.

He bolts up in the bed and fumbles, reaching over to my side to feel for me. When he finds the sheets crumpled and the pillow bare, his eyebrows fold, his lip trembles, his eyes blink blankly toward the heat.

"Jane! Jane!"

I stand in the doorway and watch, silent as I could be, steeling my nerves and scrutinizing him for any sign that it might be true, any hint of the changeling creature I have been warned to fear.

Reader, have I gone mad? I fear it and find it preposterous in turns, but I could no longer bear the agony of the questions that had been planted in me.

Through my life I have always considered myself to be rational above all else, even when my heart begged me to do otherwise. Every step I placed, I tried to set it on the right side of the line between heart and mind, between right and wrong.

I have no doubt that almost any individual you could find would agree, burning one's husband, particularly a good husband, is not on the side of good—or rational. But in this action I feel compelled, and though I fought it, I felt I had no other choice.

For I must know if what Bertha Mason's ghost told me is true. If it is, I am in dire trouble indeed. If it is not, then at least I will know for certain that I am indeed going mad.

Then, at least, I can start now to tear myself away from this man—my heart—before I, too, find myself locked away in an attic. I love him, reader, I do, but I do not have it in me to allow anyone, even him, to bind me.

Bertha's intrusions on my blissful life started only a fortnight after our wedding—an utterly blissful time of clear skies and peaceful days, filled with walks together through the fields and evenings sitting in our own Ferndean, side by side.

He did not have his riches, he did not have his strength, but we had each other, and I had enough of each for both of us. Oh, how my heart swelled and fluttered and clenched in turns, to be at Mr. Rochester's side as his own, truly and really, and to have the claim over him to care and look after, with all that had passed.

In my contentment of those days, I would not have been amenable to bad news of any sort, from even the most rational of sources—had the caretaker of the inn in town run to our door to warn me of a coming storm, I could hardly have accepted even that, from within the cocoon of the perfection of my happiness.

The ghost of my Edward's first wife hardly met such stringent criteria. The first time she appeared to me, as my Edward—mine, not hers—and I sat basking in the setting sun by the window, he rocking and I reading, I outright dropped my book to the ground.

"Is all right, my fairy?" Edward asked, reaching out, as if he could catch my book without seeing.

I leaned forward and picked the book up, not minding the crinkled pages, for I was completely transfixed upon the vision.

It was Bertha Mason, clear as a cloud in the sky. And yet it was not her, not the way she was in life as I had seen her. She stood straight and proud, her hair sleek and brushed, and dressed not in the white nightgowns she skulked through Thornfield in, but in a fine and simple dress. She said nothing, but she watched me with intent and intensity, as if waiting for me.

My heart then quaked and pounded, as I took in this strange vision, and my head turned light as the blood left it.

Most of the time Edward's lack of sight was nothing but a way for me to care for him. But in that moment, how painfully I wished that he could see, and tell me if this spirit before me were true or not.

"Janet?" Edward reached for his walking stick and stood with great bluster, as if despite his weakened state he would take on whatever had startled me.

"It is nothing," I said, hardly sure if I were telling him or myself. "Only my fingers are becoming cold in the dusk."

Edward sat back down then, his great figure easing into its relaxed state. "But then give them to me, my Jane, and I will warm them."

He reached out idly and as my hands met with his, he folded them between his own. The apparition stood there for some time, as if pleading for my attention, before finally fading away into the dusk. But the cloud on my blue skies was there to stay.

Edward's first wife continued to appear to me, silent and watching, in the days and weeks to follow. She appeared to me as we sipped our morning coffee, she watched as I tended the garden, and she hovered over us in our bed in the night. I told myself it was not her, that she was not there, that it was best to ignore her and get on with life. But her presence chilled my soul like a shadow.

Finally, as she watched me in the red room at the back of the small house, while Edward sat in the garden out front, I could bear it no more. I determined I would not allow my fear to overcome me as it did in another red room with another apparition when I was small.

I steeled my nerves, stood abruptly and said, "What is it that you want from me?"

Only then did the apparition speak.

"We are the same, you and I," she asserted.

I realized then that I had not truly expected the apparition to speak, but rather vanish upon being called out, for now though she had been watching all these days, I still did not believe that she was real. Now that she opened her mouth and spoke, I was overcome with a throbbing heat that pulsed from my core.

"We are not!" I exclaimed in reply. "I am no madwoman."

I could hear the cruelty of my words, but had no power to stop them, for I was in such a state over speaking to a ghost, and my Edward's first wife, at that.

"We are," she pressed. "In ways you could not know."

What she could possibly mean by such words I had not the slightest, and my interest in engaging an apparition had extinguished, as her words alarmed me even more than her presence. I pleaded to her not to continue, to leave me in peace, but she would not.

"What is it that he calls you?" she asked.

I could hardly understand why such a thing would interest her. But I was startled beyond the point of argument.

"Different things, depending on the mood that strikes him," I reply. "Fire spirit, changeling, fairy—"

And so I could have gone on for quite some time listing the many things my Edward has called me, from the quite strange to the most sweet. But it was at this word that Bertha cut me off.

"Yes, yes, yes," she said. Her eyes were alight and her expression so elated that she seemed almost like the madwoman I first knew her as. "Don't you see? Can't you guess?"

By now the shock of my fear was passing, and where it subsided from my body, it was replaced with a fierce anger.

"Guess? Guess at what? What are you after, intruding into our home and our life here?" I demanded.

"Think on it—it will not take you long to see," the apparition pressed. "Have you not experienced strange occurrences through your life?"

I hardly have to tell the reader of the many inexplicable incidents that have at points shaped my life's direction.

From that first time my uncle's ghost thwarted me at my aunt's home, to the many other oddities that have, at most strange times, punctuated my life.

It was such an occurrence that brought me back to my beloved Edward finally, when his voice reached out to me over inexplicable distance as I sat praying, considering whether to leave this continent for good. It was that voice, in that moment, that brought me back to this place.

"And what of it?" I demanded.

But it was as though I already knew what she was about to say.

"We have something in common, you and I. Something beyond the man we wed. We are both fey. And it is of no coincidence that we both found ourselves in this man's home."

I must confess I did laugh at her then. For it seemed to me then that despite her outwardly collected appearance, this apparition-Bertha was, indeed, still as mad as I witnessed her to be in life.

It was then that Edward called for me. I answered, and when I turned back to the room, Bertha was gone.

And though I told myself she was mad—that *I* was mad, for fancying I was speaking with spirits—what she said plagued me and would not be banished from my mind.

If only I were capable, then, of comprehending, the full of it.

After Bertha's visitation upon me, I set out determined to put the whole business right out of my head. I told not a soul of it, for fear of what they might say or think.

Instead, each and every one of Bessie's old stories began coming back to me, tales of imps and fairies and other creatures—tales that to me, as a child, always felt too real and too close, so much so that I sometimes fancied I saw them in my own mirror.

Other instances, too, haunted me. The ghostly flash that visited me within the red room of my uncle's old home; the lightning that struck the tree at Thornfield upon Edward's first proposal; the way his voice reached to me across so much distance and drew me back to him here. These and other things, which I had before easily reasoned away, now came back to me.

Do strange occurrences happen to one over the course of a life? Most assuredly. But in my experience most are easily explained away with the mundane in the end. But now, explanations that before had settled my nerves seemed flimsy and absurd.

For what other did I know who had any experience equal to some of my strangest moments, the ones that I must now confess went against all the laws of the natural world? What was Bertha's end in telling me such wild things? For if I accepted her claim as true, she had more to tell me.

How I fretted and vexed and lay awake next to my Edward in the nights, tossing over these terrible seeds the apparition had planted in my mind. It was a relief, then, that he could not see my face, for I blushed heatedly whenever his pet names for me strayed onto Bertha's claims.

To find peace again, I finally had to admit to myself that I must know more. On the next fine day, I set Edward by the garden and took to the red room. I sat there so long, waiting for that specter to haunt me, that I began to believe that it had never been real at all, and began to feel quite silly indeed for allowing some strange daydream to overcome me as it had.

The relief began to loosen the tightness of my shoulders—but when I looked up, she was there.

"Are you ready?" she asked.

"Yes," I replied. "In truth I do not know yet what to make of your claim, but I will have the last of it, and then I will determine what to do with it."

Bertha nodded. She wasted no time, having acquired her audience, in telling the rest of her tale.

"We are fey, Jane, and it is no coincidence that it is the two of us Rochester has collected as companions, among all his acquaintances and lovers. For he is no true man, but a goblin."

At this most unusual accusation I stood abruptly, a powerful current rushing to my cheeks and my fingertips—who was this madwoman, to come to my home and haunt my steps and make accusations of my husband?

"You're jealous," I said then. "And you're not real."

"You could dream all this up on your own, then? You said you wanted the full of it, and this is only the start."

Bertha waited for my rebuttal, but I had none. Indeed, I wanted to have all she had to say, no matter how mad it might be, so that I could make an assessment of the full—and now, so that I could be done with her. I sat back down.

She watched in quiet as I stilled myself before she continued.

"He wants your powers, Jane. He wants to bind you so that it is his own."

That was enough. Anger coursed through me like a flash of lightning, splitting me like a struck tree.

"And how exactly would he go about taking it, if that were something he could do, and something I had to be taken?" I demanded.

"Slowly," Bertha said. "Until finally, without you even noticing, you have none left at all."

"Would it make him better? Would he see again?"

The thought quivered within my soul, for perhaps then I would give it to him willingly, if it meant seeing my terrible Edward whole again. I had not missed any such magic I might possess before, nor did I have any great plans for it. What I wanted most in this world was a home where I belonged, and I had that finally here.

Her silence I took to mean that it would. My heart fluttered violently at the thought of him whole again, the same strong Mr. Rochester that I first met at Thornfield, and especially to think that I, little and plain as I am, might have it within me to grant it to him.

"It would make you as mad as I was in life," she finally said.

At these words, my spirit shut tight as a trap, for my mind is one thing I shall never forfeit, not for anything. I was then overcome with a peculiar rage I had never felt before, and I hardly knew who or what it was for. It did then cross my mind that I may already be just as mad.

My anger closed me against the apparition—for as of that moment I still had my mind. I would use it.

"Prove it," I ordered.

Her face then fell into a most solemn expression. "Show me your hands," she ordered.

I stretched them out in front of me, hardly knowing what to think.

She placed her own hands so that they hovered around mine. The energy between her hands and mine, between my own two palms, began to tingle, and then to quiver. Finally I could bear it no more and gave in to release.

In response, a flash of green bursted from my fingers.

"No. This may all be my own strange daydream. How will you prove to me what *he* is?"

"The same way I have tried before, to expose him to you in life. The only way. In fire, he must show his true form. You must surround him in fire."

Then, indeed, reader, it was as if all the pieces of the puzzle were cast into the air and rearranged, falling into a new pattern, and suddenly a picture was made clear that I had not seen before. A gasp escaped me. When I looked back to the specter, ready with a flood of questions, she was gone.

Reader, I am no fool. I knew my Edward to have monstrous things within him—but who does not? This alone did not make him the terrible creature Bertha claimed.

But there I went, going on as if Bertha's apparition were as real as myself, when in fact, that was as unlikely as the rest of it.

I fought the idea. I fought it for days. For weeks. It was ridiculous. It was impossible. And even if it were true, what then? For I could not abide the thought of parting from him again, ever. The last time had duly wrenched my heart out thoroughly enough to last a lifetime.

In secret moments when I was sure Edward could not know of it, I cupped my hands the way Bertha showed me, and summoned forth the tingling light of my powers. This, of all of it, could not be argued away. It is as true as my own soul. And yet, even in the short time I knew of it, the light became dimmer with each summons, and harder to draw forth. Bertha was not lying on one account: There was something drawing it away from me.

And then, I started to fancy that I felt something when I was near my Edward. Not the thrill of his touch or intensity of his gaze in my direction, but something else, something I had never before noticed; a faint draining sensation.

*Impossible,* my heart protested. But a small voice from within me began to grow that pushed back against it: *Possible. Possible.*

The idea would not let me alone. It came at me in dreams, and then increasingly consuming daydreams—fire, and a terrible form within in. I finally confessed to myself that it must be done. For my own sanity was hanging on by a mere thread.

And this is what drew me to set the candle to the bed's edge this night.

I stand just outside the door watching as the flames grow hotter, and I clench the bucket waiting in my hands, filled to the brim and ready. Edward pulls in his legs and reaches for his walking stick, clutching it as if it is life itself; a fit of coughs overtakes him.

*Just a moment longer,* I tell myself, *just another moment,* for I have to be sure.

The flames are growing quite fierce now, and the heat is drawing beads of sweat to my brow even from the threshold where I now stand.

Surely, if what Bertha said was true, I would be seeing it by now, would I not?

It has been almost a full minute now since the flames took, and the fire is a terrible one. It has begun to work its way up the foot of the bed. Guilt consumes me as rapidly as the fire consumes the bedposts, for in this moment madness seems the more likely of the possibilities before me. Bertha is, after all, dead. And now here I stand watching my husband become surrounded by flames, all on her suggestion.

He sits, pulling away from the heat, frantic, the flickering of the flames causing terrible shadows to throw over his face, turning it monstrous by degrees, but it is still his own.

I wait for the screams to come when it starts to burn him, holding my breath to listen closer. They do not come.

And just when I think I can bear the terror on his face no more, a flicker of the light cast over him reveals he is changed— his countenance is not the puzzling, brooding face of the man that I know, but something much more hideous, a hooked nose and strange crinkled skin, a brow that folds oddly over the rest of his face like the lip of a melted candle. *This* is not my Edward. This is a wholly different, horrid creature indeed.

As I watch, his fear leaves him; he straightens and pushes his palm out toward the flames. As he does, the flames recede, regressing toward the foot of the bed.

It is slight and sudden, these changes, and then they flicker away in the fire again. All returns to normal, but I am sure in what I saw.

Relief drops over me like a sheet, chased quickly by rage—it was all true. I am not mad. The man I have bound my life to is no man at all, but a thieving goblin, slowly draining my gifts from me.

"Fire!" I shout, running into the room. I lift the bucket I hold tightly in my hand and pour out the water, dousing the flames.

"Oh my fairy," Mr. Rochester exclaims, "My nymph. Is that you? You came just in the nick of time."

I do not answer him, but exit the room as swiftly as I entered, and lock the door fast behind me.

"Jane?" There is a pleading in his voice that I cannot stand.

"I have discovered you, you fiend!" I call through the door.

"Discovered me, Janet?" he replies. "So you have found me out, finally? That I am nothing but an old, crippled man who has no right to a creature such as you at all?"

"*You* are the creature," I call to him.

Oh, how my heart pounds, how my soul sobs. But I will not be siphoned from like mere oil to a flame, until I am a burned-out husk with no mind left. Already my mind seeks other answers, other explanations—a trick of the light, a mind too active and weak, too susceptible to influence—but I know what I saw.

Bertha was right.

Had he ever feelings for me at all, beyond taking from me all that he could?

Or had it all been part of luring me in? Was the thing's plan to lock me away, in time, as he had Bertha? I know the answers to these and all my questions even as I ask them, for now my eyes are opened, and I see all, even what I do not wish to see.

My heart hardens. I am no bird, and no net ensnares me.

"Jane! My Janet!" he calls.

Even now my soul cries to forget it all and surrender to him, to let him take what he will, so long as I can be near him. But I will not let him be free to siphon from me as he pleases. My mind is my own, and mine only.

With Bertha's proclamations proven true, there is only one choice left to me. I steel myself with resolve against my heart's pleas and take the key from my pocket and lock him in.

He must have heard the click of the lock, for as I step away and tuck the key back into my pocket, he pounds on the door and calls to me. But I do not turn back.

## AUTHOR'S NOTES – E.J. WENSTROM

JANE EYRE'S strange story is like a mirror, forcing me to reassess Jane, the story, and ultimately, myself, every time I read it. A few years pass, I pick it up again, and it shows me how much I have changed by how different it reads.

Because it is constantly changing on me, I cannot say what to make of Jane's relationship with Mr. Rochester. I can only say that, as much as I want Jane to be happy, the story's conclusion has always had a feeling of unfinished business about it.

*—EJW*

# TREASURE IN MY POCKET

## T.L. WOOLSLEY

### 1. The Old Captain

The bloody, disembodied head stared at her with glassy eyes. Jaquie looked away. Gore covered the small room, body parts scattered over the narrow bed and wooden floor. Blood spatters ran up the walls across the ceiling, as if dispelled by great force.

Jaquie gulped and closed her eyes. Only her father's warm presence at her back kept her from screaming. His firm hands on her shoulders steered her into the hall.

"You okay?" He leaned over to look her in the face, and his breath was soft. She nodded, not trusting her voice.

Her dad called the authorities. His voice seemed far away, and Jaquie missed a few words while she concentrated on not throwing up. "Yes, the Admiral Benbow Berth, second floor. In the lodging rooms. First door as you get off the lift. Yes ... I'm Bo Hawkins, the owner. No." He paused. "No, there's no chance she's alive. She ... she's been dismembered."

Jaquie gulped again. It was hard to believe that was all that was left of the Old Captain. They had talked only yesterday. The Old Captain had been in her usual spot, a small table near the kitchen, when Jaquie passed by with a bin of dirty dishes.

"Jaquie."

A voice hissed her name, and she stopped. "Yes, Captain?"

The Old Captain—never referred to as such to her face—crooked an index finger at her. "What the hell are all these people doing here, girl?" The scowl on the older gara's face wrinkled her forehead and arched high into the mess of her curly salt-and-pepper hair.

"Ships docked this afternoon. Four of them, Dad says. Lots of business. I have to go—"

"Bring me another drink, would you? And a sammich."

When Jaquie returned with the sandwich, the Old Captain touched a finger to the bromeliads that lined a long tray on the upper edge of the booth.

"Where's my drink?"

"Dad will bring it. You know I'm too young. I'm not even three fives yet."

"No one will ever know. Now this plant—" she pointed to the Scarlet Star nearest to her— "likes gin, just like me. It's these other ones—the posies—that don't. They like bourbon. Expensive tastes, for a plant."

"You said you would stop pouring your drinks in the flowers."

"Eh? Did I say that? But they like it. I'll drink the good ones m'self."

"I have to go—"

"Wait." The Old Captain waved Jaquie closer. Jaquie took two steps. Stopped. She could already smell the Old Captain's breath.

The gara slouched to Jaquie's level, and her voice dropped into a conspiratorial whisper that couldn't have been heard more than six or seven feet away. "You been lookin' out like I told ya?"

Jaquie nodded. "A one-armed gara. Haven't seen her. Gotta go." Jaquie pivoted on one heel, but not fast enough. She gasped as the

Old Captain's narrow hands grabbed her elbow. Reluctantly, Jaquie turned to face the old gara.

"What else did I tell you? How will you recognize her?"

"She has one arm, and she'll be wearing a ship's patch on her uniform. Probably green background with a blue rectangle. And you'll pay me 27 credits if she actually shows up."

The Old Captain looked astonished for a moment before regaining her composure. "That much? Well, yes, if she shows her face, you come tell me and I'll pay you the 27." She leaned back and thumbed her chest. "That one-armed gara wants to know where the treasure is, and I ain't tellin' her. That treasure map's worth 27 right there. Three a week in the meantime, though. Isn't that what I said?"

And The Old Captain had been saying it for as long as Jaquie could remember. "Yes. I ... I really have to go."

Jaquie hadn't seen her the rest of the night. Now she knew why. Had someone come looking for the treasure map? From the looks of the Old Captain's room, they had certainly been looking for *something*.

## 2. The Investigation

"NAME'S ANA," the inspector said. "Ana Hyrand." She bowed once, briefly, then she and her team poked into everything. The inspector was the shortest gara Jaquie had ever seen. She closely questioned Jaquie and her dad about the Old Captain's habit and who might have visited her. Jaquie's dad kept following Inspector Hyrand's team around, trying to get them to hurry up. "I don't want the other lodgers disturbed," he explained. "With four ships here at Athne, I'm almost full—"

"Stand aside, please." The inspector said with a wave of her hand. "We have to be thorough. Why don't you go back downstairs until we're through?" The glance she included with that remark took in Jaquie as well.

Jaquie tugged on her father's sleeve, only too glad to leave the gore behind. "C'mon, Dad."

The early-morning restaurant staff peppered them with questions when they came down to the kitchen. "It was gross," Jaquie said, her mouth stretched down and her tongue stuck out to mime the nausea she had felt. "And the blood! You remember that flick that came out last year? The one with the killer on the space station? This was worse than that. Body parts were everywhere."

Breakfast was in full swing by the time the inspector came downstairs. Jaquie managed to be nearby, making a fresh pot of tea, when the tiny woman spoke to her dad. "Can you tell us if anything is missing from the room?"

"I don't think so. To tell you the truth, I didn't look too closely."

The inspector shrugged. "The room was torn apart. She tried to put up a fight, it looks like, but we can't tell if they took anything away with them."

"I doubt she had much worth stealing."

"The treasure map," Jaquie blurted.

"What?"

Jaquie explained to her father and the inspector her arrangement with the Old Captain. "She was worried about some one-armed gara who was after a treasure map."

Her father grunted. "Sounds like you've been reading too many stories. Like that one you read last week—the one with the treasure on some island."

"She really believed it. Why else would she pay me three-a-week?"

The inspector shook her head. "I agree with your father. I doubt there ever was anything like a treasure map. The 'Old Captain'— her real name was Ellen Moss—was just an old drunk with a vivid imagination. There was nothing valuable in her room. Worn clothes, mementos, a couple of used uniforms with ship's patches on them, that's it."

"Okay, thanks, inspector," Jaquie's dad said. "Jaquie, go to the kitchen and see if they need some help."

All through breakfast, even after the inspector left, Jaquie glanced at the little table where the Old Captain usually sat, still shaken that the older gara would never sit there again.

In the lull between breakfast and lunch, Jaquie crept into the Old Captain's booth. What had the old gara always said? *That one-armed gara wants to know where the treasure is and I ain't tellin' her.*

## 3. What the Data Crystal Showed

THE OLD CAPTAIN'S booth was the worst seat in the restaurant—right near the kitchen and the stand where Jaquie sent dirty dishes to be washed. Jaquie sat where the Old Captain had always sat, and looked out. The horizontal garden wound its way through the restaurant, blooms peeking out from beams and overhead lattices made to look like wood. By contrast, the vertical garden, stretching high above Jaquie's head, contained only edible plants—vegetables, fruit trees, and herbs combined into a spicy smell that balanced the sweetness of the flowering garden below. All of it fed on the nutrient solution that flowed through narrow tubes and filled tanks holding larger growth.

The restaurant itself lay mostly to her right, with a large view screen providing a stunning sight of the stars outside Athne Station. It wasn't a window, of course, but a relayed image from cameras—but the spot was popular anyway. The Old Captain wouldn't have been able to see much of the scene from her table. The bar was up ahead and to her left—trust the Old Captain to pick a spot close to where the liquor was kept. *She sure liked her drinks, although she also liked to "share" them with the flowers.*

Jaquie knelt on the seat to look at the bedraggled bromeliad floating in a tank of nutrient solution suspended a little above her head. She wrinkled her nose at the reek of the Old Captain's last baptism of whiskey. There was nothing else—

Something opaque glinted, right where the stem of the bromeliad entered its tank. Jaquie reached in and felt something hard about the size of her little finger. After a little tugging it came free.

"That," said her father when she showed it to him, "is an old-fashioned crystal media spike. Much bigger than the ones we use today. Haven't seen one like this in quite a while."

"Wonder if it's got the treasure map on it."

Her dad shook his head. "We'll have to use an adapter to read it. You sure it was the Old Captain's?"

"Who else would put it over there? She was the only one who sat there. And she sure wanted to hide it from that gara with one arm."

"I'll find an adapter," Jaquie's father said. "Let's see what that data crystal shows." After rummaging around his office, he found an adapter in the back of the office supply closet.

He plugged the crystal media in and slid both into a slot on his desk. Thrusting his hands into the holographic field, Jaquie's father waved the computer interface to life.

Jaquie peered over his shoulder as numbers flowed in the holographic field above his desk. The first set of data appeared in groups of three, the second set in groups of two.

Jaquie frowned. Unlucky, unstable twos. Why twos? Jaquie shivered. Bad luck twos. It had certainly been bad luck for the Old Captain. *Why would the Old Captain protect such data?* She went back to the groups of threes. Except for the first set, all had a small symbol near each grouping. "Numbers. What are those—"

"I see them, Jaquie. Okay, let's take those—" her father clutched the holographic numbers and threw them into another section of the computer interface "—and see what this program can make of it." Colors bloomed like flowers and expanded into orbs. "A solar system," Dad said softly.

"Which one?"

"I have no idea. Let's see if it's in any of the databases we can access. The Athne General Databank hasn't heard of it. Hmm…oh, here's some information that was uploaded to public domain. Let's see if we can find a solar system that matches the one we're looking for."

"What about that one?" Jaquie asked, pointing.

"Hmmm … not quite. See, the one we're looking for has big, rocky moons. It looks like it's this one way out here, near The Rim. What are these symbols? Oh, that language is Sepa. Let me see if I can dig up a translator. Okay, we can buy one."

"What does it say?"

"Patience, Jaquie. Oh, here it is." The simple geometric symbols turned into familiar letters as they watched.

"Apparently, those symbols are directions in Sepa. The numbers are a series of coordinates that guide you through grivers to some destination."

"Grivers? Gravity rivers?"

"Yup."

"What about the other stuff? The unlucky stuff?"

"Wait. There's more Sepa to be translated, give it a minute. It's talking about tacey, see?"

"Tacey powder? The stuff for artificial gravity?"

"No…" Jaquie watched as her father puzzled through the rough translation. He set his mouth in a line. "It doesn't make any sense. Something about the tacey itself, before it's made into powder."

"What about the other numbers?"

Her dad grabbed the second group of numbers and threw them in to the reader. "Not the location of a solar system. It doesn't know what that data is."

He turned off the reader and retrieved the data crystal. "It still doesn't sound like enough information for someone to kill the Old Captain."

Indistinct noises and shouts caught their attention. Jaquie's dad ran out the door as the noise level rose. "Stay here, Jaquie."

*The Old Captain sure wanted to keep this stuff secret. Maybe I should hide it, too.* She wandered to her own room and looked around. The bright bedspread in her sleeping alcove, posters on the wall, and stuffies did not look promising.

She remembered "Partense," her favorite stuffed elephant as a child, had a tiny tear in it. Perhaps that would do. Jaquie slid the crystal spike into the gap and closed the fake fur around it. She put Partense back on its shelf and went to see what the commotion was about.

## 4. The Fight

DOZENS OF GARAS—MALE, female, and indeterminate—had spilled into the restaurant and bar. Shouts and accusations flew as frequently as fists and feet. One gara yelled as another deliberately poked him in the eye. She lost sight of her father in the fray.

Jaquie spotted a tall gara with long hair—and one arm. Jaquie turned away from her, but someone grabbed her, hard. She had just enough time to squeal, "Daddy!" before another gara joined the one-armed one and picked her up. Jaquie fought back. A flash of fists, glimpses of her father's shirt. The smack of flesh on flesh, the stink of booze and bodies, the cacophony of shouts and curses. Whoever held her collided violently with someone else. Strong hands pulled at her. "Daddy!"

Jaquie heard his deep voice, but she couldn't discern the words amongst the chaos. The sizzling sound of stunners. She fell to the floor and curled in a small ball—someone stumbled over her. She crawled, tripping someone else. More stunners.

"Jaquie." Her father's voice, tense though it was, was filled with relief.

"Daddy." A small pocket of peace surrounded him. She sprang up from the floor and buried her head in his shoulder as he picked her up, tears streaming from his face.

He spoke to someone else, calmly now. The other voice was strong—someone in charge. "What about that gara over there? Is that one with you?"

Jaquie lifted her head from her dad's shoulder. Bodies lay all over the floor, all still. Ana Hyrand and a couple other authorities, all armed with stunners, stood to one side.

Jaquie's dad was silent for a moment. "No. I don't recognize anyone. Do you have the one that grabbed my daughter?"

"I don't know. Do *you* see the one that grabbed your daughter?"

"Jaquie." Her dad's voice was soft as he set her down. "Are you all right?

She nodded her head.

"Which one grabbed you?"

Jaquie looked at the bodies sprawled on the floor. "Is—is the one-armed gara there?"

"I don't see anyone with just one arm. Is that who grabbed you?"

"N—no. It was another gara, with the one who had only one arm."

The inspector interrupted, "Can you recognize that person?"

"It was too fast. But I saw the one-armed gara, Daddy. She was here."

Jaquie and her dad explained to the authorities the warning the Old Captain had given Jaquie about the one-armed gara. "And the data spike. Daddy, tell her about the data crystal."

The inspector held it in her tiny fingers. "It's big."

"We found an adapter," Jaquie said.

The gara's eyes glanced from her to her dad. "What did it have on it?"

Jaquie's dad shrugged. "Just numbers. Nothing we could make sense of."

The gara dug in a pocket and produced a small sealable bag. "I'll just—"

"No." With a sweep of his hand, Jaquie's father snatched the crystal spike from Inspector Hyrand. "We'd rather keep it for now."

"That's evidence!"

"It was not found at the crime scene and we don't know if it even belonged to the Old Captain. It was found in my restaurant. Someone may have lost it and come asking about it later."

The inspector scowled, but did not say any more. "We'll keep an eye out for this one-armed gara. Not too many around with only one arm. We should be able to spot her, even on a station this big. In the meantime, we'll haul off the others and start questioning them."

Her father wanted to take Jaquie upstairs and put her in bed, but she refused to leave him. She kept close to his side as he watched the inspector's crew remove the unconscious garas. She sat next to him as he called in cleaners to mop up the mess left behind by the brawlers. Her eyes grew heavy with fatigue until her father scooped her up in his arms on their way to their apartment. *He hasn't carried me this much since I was little,* she thought sleepily. He paused at the door of their apartment then headed back down the ramp.

"Where are we going?" She managed to ask her dad.

"We're going to stay in one of the lodging rooms instead."

Jaquie barely remembered being placed in a big soft bed and her father lying down beside her. She slept.

## 5. A Change of Plans

THE NEXT DAY, Jaquie stayed close to her dad's side as he went through his tasks for the day. Every time someone came into his office, or new diners appeared in the restaurant, she looked them over to see if the one-armed gara was among them. The four ships left Athne Station, and while others came, there were no more fights at the Admiral Benbow. The Inspector reported no useful information from questioning those who had been stunned and hauled away.

"How are you doing?" her dad asked her often. "I know it was a scary experience."

"I'm okay," she told him. "I just keep thinking I see a one-armed gara everywhere." But the one-armed gara had not been found.

"She probably shipped out on one of those tugs that were docked here."

"I guess so."

Jaquie and her father got back to their old routine. One day Jaquie stood behind the Admiral Benbow's bar on a step stool, setting glasses on shelves, when a familiar swish of gold and burgundy caught her eye. A male gara wearing similar colors stood behind Lady Aurnice.

"Jaquie, I need to see your father."

Jaquie found him stocking shelves in the back. He sighed but followed her. Lady Aurnice had seated herself at a booth. Her husband sat at a table nearby.

"Lady Aurnice, Gara Aurnice." Jaquie's dad glanced from one to the other. He stood between them and did not bother to unroll his sleeves.

Lady Aurnice smiled at him. "Please sit down," she said, as if it were not his establishment. Jaquie's dad glanced once more at the husband before taking a seat facing Lady Aurnice. "Jaquie, go count that shipment of meat in the freezer. Make sure we got what we ordered."

Jaquie headed toward the back of the Benbow, but took a sharp right once she was out of the others' sight. She crouched in a booth three meters away and peeked between flowers.

"I understand there's been a recent development in the murder case," Lady Aurnice said.

Jaquie heard nothing for a moment then her father said, "If so, I haven't heard anything about it."

"A—something about a treasure?"

"Oh." Her father sounded disappointed. "That's just a theory. Probably an old gara's fantasy. The Old Captain was a bit odd, you know."

"I heard there is … data."

Her father sighed. "Yes, there is something on an old data crystal, but we don't know exactly what it is. And we have no idea if there is any real treasure."

"I spoke to the inspector who is investigating the murder."

"Oh?" Jaquie knew her father's irritated tone well. *Lady Aurnice is getting nosy again.*

"The inspector said that The Old Captain—Ellen Moss, I mean
—had been a hauler at one time."

"So?" *Yup, he's annoyed.*

"There is—information—that this treasure might be real."

"Humph."

Jaquie heard a clink that might have been Lady Aurnice's
bracelets on the table between her and her father.

"There is—was—a cartel. The Old Captain was a part of it.
She was one of the biggest haulers for a corporation running all
sorts of things out on The Rim."

"Yeah. Look, Lady Aurnice—"

"No." She interrupted Jaquie's dad sharply. "You cannot dismiss
me so easily. *Listen*, Bo. This is important to your interests, too.
Apparently a barge broke down and took refuge somewhere in The
Rim. They found something important. Something—" Her voice
dropped, and Jaquie could barely make out the word that came
next. It sounded like, "valuable."

"What did they find?"

"I—no one knows."

"Still sounds like a fairy tale to me."

Lady Aurnice's voice rose. "Albon, come here."

Jaquie saw the husband rise and move closer. He stood next to
the booth.

"You may know Albon, my only husband. He used to work in
the lanes before I took him away from all that. He worked on a
barge that belonged to the cartel. One of the garas he worked with
found out about the...treasure. Poor gara was murdered the very
next stop the barge made."

Albon nodded. Taller than Lady Aurnice, his waxed eyebrows
stood out at least an inch just like many of the noble male garas
wore. "It's true. I met the Lady shortly after that, so I never found
out what the treasure was, or where. But I remember the name they
mentioned as part of the cartel. It was Ellen Moss."

Lady Aurnice's voice dropped again as she leaned closer to
Jaquie's dad. "I'll bet that data crystal points to the treasure, Bo."

"You don't even know what this 'treasure' is."

"Something worth snatching your child!"

Parting the blooms to get a clear view, Jaquie saw her dad freeze.

Lady Aurnice sat up straight. "I can finance such a venture, if we can find something valuable. You know where this treasure is."

"And how do you propose to find it? Just go flying out—in a ship we don't have—and looking around, based on a bunch of numbers on an old data crystal?"

"We can hire a ship. I have business interests that could justify it." Lady Aurnice dismissed that obstacle with a wave of her hand.

"I can't leave my business and my daughter."

"I wasn't thinking of that."

"What were you thinking?" He looked askance at the noble gara.

"I could hire a ship and send Albon."

"With our data crystal?"

"With Jaquie and your data crystal."

A wild excitement took hold of Jaquie. Could she go looking for treasure?

Jaquie's father looked as if he'd bitten into something sour. "I'm not sending her alone."

"She'll be with Albon, I tell you. We can tell the haulers that they're father and daughter. I'll bet she could get an apprenticeship."

"She's too young. She's had three-threes, but not four."

"Call it a fact-finding trip. She can find out if she wants to become a hauler. If I hire the ship, they'll allow it. And Albon still has his loadtech ratings with the guild."

Her father did not look convinced.

"Your half would allow you to fix up this place." Lady Aurnice waved a hand that encompassed The Admiral Benbow. "Fix that auto feeding system for the gardens that almost flooded you out last year."

Jaquie's dad's face didn't change.

"Jaquie would be safer," Lady Aurnice said gently.

His head rose to look her in the eye. "What do you mean?"

"If someone almost made off with her just recently, what is to stop them from making off with her tomorrow? Or the next day?"

She paused, before continuing, "Yes, the business venture is attractive to me. And I know you must keep your little girl safe. Why not combine the two?"

"Lady Aurnice is right," Albon put in. "Athne Space Station is not safe for your daughter. If we hire a ship, we can search for the treasure under the guise of setting up a new hauler's route between The Rim and this station. No one would know Jaquie was on the ship, so there would be no reason to follow it."

Jaquie's dad nodded slightly. "I see what you mean, but I still don't like it."

"By the time they get back," Lady Aurnice said, "the inspectors may have caught these people. Keep her safe away from them."

He froze again. Took a deep breath. "Okay. I'll send her."

## 6. Departure

"JAQUIE, would you bring down some peaches for me, please?" her father asked one morning a nine-day later. "I want several of those near the top of the big tree. They're not falling on their own, and we need some for a dessert the cook is planning."

"Sure, Dad." Jaquie's face lit up. Despite the vertical garden's beauty, her favorite part was climbing the catwalks and girders to harvest fruit or vegetables. The catch net at the bottom not only saved diners below from being bombed by ripe produce but was strong enough to hold anyone who fell from the upper level.

"What am I going to do while you're gone?" he asked as she handed him the peaches.

"You'll have to get one of the waiters to go up there. Or, you know, get over your fear of heights." She grinned.

"Huh. Not likely at my age. Say, Albon tells me the ship's almost ready to go."

"Really?" All the delays had pushed the excitement and possibility of treasure into uncertainty. Now that future was coming much closer. "When?"

"A couple of days. You better start packing."

"Oh." Jaquie said nothing for several minutes. In a voice barely above a whisper, she said, "I wish you could go."

"I know, honey. I wish I could go, too. But we can't shut down The Admiral Benbow. And you'll be safer away from here. Once we get this 'treasure' business settled, one way or another, you'll be safe, and we can move back into our old apartment."

Jaquie smiled. "Or own the whole station with the money the treasure brings!"

He grinned back. "Or that."

Jaquie's dad took her down to the docks two mornings later. "Which one am I going on, Dad?" Jaquie peered at a viewer mounted on a wall near the dock entrance ramp.

"That third one, there. The *Hispaniola.*" He used his finger to trace a hub that extended from Athne Station to a narrow end where a ship lay tethered.

She studied the ship while her dad spoke to Lady Aurnice, who had come to see Jaquie and Albon off. Jaquie had seen many ships dock at Athne Station, but knowing one of them would be her home for a while made her look at it more closely. It was beautiful, with long swooping pillars supporting a graceful main compartment. Two long sections on either side, slightly smaller than the main one, were connected by arching bridges above and below. Unlike the smaller, aerodynamic tugs that sometimes docked at the station, the *Hispaniola*'s shape showed that it had never entered a planet's deep gravity well—it was purely a craft for space. Any ship could land in an emergency, of course, but this one looked as delicate as an egg shell.

"Albon tells me he has hired the best crew he could find," Lady Aurnice told her dad. "We vetted them as best we could, but you will understand that the choices were limited."

Jaquie's dad glared. "I understand, Lady Aurnice, but this is my daughter's safety—"

"I'll take good care of her," Albon said. Below his shelf-like brows, his eyes were kind. "We'll be fine. We'll find out about this treasure and be back as soon as possible." He looked down at Jaquie. "Take good care of your Go-Suit."

Jaquie shrugged. The customized suit had been hers since she was nine years old and provided total body protection—including air and waste removal—in space or in harsh environments. It was flexible enough to dance in and had grown as she had gotten taller. It fit over any clothing and except for the helmet, was clear.

Her dad continued. "Did you remember to pack the data crystal?"

She nodded. "And the adapter. Dad—"

He knelt down to her level. She saw the look on his face: a little sad, but also kind of proud. "Are you ready?"

"I guess so. I'm going to miss you, Dad."

"I know. I'm going to miss you, too. But this will be a big adventure for you, and you'll be safer on the *Hispaniola* with Albon. Do what he says. I'll see you soon."

Albon cleared his throat.

"Guess you better go now. Give me a hug."

The embrace was strong and lengthy, both of them trying to put into words what they couldn't say. Jaquie headed down the ramp next to Albon, bag in one hand and Go-Suit in the other.


## 7. On the Ship


ALBON FOUND Jaquie wandering the hauler. "Hi, Jaquie. Would you like a tour?"

They made their way through the passageways of each of the three levels on the ship. Several crew members hurried past, not stopping to talk.

Albon took pains to point out which areas were not safe for passengers to enter. "See this mark? That means Stay Out."

"You used to do this? That's why you know all this?" Jaquie asked part way through the tour.

"Yes, and I will be doing it again while we're traveling. We will be picking up some cargo and some more crew at our two stops."

"We're not going straight to the treasure?"

Albon laughed. "No. We have to pay for the *Hispaniola* and all its repairs. And Lady Aurnice wants to see if she can make some money in the future with this ship, too. Might as well find out right away. Here's where you'll be staying."

The tiny room held a small desk and three chairs, plus three beds, each on top of the other with stiff curtains to close off the space. The bottom bunk had a bag and two smaller boxes on it. "Whose stuff is that? Can I have the top bunk?"

"The senior crew member gets to choose which berth they want. Looks like your bunkmate has chosen hers, but you might have another in here after we add crew. Go ahead and take the top bunk for now. But be careful.

Why don't you get settled while I talk to the ship's captain? I'll see you in the common area in a little while."

Jaquie unpacked her clothes into the shallow drawer below the top bunk. Partense fit snugly in the corner where the bed met the wall. *I wonder what the other gara in here is like. Nice, I hope.* She sighed and went to the common room.

THE LONG, narrow room was deserted, but she could hear laughter through the window that led to the kitchen. Cautiously, she opened the door marked "IN" and stepped through.

"Well hello there!" A short, rotund gara leaned on a countertop and greeted her right away.

The other gara had closed one cupboard door and locked it, then unlocked and opened another.

"Who are you?" The first gara asked.

"Jaquie," she replied, feeling shy all of a sudden.

The other gara turned around to look at her. "Are you lost?"

"I don't think so. Albon told me to meet him in the common room, but there's no one in there right now."

"Oh, Albon!" The first one said, as if that explained everything. "I heard we were going to have a passenger, but no one said you'd be so young. What's your name, sweetie?"

"Jaquie."

"Jaquie, I'm Renna, and this is Del."

Renna wore her hair shoulder length except for two strands that grew from each temple. Green beads had been woven into the strands on either side, with six beads on the right side, three on the other.

Del nodded once in greeting before turning back to examine the contents of the cupboard. His hair was much shorter, but he, too, kept two strands of hair long at his temples. His beads—one on the right and eight on the left—were a dull red.

"What do the colors of your beads mean?"

"Oh." Del stared down into his plate. "This color"—he touched the beads lightly—"is for atmo-to-space loadteching. I'm getting special schooled in that. In the meantime, I help out in the kitchen."

Others in the common room introduced themselves. Some of them were loadtechs, like Albon but on different shifts. Others were pilots or navigators, or like Del, ordinary crew. They chatted for the whole meal and were surprised to find that Jaquie knew so much about haulers. "We get them at the Admiral Benbow all the time," she said.

JAQUIE WANDERED THE *HISPANIOLA*, avoiding rooms where crew worked. She peeked once in engineering, but a handful of garas stared at her, so she quickly withdrew. No one spoke to her until she found a large room with tables and chairs that looked like a dining room. Albon found her there. He looked very different in his ship clothes, and his eyebrows had been freshly waxed.

"Go on back to your bunk. And when you hear the announcement for Stage 3 prep, make sure you're lying on your bunk. It's a safety precaution. I've got to go—I need to make sure the cargo is secure."

Then he was gone. Jaquie took her time heading back to the bunkroom. In one cross-corridor, she caught sight of another crewmember hurrying up a steep ramp. Everyone had something to do—except her. She decided to explore, at least until someone announced Stage 3 preparations.

One door led in to a walk-in cupboard off the kitchen. Jaquie looked at shelf after shelf of neatly labeled bins, bags, and jars. It reminded her of the storeroom back at the Admiral Benbow Inn. She wondered what her father was doing, and felt a little pang. She missed him already. Would he finally get over his fear of heights and climb the girders and walk the catwalks to take care of the Vertical Garden by himself? Or would he get someone else to do it for him? He would have to. Perhaps a snack would get him off her mind.

"Stage 2 preparations should be complete. Begin Stage 3 prep," the low voice said, followed by a different sharp tone. Jaquie looked around and found a bin marked Fruit. She thumbed off the stasis field, grabbed an apple and dashed for her bunkroom.

The ship vibrated, reminding her that she needed to be in her bunk. She climbed to the top bunk, awkwardly with the apple in one hand. The vibrations increased. She dropped the apple.

The low voice was back. "Stage 3 preparations should be complete. Prepare for liftoff."

With an impatient sound, Jaquie climbed back down to look for the apple. Where was it? It had rolled against the lowest bunk.

With shaking hands Jaquie picked it up, bit into it and scrambled up the ladder to the top bunk. She was flat, apple in her mouth and Partense under one arm, when the *Hispaniola* lifted.

AS SOON AS THE "ALL-CLEAR" announcement aired, Jaquie heard her name called over the speaking orb in her bunkroom, commanding her to come to the kitchen.

She entered to see Albon, a gara new to her, and Del standing behind them both. "I'm Moa, I run the kitchen," the new gara said briskly. She was just a little shorter than Albon. Her cold blue eyes bored into Jaquie's. "You must be Jaquie." As she pointed into the storeroom, Jaquie could see that all the nails on that hand were bitten down to the quick. "Have you been in here since you came on board?"

Her heart pounded, as all the adults looked stern. "Yes."

"Take a look," Moa said.

Jaquie peeked in to see the storeroom covered in apples. There must have been hundreds on the floor, and they had rolled into every corner.

"Oh."

Moa glared at her. "You didn't latch the bin or turn the stasis field back on, so this happened during takeoff. Weren't you taught to put things back the way you found them? All those apples are bruised and dirty. What were you doing in here?"

"Just looking for a snack. I'm—I'm used to getting my own stuff." Even to her ears, Jaquie's voice sounded like a little kid.

"Well, get used to asking from here on out," Moa snapped. She glanced at Albon. "You need to do a better job of training this little gara about courtesy. If she's going to be working for me, I can't have her messing things up all the time."

Albon bowed his head. "Yes, Moa. I'm sorry. I will make sure she understands."

"Okay, Albon, no dessert for either of you for a nine-day. Jaquie, get an apron. You're going to pick up every one of those apples and clean them before they go back in the bin."

Once the apples had been put away, Moa gave Jaquie a list of chores, mostly cleanup after meals. Her rating, she was told, was "Kitchen Support Crew, Third Class." She fetched coffee and snacks for the senior crew on duty and wiped down tables in the common room. It was depressingly like her chores at the Admiral Benbow.

She was surprised to find that there were three shifts of garas working, resting, or sleeping at any one time. Jaquie decided that the gara who slept on the bottom bunk had a different shift than she did, because she rarely saw anyone awake in there. The middle berth remained empty.

Sometimes Jaquie worked with Del, but he did not strike up conversations and only responded to her in one-word answers. His rank was "Kitchen Support Crew, Second Class." He was supposedly her supervisor, but only gave instructions in terms of what Moa wanted: "Moa wants you to bring sandwiches and coffee to the captain's conference room."

One day, almost half a nine-day later, Del said, "Moa says the captain wants to see you."

Jaquie looked at him. "Why?"

He shrugged. "The Captain asks to see you, you go."

"Does she want something to eat?"

Exasperated, Del's shoulders slumped. "Just go."

Jaquie raced to the captain's conference room. She knocked on the hatch. A green light glowed, and a faint click told her that the hatch had unlocked.

Captain Po and Albon were the only garas in the room.

"Hi Jaquie," the captain smiled. "Have a seat."

Jaquie chose one close to Albon, facing Captain Po. Tall and wiry, the captain had long brown hair that fell to her back. She appeared to be younger than Albon. She sat tall in her seat, shoulders back.

The captain continued. "Lady Aurnice told me why she hired this ship. The real reason, I should say."

Jaquie nodded.

"I brought you here because—well, there are a few reasons. One, I want you to be quiet about this treasure. You haven't told anyone, have you?"

"No."

"Good. Albon also told me that there are some people after you. Is that right?"

Jaquie glanced at Albon. *How much did he tell the captain?* "My dad thinks so. That's why I'm here."

Captain Po nodded. " I think we need to change our plans. We're currently headed to a space station called Surann—you may have heard of it, it's the closest one to Athne—but now I don't think so. Just in case there are people looking for that information you have, I think we ought to go straight to where this supposed-treasure is."

"Okay."

"Only one person besides me needs to know that, and that's my pilot, Aida. I trust her."

*Why is she telling me all this?*

"So, to find this place where the treasure is, I'll need the coordinates on that data crystal." Po put out a hand.

Jaquie hesitated.

"What's the matter?"

"How do I know I can trust you?"

Captain Po withdrew her hand. "Oh. I see what you mean." She glanced at Albon. "Well, would it help if you knew Albon trusted me?"

Jaquie gave Albon a long, searching look.

"We have to trust someone, Jaquie," he said. "The captain is known as an honest gara. She has a good reputation among haulers. I've explained to her that Lady Aurnice wants to set up a new trade route from Athne Station, so she's eager to get future business."

"What if she wants to steal the treasure for herself?" Jaquie kept her eyes on Albon. *I hope she's not angry that I don't trust her.*

Albon nodded gravely. His long waxed eyebrows were freshly combed. "Captain Po will get a reward if we find the treasure, and will get an exclusive contract to transport goods from Athne Station. She said that's all she wants."

This time Jaquie did look at Captain Po, who smiled, a relaxed, friendly smile. Jaquie remembered the haulers who came to the Admiral Benbow Inn. Most of them were nice enough, even when they were drunk.

"I've already got a good ship, Jaquie. With a regular run, I can expand my business and work with Lady Aurnice to bring more garas to Athne. That'll help your dad's business, too. What do you say?"

"Can I learn how to work on a hauler?"

"If you like. Next time you're on the bridge, we'll start showing you what the controls are."

*Sometimes, you have to trust somebody.* "Okay. I have to go get it, though. It's hidden."

Captain Po nodded. "That's a good idea, I think. Bring it back to me here."

Back in the room, Jaquie handed the crystal spike to Captain Po.

"I'll take good care of it," she said to Jaquie.

## 8. Rough Landing

JAQUIE FOUND her work monotonous after having navigated a crowded floor full of drunks at the Admiral Benbow many times. Once last year Athne Station had seven ships all docked at one time for refueling, and fights had broken out at the Admiral Benbow every day. Shuttling food and drinks in quiet, calm rooms and cleaning the common room on the *Hispaniola* was downright boring.

One shift that all changed. She had brought snacks to the control room and paused to chat with Cate, the navigator. Of the bridge crew, Jaquie found her tasks the most interesting. "See that?" Cate asked, pointing to a shape in a display. "That's a fancy yacht that's out here, too. You could buy this ship and a couple of others for what that one cost."

An alarm screeched. Jaquie fumbled the capped tumbler of juice she had been holding and caught it just in time. She felt more than heard the ship rumble and took a step to regain her balance. "What was that?"

"Incoming! Emergency response initiated," someone yelled.

The Captain threw down the cracker she'd been holding. "Get us out of here. Jaquie—sit down, strap in, and shut up!"

"We're hit, Captain! Hull damage, but no breach," Cate called out.

The ship banked as it swooped to avoid the yacht. "What was that?"

"Dark missile. Have no idea what it's capable of," Cate said.

Another rumble, stronger than the last, shook the *Hispaniola*. "The yacht is moving away, but we've got damage this time."

"How bad?" Captain Po's calm voice sounded as if this happened every day.

"Reports coming in."

Aida, the pilot, was busy at her clutchboard. "We can put some more distance between us and that yacht. Maybe duck behind that moon over there."

"Do it."

"What happened to Surann Station?" someone wondered aloud. "Are we lost?"

The engineer's voice sounded on the speaking orb at low volume, murmuring about the damage and what was being done to counteract it: "Fire in the lower level, but it's almost out. Hull breach in forward quarter plugged, should hold for a while. But we need repair time when someone isn't shooting at us. How close are we to Surann?"

Aida flicked her eyes to Captain Po. Po raised her voice. "We're near a moon, Renna. We'll see if we can put down there. Just pay attention to your work. We'll give you notice when we get close to hitting dirt." The moon flickered to life on the display nearest Jaquie.

"You mean rock," Renna retorted. "That's all I see down there on the display."

Aida flinched.

"Shut up, Renna," Po snapped. "I want only reports, not running commentary." She said to Aida, "You're doing fine. Navigation—you spot a place to land yet?"

Cate spoke up promptly. "Several, Captain. Nothing really good. A narrow valley, trouble if we're off vector by too much. Mountain coming up soon, but don't know what's on the other side."

"That's it?"

"No data. I could tell you more if we could make one orbit."

"Nope. We have one shot at landing."

The pilot made adjustments on the clutchboard as the *Hispaniola* descended.

The minute sounds that filled the control room—breaths heaving and hands working—changed as the ship listed to port. Muscles tensed as they waited for the *Hispaniola* to right itself. The list deepened. Jaquie put out an arm to keep herself from falling.

"Need to put you big dumb guys outside to push us level again," Cate remarked to Jaren, a muscular tower of a gara. Jaquie was a little afraid of him. His eyebrows stood out even longer than Albon's, giving him a sinister look.

"Us big dumb guys would never have mistaken a little moon for Surann Station," Jaren retorted.

"I just put in the course we're given," she replied.

Captain Po activated a speaking orb and rapped out a command. Renna's whining voice echoed through the room, "I'm trying. There's a limit to what I can do."

Po spoke through clenched teeth, but her volume remained low. "Fix it or die, gara. You'll be the first one into the dirt, Renna."

Almost imperceptibly, the *Hispaniola's* list eased just as Cate called out, "Found a landing spot, Captain!"

"Where?"

"Sending to stations!"

Jaquie sat at an unoccupied station and read the numbers that hovered in front of her. Beautiful numbers, containing some kind of data. The numbers looked familiar. With a start, she realized why. "Hey!" she shouted. "It's the same!"

Captain Po said, "What is, Jaquie?"

"The numbers. Captain Po, the numbers on the display look like the same as the last ones on the crystal media."

"Jaquie, throw those numbers to Cate's station *now*."

"Got 'em," the pilot called out. "I can follow this."

"Looks good," the navigator said. "Not incredibly easy, but— wait, I have structures!"

"What?"

"Looks like some garas built something down there. It's not natural. Well, some of it is. Caves, maybe."

"Never mind. We need to get down first before we worry about structures. Helm, you good?" Aida nodded once.

Captain Po activated the speaking orb again. "Renna, landing soon. Can we handle it?"

"Yeah." The sour voice replied quickly. "The fire's out and the hull patch is holding. Better be a soft landing."

Her voice steady and firm, Po replied, "It will be."

The *Hispaniola* glided, glided, glided. Jaquie followed the process on the display in front of her. Within minutes she could see the long plain curving to the horizon and beyond it, low hills. She tensed when she realized that their destination lay at the foot of those hills. *We're going awfully fast. Are we going to crash into them?*

Numbers flowed past on the display, some of them depicting their speed, height above the surface, and more details than she had ever considered. She clutched at another part of the display and information on the moon blossomed—size, gravity, atmosphere, and the familiar series of coordinates that lead to their destination. The moon was small, but had enough gravity to keep objects—and atmosphere—from floating away. It was cold, but nothing an ordinary Go-Suit couldn't handle.

"Prepare for landing in ten," Captain Po called into the speaking orb. The *Hispaniola* listed again as the moon's gravity took hold. Po called Renna on the orb, but got only cursing in reply. The captain waved off the orb without saying more, and the list once more eased. Not completely, but more even.

They hit once, hard, and bounced up. Someone swore. The *Hispaniola* shed some speed and lowered more smoothly. The ship settled on its landing gears. They were down.

## 9. Big Discovery

. . .

CAPTAIN PO PLACED her hand on an orb, which immediately glowed faintly. "All departments—report, emergency priority!"

"This is Renna. Life support steady, no current threats. Gravity adjusted for landfall."

"This is Moa. A few bumps and bruises, but no serious injuries."

The rest of the reports were much the same—some damage, but none life-threatening.

"What do we have outside, navigation?"

"Go-Suit weather. Thin, cold air, not really breathable. Not much in the way of sights to see. Rocks, hills, dust. A structure of some sort a few kiloms away, built into a hill, looks like. No sign of movement."

"What happened to Surann Station? Did we miscalculate?" Jaren's voice, pitched high, carried throughout the control room.

"No," Captain Po replied. "I changed our destination. We're here on purpose. Our patroness has commissioned us to look for something valuable in the area."

"Did she lose an earring?" Renna's comment came through the speaking orb.

"A little more important than that, Renna. She refers to it as 'treasure' and we'll stand to benefit if we find it. Just concentrate on your jobs for now. I want a repair crew on the hull breach and the fire area, and anything else that might give us trouble lifting later. Get to work, people."

Moa tasked Del with preparing sandwiches and tea for Jaquie to deliver to the repair crews. By the time Jaquie made her last stop at the control room, her muscles ached and any flat surface beckoned her to lie down, even for a few moments.

Captain Po glanced at her as she took a sandwich from the cart. "You look like everyone feels, gara. Sit down."

Jaquie nibbled on a cookie as the captain called for another round of reports, all of which detailed the damage and efforts for repair. Po sighed. "Three-hour break for all. Go to your cabins and rest. Check in with me before you go back to repairs."

Jaquie stumbled back to her bunk and slept—really slept—for all three hours. A persistent chime roused her. Groggily, she sat up.

"'mup," she mumbled to the speaking orb. Her head felt like it was wrapped in mist.

"Good," Moa's voice replied. "Meet us in the common room."

She stumbled to the meeting. Despite the fatigue still evident on their faces, they all wore fresh clothes and looked more alert than Jaquie felt. Her cheeks felt hot. She rubbed her eyes and found them gritty.

To make it worse, Moa focused on her, smiling. "You awake, Jaquie?" *Why couldn't she just leave me alone? I can't be the only one who had trouble getting up.*

She nodded. Moa raised her voice to speak to everyone. "Some garas have volunteered to stay and work on the repairs while the rest of us go exploring."

Jaquie's fatigue and embarrassment burned away as her pulse hammered in her ears. *The treasure!*

The faces in the common room showed their excitement, too. She and Albon were going, as well as Moa and Cate.

The group each pulled Go-Suits out of bags. The suits, recognizing their bio-signatures, oozed up over them and gently covered them from their neck down to their fingertips and over the integrated shoes. The helmets, made of a separate material, went on last. Jaquie watched Moa put her helmet on with steady, practiced hands. The fingernails on one of Moa's hands were ragged and bloody where she'd bitten them. The nails on her other hand were tidy and filed neatly into half-circles.

In the airlock, Jaquie felt a tug on her Go-Suit as the airlock vacuumed out the ship's atmosphere and the moon's atmosphere seeped in.

The airlock hatch opened, and Moa took several steps to give the others behind her room to exit. She spread her arms wide. "Come on out, the weather's fine."

*Breathe,* Jaquie reminded herself. She had never been off Athne Station. She kicked a little at the ground. *Dust. What makes the dust?* The hills looked odd; she did not know what she had expected, but the dark rock looked ugly and uninviting.

She looked up—and immediately regretted it. Something—she

supposed those were clouds—hung over her head. Beyond them stars peeked down at her. *Where is the ceiling?* She swayed and her stomach heaved once.

A hand clutched her arm. She gulped air from her suit. "Look down," Cate's voice sounded close in her ear. "Look at your feet."

Jaquie obeyed, still fighting dizziness. The familiar patch on her right Go-Suit boot steadied her. *I had to patch it after Go-Suit practice when I was nine. I scraped it coming back in the airlock.*

"Everything okay back there?" Moa asked.

"Yeah," Cate replied. "Just a touch of vertigo." Her close voice sounded in Jaquie's ears again. "Just keep looking down or at the horizon. Not up. Got it?"

Jaquie nodded until she realized that Cate couldn't see the gesture. "Yeah," she replied, remembering at the last second to send her reply to Cate's suit alone.

The structure that Cate had seen from space turned out to be an opening into a cave. They stepped under the overhang and dull metal beams came into view.

Go-Suit lamps snapped on almost in unison, reacting to the darkened interior. The walls were rough rock, exotic to Jaquie.

Only a few steps into the passageway, the explorers saw a familiar sight ahead: a hatchway, with controls. An airlock.

"Shall we?" Moa said. They crowded inside, and once again Jaquie felt the tug on her Go-Suit from pressure changes. When the tell-tale showed green, Moa unlocked the hatch and stepped through. The door closed behind them with a soft hiss.

Lights flooded the interior room, obviously triggered by their movements. The cavern was large enough to enclose several Admiral Benbows, even with the lodger rooms included. Rough rock continued here—knobby and broken here and there by protrusions. The floor was relatively flat, but not without its own rough spots. Jaquie took in a breath at the beauty of the rock, striated with layers of blue-grey, cream, and tan.

"We can take off our helmets," Cate said, tapping on her cuff controls. "There's plenty of good air and pressure."

The cave smelled musty and stale. "This place is huge," Albon said in awe.

He stepped to one side of the cave and ran one hand over the wall. "Do you know what this is?" he asked in amazement. "I used to haul for a mining consortium on Outside. This rock is tacey. *Golden* tacey."

"Huh? The gravity stuff?" Jaquie bent and picked up a rock from the floor. "Doesn't look like much."

"Yeah. They use it everywhere they want to control gravity. From space stations and impeller ships on down to gravsleds and everything else."

"I've never heard of golden tacey."

"I'm not surprised. It's pretty rare. Two or three *times* as powerful as the regular stuff."

"That would be worth quite a lot," Cate remarked.

Moa turned. "Only if they recognize what it is. I'll bet not one gara in nine knows what tacey looks like in its raw form."

Jaquie ran ahead, exploring. Each part of the cavern was crowded with beautiful rocks in all sizes.

## 10. "I Want to Go Home"

A DEEP BOOM rolled through the cavern. Small tremors shook Jaquie off balance. Motes of dust and a pebble or two came down. The enclosure smelled musty and old, causing Jaquie to sneeze. Captain Po's voice came through their helmets. "We've got guests, folks."

Everyone dashed for the exit, and Jaquie followed, heart pounding. She tucked the rock into a pocket on her Go-Suit. Albon gently steered her in front of him to make sure she didn't get left behind. The airlock still showed green, so they jammed on their helmets—which auto-sealed to their Go-Suits—and cycled through quickly. From the shadow of the entrance they could only see the *Hispaniola* sitting as it had when they left. Cate stepped toward the ship, but cursed once she glanced up and behind them. "A skiff landed on the hill. Probably from that yacht that shot at us."

Sure enough, a small skiff had settled atop the cave. As they watched, an airlock hatch opened, and Go-Suited figures stepped out, stunners holstered on the suits.

"Quick, back in the cave!" Cate commanded. "There isn't time to make it to the *Hisp*." Once through the airlock she hit the emergency override. "That should keep them out for a while."

Albon asked, "How can we keep them from getting in?"

"What do we do if they *do* get in?" Cate asked.

Jaquie looked around. "Is there a place to hide?"

"Won't do any good. If they know we're here, they'll search until they find us," Albon responded.

"Can't we just let them have the tacey?"

"Sure, but they'll probably kill us to keep this location a secret," Cate said. "Spread out and search," she ordered. "Look for anything we can use as a weapon, machinery that might work, anything. I'll tell the *Hisp* what's happening."

Jaquie strode over to a part of the cavern where several boulders, some of them taller than she, still protruded from the stone floor. She found nothing except more rocks and dirt.

Someone cried out, and she whirled to see Cate and Albon crumpled on the floor and Moa facing three Go-Suited garas, each with stunners in their hands. They were unrecognizable through their helmets. *They shot them!*

As Jaquie watched, she realized that the people in suits didn't know she was there. An idea occurred to her—the nearest boulder had rough edges that just begged to be climbed.

At first, Jaquie found plenty of toe holds and protrusions to grasp. The higher she ascended the more difficult the climb became. At last she stepped out onto the top of the boulder.

Cate and Albon had not moved since Jaquie had heard Cate yell. *Hope they're just stunned. But what can I do? How did they get in?* From her view atop the large rock, Jaquie could see the people in Go-Suits talking to Moa, but not what was said. She stepped gingerly on the big boulders. *This is even taller than the vertical garden back home.* She moved from rock to rock, looking for a way to get closer to the new garas and find out what they were saying. One stone outcropping blocked her view, so she stepped around it and found herself looking down at a stone archway leading deeper into the cavern. *Away from garas with stunners is good,* she reasoned. Heart pounding, she listened. The voices were still too far away to understand. She climbed down as quietly and quickly as she could.

Several dozen steps into the tunnel she found another airlock. This one was clearly designed to bring equipment and large materials in and out.

Jaquie stood, hand on the airlock control, trying and failing to breathe naturally. *I shouldn't leave the others back there alone. Wonder if there are more garas outside with stunners? But I could go to the* Hispaniola *and get help.* Jaquie grasped the control and stepped in.

She exited on a different side of the hill from where the *Hispaniola* had landed. Ahead on a bluff, Jaquie could see a sleek, dark needle-shape—the skiff. It was much closer to her than the *Hispaniola.*

Jaquie skirted the hill, now and then climbing over rocks and through little eddies filled with dust. Scrape marks showed where equipment had tracked through the dust into the cavern. She kept in the shadow of the hill as long as she could. *Wonder if they left anyone in the skiff? Would they stun me if they saw me?*

She stared at the *Hispaniola* looming some distance away. The yacht was nowhere in sight. *If I call the ship, someone will know I'm out here and will come after me. If I run, I might get to the* Hispaniola *before the people in the yacht notice me.* As she had practiced ever since she had been fitted for her Go-Suit when she was nine, Jaquie checked her oxygen, filters, and fluids. *I can make it. I'll get help and we'll come back and rescue the others.*

She dashed, remembering not to look up.

The Go-Suit made her steps clumsy. The entire suit, not just the part covering her torso, had small pockets storing water, air, and small tools. Still, it felt as if she were running in slow motion. The *Hispaniola* came closer. Closer still. Almost there ... breathing hard, she stopped abruptly at the airlock they had come out of. *How long has it been?*

Inside the *Hispaniola*, Jaquie yanked off her helmet to the sound of screams and yells. A tense voice—Captain Po—came from a nearby speaking orb. "Who came through the airlock?"

"Jaquie. A skiff came—"

Po cut her off. "Never mind that. We've got a revolt. Some crew want the treasure for themselves and are trying to take over the ship…"

Noises in the background cut off her voice.

"Captain. Captain Po!" Jaquie got no reply, and after a few heartbeats the orb shutdown on its own. *Who's revolting?* Jaquie's stomach cramped. *Who can I trust?*

*I wanna go home.*

The screaming and yelling had faded away. Jaquie crept into the hallway. She saw no one. She stood in the hallway leading past the common room and listened to a babble of voices, all angry and strident. Jaquie backed up and made her way down a different corridor, but the voices sounded closer. She could hear the both female and male voices. They were behind her, shouting curses.

*What if they shoot me? Will it hurt?* With a shudder, she pushed that thought aside. She turned away from the voices. *The control room. I'll bet everyone is in the control room.*

The nearer she got to the control room, the louder the sounds became. Now she could hear heavy footfalls and the sounds of people breathing. They were running. Then stunner sounds and loud thumps. *Did they just stun someone? What do I do?* Jaquie ran down the corridor until she got to the control room hatch. It wouldn't open for her. She banged on it while the voices got louder. "Let me in! Let me in!" she cried frantically.

"Who is out there?" a voice called.

"Jaquie."

"Anyone with you?"

"No."

"Come in the control room—but slowly."

The hatch opened. Renna lay on the floor near the hatchway,

dead or unconscious. Captain Po, several crewmembers behind her, stood facing Jaquie. The control room was crowded, but Jaquie only recognized a few faces as she glanced around: some garas from Albon's loadtech crew, the relief pilot, some engineering garas.

Jaquie stared at the stunner in the captain's hand. "Come all the way in," Captain Po said. As Jaquie complied, the hatch closed.

"Where are the others?" The captain said, without lowering her weapon.

"That's what I came to tell you," Jaquie replied. "A skiff landed on the top of the cavern, and some garas got into the cave by a back entrance. Cate and Albon were on the ground when I left." Jaquie glanced at the still-unmoving form of Renna, then back up to Captain Po.

"How was Moa?" Po asked.

"I couldn't see her. That's when I left."

"No one saw you leave?"

Jaquie thought about that for a moment. "Maybe someone in the skiff."

The captain's expression changed. "Okay, Jaquie—get over there by the wall."

Jaquie obeyed, watching Captain Po's eyes flick to a display showing the empty corridor leading to the control room. *Of course— cameras would show everywhere in the ship.* Other displays showed corridors and rooms full of garas.

Eyes on the displays, Po made an adjustment on a clutchboard in front of her. "There," she said, almost to herself. "That should keep them busy. Aida," she said to the pilot. "Take the aft corridor to get to that weapons locker and grab all the stunners. Don't take any other route. I've got the traitors" —she said that last word with great venom— "locked off in one part of the ship. You should be fine, but get back here fast." She lowered her stunner a bit. "Jaquie, Renna tried to take over this ship, but we stopped her. Those garas" —she nodded toward the display—"are rioting. I think it has to do with that treasure that's out there. Any idea what it is?"

"Tacey powder...um, rock," Jaquie replied. "Albon said it was golden tacey."

Captain Po's eyebrows rose. "Really? That would be worth quite a bit. Del—" the slim gara behind her took a step forward. "Pick a station and monitor those cameras. If anyone approaches the *Hisp*, signal me."

"Will do."

Aida returned, sliding into the control room without showing her back to Jaquie.

"Give one to Jaren and keep one for yourself," the captain commanded. "Keep yours on Renna. If she starts to wake up, stun her again." Po focused on Jaquie again. "Which side are you on, gara?"

Jaquie gulped. "I—I just want to go home." The treasure did not seem worth it if Albon and her new friends were dead.

Captain Po looked at her, eyes hard and lips tight, before lowering the stunner. "Aida, Jaren, Del … keep an eye on her."

"Captain! Garas approaching our airlock," Del said.

All eyes went to the display. Jaquie saw Go-Suited figures waiting as another worked the controls.

Captain Po nodded at two garas in that quick, jerky way of hers. "Del, Jaren, take this group down the aft corridor and go to the freight airlock. Be quick and be quiet. Get into your Go-Suits and wait for us there. Aida, you and Jaquie and I will stay here." Quietly, the group in the control room obeyed. Jaquie took a deep breath as the hatch closed behind them and the tension in the room diminished.

On the floor, Renna twitched and moaned softly.

"Good," Captain Po said. "Our little traitor is coming to."

Renna rolled over and cursed. Without looking or changing expression, Captain Po shot her with the stunner. Once more Renna slumped into unconsciousness. "I despise traitors." Po focused on the display and muttered, "C'mon… just a little further…"

"What are you going to do?" Aida asked.

"Let them have the *Hispaniola*. You two get ready to go."

Aida and Jaquie exchanged a look.

"There!" Po shouted with a pump of her fist and grasped something on her clutchboard. "Let's go. Aida, you go first and keep that stunner ready, just in case."

"Where are we going? What did you do?"

"We'll meet the loyal crew at the freight airlock. I dropped the airtight hatches between compartments on those garas there—" she nodded at the display. "They'll be trapped in that hallway for at least an hour. The rest of the traitors have a few parts of the ship, but can't get past the hatch overrides I've triggered." Captain Po grinned. "Captains have lots of tools in case of a mutiny."

Aida's face transformed as she caught on to the plan. "And we'll be off the ship by that time."

Po nodded. "Once we go back to the cavern and get Cate, Moa, and Albon, we'll see if anyone else is on that skiff on the hill. One way or another, we'll go up to that yacht and make it our ride home."

The little group made their way cautiously through the ship's corridors. They met no one, but heard plenty of banging and cursing. Del and Jaren had everyone clad in their Go-Suits and kept guard while Captain Po and Aida donned theirs. They stepped through the large freight airlock together. Outside, the group bunched together, unmoving. A murmur ran through them.

A gara in a Go-Suit stood outside the airlock. Even in the twilight of the moon, the figure stood out among the dust and rocks. In place of one hand, a long, curved blade with deep serrations stood out from a stump below the shoulder. The Go-Suit fabric bunched up a little where it covered the stump, but not the blade. The other hand held a stunner.

Jaquie's blood ran cold. *The one-armed gara!*

Aida pointed her stunner at the one-armed gara.

"Stalemate," Aida said softly. "You stun us, we stun you. There are more of us. We still win."

Jaquie looked at the stunner in the gara's only hand and wondered how many people the gara had already shot. Then she saw the hand that gripped the stunner. The fingernails had been bitten down to the quick. "It's Moa!"

With a lightning-fast lunge, Moa snatched Jaquie's arm and dragged her away from the others.

Jaquie whimpered, wide eyes on the blade so close to her helmet. The metal was dull in places, marked by what looked like dried blood. Her knees shook. She looked at Captain Po and the others and saw stunners trained on her and Moa. Her arm hurt where Moa held it.

"I'll take this little gara for now," Moa said. She sounded oddly happy. "I'm going to send her back in *pieces*." Jaquie gulped as Moa continued talking. "That ought to keep her people away from here while we mine the golden tacey. We've got enough garas to work the mines, and the *Hispaniola* can take it to our buyers." She gestured with the stunner. "Now get out of my way," she growled.

The crowd moved to one side. Moa gripped Jaquie's arm even tighter, pulling her until her feet barely touched the dusty ground. Tears came to her eyes and ran down her cheeks. At the airlock, Moa paused. She couldn't activate it while holding Jaquie and the stunner. The blade slid uselessly off the control. Frustrated, Moa let go of Jaquie for a brief instant to hit open the airlock.

The sudden release of pressure caused Jaquie's knees to give way. She collapsed. Her vision was cloudy, but she heard the sound of a stunner.

Then there were voices and gentle hands helping her up and checking to see if she was hurt.

She heard Aida say, "I got a chance to shoot, so I took it."

Jaquie took a few shaky breaths and felt better. Moa lay unconscious outside the airlock.

"Good work, Aida," Captain Po said. "Stuff Moa into the airlock and cycle it. Everyone got their stunner ready? Let's go check on Albon and Cate."

No one else approached them as the group made their way back to the cavern. Captain Po barked, "Jaquie, are you well enough to show Aida and Del where the back entrance is to this place? Yes? Okay. Be careful, we don't know where those other garas are." Jaquie still felt a little dizzy, but kept her mind on navigating the rocks and boulders outside the cavern. *I have to help. I'm the only one that knows where this back entrance is.*

Jaquie stood back as Aida and Del stood in front of the large airlock as it cycled with the familiar feeling of unseen hands tugging at her Go-Suit. She heard Aida mutter to herself, "There's no way to sneak through an airlock."

No one confronted them inside the cavern. They stood, stunners ready, for several heartbeats. Jaquie recognized the tall rock she had climbed down just a while ago. *It seems like it was yesterday or something.* She turned on her helmet mike and called Aida. "This is the rock I was on before. Do you want to climb on top so you can look around the cavern?"

"Yes!" Aida's voice was breathy and high with tension. "You and Del stay down here, toward the airlock. If you have to, get into it and go back out."

Del moved in front of Jaquie as Aida climbed. She came back down quickly. "C'mon. Captain Po has everything under control."

Po stood over Albon and Cate, who were just stirring. Jaren crouched down beside a row of unconscious garas stretched out a few meters away. Jaquie stared at them. "Who are these people? Did you stun them all?"

Jaren chuckled. "These must be the ones who came from that skiff up on the hill. Captain Po got three; I got one. That gara is *fast.*"

Captain Po issued orders. "Okay, Aida, stay here and make sure no one gets in. Jaren, you guard the back airlock and hope there are only two ways into this place. I'll go up to that skiff and see if it's empty. Del, come on out and look for my signal. I'll wave one arm if it's safe, in honor of our one-armed traitor back in the *Hispaniola.* Got it, Del? If I do anything but wave one arm, don't let anyone out."

He nodded once in imitation of Po's quick nod.

"Captain," Aida interrupted. "We ought to take one of these garas with us to the skiff. I'll bet that skiff is bio-locked to one of them. We won't be able to get in without them."

Po nodded one jerk of her head. "Good point. Jaren, once Del has the signal, you grab one of these garas and drag them along. Don't bother being gentle. Jaquie, can you help Albon and Cate make it to the skiff?" Jaquie nodded, then the captain stepped into the airlock, stunner in her fist and with Del trailing.

"How bad is it, Albon?" Jaquie asked.

He sat up slowly, clutching his head. His eyebrows were tangled and untidy. "I feel like I spent all night drinking at your dad's place."

Aida crouched down where Cate lay. "Can you stand, Cate?"

She gave a small nod. "The question is, 'Can I stand without throwing up?'"

"Yeah, a stunner's nasty, gara. Throw up or don't, but you gotta stand if you want off this rock," the pilot replied.

Cate stood with Aida's help, but hunched over again, knees buckling. "I don't think so." She did not so much sit down as she fell into a sitting position.

Del came back through the airlock. "I got the signal. Everyone out."

Aida called him over. "Help Cate. She's too stunned to walk by herself. Let's go, everyone."

Jaren slung one of the unconscious garas over his shoulder.

Jaquie helped Albon to his feet. He used her shoulder to steady himself.

The group made their way up the hill above the cavern and to the yacht's skiff. Jaren held the unconscious gara's Go-Suited hand to the lock and it clicked faintly.

Its airlock, too small for any but one gara, presented a problem, but they took turns going through while Captain Po stood guard. She was the last to enter the skiff.

Jaquie discovered the skiff was just a transport with individual cushioned capsules. Jaren stuffed the mutineer in one capsule and locked it.

Captain Po made her way to the co-pilot capsule and sealed herself in. "Aida, can you drive this skiff?"

Aida looked over the controls. "Um…maybe. I recognize some of these symbols. This should be the altitude control, and this—"

"Don't tell me, show me," Po snapped. Turning her head, she

barked, "Everyone else take a capsule and strap in. If you don't know how, ask someone. I want to lift in three minutes."

The capsules resembled over-cushioned lounge chairs enclosed by a transparent front. Once seated, the occupant connected their Go-Suits and closed the front panel. Jaquie felt safe and snug. Air, cool and fresh, hissed as it entered. She heard voices through the capsule connection.

"Where to, Cap'n?"

"Let's go check out this yacht I've heard so much about."

Cate drew a breath. "Okay, you're the boss. I'm pretty sure this skiff doesn't have any shooting capability."

"They won't shoot at their own skiff. They'll think we're their own garas."

"If you say so. Let's hope they don't call us and ask us how everything went down below."

Jaquie felt the skiff surge as it lifted from the little moon. *Not much antigrav on this skiff.* She had to stop herself from giggling. *But there's plenty of tacey on the moon, if someone can mine it!*

Shortly Aida said softly, "There's the yacht."

"Nice," Captain Po said.

"Okay, approaching to dock. There's a spar to the stern, there —see?"

"Nothing on comm?"

"Nothing, Captain. You would have heard."

"Hmmm. I don't much like this."

"Me, either."

As soon as the skiff docked with a barely perceptible thump, Captain Po stood. "Jaren, you're with me. Bring a stunner for each of us. Aida, you stay here with the others, ready to shove off at the first sight of trouble. Everyone, stay in your capsule for now."

The skiff's exit mated to a hatch that led to an airlock. Po and Jaren cycled through, stunners in hand.

Jaquie felt her eyelids droop while they waited. The quiet murmurs of the others talking amongst themselves faded into the background.

She jerked awake some indeterminate time later when Captain

Po's voice loudly broke into the still, quiet cabin of the skiff. "Aida, bring the others aboard. There's a handful of crew, but I think we can take them. The yacht will barely fit us all, but we can squeeze in." The captain's voice changed as she directed a question to Jaquie. "Hey Jaquie, you may learn to navigate sooner than you expected. Cate's going to need help getting us back to Athne Space Station. You ready?"

Jaquie sat up straighter in her capsule, even though she knew Captain Po was teasing her. "Yes, captain," she replied in her best grown-up voice. "I'll help Cate navigate.

"And," Jaquie whispered to herself as she patted the rock she'd tucked away earlier. "I have the treasure in my pocket."

## 11. Epilogue

JAQUIE ALMOST SQUEALED as the shape on her display responded to her touch.

"That's it," Cate said from her station nearby. "Just keep that shape on the line you see. You're doing fine."

"This is all there is to piloting?" Jaquie asked.

Cate laughed. "Oh, no. There's *much* more to it. That's just the easiest simulator we have."

"Oh." Jaquie dropped her hands.

"No, keep going," Cate urged. "It gets more interesting soon. And in a few hours we'll approach Athne Station. You can sit near me and watch me pilot this yacht all the way in."

Jaquie did not look up from her focused stare at the display. "I'd like that, Cate. Maybe one day I'll be a pilot just like you."

## AUTHOR'S NOTES – T.L. WOOLSLEY

WHEN I SET out to write this story, I realized that, for me, *Treasure Island* by Robert Louis Stevenson was one of those stories I *thought* I had read.

I was wrong.

Apparently, much of the lore about pirates (the wooden leg, the bird on the shoulder, etc.) comes from this tale and so much of it pervades our culture that I was rather familiar with the contents. I knew it well enough for casual conversations, not so much to write a story based on the plot. Nonetheless, I enjoyed the yarn and adapting it to my needs.

If you'd like to read the original, download it from Project Gutenburg for free, or look no further than your local library. Have fun!

*—TLW*

# WHEN THE HURLY BURLY'S DONE

## KEN PELHAM

M otivations to evil are often primal, lustful, and powerful, and have changed little over the centuries. William Shakespeare understood this, and his work resonates with such unpleasant truths even today.

    —KP

BRIGANDS KEY, *Florida, 1934*

SUNLIGHT SLANTED gold through the wooden blinds, alighting Sam Hawke's face, nudging him awake. He squinted, picked up his pocket watch, swore softly. The sun was already up and here he lay, still in bed. *Her bed.*

His fitful sleep ended, he was sure, not by morning sun but by a dream of gathering darkness, and three pairs of glowing white pinpoints—eyes—circling him, studying him. Judging him. He sensed something expected of him.

Good thing dreams and nightmares were ghosts and not real.

Mary MacGregor stirred next to him. He leaned in and kissed

her on the cheek, and patted her shoulder. She opened her eyes, the fog of sound sleep evaporating from them, and smiled.

He kissed her again, this time on the mouth.

In the soft yellow light, he appraised her again and congratulated himself. She was one knockout of a woman, the most beautiful on the whole damned island of Brigands Key.

He drew a strand of blond hair back from her face and tucked it behind her ear. "I got to go, Darlin.' Fred will be back up from Tampa soon."

Mary stretched and rolled toward him, slow and sinuous. "Oh, he won't be back for a couple hours. We've got time for more."

"Time ain't the point. It's Saturday morning, and even if most of the fleet's sleepin' off a drunk, there're always a few busybodies up and about. I can't have them seeing me sneaking out of your house while your husband's away. Bad for business."

"My husband. Your boss. It doesn't matter, sweetie. We're going to make it official and respectable someday. Right?"

"Someday. It takes a long time to climb that ladder, even in good times. Maybe you ain't heard the news; the whole damn country's out of work."

She giggled. "Work. Yes, I heard of that somewhere, Baby."

He studied her for a moment, refusing to smile back. At times, he wondered what he saw in her. Lines around the block at Relief Offices and soup kitchens all over the damned country, but she could still buy anything and everything. Worst part was, she came from as meager a background as anyone else on Brigands Key, her daddy a fisherman like all the rest. A bad heart killed him young. She was way too young then too, maybe seven, left with a drunk mother. Hardscrabble, like most in town.

But her *looks*. Damn, was she pretty. Movie star pretty. She'd turned heads from the moment she got to high school, and soon as she got out, the springtime after the stock market crashed and sent millionaires jumping off buildings in New York, she'd turned the head of the richest man on the island. Hell, the *only* rich man.

But he was three times her age.

Sam flipped the covers and swung his legs off the bed. He stood, stretched, and wrangled a satisfying pop from his back. He reached for the bottle of rum on the nightstand, good Cuban stuff from the smuggling days, and took a pull. Wouldn't burn a hole through your stomach like the domestic shine.

Mary said, "You don't have to go, Baby."

Sam grunted. "Yeah, I do. You wouldn't be able to live like the Queen of England if Fred ever caught wind of his wife and his foreman."

"Maybe I could."

He turned to look at her. "Ha! Just how's that, Darlin'?"

"Oh, I don't know. I just can't live with someone that old forever."

"Well, stick around. Fred's sixty-two and drinks like a fish. Can't live forever. Time comes, and you'll come out like a rose. A rich, beautiful rose."

"His daddy's eighty-eight and fit as a fiddle." Her face drew into a perfect little frown.

Sam shrugged. "You picked this life of the waiting game yourself. Might take a bit longer than you'd like."

She hesitated. "It doesn't have to."

He studied her for a moment. "What do you mean?"

"I think you know."

"You're going for a divorce?"

She giggled, the sound of her voice like honey. "Divorce! If I filed, you think I'd come away with *anything*?"

"I don't know why not."

"Then you don't know a thing about money and how it works. How the courts work when you sew 'em up with money."

Sam snorted. "You got money."

"I *live* on money. Fred's money. It ain't my money."

Sam watched her, struggling through things he might say. None seemed to fit.

"Sam?"

"Yeah?"

"I'm not going to wait out my life."

He held up his palms in exasperation. "Run away with me

then."

"And be poor? I love you, Baby, but not that much."

He wouldn't put words to what she was saying. That would be stupid. "Guess you're out of luck then."

"I don't know. Like you said, Fred drinks like a fish. Who knows, maybe he'll fall off one of his damn boats and drown. Accidents happen all the time." She rolled onto her stomach, laced her fingers together and propped her chin upon them, her eyes bright. "Then I'll be rich! And still young, and needing an upstanding husband that knows Fred's business. Think of it, Sam!"

*Accidents happen all the time.*

Silence hung in the space between them. At last Sam turned and pulled on his clothes. "I got to go."

"Wait, Honey. You going to that thing at the high school Fred's all excited about?"

"What, that Shakespeare play?"

"Yeah. I'm going with Fred."

"I don't know."

"Go. It'll do you good. You got to start looking smart if you want to be my husband."

"Smart? Like Fred?" He snorted. "Fred's only going 'cause it'll make *him* look smart."

"No, that ain't it. He is smart. Real smart."

"He finished high school like the rest of us. Nothing special."

"He couldn't afford college. He worked to get where he is. Promise me you'll go see that show."

"Don't know why."

"God, you are a dummy. I want it to look like you and Fred are pals. Like he wants you to succeed." She opened the bedside drawer, rummaged a bit, and tossed a yellow card flyer to him. He picked it up.

"*Macbeth,*" he said. "I heard of it."

"It's got witches and ghosts and sword fights. Freddie said it's real good. Course, he's never been to a play his whole life. It's a big deal it's even coming to Brigands Key, and folks are even coming over from Cedar Key and Chiefland to see it. Folks with money."

"Puttin' on airs, ever last one of 'em." He shook his head, headed for the door. "Eight o'clock tonight, huh? I guess I better go."

"You *will* go. For me." She paused. "For us."

"Us?" He half-turned toward her, not wanting to hear what was coming.

"Sam. I want *you*, Darlin.' I love you. Not that hateful old man. And the only way we are together is if he's dead. You understand? I want him dead!'"

Sam stood still, the words caroming through his mind. He began to speak, thought better of it, and opened the door and stepped out into the heat of a Gulf of Mexico morning.

SAM STOPPED at the biggest boat on the dock, admiring it resentfully. Gleaming white hull, and the faint aroma of richly oiled and polished wood, the scent of a rich man's boat. A beauty. *Ellenore*, the painted name on the transom announced. *Ellenore*. Fred never even bothered to rename the boat after his first wife died and he managed to wed and bed Mary.

Fred had hired him back when he got back from Texas and the oil rigs and just a little jail time for drinking and fighting. Needed a guy with a little wildcat in him, he'd said. A guy with a little good in him and a little bad. And that's what Fred got; a guy who was loyal and knew how to work hard and when to keep his mouth shut. Better yet, a guy agreeable to do a little extra if a job needed to be out of sight. And Fred rewarded Sam and made him his right-hand man, which was the closest thing to a friend as Fred was likely to get.

Folks around town lumped Sam in with Fred. They liked him or hated him, or didn't care one way or the other, pretty much based on how they felt about Fred. That suited Sam just fine, just as long as he got a little of the same respect Fred got.

Fred came around the cabin and spotted him, beamed, and waved him closer with a whiskey bottle. "Sam!" he bellowed. "Come aboard. I'll name you first mate. Bet you never figured you'd be mate on a boat like this." When Fred wasn't bragging about his giant power boat, a 29-foot Richardson, he would brag about his giant damned car or his giant damned house. Always showing off. Rambled about his trip to Paris the last year, about London and King George. Like he was one of them.

Sam pulled his pocket watch out and flipped it open. Seven o'clock. Fred had insisted on a little something before the show, just like they do in Tampa. Like he needed an excuse to drink.

Fred fetched a highball glass, grabbed a handful of ice from a box with his greasy fat hand, shoved it into the glass, smothered it with whiskey, and shoved it at Sam.

Sam forced gratitude and a smile and took the glass. He'd never turned down a drink before, not a free one at least.

"You ready to go get you some culture, son?" Fred roared. He clapped Sam on the back.

"You bet, boss. I heard this will be good."

Mary emerged from the cabin, her own drink in hand. Sexy as ever. Dressed to the nines. She looked a little wobbly.

"I heard of this one, *Macbeth*," Fred continued. "Sword fights and stuff. It ain't no Roosevelt WPA touring number either. Nothing communist about it."

"Now, Fred," Mary piped in. "The WPA kept my daddy employed when there wasn't no work for him. They built this dock, remember?"

"The old one was just fine."

*The old one was about to crash into the water on its own*, Sam thought. But he kept his mouth shut and just nodded his support. He took a sip of whiskey, raised his glass in acknowledgment. "This stuff is sure better than what we used to haul, boss."

"Better tasting. Ain't better for us, though!" Fred snorted and held the glass up and peered into it. "Probably send me to an early grave."

"Prohibition had its good points and bad points, didn't it?"

"Made me a rich son of a bitch."

Mary laughed. "I'll drink to that." She took a quick sip. "Fishing has made you respectable though, Honey. Kind of."

"Respectable *and* famous." Fred added.

"Fame ain't a good thing for a smuggler," Sam said. "That night Capone dropped in to check up on you on his way to Miami, I thought I was gonna die."

"You and me both. But he liked your hillbilly jokes." Fred raised a toast. "To Samuel Ross Hawke. My right-hand man and best hillbilly foreman!"

Sam took another drink. "Bootlegging's done with, though, and fishing just ain't as lucrative as liquor. Course, nothing else is, either. Ever thought about lumber, Fred?"

Fred looked at him with watery eyes. "That's a whole different game, son. I ain't changing my game this late."

"But it's money that just grows on trees. Fine. Oranges. How about oranges?"

"It'd take me years to get a cash crop. Nope."

"We'll spend his money 'til it's gone, Sam," Mary said with a giggle. He looked at her. The giggle was a lie. No laughter in her face, just a what-about-it look.

Twilight and stars gathered above. Venus hung low and silver over the sea. Sam stared at it. "Goddess of Love," he said. "Pretty, ain't she?" He glanced at Mary.

Fred grunted, and pointed into the sky opposite. "And there's Mars. God of War. A better planet for watching *Macbeth*."

"Guess we ought to get over to the high school, boss. That show'll be up directly."

Fred turned narrowed eyes to him. Sam hated that look. Knew it came with a scolding. "We'll go when I finish my drink." He brought the glass up slowly, making sure Sam and Mary knew full-well they'd leave when Fred was good and ready.

Sam couldn't wait to knock that smug grin off his face one of these days.

A BUNCH of the high school boys were still dragging oak chairs noisily across the gym floor and lining them up in rows when they arrived. Brigands Key High didn't even have an auditorium yet, but rumor had it they'd start building one in another year. Or two. Or never. In the meantime, the school had a makeshift stage they'd drag out and set up for events and graduations and such, and it never looked better than tonight, decked out with a heavy curtain the color of red wine.

Fred had brought a fifth along with him for good measure and kept hitting it. Though with the way he smelled, he didn't need anymore.

Chief Toomey drifted over, his bulk and attitude filling space. He nodded and gripped Fred's hand. "Knew you'd be here, Fred. Course, ever'body in town is here." His usually gloomy face almost looked to carry a little pride and excitement. He lifted his chin in a ghost of a nod to Sam. And turned his eyes on Mary, looking her up and down.

Being the richest man in the county, Fred sauntered to the front row and took a seat. Sam and Mary sat on either side of him.

The kerosene lamps dimmed and footlights flickered and glowed. A murmur of anticipation pulsed through the crowd. Some slick Midwesterner—already in costume of a medieval warrior—came out and announced in a loud voice, and with a sweep of his slender arms, that he was Jerry Kowalski or something, of the Minneapolis Players or something. He blubbered about how happy he was to be here in Briggins's Key. Sam knew it wasn't lost on the crowd that the guy couldn't be bothered to get the name right. Blathered on a minute or two about Shakespeare and how this stuff was three hundred years old. Talked about the blood-soaked Scotland of Macbeth's day. His flat, nasal accent didn't fit the costume. Sam hoped it got better than this. The man strutted, almost pranced, off the stage and disappeared.

Silence filled the gym, and the curtains rustled and parted. A wisp of white mist drifted out and around, hugging the floorboards and curling around fake rocks. Light flickered and flashed from somewhere and a sound of thunder pealed and rolled and lingered and faded. Sam glanced about, startled. It sounded like the real thing. Maybe there was something to this live stage stuff. *Oohs* and *ahs* peppered the crowd. More lights lit the stage.

Three gaunt, hunched figures, each carrying a glowing lantern, moved from the shadows in the rear of the stage and crept closer, almost gliding with a sinuous movement to the front of the stage, not more than twenty feet from Sam. Women, of indeterminate age, dressed in torn, filthy rags.

Fred leaned toward him. "Them's the witches," he whispered. "Macbeth's witches." Like Sam was too stupid to figure that out.

The gym grew silent as a windless night on the water. The witches became still and glowered at the audience. Their heads swiveled slowly, side to side, as if searching each person in turn. Their eyes seemed to glow, points of white, in the lantern light. Three pairs of white pinpoints.

Just like Sam's dream.

He found himself leaning closer.

Seconds passed in utter, profound silence. One of the witches locked her eyes upon his and held them for a moment. Her face, though filled with menace, held a certain seductive beauty, her features flawless and smooth. Her eyes came alive, glowing with bottomless depths of white. She whirled upon her companions and spoke at last. "When shall we meet again, in thunder, lightning, or rain?" Her voice rang clear and sweet and strong.

A second witch, the tallest, answered, her voice like the rustle of cracked and brittle leaves. "When the hurly-burly's done. When the battle's lost and won." She drew a slow circle in the air with a thin outstretched finger. The circle glowed, a thin, drifting wreath of white fire. It hung in the air, and dissolved. A murmur stirred the crowd.

"How'd she *do* that?" Mary whispered.

The third witch, an ancient being, leaned against her staff, and looked to an imagined horizon. "That will be ere the set of sun."

The first witch spoke with a sudden menacing grin, "Where the place?"

"Upon the heath," the second witch answered.

The third witch nodded. "There to meet with… Macbeth." Her head swung suddenly and her eyes fixed, glaring, upon Sam's. A bony, trembling finger pointed at him.

All three witches glared with white, pupil-less eyes at Sam, and spoke in unison. "Paddock calls, anon! Fair is foul, and foul is fair; hover through the fog and filthy air."

The mist boiled higher and the lights dimmed and brightened again.

The witches evaporated.

The audience, shaken from silence, clapped furiously.

Sam felt swept into the story. The scenes of the play rolled and surged with grim urgency. King Duncan received the news of Macbeth's rousing victory with Banquo over the rebel army of the traitor MacDonald's. The field of battle lay littered with the bloody and dismembered dead. Macbeth and Banquo, exhausted, bloodied, triumphant.

And the witches. The witches drifting among them, planting the dark idea into Macbeth's mind:

*All hail Macbeth! Hail to thee, Thane of Glamis! Hail to thee, Thane of Cawdor! All hail, Macbeth! That shalt be king forever.*

The witches again locked their eyes on Sam.

He felt his heart racing, his forehead slickening with sweat. He sensed both Fred and Mary looking at him, but he couldn't turn away from the players on the stage.

The tale grew darker. Evil compounded evil, and ambition and deceit and murder took their tolls, the spoils of evil raising Macbeth to the throne, and dashing the new tyrant and his queen into ruin. The mists and stones and trees and banquet halls and moors of the set became real; the cold windswept Scottish moor and highland, and the blood-soaked stones, and the clash of metal upon metal, and metal upon flesh and bone, and the oaths and fury of pitched battle to the death of Macbeth and MacDuff, sparks flying from striking blades, sweat flying, threats, shouts, blood, death, and over it all the glowing, greedy eyes of the witches, the Weird Sisters, those leering puppeteers of lust and hate and murder.

And Macbeth, realizing at last the great lie of prophesy, of his invincibility, of the gifts imbued by the witches, casts aside doubt and crying, "Lay on, Macduff, and damned be him that first cries, Hold, enough!" And Macbeth sinking, sinking, falling, redness welling and splashing onto the cold earth, dying at last, his evil undone, the victim of his own ambition.

And with the final curtain, the shouts and roars and thunderous clapping, Sam shaken as if from a dream. He found himself on his feet with the hundreds of friends and enemies, the islanders, clapping as never before.

The players assembled afterwards in a line on the stage, clasped hands, took their bows, basking in the rapturous applause.

The Weird Sisters were not among them.

THE CROWD FILED out from the little high school, buzzing with excitement, and into the dark streets headed for home.

Sam watched silently as his boss lingered on the broad steps of the school, collaring and jabbering at anyone and everyone about what they'd just witnessed. Fred withdrew a bottle from his jacket, took a long swig, and passed the bottle to Sam. Sam obliged, cast a furtive glance about, and took a sip. Mary too. Propriety and sobriety be damned, Prohibition was done forever and even though it had made him a pile of money that would someday run out, Fred could drink in public as much and as loud as he wanted.

"Toomey!" Fred yelled, as he grabbed the Police Chief's sleeve and pulled him closer. "Did you see that? Damn that was good. Best thing ever to hit Brigands Key, don't you think? Here, have a drink, pal." He shoved the bottle at Toomey.

Toomey shook his head. He gave Mary a quick anxious glance. "Fred, much appreciated, but I still got some inspections before I get home. Mary, you see him safe to bed now, you hear?" He returned his focus to Fred.

Sam watched closely. Mary glanced his way, her eyes penetrating, with that look again, that look of expectation, of demand. She kept her eyes on him, the urgency and heat in them growing. And she swung back to Toomey and her husband, all smiles and youthful happiness.

The images and words of the play swirled through Sam's mind. The spiral of lust and greed had dragged the characters to their ends. But the retribution and repaid debts for misdeeds made no impression on Sam. He had seen himself in Macbeth, had seen the witches ordain him for greatness and set him upon its path, murdering his beloved king.

Fate. There was no such thing, Shakespeare was saying. But there was destiny, only it had to be made. It had to be *taken*. And for the first time in his hard, bruised life, Sam saw his destiny, saw himself sweeping aside the most powerful man in Brigands Key. Brokering deals, controlling the high-and-mighty, maybe becoming even the most powerful in all of Florida. The witches made him see when they turned their bright shining eyes upon him, even as they schemed and ordained the faraway Macbeth's future.

Macbeth listened, acted, and made his own destiny happen once told it truly was his destiny. He had no choice.

But wasn't there always a choice?

The idea gnawed at Sam, consumed him. Unlike Macbeth, he didn't have a driven outsider like Lady Macbeth pushing him into action. But he had an insider. The ultimate insider.

He had Mary MacGregor.

He had the king's own queen on his side and in his bed.

All he needed was the backbone to see the thing through.

Toomey continued to listen to Fred. He had to, the poor sap. He was paid to listen when the town's richest man opened his mouth.

"Damn, that was good," Fred shouted. "We need to celebrate."

"Beautiful weather tonight, Darlin'," Mary said. "Perfect for celebrating under the stars!"

"Honey, you're beautiful and smart! It is a perfect night! Let's take *Ellenore* out on the water."

Sam shot a glance at Mary. She ignored him and sipped her drink. "Are you sure, Honey? We can sit on the dock with all our friends and listen to the current." She slurred a few words. "We don't need to go out on the water. Sheriff Toomey can join us!" She giggled. Damn, she was good.

"I'm not a sheriff," Toomey said drily. His eyes drank her up and down. If Fred noticed, he didn't care. "And besides," Toomey continued, "I still got inspections, and to see folks home all right.

Got to make sure this bunch of Gypsy actors gets squared away too. For their own good."

Fred hoisted his bottle. "To the Gypsies!" He took another drink, spilled some, and wiped his mouth on his sleeve. "And you make sure and tell 'em to come back around next year. Let's get to the boat. I think there's a case or two aboard."

THE ENGINES of *Ellenore* grumbled and smoked. Sam lit fore and aft kerosene lamps, and cast off the lines, and Fred eased the boat away from the dock. The tide was up so they should be able to get out okay, that is, if Fred didn't manage to run them aground in his drunken stupor. A channel dug into the waterway would sure be a handy thing for a town that relied on fishing, Sam thought. Someday they might get one dug, but it might take another world war before anybody drag-lined the first bit of bottom out.

Fred negotiated the passage well enough for a drunk and they rounded the corner on the north end of the island. Overhead, the Hammond Lighthouse swept its lantern across the island and sea. The shadowed form of Old Man McConklin perched like a buzzard on the lighthouse catwalk high above them, presumably glaring down at the nighttime fools in the boat. Old Man McConklin glared at everyone.

Wispy clouds cleared away, revealing a glorious night sky, glittering with stars like diamonds. A cool breeze brought on a shiver. Fred cleared the island and turned *Ellenore* out to sea and cruised slowly west. Minutes passed. Sam searched the sea for other boats. No running lights, but that didn't guarantee there were no boats out. Some fools clung to the old Prohibition habit of lights-out to avoid the Coast Guard, and some few still smuggled illegal hooch anyway. Some were just fools. Sam looked aft to study the dim points of light that marked Brigands Key. No one followed, as much as he could tell. The sea rolled low and long and slow, the gentle waves lapping the bow as *Ellenore* eased through them.

Five miles out on the Gulf, Fred cut the engine and the boat drifted forward. Silence embraced them. "Hell of a night," Fred bellowed. He had not for a moment let the whiskey bottle wander more than an arm's length away. He waved it, drank, and passed it to Sam.

Sam obliged, mumbled his thanks, and took a sip. He passed the bottle to Mary.

Her eyes glinted in the dim flicker of the boat's lamps. She gave him the tight-lipped look again. The look that said *now or never.*

Sam felt his resolve fading. Murder, he thought. *Murder.* Had he come to this? Fred MacGregor was an ass, but who wasn't?

Fred was drinking himself into an early grave anyway. How many more years could he have? Would it be such a loss? The guy had no children that would grieve for him. His two brothers both died of heart attacks, like the one Fred was working towards. The only family he had left wanted him dead.

Tonight.

Fred headed aft, stumbling. "Look way down yonder," he said, pointing south along the black line of coast. "Cedar Key. They got the right idea, y' see? They got the trees and that means they got the lumber, and are making it pay off."

A fine idea, Sam thought. When he'd pitched it not three hours ago, it was a lousy idea. Now it was Fred's idea and a damned good one. A fine idea. Just fine. Just like every other idea Fred had stolen.

"Lumber," Fred continued. "That's what I need to get into. Lumber. Don't you think, Mary?"

"Sure, Honey. There's a lot of money in lumber. That is, 'til you cut all them trees down. Then what? Cedar Key cut down all the cedars a long time ago and the pencil company up and left. Now they stumble along like all the rest of us."

"You got no vision, Mary, so just sit back and look pretty. Let the thinking to me."

"Lumber." She took another drink.

Sam shook his head slightly. She glared at him. He wondered if she were becoming a problem herself. At least Fred could recognize a good idea, once he'd taken credit for it.

Mary went to Fred and squeezed his arm, brushed against him, whispered into his ear, giggled, kissed his cheek. She topped off her drink and took another sip. He turned to her, soft-eyed, with a widening grin. He reached down and pinched her ass. She giggled again and swatted his hand away. But her own hand traced lightly down his shoulder, his chest, his stomach, and lingered there, and moved lower. He pawed her and she skipped away from him, giggling again, so light and sweet, and headed forward, to the bow.

She winked at Sam as she passed. "Freddy, come on up and let's enjoy the bow. Sam, you go down to the transom and turn your back and sulk, why don't you? Me and my honey got some things to do."

Fred, clutching his bottle tight, lurched after her. Determination and lust lit his dull eyes. He ignored Sam, shoved past him, his eyes locked on his wife.

It dawned on Sam; this was it. The moment. They had been aft, at the transom. The boat's sides there were high, not at all good for falling overboard. She lured him fore, to the bow, where nothing but a low rail atop the low gunwale separated the deck from the sea. A little water on the deck, a little slip, and over you go. Damn, she was so good and so cool.

They reached the bow and Mary drew Fred close and kissed him hard, savagely. His hands roamed clumsily over her body. She twisted, maneuvered him closer to the side of the boat. But he outweighed her by double. There was no way she was ever going to shove him anywhere he didn't want to go. She angled her head, still kissing him, and looked straight at Sam. That demanding look again.

Sam could hear the witches of Macbeth in his mind.

*For a charm of powerful trouble,*
*Like a hell-broth boil and bubble*

He drew a breath, and another, and moved slowly toward them. He measured his steps, planted his feet as softly as he could. An old sea dog like Fred would feel the boat shift almost imperceptibly with each step.

Closer, he came. Closer. Ten feet away. Eight.

Mary pushed herself free from Fred's hands and stepped back.

He glared at her and moved in again. Sam had his instant, his opening.

He hesitated.

"Do it!" Mary hissed, her eyes still on her husband's.

Fred stared dully at her.

*By the pricking of my thumbs*
*Something wicked this way comes*

Sam rushed forward and threw himself at Fred, striking him high in the back, between the shoulders, like throwing a block on the field with his arms tucked tightly in. The last thing he wanted was an open-armed entanglement, one that might end with his going overboard along with his victim.

It felt like running into a wall of muscle. Fred grunted and staggered and began to twist about, and Sam struck him again. Fred's heel caught on the rail. The big man teetered, seemed about to right and catch himself. The slight swell of a wave rolled past the boat, nudging it, adding imbalance. Fred clawed at the air, swayed, disappeared over the side, and plunged into the Gulf of Mexico with a splash.

Sam leaned over the side, his hands clenched on the gunwale. Bubbles stirred the water, but Fred was gone. Mary darted forward and fell to her hands and knees, staring down at the black water. Fred could swim like a fish. It came with the job for a rumrunner. But he was drunk and waterlogged in full clothing. He had to sink. He had to. In silence, they waited.

*Show his eyes and grieve his heart*
*Come like shadows, so depart!*

"It's done," Mary whispered. "Done!"

A splash. Fred's hand broke the surface and flailed, followed by his face. He sputtered and coughed.

"No!" Mary cried.

Fred thrashed about and clawed at the hull. He reached upward for the gunwale, but *Ellenore* was built to ride high in the water and her sides slanted steeply out over the surface.

"Help me," Fred cried. "Mary! Sam, pull me up!"

Sam shook his head. "Don't think we will, boss."

A flash of terror, and a slow turn to anger transformed Fred's face. "You son of a bitch! You whore. This is what it's about then."

Mary shrugged.

They watched him struggle. He regained his composure, steadied himself. Sam knew Fred was a strong swimmer and could stay afloat for an unknown time, maybe even hours. This was a new wrinkle. But Fred was fully clothed, boots and all, and even the strongest swimmer couldn't last weighted down in drowned clothes.

Fred pushed himself away from the boat and peeled off his jacket.

Sam pounded the gunwale. So it would be a waiting game now. Fine, time was on his side. No. They couldn't wait and hope. If a boat chanced by, Fred would call out.

"Mary," Sam said, "fetch me an oar." He would beat the man until he sank, and pray that the battered body never drifted ashore. No. He would beat him to death and wrap the body in chain so it would never come to the surface.

How did simplicity just become so complicated?

Mary continued to stare down at Fred.

"Mary, get me an oar! Now!"

She started, shot him an angry glance, and scampered toward the rear of the boat.

Sam continued to watch. Fred appeared to be removing a boot.

A movement, a short distance out in the water, maybe sixty feet, caught Sam's eye. He glanced in the direction and saw nothing. He returned his attention to Fred.

The movement, again. He was sure of it. Something in the water, closer than before. Had the commotion gotten the attention of a shark? Maybe, but it was nighttime. He'd not see a shark under the water if it was two feet away, much less sixty.

He saw it. The faintest hint of pale light under the water, coming swiftly toward them. Like a ghost.

No. Like *three* ghosts. Three apparitions of glowing whiteness.

They drew near, and within each apparition there appeared two glowing points of white.

The witches of *Macbeth*.

They encircled Fred, mere feet away and not more than two feet below the surface. Their faces turned upward, their long hair fanning and drifting about, and their pale, burning eyes fixed upon Fred, and malevolent hungry grins formed. One of the witches looked up at Sam. A claw of a hand broke the surface, glistening and dripping, and pointed at him. She mouthed a word. *Macbeth.* And withdrew her hand.

Behind him came the clatter of an oar onto the deck, a small curse, and Mary's footsteps returning.

Fred stared, terror-stricken, into the water about him.

The witches closed upon him.

Soundlessly, he disappeared under the water and was gone.

Not a sign of any of them remained.

Mary reached his side and dropped the oar onto the deck. She stared into the water, this way and that. "Sam! Where'd he go?"

Sam continued to peer into the deep, wanting to see, hoping that he would not.

"Sam!"

"He sank, Mary. He got tired and just...sank."

She gasped. He stood and backed from the gunwale, still watching the water, trembling, and drew her into his arms. "He's gone. Fred's gone. It's just us now." He at last looked at her and drew her close and kissed her.

SAM PILOTED the *Ellenore* back into channel, dropping speed as he rounded the north point, under Hammond Lighthouse. They worked it all out, having gone over it again and again. The thing would raise an eyebrow or two—everything that happened on this coast did—but tear-choked grief would sell it. On account of money.

Fred MacGregor lorded over the island as its richest man and sometime benefactor. *Ellenore* was the first boat in several counties to get a wireless. Even the yachts down in Tampa didn't have wireless. What's more, Fred bought Chief Toomey's office a wireless radio and mechanically recharging batteries, when the island didn't even have electric power yet. Made quite a grand show of his gift to Brigands Key.

Sam had wired Toomey on the way in, the bearer of awful news that drunken Fred stumbled and fell overboard and sank to his death. Once Sam discovered his best friend and boss missing, he'd dived in to search in futility. He shivered now in believably drenched clothes.

The story would work.

He neared the dock and eased *Ellenore* into her slip. Toomey waited on the dock, watching, his thumbs hooked into his belt. Two cops, Jenkins and Merriwether, stood to his left and right, each carrying a bright kerosene lamp. Sam throttled down and the boat bumped gently into place. He killed the engine, moved fore, and tossed a line to Deputy Jenkins.

"Hell of a thing, Sam," Toomey said.

Sam stepped onto the dock and took Toomey's hand. "He went up to the bow, was up there alone." Sam's voiced cracked. He looked at his feet, then back into Toomey's face with carefully applied tears. It was important now that he retold the story like he'd done over the wireless. Mary had tearfully corroborated his story on the radio. They were in lockstep. Quite a pair. A year and a half from now, after dutifully comforting the grieving widow and helping her out with the business, they would get engaged and no one would bat an eye. A woman needed a man, after all. "I was aft, shining a light on the prop. I heard a splash, thinking a fish jumped. Mary was in the cabin; she screamed. And then I looked. He was gone." He shook with nice sob, inspired maybe by the glories of theatre. "Just… gone."

A movement, a pale light under the dark water, caught the edge of his vision. He turned to see, but the light had vanished. He stared into the darkness.

Toomey followed Sam's line of sight for a moment, and turned back to him. "Hell of a thing," he said. "I appreciate you looking for him. But I could see he weren't in no shape to be out on the Gulf at night." Toomey glanced up and down the boat. "How's Mary taking it?"

"She's all tore up. Down below in the cabin, bawling her heart out. Can't believe what's happened. All tore up."

Toomey nodded, and patted Sam on the shoulder. "Jenkins, go fetch her and be real gentle about it."

Jenkins eased onto the boat. The *Ellenore* shifted, as if unsure of the stranger. He went to the cabin door and knocked softly.

A moment later, the door flew open and Mary emerged, wide-eyed, gripping and brandishing a fish gaff, its wicked barbed hook glinting in the light. "Stay away," she cried.

Jenkins took a step back. Mary seemed surprised to see him, her eyes wide and darting about.

She was off-script. Way off.

"Back away," she screamed.

Jenkins held his lamp high, casting her in a pool of shaky yellow light.

Her lip was swollen and cut, her eye blackening and nearly shut. She spotted Toomey, then Sam. She screamed again, and swung the gaff in the air. "Keep him away from me!"

Sam took a step and said, "Mary, what…"

She swung again. "Keep him away from me! It was him! Toomey, it was Sam! I saw him. I saw it all." She shook and trembled. "He lied about it to me but I saw it all. He shoved Fred over and watched, just watched, and kicked him down. And Fred was drunk and clothed and sank. He killed my Freddie!"

Sam overcame his sudden shock. "No! That ain't true at all! She saw it all right, she stood right there watching him go over."

"A second ago she was in the cabin," Toomey said. "You changing your story that quick?"

"He said he'd kill me if I told what I saw," Mary sobbed. "He choked me to make it clear. Look!" He pulled her high collar down, revealing bruises on her neck. "I was so scared!"

"No," Sam cried. "I didn't touch her! She did that to herself."

"Beat herself up. Choked herself," Toomey said. He slugged Sam in the stomach, doubling him over. "Merriwether, draw your gun and haul this son of a bitch in."

·  ·  ·

MARY WATCHED THE FILLING COURTROOM, fidgeting with a set of rosary beads her weasel lawyer said would look good. The date had been ramrodded up the calendar, and the trial would be speedy and sure. You just don't kill the town's biggest employer and throttle his pretty young wife and get away with it. Sam's word against hers, and his word wasn't worth a thing. It was as good as settled.

Judge Carter of the circuit court strolled in, stern and angry, and settled in as if he were the show, not her. Fine. There wasn't much to discuss, and there would be a hanging soon.

Mary studied the two major players. Sam wasn't one of them. He was cooked. No, the judge and the sheriff were the two biggest fish now. She needed a man, not for the sex, but for the expectations of the world. She had worked them both during the trial, a shy smile here, a gentle laugh there. They were eating it up.

Toomey was old and fat. She could control him without breaking a sweat. But he had little future, other than maybe getting elected a small-county sheriff someday. Judge Carter, on the other hand, had a slick way about him, a way of climbing. And a background in getting elected. Maybe he could win a governor's mansion someday.

Judge Carter it was, then. She cast him a sweet smile. He returned it with that look all men got around her.

She saw her future unfold before her. Lavish banquets, mansions, movie stars. And theatre. It was the same vision she had gotten that night at the gym, when the witches of Macbeth glared at her, and named her the future queen. It had all been ordained that night.

And the night before, in her dream.

All she had had to do was make the vision come true.

She smirked at Judge Carter. He wasn't going to run the show. That too had been ordained.

*No man that's born of woman*
*Shall e'er have power upon thee.*

## AUTHOR'S NOTES - KEN PELHAM

AT A STAGE PRODUCTION of *Macbeth* a couple decades ago, I sneaked into an unused front row seat. It was worth it; the clash and clang of steel upon steel, the bellowed curses, the flying sweat… this production came alive and I felt part of the action. But the thing that stood out above all was when one of the witches, one of the Weird Sisters, fixed her baleful staring eyes upon me and let me know that I existed only at the merest whim of the mysteries of darkness.

Wow.

There's a reason the witches of *Macbeth* command our attention and set the gold standard of supernatural evil. So when this anthology's premise—reimagined takes on classic lit—came to be, *Macbeth* bubbled, toiled, and troubled from the depths of memory to the top. The idea occurred to me to set this weird, wonderful tale of Shakespeare's in Brigands Key, my somewhat shady fictional barrier island off the Gulf Coast of Florida. As an additional wrinkle, I set it at the height of the Great Depression, when many touring theater troupes crisscrossed America to scratch out a meager living, playing to audiences of a downtrodden, desperate public.

I suspect that nearly all critics and lovers of the theater would rate *Macbeth* among Shakespeare's best. The story is a simple one of ambition, greed, and murder, with questionable prophecy driving man and wife to acts they would once have never contemplated. At the heart of this great drama are the elements of horror, all set into motion by the dark, prescient visions and machinations of the witches. The story is a cornerstone of Western literature, and I'd be silly indeed to try and top Shakespeare. All I ask is a bit of indulgence as I tease out its essentials of horror and ambition, and reimagine them in a new setting.

I hope you enjoyed the story as much as I enjoyed writing it.

*—KP*

# THE LOTTERY

## KRISTIN DURFEE

*" To turn back is one kind of death; to go forward is another."*
*——Elizabeth Lesser*

## I

EVE RUBBED the edge of her thumbnail back and forth over the hem of her thread-bare dress. She wondered how long she'd owned it. It felt at times as if she had been born in the garment. The days of new clothes were long behind them. There was nothing new anymore.

She stared out the window, the pane clogged with dirt from the town, and onto scenery that wasn't a view at all anymore, but just more and more grey on grey on grey. The dilapidated town hall towered across the way, whispering of past greatness, its single tall column once connected to a long-ago collapsed gable, its steps cracked and doors no longer closed all the way, like two crooked front teeth.

The houses that lined the street the other way didn't pretend they'd ever been anything more than mediocre. They served their purpose and did exactly what was needed of them, nothing more, nothing less, just like those who were left. There wasn't any point in fixing things up, even if there was the material to do it. People mainly ignored their surroundings, they knew better than to look around too much or they'd risked giving up.

The town hadn't always been like this. If Eve closed her eyes and thought back to when she was a little girl, she could almost remember the color of green grass and the smell of fresh rain.

Rain.

The thought made her dry throat contract in desperation. One more hour and she'd be able to send Albert to fetch their daily rations. It They always ran out too quickly. They never had enough and there was never any more, but there was hope.

Today was a special day. Quite possibly the last special day, and that thought made her insides twist and squirm. It was their last chance of a future, to get out, to move on with their lives, because if they weren't picked today, their loss equaled a death sentence.

Eve looked back down at the hem, now frayed slightly from a snag on her fingernail. Her dress pulled up just enough to reveal the four bruises, purple in their newness. She wondered if Jacob would notice them. Probably not. He barely registered her presence most days, which was perfectly fine with her. Long gone were their days of courtship and best behaviors. How funny, she thought, that for years he gave her bruises and marks that she tried to cover-up and hide from other people, her children, herself, and now here she was, trying to hide these from him. These marks that came, not from him, but from him.

The memory washed over her and sent a tingle deep within her belly. Hector running his hands roughly, but in a tenderly way she was not used to, over her body. Her feeling alive for the first time in recent memory. The last time she'd been so present, so in the moment, was when her babies were born, the pain making her aware of every second, every tensing of muscle.

She hadn't seen Hector in years, not since their primary school days. He'd been from a wealthy family and didn't belong in Holcon, where generations of her family toiled and failed to make lives for themselves. His parents had moved to the area as part of the recruitment effort of those who got an automatic selection and could forgo The Lottery. They helped with finding the best of who was left on Earth, to hand-pick them for the repopulation of Mars.

Mars. That glorious place of hope and possibility.

Hector's parents had spent twenty years doing research on the residents who surrounded the small towns that made up what was left of the United States.

Eve remembered learning when she was little about how grand this country was. How it stretched for thousands of miles in each direction. How there were places you could go where you didn't even see a body of water. Eve couldn't picture it. The ocean was visible everywhere she'd ever gone. It lapped at their shores like hungry dogs waiting to devour them. And really, it was.

In old text books, she had seen pictures of snow and tropical forests, and wondered how both things could have existed in the same place. All that was left were dirt and a few crackling weeds longing to be more. To think it had ever been anything else warped her sense of self, so she mostly didn't think about the past too much, or the future too much, for that matter.

Mars, though, Mars she had heard wonderful things about her whole life. Those pictures she could believe. The lush forests filled with greenery and crystal blue lakes which you could drink from! It seemed impossible to her the notion that you could just walk up to a body of water, place your mouth upon it, and drink without getting sick. It was so fantastic it almost didn't seem real.

Mars.

She had been trying to get there her entire life. And her parents had tried their entire lives, and this was it. The last ship was scheduled to leave in a week's time and she had one last chance to get on it.

The days of Hector's parents' research were long gone. They had both died about ten years prior and Hector had moved to another part of the country about fifty miles away to complete their studies. When she walked down the street to the store two weeks ago, she spotted him across the broken asphalt. Time stopped. He looked over and a brightness filled his eyes and face. They had been friends in their school days. Somehow, he was able to see past her unwashed hair and too small clothes—hand-me-downs from a petite but generous neighbor—and saw her true self.

Eve felt unabashedly naked around him like she was the first Eve, confident and without self-consciousness. Their conversations were light and deep at the same time. It wasn't until he left town that she'd realized how much she'd liked him.  But she had married Jacob, as of course she was destined to do anyway. To think that a rich boy would find interest in her as anything more than a play-yard friend was a dream. A dream that she long ago released from her nightly prayers.

But then there he was, looking of the past and promise. He crossed the street in large strides and held her in a wordless embrace. She was embarrassed to find tears stinging her eyes.

"Evie," he said, looking directly at her as he pulled away. She tilted her head down, feeling red heat flushing her cheeks. She couldn't believe he remembered his nickname for her.

"Hector!" she said his name in a breathy exhale. "It's been so many years. I was terribly sorry to hear about your parents. I wanted to tell you, but didn't know how to get in touch."

"Thank you. It was many years ago. You look wonderful."

It was a lie and while she knew they both knew it, she played along with the fantasy. She couldn't remember the last time someone had said she looked wonderful. They spoke for a few more minutes. He was there with the rest of The Lottery committee for the drawing, and he told her about the room he was renting in the old Clinton mansion. She wished him luck in his work and was convinced when they parted that she would never see him again. It was sad, but not as much as it had been when he'd left her before.

So, it was a wonderful surprise when she saw him again the day before the drawing. He flashed the same white, straight smile at her and she waved back, covering her own yellowing teeth with her other hand. He pulled her hand down as he embraced her and didn't let go, pulling her toward a small restaurant that she hadn't been to since the night Jacob asked for her hand in marriage.

The décor inside was the same as she remembered, pinks and yellows that were faded almost white by the sun, and the food like a ship itself, transporting her to a life she'd scantly remembered when Jacob had just begun to court her and she'd toyed with the idea that he might actually make her happy.

She could feel the greasy fat from the meat she ate fill her insides with energy and warmth. She wondered where the place had found it. Meat was more rare than clean water these days, but she didn't question it, fighting the urge to run her finger across the plate and lick off the flecks that clung to it. If this was the last meal she would eat before she died, she'd consider her life well-lived.

After the meal, they stood in an awkward silence on the street. Eve didn't want to leave, she wanted to live in this moment for as long as she could, but she also worried that someone would see her. Though, on second thought, it was doubtful. The people she knew didn't frequent this part of town. It held nothing for them, nothing they could afford at least. She opened her mouth to say something at the moment he spoke.

"Come with me," he said. His pupils were dilated and she could see his chest rise and fall at a quick pace. Part of her imagined that she could feel his quickened heartbeat through the cracks on the ground. She nodded, unsure of her ability to speak.

What made her follow him, she would never know. It was as if her conscience, that guiding part of her brain that warned her that she should look both ways before she crossed the street, had quietly slipped away. Her mind filled with the hum of white noise as if she walked through a dream. At his hotel room, he wordlessly took off her clothes, then his own. She stared at his body, muscles under a layer of fat that she was instantly jealous of. She was all bones and angles, nothing soft about her. His lips moved over every inch of her as she melted into him.

After, her body still buzzing, she stared at his stilled form in the late afternoon light. His chest rose and fell in shallow beats, sleep pulling his breaths into a rhythm she found hypnotic. She moved her and to place it against his chest, but stopped, noticing how dirty she was against the white sheets on the bed. Their crispness hurt her eyes. White sheets. What a novelty in a place like this. Everything she owned, including her own body, was tinted the color of dirt. She got off the bed and stepped into the white tiled shower and turned the water as hot as she could stand. Eve stood under the stream, fighting the urge to open her mouth to the recycled water as she allowed it to pour over her body, until the draining water around her feet turned from brown to clear. Had she ever been this clean in her life?

It felt grimy to put her clothes back on. She wished they matched how she now felt, clean and new again. Reality pulled her back in a greying swirl. There was no escaping. White sheets and hot showers weren't parts of her life. It was nice pretending for an afternoon though. Nice having a small piece that she could hold onto when that ship left and she was stuck to perish along with the rest of the planet.

Sure, her name was on a slip of paper, just like Jacob and Albert's names and the names of everyone else left, but she'd known it wasn't going to be picked. Just like it hadn't been picked the countless other times. It might be the last chance in theory, but she knew she'd never had a real shot at it anyway.

She longed to ask Hector the truth. To hear if the rumors were correct and that it wasn't so much a paper lottery but a genetically determined one. She knew that along with her entry, they took swabs of her cheeks and the cheeks of her husband and children. Knew that the scientists had run all the tests they could to determine her life expectancy and the traits she passed on to her children. The information wouldn't be new. She'd heard it for as long as she could remember and recalled them telling her after getting pregnant with each of her children their fates. She wanted to think that they were wrong, but it shouldn't have come to the shock it did when little Alison died when she was six just like they predicted. Ricky, June, and Albert all had better odds. Their chances of reaching one-hundred were all but guaranteed. If only the Earth would cooperate.

The planet had been dying for thousands of years, but scientists had always anticipated that they had about a million more before their planet was really at risk. It was considered a problem humans probably wouldn't be around for, anyway. But after the unexpected collision of two black holes at the edge of their solar system, shock waves slammed into the sun, causing it to expand. The destruction of Earth now accelerated at a pace no one had predicted. The missions to Mars had been going on since the middle of the last century, but with renewed risk at home, the need to make a new, livable planet became the sole purpose of any scientist on Earth. After a series of disastrous test runs, including a colony on the moon that lasted a mere forty years before a leak in a water seal lead to the death of all six-hundred and eighty-two occupants, Mars became the last, great hope of humanity.

The Mars missions weren't without their own struggles though, but for the last thirty years, the colony started to take root. Over time, plants and animals were removed from Earth and transported to Mars. With the expansion of the sun and the loss of Mercury, scientists expected Earth to last about twenty more years before all its resources heated up and floated away into the atmosphere.

Mars was the happy beneficiary of now being the third planet in the solar system. Scientists and leaders had been in the early waves of colonization. Once those people of importance were in place, the planet was opened up in a lottery system to all those left behind. Which was mostly the poor or poorly educated. Those who couldn't afford the initial transit ticket, or didn't have desirable skills that warranted a scholarship, had the opportunity once every three years to place their names in a pool to be chosen for the trip. But Eve always found it strange that while it was supposed to be completely random, somehow the best of who was left happened to get picked. As Mars took the strongest people, Earth got weaker and fell closer to Her destruction.

So close, in fact, that this was to be the last lottery held. After this, the ships would not return and the planet, and those left behind would wait around for each other's destruction.

It felt wholly unnatural to Eve to die this way. To have someone pick whether you got a one-way ticket to your future or not.

She turned to Hector to ask him, but thought better of it. Deep down, she didn't want to know.

Stepping into the street and making her way to her house, she got glances from people as she entered her part of town. She looked down at her clean arms and cursed herself. How foolish to think she could pretend to have another life. How silly to think she could have an affair with a man and his lifestyle and think she could carry on as if neither had happened. She stopped down a small alleyway and picked up handfuls of dirt and rubbed them on her arm and face, erasing all evidence of her indiscretion.

When she righted herself, she saw a movement in front of her. A small, black-winged creature fluttered up to a long-broken light post. Bird. The word entered her conscience, recalled from some long-ago memory of sitting in class. Bird.

She'd never seen a living one before. Its black eyes bore through her and she wondered if it could see the future. Its expression was all-knowing. She stood tall, rooted in place, looking up so long the muscles in her back and neck screamed for her to lower her gaze. When it took to the skies, tired of being watched by her, she stared at the speck of clear blue it flew into until the darkness of evening washed it away. She wiped a tear and headed home.

## II

WHEN SHE WALKED through the door, no one asked where she'd been. Ricky was working late, so he wasn't home. June had set the table as Albert stirred a pot on the stove. In that moment, she wondered if anyone would notice if she disappeared.

Jacob arrived home just as the watery soup was ready. She loved her children, loved them as an extension of herself, but there were times when she wished they had never existed. Never had to live in this troubled time. Her hope for winning The Lottery was just as much for them as for her. To know that they would have a mere

twenty more years to live made her lose her breath with the unfair-
ness of it all. Her life may not have been considered full, but she
would live to late middle age. There was something to be said for
the ability to grow old. Something her children would never
experience.

June told her about her day at school and how they were
learning about how the Mars atmosphere conditioners worked. The
little girl's excitement about the technology that allowed people to
inhabit a different planet brought a spark to their meal. Albert
stared at his sister. He was two years younger than June and idolized
her. Ricky was ten years older than both of them and hadn't been a
big part of either's lives. When Alison died, he distanced himself
from the rest of his family. The two of them had been best friends
and her loss had shifted something in him that never quite went
back correctly.

He quietly went to work and quietly returned like a mouse in
their midst, scurrying about the home when no one was looking.
When Eve thought of her children, Ricky was an afterthought. A
part of her soul followed him in everything he did and in everywhere he went, but it was a separate being, like a hunk of flesh
removed that would never grow back, making her feel empty at
times.

The four of them, Albert, June, Jacob, and herself, sat around
the table and slurped their soup. It tasted of warm nothingness and
both filled and emptied her at the same time. She thought back to
the meat and was ashamed. How could she have enjoyed such a
splendid meal and not thought to cut it in halves, or quarters, to
bring home to her children? How their skin hung in grey ribbons on
their bodies, not an inch of fat on them. She felt the weight of her
indiscretion in a wave and had to grab the edge of the table so she
wouldn't risk falling out of her chair or vomiting.

When she awoke the next morning, her first thought was of The
Lottery, and she sent dozens of prayers in quick succession, begging
to be a winner. Begging for her children, for once in their lives, be
winners. Ricky, at seventeen, was now considered an adult and had
an entry all on his own. If he could make it, if at least one of them

could, she would consider it a sign that her moment of weakness was forgiven by what, or who, forgives such things.

She busied herself in the kitchen, but there was little to do and she gravitated back to the window. Would this be the last day she spent in her house? If they were chosen, they'd be taken to Arendale that very night. They'd go through flight preparations and be on the ship three days later.

In the past, even when not picked, everyone still traveled to watch the train depart for Arendale. The government provided a celebration, which meant they'd at least have food. The feast would almost make up for the fact that they weren't able to leave for a new world and would die with Earth.

Almost.

Three days later, they'd travel to the edge of town. Eve would stand, her children clutching her sides, their full bellies a distant memory, and they'd watch the ship blast into the sky. Even at a distance, the noise and heat and light had always been overwhelming, but she never looked away. Never covered her ears. She wanted it to reverberate around her so she could recall it at any time. She never wanted to forget how escape felt.

To think that she could be on the next one helped her through the day. When Albert returned with the water, they drank large glasses. If they weren't chosen, she'd regret wasting so much on a single moment, but she didn't care. It felt different this time. Her doubts erased along with the dirt in the shower. Maybe it was because of her connection with Hector, but she knew, deep down, she'd be on that ship. Be racing away from this life and moving on to the next.

"Should we pour a glass for daddy, June, and Ricky?" Albert asked when they'd finished.

"Do you think we should?"

He giggled. "I can feel my belly slosh."

As if summoned by the youngest in the family, Jacob, June, and Ricky walked in.

"Water!" Albert exclaimed. He grabbed three more glasses and filled each to the top. A laugh was half-way through Eve's lips when

Jacob moved forward and snatched the pitcher from Albert's hands, spilling a few drops on the table.

"What in holy hell do you think you are doing, boy?" he boomed. Albert shrank back, the joy from the previous moment evaporated along with the water drops.

"Jacob," Eve said.

He slammed the pitcher down, making the glasses jump. "Did you put him up to this?" He moved forward and grabbed her left hand roughly, making the bones creak under his grip.

"I thought…"

"No, see, that's the problem. You didn't think. You think Ricky and I work our asses off every day so you two can sit home and drink all our water in one sitting? Is that what you think?"

"No, no, of course not." She tried to keep her voice even, not wanting to scare the children. Out of the corner of her eye she saw Ricky move forward and place a hand on his father's shoulder.

"Dad." His voice was quiet, but Jacob's hold of her softened enough that she was able to pull her arm away. She didn't give him the satisfaction of knowing that he hurt her, fighting the urge to rub her wrist.

Jacob turned and downed an entire glass of water in one, long sip. After slamming the glass back down, he turned and walked out of the house.

Had he ever made her happy? She tried to think back to when they were younger, or after each of their children were born. To search for a glimmer, a single spark of memory. There must have been moments, reasons that went beyond convenience or obligation as to why they were still together, but she couldn't think of any.

Eve looked at her eldest son. He was the spitting image of his father, red hair and all, but thankfully for all of them, he inherited his mother's disposition.

"Mom."

She waved a hand and cut him off. "Alright you two, drink up."

"All of it?" June asked, her voice filled with skepticism and hope.

"I have a feeling we are going to be big winners today," Eve said. "Drink it all up."

# III

EVE STAYED in the square clutching June's little hand as the workers started to disassemble the stage for the last time. The last time. It felt as if time was standing in a pocket around her, yet moved at warp speed outside of the bubble she was in. June knew better than to speak, than to tug on her mother's hand. The girl knew that her brothers would get them food and bring it back to the house. It would be cold, but that wouldn't matter. It would be the last feast they would eat.

The scene played over and over in Eve's head. Hector stood on the back of the stage, the white shirt under his suit jacket reminding her of the sheets at the hotel, as the man and woman standing by the microphone read off a list of names.

A list of names that didn't include hers or Jacob's or Ricky's.

It didn't make sense. After the day she'd had with Hector, she was sure, positive, that her name was going to be chosen. She thought her biggest task of the day would be deciding what items to bring and what to leave behind. Packing up her children and making it to the station in six hours to head to her new life. Getting him to agree to allow Ricky to travel with them. Deciding if she'd stay with Jacob or not when they reached Mars.

There was no new life for her. Hell, there was no life for her in general. The Lottery hadn't chosen them, and, in effect, had signed her death sentence and the death sentence of her children. The ache of that truth made her drop June's hand and clutch her chest. Still, her daughter did not leave. She held on to her mother's frayed hem and stood silently with her.

An overwhelming drive surged through Eve's body. She had to do something. She couldn't take this as the final answer.

She knelt down and faced her daughter. Her daughter with wire colored hair and a dirt-smudged face. Her daughter who would never get to grow old. Who would never get to have grandkids, maybe not kids at all. Because who would want that? Who would want to bring life into a dying world?

"June, I need you to run along and find your brothers and head home."

"But mama." She still hadn't let go of Eve's dress.

"It's okay baby. I will be there soon, I just have to run an errand. Just don't eat all my food while I'm gone," Eve teased and tickled June in the spot just above her belly button. The little girl laughed and nodded. She ran off one way and Eve turned and ran the other.

## IV

HER HEART POUNDED as loud as her fists on the door. She begged the heavens that he was still here, that he hadn't checked out and headed to Arendale in preparation for the twenty winners of Holcon to join the last two-hundred people that would be leaving Earth.

Eve wondered how many people would be left behind. They were due for a census this year, but would anyone be interested in taking it? Would democracy itself, or what was left of it, start breaking down around them? What little stability they had left—the incentive to be good because any infractions would have removed your name from The Lottery now gone—would the world implode under the pointlessness of it all? She didn't want to find out.

He opened on the second round of banging, pulling her to his chest in a crushing hug. She clung to him, sobs wracking her body.

"Eve, oh Evie, I am so sorry, I really tried. I tried to get you on," he whispered into her hair.

She looked up at him. "Then why didn't you?"

He motioned for her to follow him, the heavy wooden door shutting in a burst of noise.

"Why didn't you?" she asked again.

"Eve, I don't know," he trailed off.

"I need to know."

He took a deep breath. "The results of the health screenings. You know how The Lottery works. If one family member gets in, they all get in."

"So? All my children." A pain made her pause. "All my living children have had their tests. They are good. We are all good."

Hector took another big breath. "Sometimes the tests can change."

"What? No, the tests don't change. You get tested at birth, we all know that. We all know that. It tells us how long we will live. I mean, I know people can get hit by cars or fall down stairs, of course, of course there are anomalies like that, but the tests don't lie. If you are careful, the tests are always correct." Her voice caught. "Alison. It was right for her."

"Eve, I know. It's usually correct. But there are times that something isn't seen on the initial screen. We see it every now and then. Why do you think we re-run the screenings? If they were good forever, what would be the need?"

She opened her mouth, but didn't have an answer. Why had she never questioned this? It had just always been part of the process. She thought it was just another step.

"So, what are you saying? Am I sick? Is Jacob?"

Hector shook his head.

Panic made Eve forget to breathe. "Who?"

"Albert."

"No, that's impossible. No."

"I'm so sorry." He reached out a hand to her, but she slapped it away. "Eve, I'm so sorry, but it made you ineligible. Normally we don't tell people, they just don't get picked, but I care for you, Eve. I want you to come. I want you to escape this dying planet before you perish along with it."

Tears blurred Eve's eyes. It was what she wanted, too. An indescribable feeling poured over her. She had to get out. She had to get away from this hotel room and this person who had a whole life ahead of him. Albert? No. She'd already lost one child, she couldn't lose Albert too. Eve ran to the door, but felt a strong hand on her shoulder when she reached it.

"Wait," Hector said.

"For what?" She didn't try to hide the bitterness in her voice. She needed to hate him. She knew he had nothing to do with this, that he'd actually tried to save her, but he failed. He failed and there was no one to blame, not really. Albert's genes, that was what was to blame. So, it was her fault. She was the one who made him, who gave him his genetic make-up. When it came down to it, she'd sealed her whole family's fate six years ago when he was conceived. But she couldn't blame herself because there was no way she would have been able to carry on with their slow march to death knowing that it was her fault. Hector, Hector she could blame. It was unfair, but convenient, and at this moment, that was what she was after.

His grip softened, but he still held her. "Please, please let's talk."

Tears poured down her face and she didn't make any effort to wipe them away. She wanted him to feel bad, wanted him to hurt like she was hurting. "Talk about what? Talk about how you are going to get out of here, get back to your family, and lead a long, happy life on Mars? How you will all watch from a distance as the Earth is boiled and melts away?"

"No. Talk about you coming with me."

The shock of his statement made her release the doorknob.

## V

AN HOUR LATER, Eve was shuffling back home, lost in thought as Hector's words swirled in her head. I can take you with me.

He told her how he'd loved her when they were young. How leaving the first time almost killed him and a second time surely would. How his parents never would have approved and when he'd heard of her marriage to Jacob, thought it was pointless anyway, but he didn't care about any of that now.

She had two hours to decide. Two hours to change the trajectory of her life and future. Her life and June's. Because that is what he offered her. There was no way Albert could come, that much was true. And with Ricky being seventeen, he was no longer considered a part of their family when it came to The Lottery. He was on his own. Jacob, of course, wasn't included in the offer.

Hector could ensure passage for two. He could get paperwork that stated that he and Eve were going to be married prior to departure. Her divorce to Jacob wasn't needed. Hector knew enough people that would turn their heads to such a thing and let her on the train. When they got to Arendale, they'd go to the courthouse and make it official. Eve would say her husband died and Hector would adopt June.

Money would change hands, large sums of money by the sounds of it, but Hector could manage. He could do this for her and by the end of next week, they could be speeding at twenty-thousand miles-per-hour toward a new planet, their old lives all but a distant memory in more ways than one.

What was she to do?

When she opened herself up to the truth, she realized she loved Hector. Loved him in a way that she never loved Jacob, or that she never remembered loving Jacob. They'd had something between them once, she was sure. Hell, they'd made four children together, but Eve felt like she was with Jacob more because they'd met when they were young and everyone assumed they'd get married. She couldn't even remember considering another life for herself. One had been presented to her and she took it. Might as well.

But now. Now she had an option, a literal out. She could take a chance and leave for a foreign land. A land that appeared lush and magical in pictures. She could sit and watch birds and other animals she'd only ever read about. Each day could be an adventure and she'd get to grow old. Get to see her daughter grow and maybe have a daughter of her own. Or a son. Or a collection of each.

An image of Ricky and Albert broke through her thoughts and made her feel like a terrible mother. How could she leave them? She'd lost a child once and it nearly broke her. How could she choose to lose two more? Sure, she could justify it to herself that there was nothing that she could do for them and that she'd be securing June's future. She could save one of her children. Shouldn't she take that? Do whatever she could with what she had? But deep down, she knew it was for selfish reasons. She wanted to get out. June coming with her was a mere bonus.

By the time she made it home, she had forty-five minutes to pack her things and make it to the station in time.

June and Albert were playing with blocks quietly in the living room. They were trying to build a house, but didn't have enough materials for more than three walls. Ricky was in the kitchen, warming a plate of food for her. Her sweet Ricky. Her first born. He was a strong man. He'd lost so much in his short life and it turned him into a different person than he'd been as a child. What would losing his mother and sister do? Would he change so much he'd go back to being who he was?

"I saved you some food," he said as she sat at the table.

"Thank you, my darling. Did you get enough? I am not terribly hungry, why don't you sit with me and we can split it?"

He hesitated, but nodded and sat the steaming plate between them.

"You were gone a long time," he said between mouthfuls of creamy potatoes.

"I was."

"Can I know what it was about?"

"Nothing you need to trouble yourself with," Eve said. She longed to confide in him, in anyone. For someone else to take the burden of her choice away from her.

"I am moving." He spoke in a shaky voice, as if he didn't trust what her reaction may be.

She put down her fork and looked up at him. "Moving? Did you find a place closer to work?"

"Sort of," he said. "A place by my new work."

She frowned. "New work?" She could see the hesitation in his eyes.

"Look, I was going to tell you, but with The Lottery, I was hoping that maybe one of us would win and it wouldn't be an issue. But I got a job in Evenson."

"I don't understand." His words weren't properly computing in her head.

"There isn't anything for me here. Look, I love you, and I love June and Albert and dad, in his own way, but there's no life for me here."

"And there is a life for you in Evenson?"

"I think there will be. At least I can try. We've got, what, ten, maybe fifteen good years left?"

"Ricky, don't talk like that. The scientists said at least twenty, but maybe they're wrong. Maybe we will get even more." The lie stung on her tongue as she said it.

He shook his head. "No, mom, they're not. Plus, if we are all going to die in twenty years, I doubt it is going to be in a big bang, it's going to be a slow process. I'd like to live as much life as I can while there's still some left."

"When are you going?" Eve felt tears drip down her cheeks.

He turned his head and looked at a small bag packed in the corner. How had she not noticed it when she came in? It wasn't just that he was leaving, he was leaving now.

He stood and embraced her. She clung to him, running her fingers through his hair. She wondered if when he looked in the mirror, did he see his father? His own red hair greying at the temples, but the same fire color as his eldest boy. Would Ricky forget what his mother looked like? That her eyes were the ones that reflected back at him? Was this going to be the last time she was going to see him? If so, would it be her choice or his?

"You are my first born," she whispered into his neck. "There is a small part of my heart that is all yours. You are the only one who resides there, it is completely yours."

"I love you mom."

"I love you too."

He pulled away and wiped at his face. After quick hugs to June and Albert, he grabbed his bag and walked out the door. Eve wondered if Ricky had said goodbye to his father.

**VI**

EVE PADDED her way to her bedroom and pulled a bag out of the closet. She decided she was going to fill it just to see how that would feel. She grabbed the few items of clothing she had and placed them in the worn duffle. She left the faded dress hanging in the closet.

She walked into June's small bedroom. Albert and Ricky shared, or used to share, the larger room down the hall. June shared her room with Alison for a mere three days, what felt like a lifetime ago. And really, it was like a different life. The part of Eve that had been a mother to four children no longer existed. Would the Eve that went to Mars be a different one as well?

June's belongings amounted to little and easily fit in the space left in Eve's bag. One small duffle contained their whole lives. She didn't know if she was relieved or saddened by this.

As Eve picked her way down the hall, she walked into the boy's room. Ricky had only been gone moments, but his presence was already wiped from the space he'd spent his whole life. His side of the closet was empty, hangers still swaying. Eve tried to picture Albert alone here. Alone with his father. Or, on hearing news that his mother and sister left, would Ricky send for him? Eve decided that he would, or, at least, told herself that so she could go through with it.

Because she had decided to go through with it. If she stayed on Earth, she'd die over and over again. Part of her would perish each time she wondered when Ricky would be home from work and then having to remember that he no longer lived with them. Each time Jacob lifted a hand to her, knowing that Hector never would. When Albert inevitably died. And lastly, when the world slowly swallowed itself whole. Huge chunks of her would be cut from her body and thrown away unceremoniously until she was so light, she'd float away in the thinning atmosphere.

She couldn't bear the thought of it.

Leaving Albert was wrong. A part of her screamed to cut this shit out. To stop pretending that she was someone she wasn't, that she was entitled to a life that simply wasn't hers, but she'd rather regret doing than not doing. Her decision was a mistake and she hadn't even done anything yet, but she ignored the internal voice. Pretended that it spoke to someone else far, far away.

Eve came into the living room and noted that the toy block house had been abandoned in preference of a low-level building. "June, baby, why don't you come run to town with me?" Eve kept her voice chipper.

Neither June nor Albert looked up at her.

"No, it's okay mommy, I am going to stay here."

"June, please."

He daughter looked up at her, and, with exasperation, stood.

"Don't mess up what we're building Al."

"I won't," her brother assured.

Eve bent over and crushed his little body to hers. He squirmed and laughed, thinking it was some sort of game. He allowed his mother to kiss him one last time and went back to rearranging the blocks by color, forgetting his promise to his sister already.

There was no winning in this situation. If she stayed, she was a bad mother because she could have saved June, could have offered one of her children the chance of a future. And if she went, she was a terrible mother for leaving two of her children behind. Each decision was the wrong one. So, she decided to go with her heart, or what was left of it.

"Come on, June." Eve reached her hand out and her daughter took it. The little girl didn't question the bag slung over her mother's shoulder, but Eve could feel her hesitation as they walked through the front door.

"Mama," June's little voice whispered. It had been years since she'd called her mother that. Once she turned five she'd declared herself a grown up and started speaking more formally to her parents. It was strange at first, but Eve had gotten used to it these last two years. Now, sounding so childish, Eve paused.

"June, we need to get going, we have to keep our appointment."

"I thought we were going to town."

"We are, we are going to take a little trip, you and I." Eve tried to pull the corners of her mouth into a smile, but judging by June's reaction, it came out closer to a grimace.

If Eve had learned anything as a mother, it was that children were smarter than anyone liked to give them credit for. Maybe that was because adults wanted to seem superior at something, or felt that they'd learned enough in life that they no longer wanted to be proven wrong, but Eve knew better. And June knew better, it was all over her face.

"What about Al? And Ricky? And Daddy?"

Eve had to look away. This should have been a clue to her. If she couldn't even look her seven-year-old daughter in the eye, how would she ever be able to look at her own reflection again?

She knelt and placed her hands on either side of June's face. "They can't come with us."

Tears sprung out of June's eyes. "But, but." She may be wise, but she was still a child. She was on that precipice of frustration where she knew what she wanted, but was still at the mercy of her parents, unable to control her own destiny.

"I know this is hard to understand, and I realize that you may never truly know why I had to make this decision, but we need to go. It's time."

Eve stood and grasped June's hand. Her daughter followed without further comment, though Eve could see her other hand wipe at her eyes.

They got to the station with five minutes to spare. Hector stood on the platform in the doorway where uniformed men and women checked names off a list as people shuffled by them.

Eve watched as families, some with smiles, some with tears, waved goodbye to those left behind. There was a dividing line of the lucky and the unlucky and each side knew they'd never see the other again.

With her bag in one hand and June's small fingers in the other, Eve moved to the back of the slow-moving line. A commotion broke out as a man from the crowd tried to break through the metal barriers on either side of the platform and tried to jump onto the train. Three guards in white suits tackled the man and began kicking him before they dragged him away.

There were always people who tried to get on the train, that wasn't new, but the brutality of the officers shocked Eve. The crowd pushed and swelled around her. One time June's hand was ripped from her own as a man careened between them, making a break for the ramp. Eve lunged forward to grab her daughter before she could get trampled. The tension through the crowd was palpable. While people always tried to break through, this was the last time people could try to muscle their way on.

Something whizzed by Eve's left ear and she flinched as a large rock cracked the plastic helmet a guard wore. More rocks followed. The crowd was desperate. If they couldn't somehow get on board, they would literally die. It was their last chance. There were no more rules. The guards, sensing the same thing, started to pull the ramp in, signaling to the remaining few waving tickets that they needed to move forward. There was no time for long good-byes.

Eve felt people pushing in to her left and right and held June's hand tighter. If she was separated from her again, June was sure to get swept away, lost to her forever. Eve could feel the buzz of the crowd grow and knew they needed to get to Hector. She had seconds now to solidify her decision. This was it.

She looked at Hector, standing on the threshold of the future of humanity. He locked eyes with her. What was his expression? Love? Fear?

Out of the corner of her eye she saw a flash of red hair. Part of her was afraid to look. To see if it was Jacob, but she knew the truth. Knew that he was there watching her. Watching his wife and daughter with a man that was not him waiting for them.

It was time. She had to decide. Would she go forward, or back?

Clutching June's hand, as tears ran down her face, Eve filled her lungs with air and took one, purposeful step.

## AUTHOR'S NOTES - KRISTIN DURFEE

AGAIN, what excitement at being included in this wonderful next installment of the Alvarium Experiment! As the ideas began to be kicked around and retellings of classics was settled upon, I had my work cut out for me. My ambitions were big, but condensing a novel into less than ten thousand words turned out to be a challenge. So, I set my focus upon other short stories that could be updated. Admittedly, other than in school, I hadn't read a lot of them. A google search of classic short stories was a treasure trove of possibilities.

I had an idea of what I wanted my story to entail, some sort of lottery that would result in a trip to Mars, but the specifics were a mystery to me until I stumbled upon this gem of a story, "Eveline" by James Joyce. Written in the early 1900s, the main character was faced with a timeless question: to remain in the past or move forward to the future. I'd found my Eve.

I tried to stay true to the feel and struggle Eveline went through in her decision, I hope I did Mr. Joyce justice. For your continued reading pleasure, I encourage you to seek out "Eveline." A quick internet search will yield the story in its entirely. I hope you find it as enjoyable as I did.

*—KAD*

# PUPAK AND THE GREAT FISH

### JOHN HOPE

**Part I: Swallowed**

*Summer of 2017, at O Presidente's mansion just outside of Brasília, Brazil*

Pupak stood next to Dimas' bed, hovering over the undersized twelve-year-old boy like a dark daemon. He patted his belt that held a knife—a good, strong knife he had stolen from the garden shed. He slipped the knife out of the belt. The dim moonlight shone from behind, glistening off the blade's multiple scrapes where Pupak had sharpened it with a rock. He felt the moon's light on his back like the eyes of the gods watching over him waiting for him to commit a punishable sin. The longer he lived in O Presidente's mansion, the less he feared the gods and the more O Presidente's lust for godliness made sense. Anyone could weld god-like power if only he had the right tool.

Pupak turned the blade over in his hand as he focused on the boy. He'd wished he had such a tool back in his village. He'd had not chance to use it, until now. And nothing would stop him.

.   .   .

*Nine months earlier, off the southern coast of Brazil*

SCREAMS from the frightened men pierced the wailing winds. Pupak sat cross-legged on the metal-grated floor of the white men's great canoe, his arms to the side gripping twisted ropes and fighting the ship's ferocious heaving and rolling. He squinted as dagger rain pellets smacked his face. The wooden rainforest canoes at home were no longer than two men. This metal beast held fifty men, with poles and rope and wheels and objects that made animal growls. He gritted his teeth, sucked in quick breaths, and gripped the rope, wishing he was back home. The rain at home was never this violent. He yearned for the safety of the towering canopy of trees and tired droop of branches that protected him and his family from such godly power. He knew that this was the work of the gods. They were angry at him.

The storm had struck quick and violent. One minute, Pupak stood staring out over the great endless water, in awe of the open vastness, and the next – chaos. The great canoe rocked, men screamed, and Pupak cowered to the deck like a child.

Tupi men aboard the vessel fought the storm across the slick deck. Dressed in white men's clothing, they yelled at each other, racing from one end of the great canoe to the other, struggling with ropes and tools foreign to Pupak. Torrents of water slammed against the men, toppling them over each other, their foot coverings squeaking against the abrasive floor. They rose, fought, and fell again.

In one fall, a couple of them landed at Pupak's bare feet. They looked to Pupak and barked questions. One man stumbled forward and pushed his way toward Pupak. The side of his face wrinkled and disfigured, he appeared a victim of fire. He gripped Pupak's shoulders and demanded an answer. His Tupi language, mostly babble to Pupak, sounded different than the Portuguese of the white men of Brazil – more nasal with drawn-out sounds like rolling Rs, but just as cryptic. But Pupak knew what he must have been asking.

He had known of the Tupi. Their dark skin shared a resemblance to Pupak's Akuntsu tribe. Pupak guessed they held similar beliefs, an aligned understanding of the balance of the gods and how these gods controlled the world around them. Unlike the white men, whose aggression showed their lust for the gods' powers.

Another gush of water knocked the Tupi men off their feet.

SNAP. A pole like a splintered tree branch fell to the deck. The men rushed to the pole and wrapped ropes around it and an adjoining pole to keep it from slamming against something else.

Another crashing wave and they rolled over each other across the deck. Through the battering wind and rain, they crawled on their hands and knees back to Pupak. Again, they demanded an answer.

Pupak lowered his head and closed his eyes. Looking up, he nodded, pointed to his chest, and spoke in his native language, "Yes. My fault. The storm. The angered gods. My fault."

The Tupi eyed each other. They yelled over the wind, then returned their focus to Pupak. The fire-scarred man pointed to Pupak's chest and spoke.

Pupak nodded. "Yes. My fault. My fault."

Fire-scarred man pointed skyward. He yelled. The winds yelled back. His grotesque face mimicked the way the gods must have looked.

Pupak looked up. The rain attacked in sheets of stinging rain, striking their faces with the ferocity of thousands of arrowed darts. Pupak knew they wanted an apology out of him. Not for the men, but for the gods. Pupak knew it, as did the Tupi. And despite their separate languages, the Tupi seemed to understand Pupak's admittance to guilt.

The problem was he couldn't apologize. He had bribed the Tupi to get aboard this vessel so he could hide from the gods. Though it

was the white man who had forced him from home, he knew the
gods were on the men's side. They wanted him to go.

Pupak heaved to his feet slipping, wind and rain battering him
from side to side. The boat's sway made him even more unsteady.
He gripped the side of the great canoe, which was chin-level. With
one hand on a post, he used the other to thumb toward the water.
"Throw me to the great water." He looked to the raging waves. Part
of him wanted to leap in and end it all. But with his shaking knees
and chest, he needed the Tupi's help.

The Tupi shared looks of confusion, frowns and narrowed eyes.

"Throw me to the water." Pupak repeated. "This is my fault.
Throw me in to save yourselves."

Fire-scarred man stepped forward, legs spread to stabilize his
walk. He grunted something and pointed to the sky, his dark, crinkled face angry.

Pupak shook his head. He felt the big man's frustration. "No. I
can't beg the gods," he explained. "I ran from them. I have no
escape." He glanced at the violent ocean, waves frothing in ever-
moving spikes and sprays. He looked to the Tupi. "Sacrifice me."

Fire-scarred man's eyes widened.

Though separated by different languages, the Tupi and Pupak's
tribe, the Akuntsu, were both native to the great forest. Pupak had
learned in his rare encounters with neighboring tribes that the
language shared some words. Based on fire-scarred man's face,
Pupak guessed that sacrifice was close enough to the Tupi word – he
understood. Pupak pointed to himself and then to the water.

Fire-scarred man narrowed his eyes again and nodded slowly.
He spoke to his fellow Tupi. They argued. As frightened as they
might have been from the storm, unwarranted murder was something just as taboo. It may anger the gods even more than they
already were.

Pupak risked letting go of the ropes he used as support. He
stumbled forward and gripped Fire-scarred man's collar. "Please.
Save yourselves. Sacrifice me."

Fire-scarred man gave another nod. With a final word to his
peers, he swept Pupak into his thick arms, struggled the two steps to

the side of the boat, and with a single nasally Tupi word, "Nnd," he hurled Pupak overboard.

Pupak gulped a mouthful of salt water the second he splashed into the tropical waters. He surfaced, coughing, kicking, and fighting for life. Though he had chosen death, he couldn't stop struggling. He kicked and reached and coughed and breathed. Water splashed. Wind blew. The roar of the gods' power was the most frightening thing he'd ever witnessed in his life. Nothing from his forest home compared to the ferocity.

His fight with the water reminded him of the waterfall game he'd play at home. He and his cousins would dive into the river rapids to get dragged tossed in currents and fight their way to the shallows before reaching the falls. This life and death game was foolish, but surprisingly good training for this unexpected plunge.

Within seconds, the battering rain stopped, the winds stopped, and the noise stopped. The waves still rocked him up and down, but with a gentler motion.

Pupak kicked, spinning in the water. The great canoe of the white men rocked along the easing waves a stone's throw away. The Tupi men stood at the side, all with matching bewildered gapes at Pupak. They turned as one at the voice of a barking white man, who approached from nowhere, pointing, demanding, and appearing far dryer than his darker minions. The men stepped away from the great canoe's side and resumed working. The last, fire-scarred man, gave Pupak a final glance, and disappeared.

Pupak continued treading water as the vessel veered and moved away from him. Part of him yearned to swim after it, climb aboard, and get back home, to his family, to his cousins, to his bed. But he understood, as the Tupi did, there was no going back. The gods had been pleased–at least for now. Pupak had been sacrificed and the storm was gone. Returning to the ship could only result in the death of them all.


PUPAK'S ARMS and legs grew weak. His mouth was dry and he craved fresh water. The waves leveled out to a smooth, glassy surface. The dark clouds left and the sun baked his face as he moved his arms and legs in languid strokes. He knew he should allow himself to sink and complete the gods' appeasement. But he didn't know how to quit. He didn't quit when the white men invaded his village, tied him and his friends up, and raped the women. He hadn't given up when the survivors were forced to flee farther and farther upriver, hiding from the white men's loud beasts that consumed the trees. And he hadn't given up when seemingly kind white men that spoke of their all-powerful god sought friendship by offering the Akuntsu women and children blankets before they all grew ill and died.

Now, one of the last of his people still alive, he couldn't let go of hope. Sore, tired, and alone, he continued to tread. Exhaustion crept in. His life would soon be over.

The distant sound of bubbles reaching the surface startled him.

He wrenched his neck from side to side. The great canoe had disappeared beyond the horizon long ago. At this point, Pupak couldn't tell which way it had headed. When it left, heavy clouds hid the sun and the ocean looked the same in every direction. Now, the sun glared, making it hard to see.

More bubbles, this time an echoing screech accented its gurgle. The noise reminded Pupak of the metal beasts that consumed his forest home. He kicked and swung his weary arms. Still, he saw nothing.

At last, a definite SSSSHHHHH drew his focus in a single direction. There, three stone throws away, something glimmered and emerged from the flat ocean surface, something dark and ominous. A vast water beast, large by far than the great caimans or snakes, approached him fast, growing larger by the second, a long, narrow silver beast.

Pupak panicked. Despite his weakness, he spun away from the water monster, swimming hard. He pulled at the water and kicked. But the SSSSHHHHH grew heavier and louder. He spun back. The beast was larger than ever. Narrow vertical beams, each the width of a man's finger, stood in a line atop the beast as its silvery body emerged. The monster was seconds from consuming him.

A sharp scrape against his legs buckled his lower body. The beast rose from the water from directly beneath Pupak, sweeping him up and out into the open air.

Pupak gasped.

He rolled himself into a tight ball. Eyes closed. A cool breeze cut over him. He shivered.

A moan echoed. The beast must be angry.

Guilt overwhelmed Pupak. Hiding from the gods. Thinking he could deny their command of him. He was a fool. "Please. Oh, please. Have mercy," Pupak pleaded. "Please forgive me. Please."

Another moan.

His eyes remained tight. He touched his hot, sunburnt face, his waterlogged fingers shaking. He opened his eyes. He was out of the water. The weight of his soggy body pressed against the beast's abrasive skin. "Oh, please. Please. I was a fool. Forgive me." He shook.

But the next noise was completely unexpected.

CLANK.

Pupak opened his eyes and looked up. Squinting, he held a hand up to shade the sun's glare.

A white man dressed in white, emerged from the center of the beast's back. His opened mouth and huge eyes looked down to Pupak from a high mount. Wind flapped the man's clothing.

Pupak looked from side to side. Now clear from the bubbling water, the beast's silvery back was fully exposed. This was like nothing he'd ever seen before – sharp angles and shinier than the clearest river's surface.

The man called out in his white man's Portuguese – Pupak recognized the sound of the language in an instant. The man waved for the Pupak to join him.

Slowly, Pupak rose.


PUPAK SAT HUDDLED inside the beast on a hard seat, his arms tight around his folded legs pressed against his chest. He shook in the cool air. He repeatedly refused the blanket a white man had laid next to him. The last blankets that white men offered his fellow Akuntsu had the power to kill.

He had never been in such a place. Tiny lights like stationary fireflies flickered on every wall. The stench of white men wafted around him, sharp and pungent. A constant hum pounded against the sides of his head. White men surrounded him, all staring and speaking their gibberish to each other like he was the alien. Though clearly, this was not earth.

The men split, allowing a man with dark skin approach. He had the same trimmed hair and clothing of the white men. He spoke.

Pupak frowned. "I don't understand."

The man stepped back. He tilted his head and said, "Akuntsu?"

Pupak straightened. "Yes. I'm Akuntsu."

The man's eyes shown bright and he exchanged words with an older white man whose silvery, slicked back hair matched the color of the beast. They gibbered for a full minute.

When the man returned his focus to Pupak, he said. "Ohrooda." He tapped his own chest.

Pupak tapped his. "Pupak."

Ohrooda translated to the white men. Amongst the words, Pupak heard his name. Ohrooda looked to Pupak. "You're cold. Use the blanket." He pointed.

Pupak hugged himself and shook his head. "White men's blankets are bad."

Ohrooda breathed deep and gave a slow understanding nod. Evidently, the white men had given poisoned blankets to more tribes than just the Akuntsu. Ohrooda unbuttoned his shirt and slipped it off. "Please. Take it."

Hesitating, he took it and wrapped it around his shoulders.

Ohrooda returned to the gray-haired man, speaking.

Pupak lifted a finger and spoke, "Ah, Ohrooda."

The dark man focused on him.

"What is this?" He looked around. "This... great fish?"

The side of Ohrooda mouth lifted as if he were trying to stifle a smile. "This great fish is called a – submarine." He said the final foreign word slowly so Pupak could understand it.

"Sub-mar-ine." Pupak sounded out each syllable as he surveyed the odd surroundings.

Ohrooda drew closer. "Did your boat sink, Pupak?"

"No. I was sacrificed."

"Sacrificed?"

Pupak swept a hand across his face. "I hid from the gods. They sent a white man to bring me to his elder's son."

Ohrooda scratched his head as if trying to figure out Pupak's riddle. "Elder's son? What elder?"

"He called him O Presidente."

Ohrooda stepped back as if Pupak had just smacked him with a branch. He spoke to the gray-haired man in rapid fire. His sudden excitement frightened Pupak. He tightened Ohrooda's stiff shirt around him – it had a strange, crisp odor, similar to white men he'd encountered. It reminded him of the white men who spoke of their powerful good and who bathed in the river and used white stones that made the bubbles in the water. The same scent was fresh in his burning senses the night he held his small nephew, Bentoo, as he wheezed, shivered, and breathed his last. Still very clear in Pupak's mind, he remembered screaming into the darkness. After he lay the boy onto a patch of leaves, he stabbed every blanket with a spear and flung them into the fire. Smoke billowed, streaming wavy lines that rose above the flames like angels of death lifting over their encampment. He felt his home died that night, along with his inner childhood.

The more Ohrooda and the gray-haired man spoke, the more Pupak's unease grew. His eyes darted from wall to wall. The other white men stared. The fireflies blinked. The great fish rumbled. His knees bounced. He felt ready to dash, to flee once again. The pressure of being trapped inside this beast pressed against him. He struggled to breathe.

"Pupak." Ohrooda touched his arm.

Startled, Pupak jerked, panting.

"O Presidente," Ohrooda said. "Are you sure that was his name?"

"Yes."

Ohrooda and the gray-haired man shared a nod.

"What?" Pupak asked. "What is it?"

Ohrooda lowered his brow as he spoke. "Many people have been looking for you."

"Me? Why?" He asked, but already knew the answer. Ricardo, the man who forced him from his home, had tried to reason with Pupak. He had already explained his importance to the country, to O Presidente's son. But Pupak wanted nothing to do with them. They killed Bentoo. They killed his people.

"You have a medicine."

Pupak frowned. "I am no medicine man. White men have killed all of Akuntsu's medicine men."

Ohrooda shook his head. "The medicine is inside you."

Pupak shifted and stiffened his back. "I have nothing."

"Please." Ohrooda sat uncomfortably close. "Let me explain. There is an illness, a great illness, that kills many people. It is called malaria." He sounded out the foreign word. "Many have died from this malaria. But your people do not get it. You are immune."

Pupak frowned. "What is immune?"

"It means your body stops this illness. Even if you get malaria, it will not harm you."

"I have this… immune?"

Ohrooda nodded.

Pupak touched his chest. The thought of something called immune swimming inside made him squirm.

"O Presidente's son has malaria. He is dying. O Presidente started a great search for your people, to acquire this medicine inside of you. They found you. You were the hope of the country. But you disappeared."

"I escaped," Pupak corrected.

"Why? Why did you run?"

Pupak stood, Ohrooda's shirt falling away. "Why should I help? O Presidente and his white men brought illness to my people." He paused, realizing he was growing loud. He knew that the gods were listening to every word. His fate lay in helping O Presidente's son. When Ricardo found him, a black bird sang his song above his head. He'd known since childhood that such a sign could only mean the gods had sent this white man. Pupak had to go. Yet, he couldn't. "They killed our little ones. Why should I help save his little one?"

The surrounding men stared, suspicion written in their faces.

Pupak stiffened and motioned to the men. "They deserve to die."

Pupak shoved Ohrooda, who bounced against the gray-haired man. They tumbled. Pupak flung himself around a pole and threw an elbow at a white man's face. The man fell. He attacked the next, but a brawny man with painted arms snagged him around his neck. Pupak fought, but choked, his throat collapsing. His lips tingled and the world blurred.

Ohrooda and the gray-hair man yelled.

Pupak felt the arm around his throat relax a fraction, then slide away.

Pupak collapsed to the hard floor, gasping face down. Tears poured down the sides of his face. The weight of the gods, his responsibility, his losses, and his helplessness – it all weighed on him with an intensity far greater than the squeeze of his throat. He wheezed, his lips scraping the floor's metal grating.

Shoes surrounded his head. Ohrooda squatted in front him and offered his hand.

Pupak looked up, eyes overflowing with tears. He grabbed Ohrooda's hand and sat up.

Ohrooda asked, "Why do you fight?"

Pupak swiped his face. "Men swallow fish." He whimpered, shaking. "But I am a small man. I'm swallowed by a fish."

Ohrooda nodded slowly with a dark look. He breathed deeply. "Yes. I understand."

"You understand?" He rubbed his face again.

He nodded. "As a boy, I was taken from my village." Leaning, he nudged the blanket that had fallen to the floor next to Pupak. "White men poisoned the blankets they gave us. They lit the trees on fire. Now, they are poisoned by our home they stole from us and a fire burns within us. We are inside out and we must survive being swallowed by fish."

Pupak curled his legs against his chest. White men surrounded him and Ohrooda, both huddled close to each other. Ohrooda's deep, dark eyes stared. Though from a different tribe, Pupak saw home in Ohrooda's eyes – something familiar and warm, something he'd thought had died the night Bentoo's soul floated into the dark tree canopy. Ohrooda wasn't here by accident. There were very few still alive that even understood the language of the Akuntsu. The gods positioned him and this great fish to pluck him from the water so the white men could use the medicine hidden within his body.

Pupak said, "The gods commanded me to help them."

Ohrooda placed a hand on Pupak's shoulder. "Then that is what you must do."

## Part II: Saving the Sinners

PUPAK SAT at the edge of a bed. A breeze flapped light, translucent curtains. The warm evening sun illuminated the room. Next to Pupak lay O Presidente's small white boy, Dimas. He swept the back of his hand over the boy's forehead. For once since Pupak had arrived, it didn't feel chilled and clammy. He combed his fingers across Dimas' light hair.

Dimas opened his eyes, flickering at first. He squinted, then focused on Pupak's dark face. The boy spoke. There was a question in his tone.

"You will survive," Pupak said with stiffened lips, though he knew the boy would not understand. Tension welled inside Pupak.

Dimas' mother spotted her waken child and sprang from the door. She sat on the bed opposite to Pupak. Her face lit, she embraced Dimas, kissing his cheeks and rambling in her foreign Portuguese. "Meu bebê! Meu precioso anjo!"

The deep tone of O Presidente captured the boy's and his mother's attention. "Filho." He too joined the family reunion.

Pupak stood from the bed and joined the doctor with whom

he'd been working the past few months. Pupak's arms folded tight against his chest and his nails dug into his skin. The poking and prodding of Pupak's body had been one of the most uncomfortable experiences of his life. But there was no escape. He had already been swallowed.

Pupak stepped for the door, but the doctor grabbed his shoulder.

The doctor said, "Where are you going?" His words were hard to understand – he barely spoke Pupak's language.

"Out." Pupak pulled free.

Pupak marched through O Presidente's palace to the surrounding gardens. Dark men and women darted around his grand home, constantly trimming the surrounding blunt bushes and flowers. Everything was knee high – nothing tall enough to sit beneath. The result was a bright garden, too bright for Pupak. The late evening sun, low on the horizon, burned his face. He shaded his eyes with his hand as he walked. Every day, every hour, he yearned to return to the rainforests, to his shaded village, musty and rich with vegetation and life. O Presidente's son's recovery was just the first step of great things, according to the doctor. The medicine they found inside him had the potential to save millions of people. But none of this mattered to Pupak. He would always be homeless as long as he was here. He kicked at the ground and pulled at the collar of the white men's clothing he was forced to wear.

A green, leafy plant in the distance drew his attention. He pulled off his shirt and jogged to it. The plant appeared out of place in this flat garden, tall and shadowy. He sat beneath the plant. Vines hung low from the plant's branches and the air felt cooler within the shade.

He curled into a ball and closed his eyes. In his head, he imagined himself at home, his friends surrounding him. He breathed and for a brief instant thought he smelled the bright blooming flowers and exhale of centipedes and beetles lining the moldy bark of surrounding trees.

For a brief moment, he felt the presence of the gods. At home, their governess wind, rain, insects, stars, moon, sun, and all things greater than him brought a sense of order and comfort. His time at this mansion had been chaotic – doctors, needles, questions, and an onslaught of foreign words. Quietly, Pupak prayed for peace. His words twirled inside and Pupak drifted off asleep.

PUPAK AWOKE THE NEXT MORNING, the sun striking his face. He sat up and squinted. The leafy plant he had fallen asleep beneath appeared withered. It wiggled and moved. Standing, he wiped his eyes and focused on the plant. It was infested with dozens of fat caterpillars. They devoured the plant.

Pupak's stomach twisted and his heart sunk. The last of the shade in this open-air garden was gone. The sight reminded him of the white men with the metal beasts who invaded his home and devoured the trees. The result was a flat, splintery landscape—no life, no shade.

Pupak approached what was left of the plant, plucked off a caterpillar, and squeezed. It popped, oozing green slime.

"Pupak."

Pupak spun.

Ohrooda stepped through the maze of blunt garden bushes and flowers. The doctor walked briskly behind him.

"Ohrooda. You came." He smiled.

Ohrooda said, "The entire house has been looking for you." He stopped, his hands on his hips. He still wore the white, stiff clothes he wore when he was within the great metal fish. They hadn't seen each other since then. "Have you been hiding again?"

Pupak shook his head. "Dreaming." He looked to the plant. "But my bed was taken."

Ohrooda looked to the caterpillar-infested plant and then the dead bug pinched between Pupak's fingers. "Don't eat those caterpillars."

"Why? Have you?"

"I have."

"And?"

Ohrooda narrowed his eyes. "You're still angry." The doctor stepped next to him, folding his arms.

Pupak frowned. "Why wouldn't I be? They killed my family, yet O Presidente's son was allowed to survive. How is that fair?"

Ohrooda didn't speak.

"How are you not angry? They stole you as a boy and forced you into these things." Pupak flicked Ohrooda's collar. "Why are you happy?"

"Pupak—" the doctor started, but Ohrooda stopped him with a wave of his hand.

Ohrooda said, "White men's fate is not ours to decide. I'm happy because I chose to be."

"You chose poorly." Pupak spun away.

Ohrooda caught his shoulder and spun him back. "Really? I'm not the miserable one."

"You're just another white man."

"No, Pupak. I was born in the jungle. There, I fought to survive. I still live in a jungle. And I still fight." He pointed to the caterpillar-infested plant. "These caterpillars devoured this plant." He turned to Pupak. "Don't let them devour you."

Ohrooda's words and tone reminded Pupak of his village elders. Their counseling was always direct and harsh, as hard as surviving their rainforest home. Bentoo was certainly not the first child he watched die. His sister's first baby also died in his arms. The baby had been very small and wouldn't suck on his sister's breast. The baby shivered and went cold. By night, she'd stopped breathing. His sister refused to believe the baby's death. She wrapped the tiny form in palm fronds and tied her to her chest for days until a strong odor forced her to accept the truth. It wasn't until now that Pupak realized that he still held Bentoo's memory just as close to his chest. Maybe it was time to let go.

A tear trickled down the side of Pupak's nose. He wanted to curse the gods for forcing him here. "I hate the white men."

"I know."

Pupak looked at the squished caterpillar still between his fingers. He flicked it away, stepping toward Ohrooda, his head down.

Ohrooda placed a hand across Pupak's shoulders. "Come."

With heavy steps, they walked back into the house.

. . .

OVER THE FOLLOWING MONTHS, Pupak helped the doctor, as well as dozens of other men jabbing needles into his dark skin, to discover more about his hidden medicine. The first set of medicine that brought O Presidente's son back to life required weekly tubes of blood from Pupak's arm. The white men grew closer and closer to replicating the medicine.

He befriended Senhor Alvarez, the groundskeeper in charge of the gardens. Pupak volunteered his time assisting Senhor Alvarez's staff and learned the names of the various flowering plants. His favorite was the Heliconia, a beautiful large-leaf plant with flowers like sideways teardrops in cascading rows of fiery red and yellow, like the brightly-colored birds of his village.

As pretty as the garden was, he still yearned for the shade of home. At the far corner of the property stood a shed where the garden tools were kept. The shed bordered a patch of undisturbed forest, a rarity near the mansion grounds. Every time Pupak returned to the shed, he felt the pull of the trees. At night, he started sneaking out and walking the forest. It wasn't particularly large. An ugly city of smelly buildings and streets lay beyond the woods. The forest likely remained to act as a buffer between the city and O Presidente's property.

Pupak begged Senhor Alvarez for a larger plant for the garden, similar to the large leafy plant that he had fallen asleep beneath weeks before. Senhor Alvarez refused and claimed the plant Pupak had seen previously must have been a weed, something that they would have ripped out had the caterpillars not gotten to it first. Nevertheless, Pupak persisted. Part of him feared that his hope would wither and die like the tall leafy plant in the garden.

Senhor Alvarez relented – a little. He reserved a small patch of ground near the back corner of the mansion for Pupak to plant whatever he wished.

One morning, Pupak worked on his hands and knees, turning the soil with a trowel. Then O Presidente approached with his son, Dimas.

"Pupak," the deep-voiced man said.

Pupak stood, brushing off his knees. He focused on O Presidente, bracing for the onslaught of Portuguese that Pupak had been struggling to learn.

O Presidente said, "I wish to thank you for cooperating with the doctors."

Pupak frowned and rubbed the various needle puncture wounds up both arms.

O Presidente placed a fat hand on his son's shoulders and said, "And for my son's life. He wouldn't be with us if it wasn't for you."

Not that I had much a choice. Pupak thought. You've imprisoned me here. Stole me from my home. Murdered my village. He nodded and spoke in Portuguese, "Yes."

O Presidente nodded in return. "Yes," he echoed. "Well… thank you." He shook Pupak's hand. "Thank you." The tall man pulled him forward and hugged.

Pupak pushed him away.

O Presidente straightened, appearing startled from Pupak's move. He frowned. "You should be grateful, as well."

"Grateful?" Pupak muttered.

"You too were rescued. From that godless forest. Look at yourself. You're civilized now."

Pupak thumbed his chest. "I needed no rescue. Your people devastated my home."

"We need that wood. We all do. It builds society."

"And destroys it."

O Presidente mounted his fat hands on his wide hips. He stepped forward.

Pupak stepped back, his face tight.

O Presidente jabbed a finger in the air, pointing at Pupak. "Know your place, boy. I am the most powerful man you'll ever meet."

"You claim I am godless, but I honor my gods. You claim you have an all-powerful god, yet you pretend to be one."

SLAP.

Pupak jolted from the sting of O Presidente's hand against his face.

O Presidente waggled his finger in Pupak's face. "Watch your mouth, boy. Or you'll find yourself wrapped in the same blankets that killed your family." He spun and marched away.

"Papai," Dimas called out.

O Presidente hesitated and spun, his eyes wide.

"May I help Pupak in the garden?"

His eyes narrowed, pausing as if considering the request. "Fine. You may help the help." He walked away.

Dimas smiled at Pupak with his childish enthusiasm. The child's illness had stunted his growth, making him appear younger than the twelve-year-old he was.

Pupak glared. He wished this boy had died from malaria. Day after day, Dimas had spent more and more time with Pupak, never picking up on Pupak's subtle cues to just go away.

Dimas was useless. He was treated like a prince, yet allowed to remain an infant. He was past the age Pupak was when the village elder walked him out to the forbidden ravine and left him tied to a tree. They did this to all boys so that they would grow properly into men. But this boy was coddled. O Presidente spent almost no time with him. He didn't teach or instruct him in anything. Since Dimas woke, Pupak wondered why these white men placed such effort saving Dimas when they ignored his life, leaving his rearing to the servants.

Dimas asked, "What are you planting?"

Pupak looked to the dirt. "Nothing yet." He spoke slowly, making sure he said the correct Portuguese words. "Dirt... uh... needs prepared."

"Prepared?"

"Yes. If dirt not ready, plant will not survive."

Dimas' smile and wide eyes exposed his unabashed excitement. "How can I help?"

Pupak hesitated, then lowered to his knees.

Dimas joined next to him.

Pupak dug the trowel into the soil and flipped it over, exposing the darker earth beneath. He looked to the boy. "Earth must breathe."

"Can I?" He held out a hand.

Pupak handed him the trowel.

He went at the soil, digging and turning it over.

Pupak stood, watching Dimas work from behind. He stepped back and wrapped his fingers around the handle of shovel. The back of Dimas' exposed neck beckoned. With a swing of the shovel, he could rid himself of this menace, this useless child.

For weeks, Pupak had endured in the belly of the beast, biding his time for the day he could exact his revenge. The more time he spent with Dimas, the more these thoughts of vengeance flowered. He often recalled Bentoo, how the promise of his life was robbed. Yet the promise was given to this boy in front of him, a boy undeserving.

Dimas angled his head up. "How am I doing?"

Pupak nodded slowly. "Well." He squeezed the handle.

## Part III: Righting the Wrongs

AT NIGHT, Pupak rose from the floor. As usual, he had slept on the floor next to the bed he was given. O Presidente's mansion stood quiet and dark. Pupak tiptoed down the chilled wood-floor hallway. The occasional creak below his feet kept him alert and caused his heart to bounce.

He rounded the corner and darted for Dimas' bedroom. With a gentle push, the door swung open.

The small boy lay asleep in his giant bed. Translucent sheets hung suspended above him from the bed's four wooden posts, a slight breeze from the ceiling vent giving them a silent sway.

Pupak stood next to the bed, hovering over Dimas like a dark daemon. He patted the knife on his belt– a good, strong knife he had stolen from the garden shed. He slipped the knife out of the belt. The dim moonlight shone from behind, glistening off the blade's multiple scrapes where Pupak had sharpened it with a rock. He felt the moon's light on his back like the eyes of the gods watching over him waiting for him to commit a punishable sin. The longer he lived in O Presidente's mansion, the less he feared the gods and the more O Presidente's lust for godliness made sense. Anyone could wield god-like power if only he had the right tool.

Pupak turned the blade over in his hand as he focused on the boy. He'd wished he had such a tool back in his village. He'd had no chance to use it, until now. And nothing would stop him. Pupak tightened his grip on the knife and shifted his weight.

The floorboard creaked.

Dimas woke, slowly at first. With a wave of Pupak's knife, Dimas' eyes widen. He gasped and stared at the dark figure above him. "Pupak."

"Shhhh." Pupak touched his finger to Dimas' lips. He slipped the knife back into his belt and spoke in broken Portuguese. "Rise. Follow Pupak."

Dimas sat up. "Where we going?"

"Come." He stepped back, waving a hand.

Dimas shot out of bed and approached, wobbling at first. Dressed only in his nightshirt, his bare feet squeaked against the floor and his face lit with excitement, white teeth broad.

Pupak led Dimas into the hallway and downstairs.

Dimas kept close behind, bouncing like a snake's tail. Pupak felt his bubbling energy.

They approached the kitchen's open entrance. Though dimly lit, long, fuzzy shadows along the floor revealed the late night staff quietly attending to their duties. Pupak pressed his back against the wall next to the entrance. He placed a hand against the boy's chest, steadying him along the wall next him. He looked down to Dimas and let out a soft, "Shhhh."

Dimas nodded.

Pupak peered into the kitchen. A pair of men carried and unloaded boxes in front of an opened pantry, their backs to Pupak.

He crept past, Dimas on his heels.

Outside, the night breeze fanned them, and still Pupak's heart fluttered for what was to come.

Dimas grabbed his hand. "Pupak. Where we going?"

Pupak didn't stop until he led the boy to the far end of the garden, to the shed at the edge of the property. He spun toward Dimas and reached into his belt.

Dimas held his breath, his eyes still huge and filled with excitement.

Pupak pulled out the knife, reached for a bag tied to a bush that grew against the shed, and cut it free. Opening the bag, he pulled out a dark, rectangular cloth. He wound the cloth a few times around the boy's eyes and head like a blindfold.

Dimas asked, "What's this for?" He didn't resist.

"Pupak must hide Dimas' eyes."

"Why?"

"Dimas will understand when it is time." He tightened a knot at the back of his head, pulled out a rope from the bag, and grabbed Dimas' hand. "Come."

Dimas staggered at first, but allowed Pupak to guide him.

They walked, crossing the line of rocks that marked the edge of the forest. Dimas stumbled, but Pupak's tight grip and patient, steady steps led him forward.

Dimas said, "The ground is sharp."

"A boy's feet are soft."

They stepped over roots and through thick bushes, rounding trees and crunching dry leaves. The mansion's constant lights grew less and less discernable, requiring Pupak to rely on the moonlight that barely penetrated the tree canopy. Pupak breathed. The sharp mustiness flooded his senses. The scents weren't quite like his home, but it felt a step closer. The ghostly atmosphere was warm and comforting. He felt himself smiling.

"How much farther?"

Pupak tightened his grip on the boy's soft hand. "Soon."

They descended a slope. Dimas lost his balance and slipped. Pupak caught him.

"Pupak." Dimas whimpered. "I'm scared."

"Dimas has no use of fear."

He led him to a clearing. Here, the moon shone brightly against a patch of leaves and the side of a tree. Pupak stopped. He had scouted this location in the daylight. With the break in the trees above, he suspected the moon would light the tree. It was perfect.

He backed Dimas up against the tree.

Dimas reached for the blindfold, but Pupak stopped him from removing it.

"No. Keep it on."

"Where are we?" He shook.

Pupak smiled again and looked at the surrounding trees. "A sacred place."

"I'm scared." Dimas lips quivered.

"Shhhhh." He touched Dimas' shoulder. "Fear not. Trust Pupak."

"Um, okay."

"Do you trust Pupak?"

He sniffled. "Um, yeah."

"Good. Don't cry. Be a man and Dimas will not be harmed."

Dimas nodded, still shaking.

Pupak lowered him to the ground. He tied his feet together, pulled Dimas' hands behind his back, wound the rope around them, and tied the remaining rope around the tree.

Dimas wiggled. "I can't move."

He placed a hand on Dimas' chest. "Dimas need not move."

"Why?"

"Tonight, Dimas will be a man."

"A man?"

"The forest surrounds. The earth threatens to consume. But this is destiny. If Dimas fights, the gods will ensure Dimas will die. Accept your fate and Dimas will live through the night." Pupak rose, stepping backwards.

Dimas cried. "Pupak. Pupak, what do you mean?" He shifted, kicking up leaves. "Pupak. You're going to leave me here? You can't leave me here."

"Stay calm, boy. Survive, and Dimas will be a man."

"No. No, Pupak. Don't leave me here."

Pupak backed into the darkness.

"Pupak? Pupak! Where are you? Pupak, please. Don't leave me here. Please."

No response. Quiet.

Dimas cried. "Pupak! Help! Mommy! Daddy! Help!"

Nothing. Just the disturbing quiet of the forest. In the distance, crickets chirped.

Dimas kicked, struggling to free himself, leaves and dirt flying. He cried, shivering. "Help! Help! Help. Help... Mommy... Daddy..." His voice tapered off into a phlegmy whimper. He breathed and coughed, choking on his tears.

The night's stillness pressed into Dimas. He pulled his legs up against his chest.

Dimas' shaking settled over the following hours. They passed slowly. He didn't sleep. Every distant chirp, snap, and squeak quickened his breathing. Bugs inched over his exposed skin. He jerked, knocking them off. He shivered. Quiet. More sounds. The cycle continued.

A growl echoed.

"What's that?" his voice cracked. Dimas kicked. "Go away. Git!"

The growl grew closer. And closer.

Dimas kicked, crying. "Go! Go away!"

A snap of twigs. Rustle of leaves. YIPE.

Dimas gasped.

Silence.

He kept his legs tight against his chest. Breathing rattled. He waited. And waited. And waited.

Hours passed.

The morning sun rose, slowly drying the ground and warming Dimas' face.

His heart quickened. Mouth dry, he tried to scream, "Mommy. Daddy." The words were barely audible. He forced a swallow, but his mouth was far too dry.

He pressed the back of his head against the tree's rough trunk. He rubbed up and down. The blindfold slowly loosened. He continued, scraping his head. He winced in pain, but didn't stop. The blindfold loosened more. It rolled upward. He continued the roll until one eye was exposed.

Looking forward, he spotted him.

Pupak sat on the ground, his back to an opposing tree. He stared at Dimas. A dead jaguar lay motionless next to Pupak. He held a bloodied knife.

"Pupak," Dimas spoke, his voice harsh and scratchy.

Pupak rose and approached the boy. He squatted in front of him. Reaching, he cut off the blindfold.

Dimas stared. "I thought…" He swallowed. "I thought you left me."

He shook his head and combed a hand through Dimas' soft hair. "No. Pupak and Dimas, forever connected. Forever men." He waved the knife at the surrounding forest. "For now Dimas knows, as Pupak knows…" He looked him in the face. "…how to survive the belly of a great fish."

## AUTHOR'S NOTES – JOHN HOPE

BASED on the Book of Jonah, "Pupak and the Great Fish" tells the fictional story of Pupak, a real-life native to the Amazonian rain forests and at the time of this story's publication was one of the last surviving members of the Akuntsu tribe. The genocide of the Akuntsu remains an ongoing point of controversy in South America, not only for the sake of the native people but for the thousands of unique animal and plant species that are being killed off at alarming rates. For more information about this tribe and their history, visit the website, *www.survivalinternational.org/tribes/akuntsu.*

Some regard the Book of Jonah as a work of fiction, an allegorical fable taking place in the 8th century BC. But whether the story is fiction or a true historical account, it beautifully illustrates how God's perspective of man's wrongdoing is far different than that of man's. Rather than seeking revenge, the story shows how God has compassion and patience. In the New Testament, Jesus references the story of Jonah. He parallels Jonah's three days in the great fish and his rescuing of the Ninevites with his own death, resurrection, and being the savior of mankind. "Pupak and the Great Fish" is told from the perspective of Pupak, whose journey echoes Jonah's experiences. In this story, Pupak's tribe has largely been killed off by invasive efforts of Portuguese-speaking Brazilians and Pupak is forced to learn, as Jonah had, that despite his anger toward the Brazilians, revenge is not the answer.

The following pages include the entire text of The Book of Jonah, using the King James Version. As you read this, note the parallels between Pupak's and Jonah's stories: their vengeful feelings toward foreign people, the powerful symbolism of being swallowed by a great fish, and their self-centered anger toward unearned compassion. The Book of Jonah ends abruptly following a narrative about Jonah's discontent. "Pupak and the Great Fish" has a couple additional scenes, involving Pupak's relationship with O Presidente's son and his attempt to teach how to survive the allegorical belly of a great fish. These added scenes help to bookend the previous themes and to bring a sense of closure to Pupak's story. In both stories, however, central themes remain the same.

*—JH*

# THE COUNT OF THE ALICIAN APOCALYPSE

## BRIA BURTON

A lice! *A childish story take,*
*And, with a gentle hand,*
*Lay it where Childhood's dreams are twined*
*In Memory's mystic band,*
*Like pilgrim's wither'd wreath of flowers*
*Pluck'd in a far-off land.*
*~Lewis Carroll*

THE RISING sunlight kissed the top of a towering Stonehenge monolith. Alice raised a camera. While she couldn't replicate the scents of fresh grass and the hint of ocean on the gossamer wind, she could capture the beauty of the monument stones. She stepped off the cement path into the grass as the tour group proceeded forward. With no one obstructing her view, she pressed the silver button. That starburst of sunlight remained, encapsulating Stonehenge in radiant light for a few seconds before the screen transitioned back into camera view.

The group of thirty or so continued on, and she stared at them through the camera lens. The women wore dresses, slacks and short sleeves, jeans and jackets. The men wore tweed, business suits, and khaki. A head of fiery red hair that stood out like a bloody mop turned toward her. Alice dropped the camera.

She didn't wait for his gaze to find her. She turned and bolted. And she had no idea why.

Fifty feet away, a building of patchwork stone with flower-filled planters beneath each window appeared from nowhere. She ran around the side to the front entrance where the sign proclaimed, *Tea Shoppe*. She pressed her back against the hard stone between the front door and a window, knees bent and catching her breath. Wisteria curled overhead on the wall.

Fear prickled her skin and the taste of iron filled her mouth. Yet it was unexplainable. That red hair had felt like an ominous warning. She knew him from somewhere, but where? She remembered his name was J.J. But that was all she remembered beyond her body's instinct to run.

Why couldn't she remember anything about him? Why did he terrify her?

The open field of short grass on the Salisbury Plain beyond promised no place to hide for a thousand yards. She took slow, steady breaths to calm her rapid heartbeat. Why had she failed to see this tea shop until now? The anticipation of her first visit to the monument had made her unaware of her surroundings. Either way, she made her decision and went inside.

The herbal, green, black, white, rooibos, and other tea varieties scented the air along with freshly baked muffins. A bell chimed as she entered, but no one glanced her way. At all the tables throughout the shop, pairs and trios chatted in polite tones while sipping and stirring their tea. Except one gentleman in the far corner holding a book in front of his face. He sat alone.

With a glance out each window and no sign of J.J., Alice approached the stranger and took a seat opposite him. The book concealing him was *The Count of Monte Cristo*.

"I hope you don't mind," she said. "No other seats are available."

He lowered the book and placed it on the table. Alice was immediately struck by his heart-shaped face. His defined, symmetrical features made her heart jump. An attractive goatee graced his chin. He had dark, wavy hair with tasteful sideburns, piercing yet gentle brown eyes. A smile graced the edges of his lips.

"I didn't mean to interrupt your reading." Alice smoothed her green sun dress to make sure her thighs were well covered as she sat.

"Whom are you avoiding?" he asked.

With another quick glance at the windows, Alice hesitated. He was a stranger, after all. "Just a guy. I don't really know him."

"Was he bothering you?" The stranger's dark eyebrows drew together in concern.

"No. Not exactly." How to explain when Alice had no explanation to give to herself?

"Following you?" he asked.

"I'm not sure. Maybe." She checked the windows again and breathed out a sigh when no one was there.

The stranger tilted his head as if in thought, and Alice assessed him more thoroughly. He wore a brown leather jacket, a polo shirt, and trousers. An expensive watch on his wrist suggested he or someone related to him had money. The classic literature implied taste and education. A sensitivity lingered in his eyes.

"Have you read it before?" She tapped the cover of *The Count of Monte Cristo*.

"It's my favorite novel. What about you, Alice? Do you have a favorite?"

"I didn't tell you my name." She was wary but not alarmed. This stranger made her curious, not afraid.

He cleared his throat. "No, I guess not." His fingers raked through his hair. "And that means you don't remember me."

Should she? "I'm sorry, no. Have we met?"

"Yes, we've met. I'm Edmond."

Now it was Alice's turn to clear her throat. "Edmond. Like *The Count of Monte Cristo*?"

He nodded. "Exactly like that."

Something about him was familiar—his name and the connection to the book. But why couldn't she remember meeting him, too? What was going on with her memories? A sense of urgency rose within her. When she checked the window again, she cringed.

J.J. peered inside. His hands shielded his gaze from the glare of the sunlight as he searched the shop. Nothing could shield Alice from the glare in his eyes.

"There's a better place to hide than here," said Edmond. "Do you trust me?"

Inexplicably, she did. She seized *The Count of Monte Cristo* and hid behind it while addressing Edmond. "Okay. Where?" she asked, desperate to know how to escape J.J. and her feeling of dread.

The grin rising on Edmond's lips left a taste on Alice's tongue like sweet apples. "Let's go out the back."

It was fortunate the place had a "back" because J.J. now pushed his way in through the front door.

Edmond's firm grip tugged at Alice's limp hand. She squeezed, the sensation familiar as if she had held his warm hand before. He pulled her through the back door and out into the open grassy plain toward the cement walkway.

"Come on," he urged.

Alice didn't look back. She knew J.J. must've seen her. When Edmond ran, she kept up alongside him as they raced on the path toward Stonehenge.

He brought her into the center of the monument where the pillars encircled them. The tour group had moved on and the pair of them were alone. Alice released Edmond's hand and caught her breath. At the moment, no one chased them. But it wouldn't take long for J.J. to figure out where she'd gone.

"We need to climb," said Edmond, pointing in an upward direction.

Unsure what he meant, Alice opened her mouth to ask a question. Instead, she froze with her jaw hanging open.

Edmond planted each foot on air, rising with each step he took as if he climbed an invisible staircase. Alice gasped when he stood on top of one of the pi-shaped sculptures some twenty-five feet above her. "Find the first step and the rest will follow," he said.

She stared at the grassy spot in front of her with no visible stairs. "How?"

J.J. emerged from the tea shop like a raging bull. He stomped toward her, arms rigid and hands clawing the air with each step.

"Alice! You saw what I did. You can follow. Trust me." Edmond's voice echoed as if they were in a chamber with walls rather than a wide-open space surrounded by ancient architecture.

There was nowhere else for Alice to flee. She took hesitant steps forward until her shin knocked into something. With a last glance at J.J. charging along the walkway leading straight to her, she lifted her ballet flat and placed her foot on what felt like a stone stair. She hovered on one foot inches above the ground. She'd found it. Her next step took her a few inches higher. The step after that, higher still. Her gaze locked on the man waiting for her at the top.

Edmond reached out toward her. Alice's heart lurched as she clasped her hero's hand. He assisted her final step up before letting go. She was mesmerized not only by the impossible stairs, but also by the sweetness of Edmond's smile. They had met. When? Why couldn't she remember?

"Alice!" J.J. and his fiery mop stomped onward.

She'd done it. On a single horizontal stone slab suspended across two pillars, Alice stood gazing down at the mysterious pursuant who couldn't touch her. "How did you do that?" she asked Edmond.

He shook his head. "Someone else made it possible. But we've still got farther to go."

"Alice, I swear I will kill you!" J.J. yelled, his rage turning his face the color of his hair.

"I don't remember meeting him, either," Alice confessed. "But I feared him as soon as I saw him. Somehow I knew his name was J.J."

"I understand," said Edmond. "Let's get rid of him. Forever."

J.J. spat out a string of uncreative profanities at them.

"Yes, let's," Alice agreed.

Edmond took her hand. His handsome smile lit up his eyes. "Now we jump."

"Wait." Alice hesitated, not sure she liked the sound of that. "Where?" she asked, worried that Edmond meant on top of the villain's fiery head.

"Into the hole. Follow me. The landing won't hurt, I promise."

There was no obvious hole, but there hadn't been visible stairs, either. She took a deep breath as she stared down at J.J. Too late to turn back now. "Okay. I'm ready."

With that Edmond took a step backward and dropped into the stone as suddenly as if he had stepped off the edge.

Alice's eyes widened to tea saucers. He was gone.

"I'll kill you both! Right after I tear you to pieces," J.J. threatened as he approached the monument.

All Edmond had done was take one step backward. That meant all she had to do was take two steps forward.

"Here goes nothing." Alice took one step, and then the stone swallowed her whole.


ALICE HAD NEVER BEEN SKYDIVING, but she'd seen videos. Horizontal bodies splayed like starfish while the speed of terminal velocity pushed faces into a balloon-like smile—or a scream, depending on the person.

The sensation of falling she now experienced defied the laws of physics. Her feet remained beneath her and the speed didn't increase. She wasn't floating, exactly. Her dress didn't flip up over her head as it would under normal circumstances.

This was anything but normal. And yet vaguely familiar, too...

From J.J.'s pursuit to the stranger named Edmond who had rescued her, nothing about this made sense. Edmond, who said they weren't strangers, who walked on air and made holes in stones leading—where were they, anyway?

She lifted her hand and saw it plainly, but everything else was blackness. Curious.

"Hello?" she asked.

"I'm here, Alice," said Edmond.

"Where?"

"Reach out your hand."

When she obeyed, a warm grasp squeezed hers. At the same moment, her feet touched a solid surface. She felt the tug of his arm.

A bright light pierced the dark. She squinted, shielding her eyes. Edmond's form materialized. As the light dimmed, her eyes adjusted.

Cinnamon and pine scented the air reminding her of Christmas. Together they entered a grand hallway with red carpet. Alice clutched Edmond's arm. He took steady strides forward. Chandeliers sparkling with diamonds hung from the ceiling. Stringed instruments played in some distant room. She heard voices and indistinct words.

When Alice glanced down, she now wore a strapless blue ballgown with white ribbon at the waist and heels instead of her green dress with ballet flats. As they passed a gilded mirror, she let go of Edmond and stopped.

Her hair was in a soft twisted updo with a small tiara crowning her head. A mask glittering with blues and golds covered only her eyes.

She turned to face Edmond's seductive smile, wondering how they arrived at this most unlikely scenario. He was finely dressed in a tuxedo. His hair was slicked back and he wore a black eye mask. He looked more familiar now, but she couldn't recall their introduction. "How did falling through a Stonehenge stone lead us to this palace?"

"I will explain. I promise. But first," he said, raising his arm, "I need to introduce you to some people."

"What people?"

He waited with his arm at the ready.

"This is where we're hiding from J.J.?"

"In a way, yes."

She pouted her lips and crossed her arms. "I'm so confused."

"You don't see him anywhere, do you?"

No one else was in the hallway.

"Soon he will be gone forever, just as you desire. Please humor me."

Alice finally accepted his arm and they continued down the hall-way. "Are you a wizard or something?"

He laughed. "No. I'm a count."

"A fictional character from a book you're reading. Is Edmond your real name?"

"Yes, it's my real name."

Alice stared up at his chiseled chin marked with the goatee. Why didn't she immediately label him an insane person? Perhaps it was the way he brought her here, seemingly by magic. And the distinct feeling that he was telling the truth.

He promised to tell her everything. It better be soon.


THEY REACHED the carpeted stairs leading down into a courtyard-style ballroom where the violinists played and the guests danced, drank, and gossiped. A balcony wrapped around the second floor. A vaulted ceiling rose many stories above featuring another exquisite chandelier. Edmond escorted Alice down to where the hardwood served as the dance floor.

"This is Alice, my fiancée," said Edmond as he introduced her to a group of ladies in extravagant gowns and elaborate masks. They each held a fan.

Alice gawked at Edmond. "Your what?"

"Pleasure," one of them said, bowing low. The rest of the ladies mimicked her. "I am Madame Emmalyn. These are Mademoiselles Gracie, Rebecca, and Macy."

When they straightened up, they fanned themselves as they sashayed away.

*Fiancée?* Why would he say that?

"Madame Catharia, I'm pleased to see you," Edmond said to one of the passing ladies.

She turned her peacock mask toward Edmond. "Dear Count, it is an honor." She bowed.

"Monsieur Atlas. Mademoiselles Lacy, Bella, Althea." Edmond

walked Alice around the room, introducing her as his fiancée, and avoiding any small talk by continuing to follow the edge of the dance floor until they had returned back to the staircase.

On their second turn about the room, he spoke only to Alice in a hushed whisper. "Mademoiselle Amelia. A kidnapper. Monsieur and Madame Brighton, spies. Madame Venetia, a poisoner. Monsieur Petrecus, an assassin."

The more Edmond spoke, the more confused Alice became. He listed too many names for her to keep straight while attaching despicable crimes to each one.

"I don't understand," said Alice. "None of these names are characters from *The Count of Monte Cristo*."

"Is that what you expected?" Edmond asked. "These are not story characters. They are my enemies."

"I thought you meant you were, you know, *the* Count of Monte Cristo."

"Not the fictional one, no. I did borrow the title from the book. That was your idea."

"What?" Alice stared up at him as he absently nodded to guests who failed to steal his attention from her. "Why," she whispered, "did you say I'm your fiancée?"

"Not here. I promised to explain, didn't I?"

"You did. So when?"

"Very soon, my love." He stopped them at the base of the stairs again.

Alice swallowed the frog in her throat. Her body quivered involuntarily. Why did his words affect her so? "Are we going to dance?" It was the only thing she actually expected to happen.

"I don't think there's enough time." He gazed down at her. "I would be delighted to dance with you at our wedding."

Alice's cheeks warmed. Stranger still, he seemed to mean it. She sighed. "Not enough time why?"

His gaze moved over the ballroom, but he didn't answer.

"Everyone here is your enemy," Alice deduced. "Then are we here so you can exact your revenge on them?"

"Yes," he admitted.

Alice didn't like the sound of that. "Did you read *The Count of Monte Cristo?*"

"Many times."

"All the way to the end?" challenged Alice. "Because the count realizes the error of his ways. God is the only one who can administer true justice."

"True," he conceded. This time his amused smirk irritated her.

"I appreciate you helping me get away from J.J.," she said, "but I'm uncomfortable with whatever scheme you may have concocted, especially if you're anything like your namesake."

"You have nothing to fear, Alice. None of it is for me alone. It is most importantly for you."

"For me? But I don't know any of these people."

"Don't you?"

The musicians played their soft music. The din of the ballroom faded into background noise. Alice's throat went dry. A feeling of dread lodged in her sternum, pressing into her diaphragm, making it difficult to breathe.

There *was* something familiar about this place and these people. She struggled to remember why. When had she been here before?

A tremble shook the chandelier, interrupting her thoughts. The music stopped at the sound of clinking crystals. The guests who had been dancing paused.

Alice gazed up at the swaying chandelier, and then met Edmond's pointed gaze. "What was that?"

"An earthquake?" someone suggested as if they had heard Alice's question. The rest murmured, inquiring as to other possibilities.

After climbing an invisible staircase and falling through a hole in a stone, Alice didn't believe anything probable could be the solution.

The next shudder shook the entire room. Several guests were even thrown to the floor. Ladies shrieked. Gentleman cried out. A waiter with a tray dropped the wine glasses. They shattered on the dance floor. Men and women tripped over themselves and each other.

Alice gripped Edmond's arm. He kept her steady on her feet.

Madame Catharia shuffled toward them. "What should we do, Count?"

"Have no fear!" he cried. "Please exit the building before this room comes crashing down on our heads. Everyone outside."

At his words, the party devolved into a frenzied mania. The hustle and bustle of the guests gave Alice the impression of a herd of cats clawing and scraping their way out. Men and women pushed past anyone blocking their path toward the French doors. Some fell to the floor, dresses tore, and masks dropped aside. Blood was drawn by the tipped nails of a buxom lady who clawed at the faces of anyone in her way. Screams erupted, more glass shattered, and the mass forced its way out through the exit like a giant serpent squeezing through a too-small hole.

As Alice prepared herself for whatever might come next, she took a step forward. Edmond's grasp tightened, pulling her back. "Wait."

"Aren't we getting out of here?" she asked.

"Not that way."

The room had all but cleared. The waiter and all the other servants scurried upstairs.

"Why aren't they fleeing?" she asked.

"They are. And they will be safe."

"Safe from what? No more riddles." Alice forced her arm free from his grasp and faced him squarely. "You know what's happening. What do I have to do with any of it?"

Edmond gently took her hands. He kissed both of them.

If her mask had not concealed so much of her face, he would have seen her brow knitted in confusion and the red rising in her cheeks.

"Come to the roof and I will explain everything." He took her hand and led her back up the staircase. Instead of returning to the second floor, he continued leading her higher.

The roof. Yes, there was something important there. She needed to do something...

"Do you remember the portals?"

*Portals.* Alice knew the word was significant. "Why, yes. I'm not sure why."

"When we first met," he said as they climbed toward the third story, "your sister had arranged our blind date. You told stories about Wonderland, expecting me to excuse myself and vanish like all your other dates had. But I had no desire to be parted from your company."

A flush rose up her neck that the mask couldn't hide.

"I asked if I could court you, and you said yes. We fell in love. Soon I learned that you were telling the truth. You are truly Alice of Wonderland."

She was, wasn't she? Alice nodded, the familiarity forming a scene. "Our first date was in a tea shop."

"Yes, Alice, yes!" Edmond stopped them on the staircase as they neared the fourth story. He held her shoulders. He removed his mask, staring into her eyes. "You remember?"

"Only bits and pieces," she admitted. Her sister had been so pleased that Alice had finally found love. "But the portals. I can't quite—"

"Come." He led her onward, past the fourth story and higher still. "Mr. Carroll believed you, but he knew no one else would. He had to tell your story as if it were a children's fairy tale. We now know that each adventure you had was from traveling into a portal. The rabbit hole led to the first portal. The looking glass, to the second portal. By the time I proposed, you had 'discovered' a third portal in the front yard of the home where you and your sister lived. Together we entered, and it was then we realized you were creating the portals, not finding them. Within that third portal, you created and we entered the fourth. We were both twenty-five at the time and we haven't aged a day since."

"What? How long ago?" asked Alice.

"Over one hundred years have passed since then."

Alice stopped on the staircase. They were nearly to the fifth story, and she needed a moment to catch her breath and process all this impossible information that she knew to be true the moment Edmond said it. "How do I do it? Create portals?" She needed to do it again. That truth she recalled, and it would mean life or death if she could not.

He hesitated, glancing up and down the stairwell. "I don't know."

"A side portal," she said. "That's what I need to create!" She was remembering, but the how...still she wasn't sure.

"My darling." He smiled, embracing her. "You are coming back to me."

She held him, more memories unwrapping like presents, even though it wasn't her birthday. "*I called you the Count of Monte Cristo so that I would remember you. And it worked*," said Alice, recalling pieces of that conversation. "You started carrying the book around for that purpose."

As he leaned back, nodding, she grabbed his hand. "We must get to the roof, mustn't we?" They climbed to the fifth story.

When Edmond opened a wooden door that led to a rooftop garden, Alice followed him through and onto a brick pathway between colorful wildflowers. Lemon, orange, apple, and other fruit trees arched overhead.

"We believe the real world and the portals are mirror images," said Edmond. "In the portals, we expect the same advancements in technology have been made, but we haven't been able to return to the real world in all this time." He held the balcony rail and Alice did the same, still catching her breath.

He placed his hand on top of hers as she peered over the balcony overlooking the hedge mazes on the grounds below. The guests had scattered, giving Alice the distinct impression of pieces on a chessboard.

"We don't know why you have this ability and we also had no idea the catastrophic effect of creating a portal within a portal. That's when your memory problems began, and that's when your life became truly endangered."

A piercing scream ripped through the air, and Alice noted a woman pointing up at them. The smell of smoke singed Alice's nose and she turned in search of a fire.

Instead of flames, a terror like nothing Alice had ever seen clung to the tower above. The giant claws of the winged, crimson beast dug out pieces of the turret as its yellow eyes gazed not at Alice or Edmond, but fixed on the guests in the garden.

Alice grabbed Edmond's arm, aware that her mouth had opened, but holding her outcry in her throat.

"Alice?" Edmond's voice seemed far away, but she heard the words he had spoken in the past: *You alone can save us.*

She had to make the portal.

Head reared, the red dragon's roar struck the air as a gale-force wind. Alice's ears rang, making it difficult to think. She covered them as her heart pounded in her chest.

*Beware the Jabberwocky.*

The words echoed in the beast's roar. She remembered a creature that had haunted her dreams as a child, but this was different. It must be another dragon.

"Now, Alice," Edmond urged.

The creature spread its wings at least forty feet wide and dropped with the ease of a lightning bolt toward the earth. It swooped over the screeching crowd, all of whom appeared to duck. The beast eased through the air like a bat, curving to dodge trees and circling back. It headed straight for them.

FALLING IN DARKNESS. Alice reached out and a warm hand grasped hers. The flash of light blinded her as it had before.

*It's as easy as a thought.*

The world opened up. Alice held Edmond's hand. They hadn't moved from their position on the balcony, but something like a bubble surrounded them, giving a watery, impressionistic ripple to their surroundings.

The dragon still approached. Maw wide and razor-sharp teeth bared, the fire from its red, scaled belly poured out from its mouth in a spray of hot fire.

Alice screamed, covering her face as the fire connected with the bubble. She could feel heat, but nothing burned her. She lowered her arms. Smoke danced around them. "Edmond?"

The dragon coughed out another spray of flames as it circled high above their heads, disappearing in and out of the clouds.

"You did it." Edmond embraced her again. She felt secure in his arms, and the side portal clearly protected them from the dragon.

Another memory: she had taken a bath right here in this palace, and she described the side portal as a soap bubble. She didn't know exactly how she had created it, except something that crossed her mind before. It seemed to be as easy as a thought for her.

The scarlet terror swooped again, scalding the balcony on which they stood to a black crisp. Bits of stone broke away and dropped toward the gardens below. The pieces beneath Alice's feet fell.

She screamed, wrapping her arms around Edmond's waist. To her amazement, she and Edmond didn't fall. The bubble floated in place. He held her tight, and she hoped he wouldn't let go. The guests scurried out of the way of the falling debris.

Time and again, the dragon bathed the rooftop garden in flames until nothing remained but smoking bits of blackened roots. The dragon crashed into the tower shaped like a rook, and the falling stones harmlessly passed through Alice and Edmond. The same could not be said for the guests screaming in horror below.

"He'll kill them!" Alice buried her face in Edmond's chest as one of the larger stones of the tower dropped onto a group of people.

"Alice," Edmond said softly. He touched her chin, lifting it so her gaze would meet his. Alice sighed at the vulnerability exposed in his eyes. "This is how we wanted it to happen. This is our apocalypse."

A cold horror froze Alice's gaze to the scene of the massacre below. She *had* wanted this, but why?

The dragon hurtled into the side of the palace. Fire blasted out of shattered windows on the opposite side.

"The people inside!" cried Alice.

"They escaped to safety already, I promise," said Edmond. "Let me explain the rest of our story."

Alice clung to him, trembling. True, she stood on the bubble as if it were a sturdy floor and nothing the dragon had done affected either of them. But how long would it last?

"We're safe. J.J. has a lot to destroy. He'll be busy for a while."

Alice turned toward the red dragon as it sprayed every tower, dove through the roof, and shot flames through the walls before breaking out again. "J.J. is the dragon?" The palace crumbled, gradually flattening out over the grounds. The smoke and rubble obstructed her view of the guests. It made no sense, and the dragon's rampage made it difficult to concentrate.

"This is the fifth portal," said Edmond, waving his hand over the apocalypse surrounding them. J.J. had extended his fiery reign of terror to the hedge mazes and the forest. He plummeted into the palace again, determined to leave no stone on top of another. His spiked tail swung through the bubble, the pointed end cutting between her and Edmond. Alice couldn't help but flinch. "Inside the fourth portal," continued Edmond, "the first portal within a portal, things were different. You could control much of the environment around you, but your memories began to vanish. Worse, we tried to leave and return to the third portal, but we couldn't get through. That had never happened before. In the other portals, you always made your way back home. But the fourth portal didn't have a direct path to the real world, so we were trapped. From day to day, you couldn't remember who I was, and some of the people we encountered desired to steal your abilities, or kill you."

The smoke thickened into a monster of its own as their bubble no longer displayed any view of the dragon's rampage, but only a gray, swirling mass of smog.

"I suggested you make a fifth portal where we could hide from the people coming after you." Edmond brushed his fingers gently over her hair. "You created all of this: the palace, the gardens, and the woods. Every person we encountered here was kind. No one in the fifth portal appeared to want anything from you, but only desired to serve you. We hired them as staff for our palace. They knew to escape back to the fourth portal where they would be safe once all the guests had vacated the palace."

"They can travel between the portals?" asked Alice.

"You've never known how to close a portal, so it's open for anyone who finds it. Traveling between the two portals within portals—four and five—is possible. But we still haven't discovered how to return to the third portal so we can go home. It's possible someone closed the third portal."

"Okay." Alice recognized each truth, but it was so complicated, she couldn't remember all the hows and the whys. She searched for the dragon. She saw nothing but smoke.

"We lived in the palace for weeks, and no one bothered us. That's where we discovered your ability to create a side portal." Edmond motioned to the bubble encapsulating them. "Separate but still able to observe the portal we were in. We thought it might be our way back, so we returned to the fourth portal. You made a side portal while we were inside the fourth, and the only thing we learned was that we couldn't be harmed while inside. Someone on the hunt for us," he said, flicking his gaze downward, implying one of their guests, "spotted us and tried to kill us."

Alice felt less and less sorry for the demise of the party.

"One day, you disappeared." Edmond's chin dropped to his chest, and he rubbed his fingers over her hands. "I searched, but the fifth portal is not very large, and I knew someone must've found their way in and lured you back to the fourth portal. So I went there to find you. My encounters with Catharia, Amelia, the Brightons, and all the rest of the guests who have now met their unfortunate but deserved end led me to you, for a price. I promised each of them that I would give away your secret of how to make portals, but only after they released you."

"You gave them my secret?" Alice asked.

"How could I?" Edmond shook his head. "And no, I wouldn't even if I knew some way for them to steal your portal-making skills."

"Oh." Alice felt silly, realizing she had accused him of something her heart knew could never be, not only because she could hardly describe her own abilities. Edmond would never betray her.

"They led me to a house in the English countryside," he continued, "and introduced me to J.J. I learned that he was the one behind everything. He had hired all those people to find you and bring you to him. The Brightons? His spies who had followed us everywhere. They found the fifth portal. Amelia, the kidnapper, used your memory loss against you and convinced you she was rescuing you from me and took you to J.J. All of the others played their part. J.J. admitted that he wanted to steal your abilities, but when he failed, he ordered Venetia and Petrecus, the poisoner and the assassin, to kill you."

Alice remembered to exhale, grateful for the first time that she couldn't remember what had happened to her in the hands of those awful people.

"When I saw you unharmed, I knew they had failed, but didn't understand why. You seem to be invincible here, at least in portals within portals. I'm not sure about anywhere else. Once J.J. proved to me you were unhurt and not held against your will, I reminded you that I was your Count Edmond, and you could walk away from J.J. at any time. You remembered enough to trust me. But before we could leave, J.J. took me aside and asked me to fulfill my promise that I would give away your secret. He assured me that should I betray him, he would not fail to kill you next time."

A snout pierced their bubble. J.J.'s maw widened over them. Alice felt only a strong wind as the great body of the dragon rushed through that chilled her to the bone.

Edmond was unfazed. "All that time I searched for you, I had devised a plan. I told him and his followers to meet us at Stonehenge the next morning. I would give them what they wanted. In order to make sure I knew there was no escape, J.J. showed me who he really was when he transformed into this." Edmond raised his arm, gesturing in a vague direction since neither of them could see the dragon. "The son of the Jabberwocky."

"Oh!" Alice breathed. Then J.J. *was* like the monster of her nightmares. The Jabberwocky's son. She searched the skies again. Nothing but gray haze, and the occasional orange glow where the fires still burned. "Then what was the plan? How are we getting out of here?"

Edmond's chest expanded as he took a deep breath. "We returned to the fifth portal where I had to reintroduce myself to you, as usual. I told you my plan, and you thought it was worth a try. So you created our masquerade ball invitations. The idea was to give everything a very *Count of Monte Cristo* feel so that you would hopefully be willing to trust me when you forgot everything and had to blindly follow my lead."

That seemed to have worked, Alice mused.

"You had the invitations sent directly into the pockets of J.J.'s henchmen. It explained that they would be given the privilege of your secret at the end of the party, so long as they didn't tell J.J."

Alice listened, pieces of the puzzle familiar, but still not everything came back to her.

"At Stonehenge, you designed limitations for anyone entering the fifth portal. When our guests passed through, their outfits for the party would be provided. Same for us. Most importantly, only the true body of a person could pass through, and that meant only J.J. as the Jabberwocky could enter. We had no idea how long it would take him to figure that out, but it seems he has impeccable timing."

"And a furious rage," remarked Alice.

"We counted on that. The party guests had slipped into the fifth portal before the time we told J.J. to be there. And as he waited for us at Stonehenge, his rage must've built to a boiling point. We hid within a tour group knowing he would spot you." Edmond winked. "You were supposed to run toward Stonehenge, not away from it."

"I was?" Alice could only remember how frightened she had felt when she saw J.J.'s face.

"It's all right," Edmond said, chuckling. "It was the typical amount of time for you to regress into lost memories. You created the tea shop out of fear, I guess. My part was to confront J.J. while you ran for the fifth portal. I told him that you were afraid because you knew I had betrayed you, and that only when we could make you feel completely calm and safe could your abilities be taken. He agreed to give me a moment to talk to you. Instead of following you into the fifth portal as originally planned, I had to talk to you in the shop. I snuck in the back door. At that point I improvised because I knew J.J. wouldn't wait long before coming inside. Once we ran away from him together, he succumbed to his rage just as we'd hoped he would. It didn't take long for him to transform and come in after us ready to destroy everything in his path."

The rest, Alice did remember. "And here we are. Our apocalypse."

"Yes." Edmond nodded.

"So…we wanted him to destroy it all?" Alice looked around, but the smoke had blackened and nothing could be seen anymore, not even shades of color. "What happens—?"

A humming sound expanded into an explosion. Edmond hugged Alice tight to his chest, and she squeezed her arms around his waist. The blackness morphed into a swirling mass of starlight with comet-tails encircling them.

The son of the Jabberwocky roared. The starlight struck his scaled red body, tearing it apart. The pieces burst into flames until nothing remained of the dragon.

The bubble jerked. Alice and Edmond fell as blackness dimmed everything into silence.


"ALICE?"

Bright sunlight met Alice's squinting gaze. She covered the sun with her arm and sat up in the grass.

"Where have you two been? Your wedding is supposed to be tomorrow! I thought you eloped!"

The figure standing over Alice resembled her older sister wearing a pink and white striped dress, her sister's summer favorite. She held a camisole, and her hair was in a tight bun covered with a lacy day cap. The lawn was the same as it had always been with a sloping hill that led around to the side of the house. The rose and tulip gardens danced in the breeze. Her sister had left the front door of their thatched-roof cottage open.

Alice's own blue ballgown remained. Beside her, Edmond sat up still dressed in his tuxedo.

"Did you two elope? And Alice, you should cover up that bosom. I've never seen you in such a dress! Where were you, a masquerade?"

Alice lifted off her mask and placed it beside her in the grass.

She gazed into Edmond's eyes, and he smiled at her. "How is it possible?" she asked.

"And don't you think," said her sister, "that if you planned to leave without so much as a note, that you would have the decency to fetch me from the house upon your return rather than lounging on the lawn without so much as a hello?"

"You did it, Alice," said Edmond, grinning. "You thought if J.J. destroyed the fifth portal, it might be the death of him, leading to a chain reaction."

"And it must have," Alice said. "Because we're all the way back here, home in the real world. J.J. did destroy the fifth portal, and outside the safety of the side portal, he was torn apart."

"Are you even listening to me? The minister has been pestering me for weeks, and what am I to tell him? You vanished without a trace, and I didn't know if I was to continue wedding planning without you—"

"Only gone for weeks," Alice said. "Not a hundred years. We've nearly returned to the time we left. Do you think J.J.—"

"Was the one who blocked the third portal? Yes," Edmond said.

"So he trapped us in the fourth portal to steal my abilities. And once he was gone, everything must've been undone." It must be a good sign that her memories hadn't vanished. Maybe they never would again now that she was home.

"If he could close the portal, he could probably open it again. Then his threat to..." Edmond's eyes dimmed. He didn't finish that thought.

Alice knew to what he referred. J.J.'s threat to kill her might have been effective back in the third portal. She took Edmond's hand. "We may never know exactly how or why, but he's gone for good and we're safe. That's all that matters."

"—long I've been suffering in the knowledge that you two could be dead for all I knew," Alice's sister continued. "So you tell me. Are you getting married tomorrow or not?"

"Yes!" both Edmond and Alice responded at once.

"Oh." Her sister jumped back, clutching the parasol to her

chest. "Well, jolly good, then. Alice, you better come with me. There is so much to do."

Alice sighed. She rose and Edmond helped her stand. "Were all the invited guests told we were missing?"

"Of course not! I wasn't going to start a scandal. How was I to know what had happened? What did happen to you two?"

Alice pulled Edmond down to her height. She kissed his soft lips. "Edmond was given a title. He's a count now."

"A count? How did—? What! Did you meet the queen?"

"She's teasing you," said Edmond with his arm around Alice's shoulder. "But we did slay a dragon together."

Her sister's eyes narrowed. "I don't appreciate this nonsense from either of you." She turned on her heel and stormed toward the house.

Edmond held Alice close, kissing her again but this time not letting her go.

"What if," Alice said, catching her breath, "the third portal is still open?"

"Alice," Edmond sighed, stealing her breath yet again in another kiss.

She eyed the spot in the tulip bed where the third portal gave no hint of its existence or lack thereof. "What if I can still make portals?"

"Might I suggest," he said, touching her nose, "we live in the real world for a change?"

Alice sighed. "All right." As Edmond escorted her to the house, Alice glanced back. She thought she saw something fluffy and white disappear into the tulip bed. Or she might've only imagined it.

## AUTHOR'S NOTES - BRIA BURTON

DURING A RECENT CONTEST, I asked participants to name a character. The results were fantastic: a list of over a dozen names that I'm eager to use in upcoming stories. Here are several of the names that made it into this story including the person credited with the idea.

Character Name Credits:

Rebecca: Rebecca Cooper

Catharia: Elizabeth McCann

Brighton: Debbie Cocchio

It was an absolute delight to create a mashup of two (technically three) classics with a speculative twist (more so Alice's story, of course). So often the characters would take a turn I didn't expect, and yet perhaps I should have! Alice and Edmond (although not the *real* Count in this story) have been around for quite some time. There is certainly room for reinterpretation and speculation, and thanks to the public domain, authors will continue to find new ways to explore these timeless characters.

*Alice's Adventures in Wonderland/Through the Looking-Glass* is one of my all-time favorite books (my copy combines both novels into a continuing story). I've been reading it since I was young, and I'm always awed by Carroll's depth in a seemingly simple child's fantasy story. *The Count of Monte Cristo*...also one of my all-time favorite books. The length may deter modern readers, but it is worth the time. I'm thrilled that the Alvarium Experiment selected this project —speculative twists on classic stories and characters.

My favorite film adaptations include the 2002 version of *The Count of Monte Cristo* directed by Kevin Reynolds and starring Jim Caviezel as the title character. The 1985 TV movie *Alice in Wonderland* was a childhood favorite with the delightful songs, wacky costumes, and a celebrity cast.

But do yourself a favor and read the source material. There is nothing quite like classic literature.

You'll find links to Project Gutenberg free online reading files for *Alice's Adventures in Wonderland, Through the Looking Glass,* and *The Count of Monte Cristo.*

*—BB*

# ANNIE KARENINA

## VERONICA H. HART

"*All happy families are alike; each unhappy family is unhappy in its own way.*"

*--Leo Tolstoy, Anna Karenina*

"PARDON, *me permettez-vous de m'asseoir ici?*"

"*Laissez-moi tranquille.*"

When in Rome. Actually, this was Moscow, but my understanding was that the upper class spoke French, not Russian. As I'd landed in a *patisserie* full of genteel ladies, I'd hoped to complete my task and return home quickly. It didn't look like that was going to happen as Madame Levin rebuffed my first advance.

I, Lady Elizabeth Margaret Killington, born in Idaho in the United States, married a singularly memorable English lord in 2013 at twenty-three years of age and was promptly widowed at twenty-seven.

Horace, Lord Killington, died in a skiing accident before he had a chance to introduce me to his home and family—or lack thereof. He had a home, all right, but no family to speak of.

There was one great uncle who had retired to the south of France, and a thrice removed cousin, whose name I regularly forget until Christmas when one of the servants brings me cards to sign.

The three lovely years of our marriage we spent either touring the country because neither of us had seen much of the United States, or skiing. I enjoyed the resorts, so different from my life at home, but after a while, one looks like another.

Horace did not lack for funds, but whenever I asked about visiting his home, he changed the subject. The most he ever said was, "There are too many memories hanging about."

One evening after several cocktails, I pressed the issue. "I've never been to England. Why can't we please go at least once?" I unabashedly used sex as a lure to convince him. Should have saved my breath.

"I've told you the place is crowded. I could never find any peace there. Dinner parties, garden parties, people scampering about the place during the night. I do not want to return."

"But, surely that was only when your parents were alive. They died a long time ago."

He scowled. "Not long enough."

His comment sent shivers through my scantily clad body. I never brought the subject up again.

That winter, he skied straight into a tree and died instantly. My parents wanted me to return home, but I had seen too much of a new life and had no interest in their dawn to dusk existence. In spite of Horace and me sending funds, they continued to live a Spartan existence. My brother and his wife lived exactly the same way in a small house on the farm.

I decided it was time for me to see what I inherited. I called his solicitors. They encouraged me to come to London to meet with them. I jumped at the opportunity. This would be my first excursion out of the country since my senior trip in high school with my French class to Montreal.

And so it was that I wound up in the London offices of Grayson, Milton, and Perkins, a place straight out of Dickens, and learned of my vast wealth. So vast, I could pay all the taxes and the lawyers, and still have more than any human being could ever need.

That first day in London, upon hearing the news, I humbly asked if I might upgrade from my tiny bed and breakfast room with shared bath to a proper hotel. Milton could hardly control himself as he set me up in Hotel 41, explaining that he would provide me with cash and credit cards within twenty-four hours and that I was not to concern myself with any expenses.

I was raised on a farm, with nice parents, a kind brother, and then attended Idaho State University—Go Bengals—so walking into the lobby of this hotel with its black and white checkerboard floor and ornate wood reception desk left me speechless. This was far more elegant than anything Horace and I had stayed at. Standing there like a tall skinny, awkward, open-mouthed hick from the states could have been humiliating, but a man in a dark suit approached immediately and said, "Lady Killington, right this way please."

He pointed at a bellhop who swept up my two well-used suit-cases and took off toward an elevator. My new life had begun. Instead of following, I stood and giggled. No one had ever called me Lady Killington. I liked the sound of it. Lady Killington. I raised my head, squared my shoulders and pretended I was Lady Mary Crawly from Downton Abbey. It helped—a little.

After two days of recovering from jet lag and the shock of my inheritance, I hired a car to drive me to my "estate."

A line of men and women mostly dressed in black stood in the graveled forecourt of a grand old mansion. It put me in mind of the photos I'd seen of the Biltmore House in North Carolina with its turrets and ornate decorations over and around the doors and windows. I needn't have wondered who all these folk were—they were "the help". The first man in line, a gentleman in his forties, dignified in a dark suit, white shirt and tie, stepped forward and introduced himself as the head butler, James Willis. He led me along the aisle between them, introducing a few along the way, the first one being Miss Beebe, the head housekeeper. Every one either bowed or curtsied as I passed by. I wondered about stopping to chat, but remembered the Dowager on *Downton Abbey* and continued with my nose in the air, nodding in acknowledgement of the introductions.

Mr. Willis led me inside where another crowd of people awaited my arrival. They were attired in an amazing array of period dress and I felt as if I'd intruded on their Halloween party, except it wasn't Halloween, not even close.

As Mr. Willis introduced them, I sensed immediately that these were the "memories" Horace had told me about—the people who crowded his life here and sometimes ran about at night. I had not understood at all. He not only socialized with them, they had lived here with him. No wonder he felt crowded out of his own home. But I was curious to learn whether these memories were real people in costume or true memories, like ghosts flitting about the manor house.

Lady Brett Ashley stood in the line looking totally put out at being made to stand on parade. She held a cocktail and stepped back when I offered my hand. Jane Eyre curtsied politely enough, but kept her eyes downcast. She was surprisingly tiny. So many people. I was overcome with emotion and had to be escorted to my "rooms" on the second floor, which I was assured was actually the first floor. It felt like it took twenty minutes to reach it, and I wasn't sure I'd ever find my way back to the main entrance. The butler, Mr. Willis, reassured me that within a fortnight I'd know my way around the old place like the back of my hand.

I did have one important question and asked Miss Beebe. "How did all these people get here?"

"I'm sorry, my dear. Didn't Lord Killington explain it to you?" She had just introduced me to Bridget, a downstairs maid who worked in the kitchens. She thought with a little training the girl might make a good personal maid. I sent Bridget to the bathroom to alphabetize my body lotions. I still couldn't get used to the idea that another person had to take care of my personal needs. Miss Beebe and Mr. Willis both reminded me that I was doing them a great honor to offer them employment and helping the economy as well.

"*Lord* Killington said the house was overcrowded and noisy. I assumed the guests were leftovers from his parents' days."

"Oh no, my dear. His parents warned him about inviting too many people. They cautioned him again and again. Once they arrive, they never leave." She shrugged. "That's just the way it is."

NEEDLESS TO SAY, this whole process of acclimatizing took a while. More than two weeks, but in that time, I dined each night with many of the house guests, most of whom I never saw during the day. Mr. Willis and Miss Beebe told me the guests spent their days rediscovering their pasts and exchanging views on the real and fictional aspects of history.

At least they were quiet and out of sight. All that commotion would have been far too much distraction as I tried to learn the ropes of being a Lady.

With the help of Miss Beebe and my new personal maid, Bridget, I learned the procedures for daily living. One day I asked Miss Beebe, "But how does one invite fictional people to become real?" Although I accepted that they were really here and sitting at my dinner table every night and eating real food, I still had a hard time believing in them.

"It's all in the library. Haven't you visited it yet?"

"Library?" The first thing that came to mind was the small brick building in the middle of town at home.

"It's on the ground floor in the west wing. It has lovely Palladian doors that open out onto a terrace overlooking the gardens. It's a wonderful room. You must go see it, but you must also be very careful of what you think as you read." She smiled, a slightly enigmatic smile, turned to peek in on Bridget, and then left my room.

"Bridget!" I called, the moment the door to the hall shut.

She scurried into the room and curtsied. "Are you real or one of my husband's manifestations?"

"Sure, and aren't I as real as anyone in this magnificent house."

"Let me try again. How did you get here?"

"Traveled here from Ireland, didn't I?"

"And began work here right away?" I picked up a hairbrush, but she immediately plucked it from my hand and began, making quick work of my tangled curls.

"Indeed. His Lordship sent for me especially. He needed someone to tend to Miss Haversham."

"Miss Haversham? Not *the* Miss Haversham of the dusty wedding gown and cobwebs from *Great Expectations*?" I relaxed under the soothing strokes.

"That be the one. She was far too difficult to please, so he let me work in the kitchen instead."

"And what became of Miss Haversham?"

"She continues to live in her room, far as I know. She doesn't like visitors."

"How does she eat?"

"Mum, she's not real. Don't matter if she don't eat. Now, what would you like to wear to dinner? Mr. Finch, Scout, and Mr. Robinson will be attending, so I'd recommend something more plain than fancy."

I shook my head. "But these people have been consuming real food!"

"If you say so, Mum."

"I think it's time I see this library. I'll wear a white blouse and black skirt. Plain enough for our guests?" I had yet to shop anyway, so I didn't have anything "fancy." Most evenings I wore the same dress I wore to my college graduation. For lunch, I dressed in my travel suit. In my few years of being married to Horace, I mostly bought sports clothes.

"Definitely. Tomorrow night will be more fun. We're entertaining Jay Gatsby and his crowd. Mr. Willis thought you might be enjoying having all the American people. We have so many to get through every year."

Bridget led me through the maze of hallways to the library on the ground floor. She opened the right side of the double doors reverently. I half-expected to see her genuflect before we entered the room. I could barely see the top of the bookshelves nearly three stories above me. A crazy array of ladders and balconies ran along the walls. In the center of the room, which was carpeted in the largest Persian rug I'd ever seen, were an assortment of overstuffed chairs arranged in comfortable conversation groupings with small tables in their centers. Seated in nearly all the chairs were a variety of men, women, and children dressed in period clothing from ancient Egypt to, apparently, the far future. They'd been chatting when the door opened, but stopped the instant I entered and all turned to stare at me.

"I hear you're dining with Atticus tonight," a woman close to me said.

"So I'm told."

"You know Lord Killington went back and saved Tom from the hangman, don't you?"

"Who are you?" I asked the pug-nosed brunette who looked to be from the forties or fifties.

"Della Street. Perry Mason's assistant. I have several more cases, if you're interested."

"What do you mean, Horace saved Tom? He dies in the book."

"Doesn't have to end that way," she said and turned back to her own reading.

I strolled through the groupings as the occupants checked me out. I'd seen some of them at dinners, but had yet to meet all of them. Tarzan and Jane were easy to recognize, as were Sherlock Holmes and his amanuensis, Dr. Watson. Others were not so obvious. Bridget pointed out Hester Prynne and Scarlett O'Hara. Rhett Butler did not look anything like Clark Gable, but he was indeed quite handsome. He kissed my hand as we passed by. I stopped short of swooning as our eyes met.

As I approached the last group of three somber looking women, my eye caught a glimpse of someone in the gardens among the flowers. She knelt by the daffodils. Although the people in the library fascinated me and I made a note to find out when I would meet everyone living in the house, I pushed through the door onto the terrace and watched for a few minutes as the lady dug around in the flower beds. Gardening for the pure pleasure of it had never been part of my life. On the farm, we gardened to survive. Mom did valiantly plant tulip bulbs every fall in front of the house, but every winter the deer came along and ate them. The few that survived also managed to get eaten, so decorative plants never held any interest for me.

Bridget followed close behind me. "You wouldn't want to be disturbing her, Mum. She's been fair miserable these past weeks."

"Who is she?" I whispered.

"Anna Karenina."

"Leave us," I ordered.

"But I'm supposed to stay with you when you're involved with the characters, Mum. Them's my orders." She sounded distressed.

"Then stay back. I don't want to upset her."

She demurred and folded her hands before her like a chastised school girl. I approached Anna, who seemed oblivious to anyone and anything around her.

"Mrs. Karenina?" I said. I had no idea if that was the correct form of address, but she did look up in surprise and smiled when she saw me.

"You must be Lady Killington. I've been hearing so much about you." She rubbed her gloved hands to remove the soil, then stood to face me.

She couldn't have been more than five foot one or two and had to look up to meet my eyes. Her complexion was fair and flawless; her hair poked out from a sun bonnet in dark ringlets. I loved her simple beauty and her slightly chubby figure. Rubenesque, it might have been called.

"I've been referred to as the Countess since I've been here, Lady Killington." Her cheeks glowed charmingly pink.

"Please call me Beth," I said and held out my hand.

She studied it for a moment then removed her right glove and took my hand. "Then you should call me Anna. I am so happy to finally meet you. I feared it would be a year or more before I was included in a dinner invitation."

"Who makes these invitations?" I was puzzled. It had never occurred to me someone might be in charge of who comes to dinner every evening.

"Why, your social secretary, of course."

"I didn't know I had a social secretary. I've been floundering about here for two weeks trying to figure out how it operates. Willis, Beebe, and Bridget are the only people I see on a regular basis. They tend to escort me from place to place, breakfast to lunch, to tea, to dinner."

"Well, perhaps it is time you understood you are in charge and ought to take control."

"But, if you're Anna Karenina, then does that mean you didn't throw yourself under that train?"

She whirled around as if I'd struck her a hard blow.

I felt my face go red. I'd struck a sensitive subject and now didn't know how to get out of the situation. She stood with her back to me, her head bent, shuddering. Was she crying?

"I'm so sorry—"

"No!" she cried out. She turned back to me. "No. It's not your fault. Shall we go sit?" She held out an arm in invitation toward a white wrought iron bench.

"May I tell you something?" She bit her bottom lip and lowered her eyes, looking shy.

"Of course."

"I-I don't know if you understand how this works, but I am living in my time period as the others each live in their own. Well —" She gave a nervous laugh. "If we didn't, can you imagine how crowded this place would be?"

"But I see all of you at the same time," I reminded her.

"*You* may, but we don't." She once again turned away and focused on something in the distance before looking at me again. She then choked out her story in bits and spurts. "The point is, I read about Annie Alexeyevna Levin several months ago in the newspaper. The name caught my attention immediately. It was just a small item buried in the middle of the society news stating that the daughter of Count Alexei Karenin had recently given birth to her first child, Ekaterine Lizaveta, whilst traveling abroad. This was the first time I was even aware that my daughter had married. The article said her husband is Dmitry Konstantinich Levin, but made no mention of him being abroad with her."

I thought about the novel, *Anna Karenina*. I had read it at least three times and always wished it would end differently. Now that I saw it had, I wondered what could be distressing this lovely woman. "You speak of Annie, your daughter with Count Vronsky?"

I wanted to grin at being the first to know what happened to that poor baby, but I dared not because Anna did not look happy.

"It struck me as odd that a woman of substantial means would wander about Europe while in that condition and not be at home with her husband, Dimitri Konstantinich, for the ensuing birth. I desperately wanted to send her a letter, but had no idea where to post it to. Now that you are here, perhaps you can help?"

"What do you think I can do?"

"The same thing your husband did for me. Find Annie and bring her here. Her and my granddaughter."

"But you said she's married to Levin's son, Dmitry."

"If you will read between the lines, you will understand that my daughter unfortunately followed in my footsteps."

"And how do I post a letter to the past?"

"You pen the letter and take it to the library. Leave it on the silver salver on the refectory table to the right of the entrance. It will be picked up and delivered."

A flash of white caught my eye and I turned in time to see a white rabbit disappear behind a large rose bush. Anna saw where I looked and smiled. "He gets annoying after a while, dashing about the gardens with a pocket watch in his paw as if he's always late for something."

That evening I asked Mrs. Beebe to send my social secretary to my room first thing in the morning. Meanwhile, I penned a letter of congratulations to Konstantin Levin on the birth of his grand-daughter. I reasoned that I knew him well enough from reading the book.

For several weeks I worked with Heather, my social secretary, organizing dinners to my liking and spent time with Bridget exploring the house. Then one day in March, Heather brought me a letter from Levin. It was written on vellum. Heather and Mr. Willis took turns examining the old fashioned script and though it was written in English, translated it for me.

Konstantin Levin encouraged me to join him in Moscow in May of 1903, when he anticipated Annie Levin would be at home and fully convalesced from her ordeal.

I smiled at his use of "ordeal" in place of child birth. Now all I had to do was figure out how to get to Russia during 1903.

I needn't have worried. The servants arranged it all. I gladly accepted the invitation and chose Bridget to travel with me.

By this time I had become accustomed to the unusual life-style at the manor, so, although I was startled, I was not taken completely off guard when Bridget led me back to the library, to a darkened corner where she escorted me through one of the Palladian doors into the garden. It seemed nothing had changed, except when we reentered the house, gaslight lit the library, no characters filled the room, and as we moved through the house, the servants appeared in what I thought were period costumes. It didn't take long to realize I had arrived at my first destination, the year 1903.

As it was most definitely frowned upon for a woman to travel unaccompanied, I bought first class tickets for Bridget to share my compartment throughout our journey.

We arrived in Paris in late April where we delighted in attending an opera, rode in an open carriage to the Eiffel Tower, and purchased tickets to The Louvre, where we spent nearly a full week touring the rooms. I'm not sure which made me happier, seeing the artworks for myself or watching Bridget's eyes light up at the sight of each new master or a particular sculpture that took her fancy. She was like a starved plant being watered by education. In spite of being unable to read, she picked up the language quickly, and by the time we boarded the train for Moscow, she had even bought two used children's primers on the left bank where artists not only sold their drawings, but household items for desperately needed cash.

During the days on the trains, she practiced reading and writing.

When we reached Moscow, after settling in to our hotel, I sent a note to Monsieur Levin at his Moscow apartment where he had assured me he would be in residence. He invited me to call on him the following day.

I was delighted to learn he spoke quite understandable English, which saved him from having to listen to my schoolgirl French.

"I am not sure what it is you want from me, Mr. Levin," I said over a cup of strong Russian tea. Bridget, now raised in ranks to "Lady's Companion," sat with us in the plain parlor. The décor surprised me as I understood the Levins to be of high status and means. Our hotel room was far more splendid–than his reception parlor.

"Your lovely letter of congratulations to Mrs. Levin displayed a beautiful sense of pleasure at hearing of the birth of our grand-daughter. If you wondered at my writing the response, it was because your letter was directed to my country estate where Dmitry, my son, Annie's husband, resides. As they have been estranged for some time, he forwarded your letter to me. If I may be frank, Lady Killington, Mrs. Levin has few friends. Too many people remember her mother and her tragic passing."

"I understand. You need say no more." This world believed her mother had thrown herself under an on-coming train when Dimitry's wife Annie was yet an infant.

"But, there is more to say. Recently she heard from Count Vronsky, the man who is her father. Perhaps, being from England, you do not know the whole story, and it is not an easy one to tell, but if it will save her life, I feel I must convey the entire truth to you. It is perhaps not for the delicate ears of the young lady?" He raised his eyebrows and gave a nod toward Bridget, who had been listening, fascinated by the conversation.

"Never mind about me," she said. "There's enough hanky-panky in me own family that little can shock me. Thank you for your thoughtfulness, though."

Levin's face darkened and for a moment I thought our interview might end there and then. He drew a breath and recovered his pleasant demeanor. "Annie's mother, Anna Arkadyevna, left her husband of many years to live abroad with Vronsky. The count made a spectacular picture—a dashing officer in the tsar's army—

women couldn't help being attracted to him. My own wife, Katerina Alexandrovna, had hopes when she was but a girl of eighteen. When he instead chose Anna, her heart was broken."

I would never have imagined a man talking about his wife loving another so calmly. But, then, I remembered Levin and his damned agricultural reforms. They seemed to interest him more than people. "And then?"

"After Anna's death, Vronsky tried to care for little Annie on his own, but his despair at losing Anna sent him into his own dark place and he put together a unit and took it to fight in the Turkish wars. Karenin accepted the child into his home and gave over her care to nursemaids. Anna's son Sergei, who was eleven years old, loved her. He was the only one. We all thought Vronsky would do something rash, but he survived to return to his old ways, living in the barracks, gambling, drinking and living an otherwise wasted life. He never showed any interest in Annie until his letter last fall, after the birth of little Kitty."

"Katerina," I said as if he didn't know the name of his own granddaughter.

He nodded. "They named her after my wife."

As if on cue, a baby cried somewhere in the apartment. Levin pulled out a pocket watch, opened it, and snapped it shut. "She's like a little clock. Shall I have nurse bring her in?"

Children never much interested me, but I nodded to be polite. Bridget, on the other hand, was like a child herself. She clapped her hands in delight. "I'd love to see her."

He got up and stepped out of the room for a moment, then returned to his seat.

"Before she comes in, I should finish my story so you understand why I responded to your note. Annie and my son have been married for a little over two years. My wife has been like a mother to her, but Annie is far too old to erase the years of living in an emotional vacuum. Karenin did her no favors by taking her in, other than to see that she was fed and clothed. If it had not been for her brother Sergei in the early years, she never would have known laughter."

"She must have been a terribly sad and lonely little lass," Bridget said.

I shot her a look. "What happened to Sergei?"

"Nothing. Why do you ask?" Levin answered.

"You said she had him in her early years. Did he leave?"

"Oh, but of course. At eighteen, when she was only seven, he went on to university, then he himself married. He and his wife live permanently in St. Petersburgh where he is employed at court."

"And you say Annie has no friends. I must agree with Miss Benedict, a sad and lonely girl now grown into a sad and lonely woman. Do she and her husband live here with you?"

"Dmitry lives on our property in the country. He manages the estate. I'm afraid our Annie followed in the footsteps of her mother, both in her actions and her melancholy. Though her child is Dmitri's, she ran off with her own handsome cavalier, a scurrilous brigand who abandoned her as soon as he learned of her condition. Apparently she did not know of his ways when she took up with him. They spent a few months in Italy. That was it. My son no longer wants anything to do with her." At the sound of footsteps on the stairs, Levin's face lit up with a smile. "And now you'll meet our Princess Kitty."

He stood and went to the door.

I watched with interest as he took a pink-cheeked, chubby baby with large dark eyes, and hair that curled like a little mop on her head, from the nursemaid. She gurgled with joy at seeing her grandfather. He carried her into the room and sat her on his lap. She bounced and waved her arms about.

"She's adorable," Bridget cooed.

"Happy, too," I added.

"Do you see all her teeth? She creeps all over the place and needs to be watched every moment she's awake. I can't wait to teach her to ride and shoot and—"

"Ride and shoot?" I interrupted.

"You English all hunt, is that not so?"

"Yes, of course. I only meant, well, that's good." I'd forgotten for a moment that I'd gone back over a century for this trip and that I was meant to be an English Lady. He apparently took no notice of my American accent.

"Do you ride?" he asked.

"Me? I did. I used to. I don't any longer." That was true enough. My brother and I used to ride when we were kids.

"Aye and wasn't she widowed only a year ago, sir," Bridget piped in.

I half rose to prevent the girl from continuing. She took the hint and clamped her mouth shut. I questioned my judgement on bringing her with me. I do not consider myself a snob, but there are some limits on what one blurts out in public.

Levin cleared his throat. "Now, let me explain. I wish for you to visit Annie tomorrow. I've arranged for you to meet her at a French patisserie here in the city, *Le Petite Versailles*. She thinks she is going to interview a new nurse for Kitty, but I wish for you to have a serious and frank discussion with her."

"In a public setting? That does not seem discreet, Mr. Levin."

"You can assess her state of mind and decide at that time how much you wish to pursue your discussion."

"What makes you think I have the ability to assess another person's state of mind? Especially someone I don't know?"

"Lady Killington, you don't suppose I read your note and tossed all sense to the wind, did you? I wondered why a Lady of your stature would write to a fallen woman of notorious parentage. When I checked, I learned that you are a well-educated American presenting yourself as a lady, quite incorrectly, may I add. Your husband died in an accident leaving you a wealthy heiress with nothing better to do than putter about an old manor house."

I bristled at his comments. "I do not take kindly to you looking into my affairs to such a degree."

"Your secrets are safe with me. All I want is for you to speak with Annie. Let her see her perpetual state of doom and gloom can bode no good for her or for her daughter. Unless she changes her ways, we shall have to send her away and Princess Kitty shall remain here with her grandparents."

Of course, Levin had no idea of my plans to take Annie and Kitty with me to England.

"What does Madame Levin look like?" Bridget asked.

"Very much like her mother. She's short, slightly plump, lovely white skin and nearly black hair. Her coloring is much like little Kitty's. You won't miss her. She's a beauty and attracts attention wherever she goes. Perhaps her downfall," he added somewhat wistfully.

"And exactly what is it you'd like me to say to Annie?" I asked.

"This is difficult for me to say, Madame Killington, but I hoped you might encourage her to spend the summer with you at your estate in England where there are no reminders of the past."

I considered his words briefly. That made part of my quest easier. "If you will excuse us now, Mr. Levin, but I have made dinner reservations at the hotel. Bridget and I must be going."

"Will you come here after your meeting with Annie tomorrow? I shall remain at home, waiting."

I turned to Bridget. "Will you see that our carriage is outside, please? I'll follow right along." After she left, I asked Levin, "Would you want that I tell her the truth?" I wanted to know if he realized that Anna had not died that day so long ago.

"You must not lie. Whether you choose to tell the truth is up to you. Good day, and thank you very much."

The next day I left Bridget at the hotel to lunch alone, hoping she would not take up with any strangers. As she did not speak either French or Russian, I assumed that was a safe risk.

And so I stood somewhat awkwardly beside the table next to Annie. Ladies at other tables were beginning to stare. I cleared my throat and tried again. "Mrs. Levin, I have been told you are expecting to interview a new nursemaid for your daughter and also that you speak English. May I sit here?"

She begrudgingly nodded so I took my place opposite her at the table. Her father-in-law had been right about her appearance. She was indeed a lovely woman of about twenty and eight. Her pale yellow and white muslin tea gown set off her coloring beautifully.

"Father Levin knows very well we do not need a new nurse for

Kitty, and even if we did, he would not seek my approval. What is it you really want, Miss…?

"I am Lady Elizabeth Margaret Killington, Annie."

"You don't sound English."

"Indeed, I assure you I am." Technically, I could claim to be as the widow of a Lord. At least I thought so.

"What is it you want, Lady Elizabeth Margaret Killington?"

No trace of despair reflected in her glaring, dark hostile eyes. Her cheeks turned red, only enhancing her beauty and reminding me of her mother. I suddenly felt awkward and plain, a tall, skinny, brown-haired widow wearing a purple day dress, suitable for one in a second year of mourning. I hated it and how I presented. It seemed the tables had turned and I was the one in need of bolstering. "Your family is concerned about you."

She studied my face for a moment. A waitress came to take my order. Distracted by the young woman, I felt a moment's confusion. I knew what I had to tell Annie, but I did not know what I wanted for lunch. "Perhaps soup and a soufflé?"

"Tea?" she asked.

"Please."

"I'll have the same," Annie said.

After the girl left, Annie said, "Of what concern could I be to them? If you have spoken to Konstanin—Mr. Levin—then you know my husband refuses to see me and Konstantin is keeping my child from me."

"I did not realize that. I gathered you also live in the apartment."

"I have *rooms*."

"I see." I didn't, not really. "I'm sorry to hear that. Do you read very much, Annie?"

"What does it matter?" Her hands fidgeted with her napkin, folding and unfolding it.

"Only that I do and I've learned that in many cultures, certainly not yours or mine, but in history, women were treated as if they had brains. Do you know only last week I met a young woman from Cuba, now living in New York City, who flew a motorized airship over the streets of Paris? Shocked everyone, but it was exciting to see and I was thrilled to be able to speak with her after the event." Oh, and if only I could tell her about the changes to come! But, as it was, I did my best to stick to the facts in her reality.

I caught a glimmer of a smile on Annie's face. "What of it? Sounds impossible."

"It was a dirigible with a basket beneath. She tucked her skirts around her and stuffed them into the basket. The owner, a Mr. Albert Santos-Dumont, rode his bicycle beneath her through the streets of Paris, acting as her guide. Her name is Aida De Acosta. Miss De Acosta does not strike me as a woman who allows others to control her destiny."

"And what makes you think I do?"

"I understand you were told about your mother."

Any evidence of a smile disappeared. "What about her? What do you know?"

"I know what you were told."

"The train?"

"Yes, the train." I leaned forward, wanting to take her busy little hands in mine, to comfort her as I prepared myself to give her my news. "Not everything you have been told is necessarily true."

Her brow furrowed. "What do you mean?"

"What if your mother didn't die that day at the railroad station?"

"Then I would not have been left with that vulture of a man who called himself my father," she fairly spat at me. Heads turned.

"Perhaps we should eat and then take a walk in the park across the way," I suggested.

Her chest heaved as she fought for control. She poked out her chin. "No. I want to know who you are to come here and address me with such news."

A tray full of tea things appeared between us as the waitress set it down. She placed our cups, saucers and silver service, along with the teapot on the table, and then whisked the tray away. We took a moment to pour and stir. My brain raced in ragged circles.

Annie spoke in a low, controlled voice. "Are you here to tell me you know what the truth is? Before you do, let me tell you something. My brother, Sergei, always told me he knew my mother was not dead. The first time they told him such a thing, he was very young, but she came to see him on his birthday. After that, when they tried again to say she was…with the angels…he knew they once again lied. Wherever she was in the world, he knew Father kept her from us."

Dumbfounded, all I could do was nod. The soup arrived along with flaky dinner rolls and butter. The fragrance of the seasoned broth contrasted sharply with my mood. We consumed our repast like two delicate ladies at lunch. Except, unlike the other ladies in the lunch room, we did not speak until the last of the soufflé was removed from the table and a bill was laid discreetly on the table. I fished in my reticule for coins to pay. Annie helped me with the currency.

As we stepped out into the fresh, warm air scented with the residue of hundreds, maybe thousands, of horses drawing carriages up and down the avenue, we waited for an opportune time to cross to the park. Once situated comfortably on a bench in the afternoon shade, we commenced our conversation.

"Your brother has good instincts. Your mother was, and *is*, alive. She lives on my estate in England."

Annie patted her forehead with a handkerchief. "That's not possible. Why did she never contact me?" Her voice quivered with emotion.

"The day that woman threw herself under the train, your mother saw her way out. Out of the dreadful marriage to her husband, and out of the shame and humiliation of having been abandoned by Count Vronsky."

"Wait. Someone else died that day? Why did anyone think she was my mother? Why didn't my mother make herself known to anyone?" Now perspiration beaded her forehead and her cheeks glowed red.

"She was despondent. She stood on the platform staring at the tracks with every intention to throw herself beneath the next train. When it arrived, at that moment, my husband caught her by the hand. The other woman, whose name no one ever learned, took her place." How could I explain Horace invented a fictional character to replace another fictional character and now I was sitting in a Russian park chatting with her daughter? "He escorted her to England. At the estate everyone knows her as the Countess Anna Karenina."

"I can't breathe," Annie gasped.

I scanned the area and saw a fountain not far away. Children sailed little paper boats in it. I rushed over to them. "Does anyone have a cup? Anything I can carry water in? The lady over there has fainted."

A small boy of about five years turned to look where I pointed then looked back at me blankly.

I searched my brains for the correct words in French. "*L-eau, por la femme.*"

"*La femme?*" He backed away from me and I turned to the bench where we'd been sitting. It was empty.

There was only one place she could be going. I found a tram heading in the direction of Levin's apartment. If she used her carriage, she'd arrive long before I got there. I tapped my gloved fingers on the back of the seat in front of me as I watched for familiar street names. When I deduced we were close by, I hopped off at a street corner and moved most indecorously along the sidewalk, passing ladies having a late afternoon stroll with their children and little dogs. At one point, I had to skirt a group by running into the street to pass them.

I reached the steps to the apartment building, gasping for air. Drawing several deep breaths to calm myself, I pressed the buzzer and waited. And waited. I pushed it over and over, frantic that Annie might speak in haste. Finally, the door opened. The nurse-maid appeared, puzzled to see me.

"We didn't expect to see you until much later, Madame. Do come in."

"Is Annie here?" I asked.

She looked at me wide-eyed. "No, Madame, she is not. Why would she be here?"

"Where could she be? She heard some bad news and ran off. Is Mr. Levin at home?"

"He is. Please, follow me."

We went up the broad staircase to the first floor where she showed me into the same reception room where we visited the day before. In only a moment, Levin appeared.

"Welcome back. How did your meeting go?" He showed me to a chair, but I didn't sit.

"Not well. I told her the truth and she ran away."

He shook his head, stopped, then nodded. "To Karenin's."

"I thought he was in St. Petersburg." Now I did sit.

"The brother is. The father retired many years ago and stays at his Moscow apartment. Was she very upset?"

"She looked to be in shock. I went for water and when I turned around, she was gone."

"She may be angry. I know anger doesn't become a young woman, but she is her mother's daughter, after all." He rushed to the hall and shouted, "Ilyana, call a carriage. We're going out."

I followed him to the hall. "What do you think she'll do?"

He patted his pockets as if searching for something. "I need my jacket. Just wait a moment."

When he returned with his jacket, we rushed down the stairs to a waiting carriage. He directed the driver, and the horses took off at a brisk trot. Unfortunately, we got caught up in the early evening traffic with most of Moscow taking advantage of the pleasant weather. It looked like every conveyance imaginable turned out to enjoy the day. Every type except a dirigible.

"This is intolerable," Levin grumbled as we sat in traffic. "I could have sent a note by foot and it would have reached Karenin more quickly."

"But what is it that concerns you so much?"

"If Annie confronts Karenin in anger, he is just as likely to strike back in anger. Did she not tell you?"

"Tell me what?" I thought about Karenin and how he was portrayed in the novel. An unpleasant man who had no idea how to parent. Could he have been physically abusive to Annie? Would he be now?

Levin turned his face away and studied the other vehicles. Pedestrians and riders chattered in the middle of the avenue as if no one had any place special to get to. I felt his frustration as well, having nearly accomplished my goal, then lost it.

"Turn onto Lubyanka Prospekt and cross to the next lane. No one will be there," he instructed the driver.

It took nearly forty-five minutes to reach Karenin's place. From the top of the stairs at the main entrance, raised voices reached our ears. The doorman let us in and we hurried to the first apartment on the right. Levin knocked on the door, but the combatants paid us no heed. He pounded and called out. "Karenin! Alexey Alexandrovich, open the door."

The lock clicked and the door slowly opened. A young, frightened maid peeked out at us. Perhaps she thought more had come to join the fracas.

"I am Lady Killington, come to see Mr. Karenin. Will you announce us?"

She shut the door. We waited. The voices stopped and the door reopened. The maid stepped back and showed us in.

The rooms displayed every sign of comfort and wealth that Levin's did not. Persian rugs carpeted the inlaid wood floors. Chairs, sofas, and tables cluttered with ashtrays, crystal vases full of flowers, and Oriental figurines crowded the large room. A fireplace with a green marble surround and highly polished wood mantle, littered with candelabra, an ornate gold clock, a portrait, presumably of Karenin in his younger days bearing several medals on his chest, and crossed swords above the painting took up the far wall. To the right a large bay window looked out on the avenue, though white sheer curtains muted the view. Heavy burgundy draperies hung to the sides. In the center of this Victorian mélange, Annie stood with an old gentleman. I guessed him to be Karenin.

"Lady Killington?" the man barked.

"I am. To whom have I the honor of speaking?" I asked in as cold a tone as I could muster.

He tugged at his jacket and threw his shoulders back. "I am Alexey Alexandrovich Karenin, late in His Excellency, the tsar's service. Are you the person who has fabricated a story to tell my daughter? Do you see what you have done to her? She will give me no rest until I take her to her mother's grave."

"And how do you propose to do that, sir?" I asked.

"She is here in Moscow. I refused to take Annie there because it seemed a cruel thing to do."

That stopped me. How could Anna Karenina's grave be here in Moscow when I knew she was alive and living in East Sussex? "Here? In Moscow?"

He smirked. The old blackguard. "Indeed, and if it will help to comfort my daughter, I shall call my carriage and we shall go there immediately."

"Never mind, Karenin," Levin said. "My carriage is just outside. Come along." He reached out to Annie.

She shrank back from his touch. Her eyes went from face to face as if she were deciding who to trust. Without warning, she threw her head back and screamed, "I want my brother. I want Sergei."

I rushed to her side and eased her onto a nearby overstuffed chair. "Hush, Annie. Calm yourself. You've had too many shocks for one day. Perhaps you'd like to come with me and rest for a while."

She dropped her head into her hands and sobbed. "No. Leave me. Leave me be. I only wanted my daughter and now even she is taken from me, just like my mother lost her children, I have lost my little girl. I have no one. No one."

"You have me," I crooned in her ear, softly so the others might not hear. "You have your friend, Beth. And soon you'll have your mother."

She drew a shuddering breath.

I asked the gentlemen to leave us for a few minutes and they quickly acquiesced. My experience has been that men in any century do not like female histrionics, so this worked in our favor. They exited with Karenin offering Levin a drink.

"How can all this be true? How can my mother be buried here

in Moscow and also be alive in your Sussex?" Her poor face was blotched with red patches.

"You must trust me, Annie. Your mother was broken-hearted about leaving you and Sergei behind. She speaks of the two of you often, but it was the only way for her to survive. She believed Karenin would be a good father to you, but she could no longer live in his household."

"She's told you about me?" Annie looked at me in wonder, as if she could not believe her mother remembered her.

"She loves you with her whole heart. Annie, she was a young girl, raised by an elderly aunt who married her off at the first opportunity to Karenin. You can see how old he is. He was in his forties when they married. Set in his ways. Not interested in society, the opera, the theater, nothing. She knew nothing of life. And then Count Vronsky came along, your father. She loved him more than life itself, but in the end, it was that love, that passion that drove him away. It took her years to understand that. But, no matter what, you were born of love." I wrapped my arms around her shoulders and drew her to me.

"But...but that doesn't answer the question, how can she be here if she's there?"

"Don't you suppose Karenin made a show of burying the woman from the train station? No one could identify the person who died," I said. Though it pained me, I had to tell her the ugly truth. "The body was so mangled. The clothing was of the right style and mode that it could have been your mother. Your father had to save face among his peers so he created the elaborate lie. Maybe he really did believe the body was hers. According to Anna she was going through a very dark time."

"We must allow him to take us there. I want to see this memorial to a mother I never knew." She gently pushed me away and stood up. "Let us summon them. Afterward, will you take me back to your hotel? We can make further plans then."

"Of course." What plans, I wondered could she have in mind? And would they fit in with my idea of her leaving for England with me?

We arrived at the cemetery around seven in the evening. Families tended graves, others strolled in the splendid evening. Soon they would all head home for their dinners, some to retire, others to prepare for a night at the theater or opera. Perhaps a casino. This was nothing like our gloomy cemeteries in England, where little children were frightened to pass in the daytime, let alone after dark. Here, children ran around headstones and mausoleums as if it were a playground.

Karenin led us deep into the memorial park to a large stone angel hovering over the gravesite. Indeed, the inscription read, Anna Arkadyevna Karenina, Loving Wife and Mother. It listed her dates of birth and death. Her death date was many years too soon.

"Who could the woman in there be?" Annie whispered to me, while pretending to mourn on her knees by the memorial.

"I only know it is not your mother."

The men remained at some distance while Annie and I knelt by the grave.

"If you come to England with me, you can live in the same comfort as your mother for as long as you choose. You and Kitty."

Annie got to her feet and I joined her.

"What about my husband?"

Somehow I thought the estrangement was permanent. "What about him?"

She frowned as she thought about him. "He has no need of me. He chose to live in the country and has refused to see me. Perhaps I do deserve such treatment. I did, after all run off and leave him for another man. But, in the end, he could prevent me from leaving the country. I am still his legal wife."

"There's no need to speak of that now. Come, let's go to my hotel."

We left the cemetery and joined the rest of the city in its evening parade through the avenues. Levin and Karenin, never friends, both agreed to leave us off at my hotel where we would dine. I promised to see that Annie returned safely to her apartment.

As soon as they were out of sight, I clutched Annie by the elbow and led her into the ladies' parlor off the lobby. "Is there any way you can get Kitty away from Levin?" I know I sounded furtive, but if she was to come to England with me, I knew she had to have her daughter with her. The poor girl had grown up without her own mother, she never would want her own child to lack for her love.

She collapsed onto a nearby sofa. "I often take her to the park across the way from his apartment, but he rarely lets me out of his sight. What are you thinking? That I should simply abscond with her? Is that not against the law? Levin and Karenin could both have me locked up."

I frowned at the thought. She was right. Levin had even threatened as much. I had forgotten we were, after all, in the nineteenth century. Women did not have true control of their own lives in most of Western civilization. "Let me think about this."

I signaled a porter and sent for Bridget to come to the lounge. She was the one who led me through the doors and into this time period, perhaps she knew a way that I could bounce back for a few minutes. I fingered my mobile phone in my purse.

Bridget gasped as she approached us in the lounge. "I'm sorry, I was chatting with the ladies on our floor. Everyone seems to be related somehow to the tsar. Never saw so many princesses in my life."

She was right, of course. As I recalled my reading of the Russian novels, it did indeed seem like there was an abundance of princesses. But, this wasn't the time for that discussion.

"I need a word with you, Bridget." I pointed to a pair of chairs near the window. "We'll be right back, Annie, then we'll all have dinner and make a plan."

Annie twisted her handkerchief in her lap.

"What," I asked Bridget when we were seated, "do I have to do return to our time?"

"You mean right this minute? I was having such a good time."

"No, I want to go for a few minutes to do some research." I pulled my phone out just enough for her to see it.

"Oh. That wasn't very smart, if you don't mind my saying so. If you get caught with that, Lord knows what they'll do to you. What is it you're wanting to know?"

"Two things, really. Just what *is* the process of getting back, and the limits of women's rights where we are at present?"

She tittered, a mirthful little laugh. "Sure and you didn't think to ask before we left on our journey? Did you think you'd blink your eyes and be back in the library?"

I didn't like her tone. She was making me nervous. "It seemed that's how we left the twenty-first century. We went into the library, walked through a door and there we were. Is there not some way to get back to the twenty-first century from here?"

"Aye, but surely you didn't think we could just flit in and out of centuries at your every whim, now did you."

Her amusement was annoying. "Obviously. This isn't funny, Bridget. We need to rescue this poor woman before her father-in-law and stepfather come looking for her. And we need to take the baby with us."

She held up a finger. "And don't forget she has a husband. And a real father. They could come tearing in here at any moment and carry her away."

"You're having far too much fun with this. If I didn't need you to get back to the estate, I'd let you go here and now in a country where you don't speak the language."

"Sorry, your Ladyship. You can't flip back and forth. We have to travel back to the library for that. You'll have to assume women have no rights. Probably the safest."

I folded my arms and scowled at her. Not because I was angry, but unsure of what steps to take next. I thought about that Cuban girl flying that thing in Paris. She didn't worry about what others would say and do to her for her lack of decorum. I considered pretending to run away together as lovers—there certainly had to be lesbians even in the nineteen century—but I wondered how believable we'd be and assumed we'd be caught before we'd gotten very far. I tapped my teeth with my fingernails.

"There's nothing left but to do it," I said. "Find out the train schedule and prepare to leave within the next forty-eight hours. And not a word to anyone. Have a carriage on stand-by. And pack our bags, except for our nightclothes for tonight and fresh underwear for a day or two."

"I'll see to it. What have you decided?" She stood, still with a look of amusement.

"You enjoy an adventure, do you, Bridget?"

She held out her arms. "You can see that I do. I'm ever so grateful you took me on as your personal maid." She whirled around and practically skipped out of the room.

I rejoined Annie. "We'll take Kitty out to the park tomorrow for about an hour. Your father-in-law appears to trust me and he will even more so when we return her promptly on schedule." I nodded, happy with my decision.

"But, what shall I do now? I must go back to my apartment. You promised Konstantin."

My hand went instinctively toward the phone, but stopped when I remembered where I was. "I'll send a note and tell him you were overcome after the trauma of today and you'll rest in my rooms tonight. I'll tell him we'll be there at ten in the morning to take Kitty for her airing. As long as I'm with you, there will be no need for the nursemaid to come along."

With that settled, we went into the dining room and enjoyed a delightful, though somewhat heavy repast. Bridget joined us and we shared all the experiences of our journey with Annie, including the adventures of Miss Aida DeCosta. When Annie laughed, her eyes lit up, reminding me of her mother's when I assured her that I could bring her daughter and grandchild to her. We ended the evening discussing the plans for the next two days.

Our excursion with Kitty to the park went smoothly. Levin agreed, but I noticed him peeking between the curtains at his window periodically as we strolled around the gardens across the street from his apartment. Nevertheless, he agreed we could take her out again the next day.

"It seems you are a positive influence on my daughter-in-law, Lady Killington. It pleases me to see her smiling, so unlike her mother."

"Tomorrow, I'd very much like to take Annie and Kitty to the Annunciation Cathedral."

He raised his eyebrows at that. "Isn't Kitty a bit young for that?"

"Possibly, but I'd like to see it and I'm sure the images and artwork will entertain her whilst Bridget and I educate ourselves more on your culture." I knew what would be happening in just a few short years to all the churches of Russia and wanted to seize the opportunity to see them in their original form, but had forgotten about Levin's political and religious views.

"Brainwashing. As you English might say, *balderdash.* If people spent more time worrying about their crops than pouring their money into churches in the hopes of saving their souls, the world would be a better place. All that gold." He shook his head. "Can you imagine how many starving children could be fed with one gold chalice used in their services?" He threw up a hand. "Take her, if you want, but only to show her the trappings of a people's belief system that will soon be history."

It was my turn to raise eyebrows. How could he know?

My mouth was dry as we left Kitty and returned to the hotel to pack for our return journey to England. Annie brought her things from her rooms to the hotel and joined us again for dinner as we talked about the next day.

"Are we really going to the cathedral?" Annie asked.

"We are," I replied. The remarkable baked chicken and potato dish had my full attention. I was busy trying to identify the delicate seasonings.

"But—"

"But, I want to see it, and if there is time, the others in the square. Our train doesn't depart until late in the evening. I've reserved a compartment for the four of us. It may be a little cramped, but Kitty won't take up too much room." I tried to make light of our impending departure. Annie was so nervous, she could bolt at any minute and the entire trip would have been in vain.

"What if Levin or Karenin suspect? Surely, they question how and why you arrived. A mysterious stranger with no obvious connection to any of us."

"I had previous communication with Levin. That is my concern. I am on a mission on behalf of your mother."

She pushed her plate of food away having barely eaten a bite. "Now, I'm not so sure. How do I know you really know Mother and she is alive? I've been so eager to believe you—"

I reached out and patted her hand. "I know you're upset and anxious about leaving all that is familiar. Ask me about your mother. Better still, ask Bridget. She's known her far longer than I have." I couldn't add that I'd read the book. That would really throw her into a state of confusion.

Instead of responding, she picked up her wine glass and took a sip as her focus darted from Bridget to me and back again. After a minute's silence, she said, "I didn't know my mother, so I wouldn't know what to ask."

"I can tell you that Karenin is a sad and lonely man who has no ability to show love or affection," I offered from my memory of the book.

"Everyone knows that," she scoffed.

"Your mother fell in love with Count Vronsky while he was courting Kitty Levin, your mother-in-law."

She tilted her head. "Who told you that? Mother Levin never mentioned that."

"Your mother is a very beautiful woman still. I can imagine her catching the eye of any man she met as a girl. Unfortunately her aunt married her off to Karenin when she was eighteen."

A tear slid down her face, which she didn't wipe away. Bridget pulled out a clean handkerchief and reached across the table with it, like a loving mother might do. Annie didn't pull back. "I really want to believe you."

"Good. We'll finish up here, have a good night's rest and pick up Kitty at ten o'clock as planned."

"I've already shopped and packed her clothes for the trip," Bridget said. "And sure, won't she be the best dressed baby on that train."

I laughed. "She'll probably be the only baby on that train."

·  ·  ·

AFTER LEAVING our luggage in the care of the hotel, we took a carriage to the cathedral. The day was remarkably warm for May and the sun shone brightly. A good omen. Annie was distracted, disinterested in her surroundings as we walked up the steps and into a church built in 1489. I was overwhelmed by its beauty. I gawked at the artwork, the frescoes, the gilded columns, the vestments a priest wore as he crossed the altar at the front of the church. There were smaller side chapels, each one more magnificent than the others. I couldn't have ever imagined such a building, even after reading about it in school and seeing photos.

We strolled quietly until a man approached and whispered something to Annie. She drew a sharp breath and covered her mouth.

"What? What is it?" I asked her after the man stepped away.

"He said there is a gentleman waiting for us outside on the steps. That it is most urgent we meet with him." Her eyes were wide with fear.

"No one…" I started to say that no one knew we were here, but of course, I had specifically asked permission of Levin.

"There must be another way out besides the main entrance," I said. My mind raced with possibilities. "You two take Kitty and wait for me by the altar. I'll be right back."

"What are you going to do?" Bridget asked.

"See who it is and what he wants. If there's a problem and I don't return within ten minutes, you two should go on to the train station. I'll meet you there."

"What about our things at the hotel?" Annie asked.

"I'll take care of them. Now go."

I waited until they were at the far end of the church, then I went to the entrance and, standing to one side, peered out into the brilliant sunshine. There stood Levin, scowling, impatiently slapping his gloves against the palm of one hand. As he had no hold over me, I considered it safe to approach him.

"Mr. Levin," I called cheerfully as I emerged into the sunlight. "What brings you here? I thought you disapproved of churches."

"I came to take you ladies to lunch. There's someone who would like to meet with all of you and this seemed a good time. Will you join us?" His smile looked oily, but that wasn't the image created in the novel about Levin. Had I put my own interpretation on him?

"We have plans. Who wants to meet with us?"

"Kitty's father, my son Dmitri, is in town. He is reconsidering his position on Annie's exile."

*Criminy, that's all we need. He's wanted nothing to do with Annie for months, hasn't seen his child and now, suddenly he's here?* "Very well. If you'll give us a few minutes to finish our tour." If he agreed to wait at least half an hour, we should be able to get away and hire a separate carriage to get to the train station.

"Take all the time you need. I told him we'd be there at one."

"Excellent. Won't be more than half an hour. Perhaps you'd rather go sit in the shade of your carriage. It's quite warm today."

"I'll do that." He tipped his hat and turned away.

I raced back into the depths of the church and found Annie and Bridget playing patty-cakes with Kitty by a side altar at the front. "We need to hurry. We have half an hour before he'll come looking for us."

"What is it?" Annie asked in alarm.

"I'll explain on the way." I took it upon myself to not tell her about Dmitri, for I understood that Levin had sent for him, if for no other reason than to thwart her chance at happiness.

Two hours later our luggage had caught up to us at the train station where we left it in the hands of a porter. We huddled in a small group in the first class waiting room, anxious to be able to board the train and hide in our compartment.

I had chewed my fingernails as a kid and now I worried them with my teeth while the other two ladies fidgeted in their own ways. Bridget chattered to Kitty, and Annie stared out the window at the tracks as she twisted her handkerchief.

Bridget and Annie sat opposite me in a corner where no one could see them from the outside. I kept an eye on the window. Every man who walked along the platform looked like Levin, Dmitri, whom I'd never seen, or Karenin. The empty train sat with its doors closed as the porters refreshed the compartments.

Annie had bought a baguette from a street vendor and fed small chunks of it to Kitty. The little one was distracted by the novelty of riding in the carriages, the church, and now, the train station. At least one of us was having a good time.

I wished for a bottle of water or a vending machine. We hadn't eaten since breakfast, and while there were plenty of vendors out on the platform we daren't risk separating and exposing ourselves.

When the time finally arrived and our train was announced, we joined the rush of people and headed for our car. The entire time, I worried about Annie. She could bolt and then where would we be? I kept a firm hold on her upper arm as we crossed the platform. A porter helped us up the steps into the car. Tears of relief flooded my eyes as the others climbed up ahead of me. Once the porter passed Kitty up to Annie, I put my foot on the stool to step up, but then I heard Levin's voice.

"Lady Killington! Stop!"

I turned to see him rushing toward me, Karenin and another man, a taller, younger version of Levin with a full beard, also running.

"Those men have been pestering us since early morning. Will you stop them and call for help, please?" I said to the porter. I reached in my purse and pulled out a wad of cash. I had no idea how much I gave the man, but he seemed happy.

"In you go, Madame," he said as he fairly threw me onto the car and then blocked the way of the others. He blew on a whistle and soon several other uniformed porters joined the fracas as Levin shouted at them.

We found our compartment, entered and locked the door. All three of us hurried to the windows and looked out. Yet, another man scanned the windows, searching. He was a handsome man and I imagined he was Vronsky, Annie's father. She had never seen him, not even a likeness of him, but I had read about his extraordinary good looks and at sixty something, he was still a handsome fellow. Karenin remained above the fray and stood, arms folded as Levin, father and son tried to browbeat the porters into letting him through. Apparently, I had tipped well.

Now, if only the train would leave the station.

People shuffled along the passageway. I heard them but didn't see them as I had drawn the blinds on the windows to the corridor. Sooner or later someone would come for our tickets, but by then it ought to be safe for us to open the door.

Levin gave up. He signaled to his son, and they huddled their heads bobbing, hands flying. What would they come up with next? Rushing the porters hadn't worked. The handsome gentleman had disappeared.

The Levin's moved away down toward the back end of the train. And the entrance to the station. Was it possible they were leaving? I hoped so.

"They're gone," Bridget announced, though we'd all been watching.

"I need Kitty's overnight bag," Annie said.

"It should be in the overhead rack with the rest of ours," I said. I stood and examined them, pulling Kitty's out. "Here. You can change her and maybe she'll take a nap."

With Annie preoccupied, Bridget and I remained vigilant at the window. Ten minutes passed and no sign of the men.

The train lurched.

I grinned.

Bridget smiled.

Annie gasped. "This is it? We're really going?"

We travelled unmolested to Paris. Although all three of us remained on high alert at every stop, nothing happened to deter us from leaving Russia or crossing borders into France. We all enjoyed the first class service and the particular courtesy of the porters, especially their kind attention to Kitty, who adored the attention. I don't think the child had ever seen so many people nor been petted and cooed over so much. Annie basked in the reflected goodness.

We spent three days in Paris outfitting Annie in the latest fashions, and buying everything we could find to treat Kitty. While she hadn't been deprived of food and shelter, each one of us thought she deserved this fluffy lamb, that sweet dress, another soft blanket until we feared we'd never fit everything into the huge manor house. The trip was glorious and unforgettable.

I almost regretted having to return to the house and the twenty-first century, but after the three days, it was time to board the train once again, this time for Boulogne and then the ferry to Dover. We rented a stateroom with the idea of sleeping on the overnight trip, but the weather was rough in the channel. Annie spent most of her time in the lavatory. Kitty slept through it all.

By morning, passengers were encouraged to remain in their bunks until the boat docked. I clung to the rail for dear life as the ferry rolled through the rough waters. Annie moaned and Bridget prayed.

In the morning, rain clouded the porthole. I wished that my trusty smartphone worked so I could look up the weather and follow the ferry's path, but it wouldn't be in use for another hundred and fifteen years. I closed my eyes in despair, but quickly opened them when nausea threatened. Finally, with a lot of shouting from the deck and bumping and jolting, the captain announced we were free to disembark. He warned us that the weather was inclement throughout the south of England. A train delayed its departure for those of us traveling to London. We, of course, were not. I hoped we could find a means of public transport to take us back to East Dean.

We stood outside the ticket office. "How do we get home?" I shouted to Bridget. The rain pounding on the canvas awning above us drowned out our voices.

"Now, how would I be knowing never having traveled abroad before?"

"May I be of assistance?" a heavily accented male voice said from behind me. Without looking, I knew it was him, Count Vronsky.

I whirled around to face him. It was him, the stranger from the train station in Moscow.

He smiled. "I wired ahead and my carriage should be waiting."

"What carriage? Who do you know in England that you can

wire ahead?" I scowled at him, hoping to warn him away. He was, after all, the man who abandoned poor Anna in her darkest hours.

"Here now, no need to be rude. The gentleman is offering to help," Bridget said.

"You mind your place," I snapped at her. Perhaps I was harsh, but I was worried. Neither she nor Annie knew who this man was.

"I assure you, I mean you no harm, Lady Killington," the count said. "If you will permit me." He reached past me to take the baby from Annie.

I pushed myself between them to thwart his effort. He stumbled back a step.

"You will *not* take them back to Russia!" I held up my reticule like a shield. "Stay away from us or I shall call security." As fast as I said that, I remembered where I was. Probably no security and no police.

"I have no intention of taking anyone back to Russia. I want to talk with Annie and her mother and apologize."

Annie shouted, "Did he say he wants to apologize? Apologize for what?" She pushed me aside and asked him, "Who are you? Why are you here?"

"I came on the same train, Annie. I watched you in Paris. I live here-in London. Please let me escort you to wherever it is you are going."

"You don't know?" I asked.

"How could I?"

Bridget settled it for us. "We're getting soaked. If we stand here much longer we'll all have pneumonia. Let the gentleman offer us his carriage. He can sit up top. Show us the way, sir."

Within moments, his driver appeared with a very large umbrella and led us to the carriage. Once snugly installed, Count Vronsky asked if he could please sit inside. A man of his years ought not be riding outside in the rain. I relented.

The smell of wet wool and body odor filled the interior of the elegantly outfitted coach. We were a bedraggled mess surrounded by velvet and satin. The coach was well sprung and rode smoothly through the primitive and muddy lanes.

No one spoke after Bridget had given the driver instructions to the manor house until we reached the village affiliated with the manor house.

"You'll leave us at the front gate, sir," I told Vronsky.

"I certainly shall not. You'll be taken directly to your front entrance. Then, if you can find it in your heart, you will permit me a word with Anna."

The other two ladies gasped as his familiar use of her name.

"How do you know her?" Annie asked.

"I know Anna Arkadyevna Karenina from long ago," he said with the saddest expression I've ever seen on anyone's face.

Bridget studied his face and then Annie's. I could see understanding in her eyes. "I think we ought to ask Miss Anna if she wishes to see you before we agree to anything."

"Of course," he replied.

The carriage rolled to a stop under the shelter of the portico. Both Mr. Willis and Miss Beebe rushed down the steps to welcome us home. Anna stood in the shadows of the doorway.

I climbed out, feeling at least three times my age with aching bones and stiff muscles. I'd be glad of a hot bath, supper in my rooms, and then an early night.

Annie, followed by Bridget carrying Kitty, mounted the stairs as Mr. Willis and Miss Beebe supervised others with the luggage. Tears came to my eyes as Anna stepped out and held out a tentative hand in greeting. Annie flung herself into her arms. Bridget for once remained quietly to one side as the two women hugged, cried, and talked over one another in rapid French. I couldn't follow it all, but there was no question in my mind, I'd done the right thing.

Count Vronsky was the last to mount the stairs. After a few minutes he cleared his throat.

I glared at him. "You were supposed to wait——"

"Alexey?" Anna squeaked. "Alexey? Is that really you?"

I bit my lips.

"Anna, my love." He dropped to one knee and grabbed her hands, holding them to his face. "Can you ever forgive me? When they told me you died…"

She dropped to her knees. "How could you know? How could anyone know? There is so much forgiving to be done. Our daughter. Our granddaughter. Do you see your eyes in hers?" She sobbed as she spoke. "Can you forgive me?"

I rolled my eyes at all this forgiving. I knew they loved one another from the start. Why couldn't they just get on with it?

"If you'll excuse me, I'll just go inside. Bridget, let Miss Beebe know tonight will be a Russian reunion dinner. Pull out all the stops. Champagne. Caviar. Salmon in aspic. Whatever it takes for a grand Russian celebration." I shook my head, happy to be home.

Anna Arkadyevna and Count Alexey Kirillovich Vronsky stepped into the reception hall and faced one another, two lovers reunited.

Kitty cried.

"Time to head to the library, Beth," Bridget said, pulling me from my reverie.

"The library?"

"You've accomplished what you set out to do. Time to return…"

## AUTHOR'S NOTES – VERONICA H. HART

WHEN I LEARNED the theme of this years' Alvarium Experiment, I knew immediately I had to change the ending of *Anna Karenina*. Her death has haunted me since I first read the book over fifty years ago, and every time I've read it since. I always want her not to throw herself under that train. I often wondered how poor little Annie managed to survive being raised by Karenin. I pictured him cold and aloof, ordering the servants to do whatever was necessary for her care, but offering no love or affection. It seemed natural to me that she would marry Levin and Kitty's son because those were the only other people with whom Karenin might have socialized. I also worried about Vronsky, gone off to the wars. Did he ever return?

If you have enjoyed this new ending to *Anna Karenina*, I'd love to hear from you at vhhart@gmail.com. Or perhaps a review on Amazon?

Thank you.

*—VHH*

# THE BRAZILIAN MILLIONAIRE'S WIFE

## SCOTT MICHAEL POWERS

A *nd I swear, you can love somebody without it being like that. You keep them a stranger, a stranger who's a friend.*
        *~Bartender Joe Bell, in Truman Capote's Breakfast at Tiffany's*

RIO DE JANEIRO, *Brazil, 1944*

THERE USUALLY IS a dark explanation behind how someone becomes a millionaire. I learned that from José himself. They figure out how to hide their pasts and peculiar proclivities, how to build all of those walls and set all of those alarms, to keep safely stashed what must never be seen or discussed. They adopt the precautions, the ways of the respected and the dignified. They learn how to talk, how to walk, how to stand, how to dress, and how to fill their homes with all the paraphernalia of power. They learn how to deceive. I said they hide—not discard—their old selves. No one like that ever really changes. José certainly did not. I had been with him long enough to see that. And I saw it in most of his friends.

There also usually is a dark explanation behind why such a man as José goes to America to find a pretty, young, American wife, and why he settles for one from the same kind of shadows. No; "settles" is not the right word. *Targets.*

They cannot hide it from me. I see in the dark. I have that gift, passed along to me from my *Avó* Ana. My grandmother was a great *Candomblé* seer, a gifted practitioner of my people's spiritual powers. Others dismiss it as fakery, as voodoo, but we know better. She was as respected and beloved as feared for her abilities. Legendary. In an important respect, though, I am more like José. I keep my true self hidden, my *Candomblé*-self. The only thing from my past I keep is *Avó* Ana's *obé Candomblé*, a ritual knife that I always strap under my vest as a tribute to her and a reminder to myself. All else from my past is walled off, behind careful ramparts of my own construction. But I am no millionaire. I am too dark-skinned to ever aspire toward or achieve such a blessing. So I just work for one.

When José came home from his time in America, he brought his bride with him. And when they arrived here in Rio de Janeiro in the summer of 1944, her name was Olívia.

I greeted them at the door. She sparkled. José dressed her in a beige suit and wide-brimmed hat, and wrapped her in silver chains. They dangled from her ears and choked her slender throat. They slid down her wrists when she moved her arms, and jingled on her shoes as she walked. But the preponderance of the sparkle came from within, through her eyes and luminescent smile, as she glanced around the foyer, and then up at the high, carved ceiling.

The rest of the staff had lined up at the foot of the staircase for introductions, but she ignored them.

"Oh, José, darling, it's marvelous, simply marvelous!" Olívia exclaimed.

She threw her arms around his neck, planted a kiss on his cheek and, in one continuous motion, slid right off across the room, and into the den to examine José's game trophies. He caught up with her when she stopped beside the stuffed, black puma. He had had the beast mounted on a platform cut from a mahogany log that held it at eye level, She pressed close, almost nose-to-nose.

"I shot him in the Amazon," José said. "The damned thing was getting ready to pounce. I was only seconds from being mauled."

Now the beast forever snarled.

"You don't scare me!" she told it.

She slapped its face, a gentle, playful slap, but with too much force. The jaw snapped and skittered across the floor.

"Oooh! I'm so sorry!"

"Damn that taxidermist!" José snapped. "He must have used inferior glues. I knew that bastard was not to be trusted."

"Don't be alarmed, madam." I told her. I scooped up the fallen mandible. "I shall repair it immediately. Please consider this a meaningless mishap, like spilt milk."

"Oh, you speak English!" As she turned to me, her look changed from aghast to delight and curiosity.

"Yes, madam. I am the only staff member who does. However, Aline, the maid, the one on the right, there, by the stairs, wishes to learn. She would be pleased if you conversed with her."

Olívia ignored Aline. Her eyes looked into mine.

"Well," she said. "Then you and I must become good friends."

She took my hand in hers. In that moment, I knew her.

I saw deeply into her darkness. Olívia already had been many women in her young life; always, always moving on. She rode life as a surfer rides waves, grateful for the moment, never looking back, never quite sure how long the ride would last, and always perfectly content to catch the next wave after one threw her or petered out. There always is another wave. I saw occasional pain from the throws, but never disappointment in the lost rides. There also was a tender, deep fear that if she ever stopped riding altogether she would drown. So she just moved on.

People never know when I see into them, yet Olívia sensed something. I cannot imagine my expression betrayed me. I have a poker face. It is part of my construction. She released my hand with a snap, and that curious expression of hers deepened. She tilted her head. When her honey bangs rolled into her eyes, she tilted back, wiped them away, and put on a practiced smile. It demanded: *pretend you didn't see that.*

"Good friends," she promised.

We already were. Souls do not touch without affecting each another. It is my curse, a powerful, annoying empathy that burdens my being each time I see. She became someone I wished to protect as a good friend, or perhaps as a daughter.

From her I felt no reciprocal desire. She did not bear that curse. I saw plenty of men in Olívia's life who had sensed her insecurity, and who had wanted to protect her, and she had shunned them all. I saw plenty who had yearned for protection by her; she had neglected and left them all. Still, as she and José made their way to the stairs, she gave me a backwards glance. Yes, she felt it. As if embarrassed, she rotated her eyes to her pocketbook. She opened it, removed a cigarette holder, inserted a cigarette, lit it, and danced, laughing, past the rest of the staff and up the stairs to catch José.

They went out that night, and the evening wore far past midnight. It is my responsibility to stay up and attend when José returns. When José and I were younger men, this was far more difficult. I had resented José for wasting my evenings while he dined, drank, conducted business, danced, gambled, and fucked, in the clubs and hotels of Copacabana, or the penthouses of Botafogo. I was left behind to keep the home lights on and the fires burning. For me, then, the hours were consumed in that burning. It's true: I had been envious of him, and perhaps jealous of those with him. It was hard being so close to such a man, yet only serve as a functional support for him. Yet as we both aged from our 30s to our 50s, I finally understood what he really did. He robbed men with pens and handshakes, or agreed to heinous commerce, albeit over good food and wine. He took and misused women who might have good hearts, even if in the fires of passion. And all the while he walled off his own soul.

At some point, my envy had turned to contempt, yet I had grown content knowing that, as I wiled hours, I was no part of any of José's offenses. We all have jobs. Like them or not, it is best to make them work, to our fullest abilities. All my loyalties to José, which I confess I once held with admiration, pride, friendship, and, dare I say it, love for him, slowly dissolved in the elixir of his ways. Yet there was no difference, because those loyalties' functions had been absorbed by my integrity in my duties.

José would go out three, four, or five nights a week, well into the devil's hours. So it was this night. Shortly after 4 a.m., I heard the door open, and I hurried from my room to meet them.

José was alone. Blood spattered his jacket and shirt, and soaked the cuffs on both arms. His eyes glared with fury.

"Fetch me my robe, and draw me a bath," he commanded. "And when you return, burn these."

"Where is Madam Olívia?"

"She is gone. You're never to speak of her, ever again. Do you understand me? She was never here. You never met her. Make sure the staff also knows this. I want her never spoken of to anyone. There never was a Madam Olívia, and there never shall be."

José was a big man, much bigger than me, broad-shouldered and chested. Women called him handsome. When he was angry and his facial muscles tightened, his chiseled cheekbones and jawline took on frightful definition. He did not have to project physical threat, but he did anyway. There could be no arguing, no refusal, and no follow-up inquiry.

When I returned with his robe, I found him in the den in his undergarments. The rest of his clothes and shoes lay on the hearth. José drained a brandy and snatched the robe from my hands. As he pulled it on, he made a point of staring into my eyes. His told mine that his demand that I never speak of Madam Olívia was of life-or-death seriousness. And his searched mine, to see that I received this clarification on the subject. I did. Ever so gently, I nodded. José softened into satisfaction. He nodded back. He pocketed his wallet and keys from the table. He refilled his snifter. And then he rushed out, and up the stairs.

Before I tossed his clothes into the fire, I went through them. In a jacket pocket, I found the blood-soaked kerchief José had used to wipe his hands and face. I crumbled it and tossed it in. The silk lit up like a searchlight, shrank from the flame, and then quickly vanished as a small roll of ash. His jacket followed.

In the pants, I found a hat check ticket from the Novo Carioca Club, for Madam Olívia's bonnet. I put it in my pocket, rolled up José's pants, and then dropped them into the fire.

Of course I feared the worst. I was torn.

I was confident that José has killed before. In fact, I knew he had, though I did not possess knowledge of the event. I had seen it in him.

My time with Madame Olívia had been brief, little more than a few moments watching her lighting up the foyer and wrecking the puma, a few words, and a momentary caress from her hand. She had been mistress of the house for only a few hours. Yet, I had seen her soul. I suffered a deep sense of shame over my failure to protect her, a dereliction of my duties. Her hat check ticket rested in my pocket, like a last chance.

There was no prospect of sleep, so I didn't bother. I freshened up and changed my clothes, and held onto the ticket, knowing I'd keep it close until that last chance might be redeemed.

José emerged in the early afternoon and went into his study where he made phone calls. Normally he didn't mind that his voice carried through the lower house. Sometimes he enjoyed putting on a little show, arguing and ordering loudly—the big shot who could get away with bullying business associates. The staff knew to ignore him; not that we ever cared. That day, however, he kept the French doors closed and spoke in hushed tones. I glanced in once and saw him in an angry, though measured, conversation.

The police arrived shortly before dinner.

There were three of them, two plain-clothed detectives and a uniformed officer. I showed them to the den. When José arrived, he greeted the detectives warmly, like old friends, but expressed just enough confusion about their presence to look convincingly surprised. The two detectives, one an elderly, relaxed captain named Barboza, the other a nervous-looking young investigator named Leal, sat on the davenport. The uniformed officer stood behind them. José sat in his leather armchair and leaned into them. I took position behind José in the corner, beside a stuffed macaw, a magnif-icent blue and orange specimen set to fly from its perch.

"José, you were seen last night with a man named Klinghoff in the Cafe Bom," Barboza started.

"Yes, yes, we had dinner. We were there talking business. Is something the matter?"

"You were seen arguing with him," Leal said.

"Arguing? Well, I guess we were at one point. Felix and I go way back. We've had many deals together, and he's still upset that I won't invest in one particular venture. I think it has reached the tipping point, and he is desperate to get me in now, but I don't know, Francisco.

"Is that a new watch?"

Leal raised his arm. "Yes, it is. My fiancé bought it for me."

"You're a lucky man," José said. "Luana is too good for you. But I know your charms. She's very much in love. So, what's this all about?"

"Klinghoff's body washed up on Morro Cara do Cão this morn-ing," Barboza said.

"No!"

"He had been stabbed, many times, and then dumped into the water," Barboza added.

"Oh, sweet Jesus." José crossed himself. "Was it that woman? That whore?"

My body betrayed me. I squirmed. I think Leal saw that.

"A whore?" Leal asked.

"Yes, he was there last night with a whore. An English whore. I don't recall her name. It will come to me, I think. Her first name, anyway. I don't think I ever got her last name. You never do."

"No, you never do," Barboza said.

"Yes, we all left together, and shared a cab, which dropped them first. She wasn't happy. When they got out, she looked then like she could kill him then and there. I recall that distinctly. But Felix never had much sense when it came to picking whores, so it was some-thing I put out of my mind with a chuckle. I never dreamed, never imagined, that she might do such a thing!"

"Yes, there was a woman there at the cafe, according to the staff," Leal said. "They believed she arrived with you."

"They're mistaken," José said with a dismissive wave and a look of irritation. The look quickly resolved into one of revelation. He placed a forefinger to his mouth, and then shook it. "Come to think of it, we did arrive at roughly the same time. I think I might have followed her right to Felix's table. I had no idea. Yes. I was as surprised as anybody when she sat there, but not really surprised. I know Felix's tastes."

"God rest his soul."

"God rest his soul," Barboza agreed.

"What did the whore look like?" Leal asked.

José described Olívia, down to her honey bangs.

"And she was English?" Leal followed up.

"Yes. Her Portuguese was not very good. When she and Felix talked, they mostly spoke in English. I've spent a good amount of time in America, and I'm very good at English. But she was not American. I know a little bit about dialects. She had a very British dialect. In fact, I think she mentioned being from London."

"And after dinner?"

"After dinner, we shared a cab. Felix's place is on the way here. So we dropped them, and that's the last I saw of them. It must have been around…." José turned to me. "What time did I get in last night?"

I had no idea how to respond. The truth, 4:15 a.m., was the wrong answer. I hesitated, just long enough for José to play it out.

"Around eleven?" he offered.

"Yes," I lied, "that is about right."

"So we must have dropped them around ten-thirty or so. Maybe a little later. Traffic was very bad last night. You know, she wanted to go out again. I remember that. She wanted to go dancing. But I don't think that was why she was so mad."

"And, of course, you were in all night after that," Barboza provided.

"Yes, yes. Susan. Or Suzanne. Or Suzie. Or something like that.

I think that's what she called herself. But of course, that wouldn't be her real name, would it?"

"Probably not," Barboza confirmed. "But if it's her street name, we may have some luck searching for a British prostitute who goes by the name of Susan. Thank you, José."

Leal pressed him for more details about the whore named Susan and why she was upset, but José demurred. He just could not be of more help regarding that matter. Finally, Barboza thanked José for his time and apologized for the bother.

"Think nothing of it. I was very fond of Felix. I hope you catch the whore. I'd like to do anything I can to help."

"I don't think we'll be troubling you again on this," Barboza replied. "You have been most helpful, as usual."

And they left.

They would not be back. I was certain of that. Nor would they ever find a British prostitute named Susan, since it was not her name. The woman they looked for was not British. No one on the street could or would ever identify her, and the investigators probably would never bother to look for her. Plus, she surely was dead. Murders involving prostitutes as suspects or victims, sadly, were too common in Rio, and rarely worth significant police pursuits. Soon enough, there would be another, more appropriate crime to divert Barboza and Leal. Poor Felix Kinghoff's murder would never be solved, and Olívia's might never be uncovered, especially if the current washed her body out to the sea, as it usually does with most of its rubbish.

I had provided the murderer with his alibi. I could have initiated justice. Instead, my duty in that moment was all too clear. Just as when I had burned José's clothes, I had had no choice but to perform my position.

There would be other opportunities. My time would come. I could not leave Olívia entirely to the eels, crabs, and sea worms. I would find out what happened to her, and respond. That duty was not of the man servant, but of the man.

The next morning was Sunday, the staff's day off. Late in the morning I slipped out. I caught the trolley to Copacabana. My niece

Júlia is a waitress down there. She does not work at either Cafe Bom or Novo Carioca Club, but she knows plenty of people, and the people she knows know people. A man named Luis led me to a man named Paulo, a waiter at the Novo Carioca Club.

We met in a *lanchonete* a few blocks inland. A corrugated tin shutter folded up against the facade, opening the place to the sidewalk and street, with no door. There were three cramped tables inside, two outside, and a couple more in the crack between that building and the next. Paulo sat at the back table in the alley, eating. He was a young man with bleached hair, and skin light enough so that he could pass for white. From the counter, I brought him a beer and myself a coffee, and joined him.

He leaned over the table to talk quietly, although no one was nearby to hear us. "Luiz said you're a man to be trusted and helped."

"I suspect that is because he wants to sleep with my niece," I said.

"Ha!" he replied. "I seriously doubt that."

"Well, I am sure he has his reasons. You, I am not so sure about. I want to talk to you about a certain party that was in the club the night before last. There is nothing in it for you. I have no money, except to buy you a beer. I have nothing to offer in return except my gratitude."

"Let's just say we have to stick together. And maybe because I like to be amused. And I think this could be amusing." Paulo waved his fork. "I think I know what party you want to talk about."

"There was a man, José, a big man, and a beautiful American woman, and perhaps some others."

"Yes, that was them. She was indeed beautiful. She lit up the place. I can't explain it."

"She sparkled," I said.

"Yes, that's it. She sparkled. There were three or four other men. Four, I think. Yeah. One came in with José and the woman. The others were already there. They were German."

"German?"

"The club caters to foreigners. There's always people of many nationalities, Americans, Brits, Argentines, French, Spaniards. All of us who work there are multilingual. That's why we're hired, because we speak other languages. I've got a knack for languages, including some German, and so they were seated in my area. But they spoke to me in Portuguese, and so I spoke to them in Portuguese," Paulo said.

"Do you know what they were there for?"

Paulo thought as he chewed on some tough pork. He washed it down with beer.

He lowered his voice conspiratorially. "They never think we're listening. Of course, we don't want them to think that. We don't even want them to see us, unless they need us. But listening is part of the fun, right? Especially in a place like Novo Carioca Club. We get so many interesting patrons. It's like a show, every night. And what we do with it! You should hear us back in the kitchen. It's a lot of fun."

He took a sip of beer. He waved the glass, and continued. "It's also a good strategy to get to know them. A good waiter always knows his patrons. It helps in knowing how to serve them."

"That I understand," I said. "What were they talking about?"

"Are you ready for this?" Paulo set down his beer. He lifted his fork, examined it, held it up, and then slashed it downward. *Go.*

"They were talking about smuggling Nazis in from Germany," he said. "Uh, huh! The war is ending for them. They're losing and they know it. There are people willing to pay big money to get to Brazil. That's what they said. That man, José, he made connections in America. The money was all set up. He needed safe houses. These other guys would be paid handsomely to take in these people until they could get established."

"What about the woman?"

"That's where it gets entertaining," Paulo said. "She was the show-stopper. Literally. I'm sure for most of the night she had no idea what they were talking about. Not a clue. I don't think she speaks a word of German or Portuguese. At any rate, she spent most of the evening dancing and drinking. She took turns with each of them. They kept her busy.

"But that one guy who came in with them, he got pretty drunk. They were dancing. And he must have shot off his mouth. He must have told her in English what they were up to. All of the sudden she stormed off the dance floor and charged back to the table.

"'José!' she screamed. 'How dare you!'"

"She said, 'How dare you?'" I asked.

"Yes. She said the Nazis had killed her brother. She said they can't do this. José told her to shut up and sit down, but she said she wouldn't. Then she started calling them all Nazis, in English, of course. José stood up and slapped her, so hard he knocked her down. The whole club went still, though there weren't many people left to see it."

"Then what?" I asked.

"She got up and ran out."

"Alone?"

"No," Paulo responded, holding up an index finger. "That one fellow ran after her. And then José got up and went after them."

"And then?"

"The end. They didn't return. The curtain came down on that show. Good night everyone. Standing ovation, except no one clapped. We all just looked away."

"What time was this?"

"We were close to closing, so it was around 3. I think the band even wrapped up at that point."

I bought him another beer and prepared to leave. I told him I hoped I saw him again someday. He said he would like that very much, and he took my hand.

I saw. Lonely. All I got was loneliness. We all yearn for compassion and love, some of us until we give up. For a young man like Paulo the longing can remain a confusing, elusive, teasing, taunting shrew.

The Novo Carioca Club was downtown, near the waterfront. I would never be allowed inside such a club, but I could get as far as the hat-check window. The attendant, as black as I am, took the ticket without a word. She vanished.

And then she returned with Olívia's beige bonnet.

Down the street was a small pier, old and empty. It occurred to me that might have been where Olívia and Felix had run. I walked its length, imagining the scene. If blood had splashed those planks, it would be impossible now to distinguish from the century of boat engine fluids, fish blood, abuse, and weathering that the wood had endured.

But there was something.

A snag of torn cloth, a few inches in length, caught on a nail head protruding from one of the planks. I pulled the cloth free. It was from a man's trousers, and it was bloody. I pressed it into my jacket pocket.

What had become of Olívia?

I stared off beyond the peninsula where Felix's body was recovered, toward the mouth of the harbor, where the river's current took most of its bounty. Past that lay the greater bay, and, finally, the sea. My gaze followed back and forth over the land. From the pier, a seawall extended fifty yards, giving way to boulders. Among the rocks I spotted something. A glint.

I ran back up the pier and along the seawall, and when I got close enough I saw that it was a woman's shoe. I climbed down as far as I could and grabbed it. Silver chains dangled from the buckles.

José had chosen his pretty, young American bride shrewdly. Her beauty and love for life made her an ideal companion tool, to soften business associates. Her lack of Portuguese or any other language but English would keep her largely ignorant of his activities. She knew no one else in Brazil, making her totally dependent on him. Her own tawdry past of reinventions should have kept her discrete, and indifferent to his activities.

But he had not factored the dangerous independence of Olívia's spirit, nor that her young soul had not yet been scrubbed of goodness. She still had standards. She still believed in love, even if it was never a consideration when she married him.

All the way back to the house I grew in admiration for her, for how she had overcome him, until she had gone off the end of the pier.

The house was mostly vacant and dark. I found José sitting in his den.

I waved Olívia's hat and threw it at him, spinning it like a discus. It sailed over his shoulder.

"What the hell's the matter with you!" he shouted. "Is that her hat? I told you. How dare you!"

"That is the last thing she said to you, is it not? 'How dare you!'"

"You are way over the line, you insolent, little, colored *paneleiro*! Get out of my house! You're fired!" He was up now, in a fighting stance. Those cheek and jaw muscles were taught. The bones beneath pressed like bricks. "Get out!"

"You killed her, didn't you?" I screamed back. It was the first time I had ever raised my voice at him.

"You are in way over your head, you fucking, little, cock-sucker. You have no idea. Get out now before you have to be carried out!"

I pulled Olívia's shoe from my coat pocket and held it up. José's eyes widened and then narrowed. I threw it at him and missed again. "I found that in the water! And then Felix!" I shouted. "Why? Just tell me why!"

"She was a fucking whore! A *puta*! What difference does she make? Nothing! People like her and you are not worth a why!"

"You cannot get away with it," I screamed. "Not this time!"

José scrambled for the end-table drawer. I knew what was in there.

He withdrew the revolver. With a slow, sizzling tone, he said, "I'll show you who gets away with things and who doesn't! Get down on your fucking hands and knees, before I blow your brains out. You worthless piece of shit. You are going to beg for your fucking life, while I show you who's the absolute master here, and who is the *preto*! Now!"

He thumbed back the hammer. Yet he did not point the muzzle at mc immediately.

I will never know why he hesitated in doing so, whether he was so arrogant that he believed I would obey his command to die in the position he demanded, whether he wanted to savor the moment, or whether he was bluffing. It was a split-second quandary I could not risk contemplating. I pulled *Avó* Ana's knife from its sheath and lunged. With a great uppercut, I plunged the blade into his throat and up into his skull. In that instant, his gun went off. The bullet took out the stuffed macaw, blasting it in two, with a puff of feathers.

José toppled backwards from my blow and fell from my knife. As his blood spilled onto his linen shirt and then the floor, I reached down and took his empty hand. I saw his glee as Olivia, pressing a wound in her abdomen, stumbled off the pier. I saw his rage as he dragged Felix to the edge and then kicked him over. After that I saw nothing. José was dead.

I took the fragment of Felix's pants from my pocket and shoved it into José's jacket pocket.

And then I ran. I ran, and left all of that behind.

It was so long ago now, and I have hidden it well. I built my walls around it. And yet, I tore down others around my soul. I reverted to something I had not been in decades. *Me*.

Among other things since then, I have taken a young lover, the waiter Paulo. We live in his flat, in a district much like the one in which I spent my childhood, on a street without a name, in a building crowded with people whom José's kind would never know.

Soon, I will take up the practice of *Candomblé*. I can make money as a seer. This is Rio. Foreigners will pay. Before I had met José, before I had seen him and convinced him to take me on, I was too young and too inexperienced. But now I have the life understanding and the rugged look of maturity, to know what I am doing, and to make people believe. I have earned all the wisdom I need.

Paulo loves me. I have filled the emptiness that had brought him so much ache. He has much to dream about, and I am encouraging him to pursue those dreams. But I do not love him, and I will not stay with him. When he is ready, I will leave and seek my own life at last. Paulo will not betray me. He cannot pursue his dreams if he ever lets anyone know that he shared his bed with another man. He will fully understand the walls he must construct. I will make sure of it.

I regret nothing regarding José. He is gone, and I do not ever fret that I killed him, or worry that the police might find and arrest me for his murder. A long time has passed. I am now but a single ant in these many teeming favelas, the crowded slums that make up the hidden background of Rio. If the police linked the fabric in José's pocket with Felix, the spineless investigators would conclude the case to be too messy to be worth solving anyway.

I am, at last, my own man.

Of Olívia, I think all the time—now that I know she lives, that she survived her fall from the pier.

Yes, Olívia lives!

I needed more knowledge if I were to pull off *Candomblé* in full confidence, and went downtown to find books. As I emerged from an ancient shop with a door on the alley corner, I saw her.

She was across the street, scooting from a cafe to cross a sidewalk for a taxi. She was alone, wearing a white, satin blouse tucked into a black, tight-fitting, knee skirt, with black, long gloves, and a black bonnet.

I stepped from the shadow and into the street, stopping for an automobile to pass. The driver honked at me.

That is when Olívia saw me too. She froze. She wiped her honey bangs from under her sun-glasses. She dipped the glasses to get a brighter look at me over the rims. She gave me that practiced smile: *pretend you didn't see this.*

And then she climbed into the cab and disappeared again.

I should have known. With someone, somehow, Olívia had caught herself another wave to ride.

## AUTHOR'S NOTES– SCOTT MICHAEL POWERS

UNLIKE THE MOVIE VERSION, which simply dumps the mystery altogether (along with some of the story's other more-delicious aspects), Truman Capote's tasty 1958 novella *Breakfast at Tiffany's* teasingly leaves unanswered the central question haunting the narrator and his friend: Whatever happened to Holly Golightly after she disappeared? Depending on the answer, Holly's escape from her New York troubles after being left by her Brazilian lover could be seen as bold and liberating, or as foolish and perilous.

For *Breakfast at Tiffany's*, it doesn't matter. Capote's unnamed narrator and the bartender Joe Bell knew Holly as a survivor. Holly was nothing if not a throw-forward, a mid-20<sup>th</sup> century model for independent women. She could take care of herself. Somehow, she'd make it, however messy her swath. Or so they hoped. They really, *really* hoped.

What could possibly go wrong?

Inspired by the endless possibilities in answer to that question when invited to participate in *The Masters Reimagined*, I imagined another such woman, calling herself Olívia, following such a trail not into romance with her newly-landed millionaire husband, but into the depths of deception and treachery. She has come to Brazil, a land of exoticism and mysticism, where surely there is enough magic to bring forth her champion.

*—SMP*

# REGARDING MR. BULKINGTON

## ELLE ANDREWS PATT

**W**onderfullest things are ever the unmentionable; deep memories yield no epitaphs; this six-inch chapter is the stoneless grave of Bulkington. ...Take heart, take heart, O Bulkington! Bear thee grimly, demigod! Up from the spray of thy ocean-perishing—straight up, leaps thy apotheosis!
~ *Herman Melville,* Moby-Dick

ISHMAEL'S BODY *lies still abed, his two daughters attending it. A small puddle mars the worn wooden floorboards beside them. Wet footprints trail across the small room to the open window, where flower-splashed curtains flutter in the brisk breeze that brings the sharp bite of ocean salt from the storm-heavy surf rolling ceaselessly upon the golden sand of the nearby beach.*

AS I, Ishmael, have ere spoken of other happenings stricken from my record of the events befalling the *Pequod* and her destruction by the white whale known as Moby Dick some thirty years ago, I wish now to write of one which will never pass my lips, but the unfolding of which I must acknowledge upon these pages, leaving this parchment and ink as lasting witnesses to the full and unadulterated glory of God's creative endeavors.

In the years since that singular disaster, though singular only to me, the apparent lone survivor, as Moby Dick had destroyed many a boat and other mighty bull whales have stove in whaling ships, most notably among them the Essex, only several years before we set sail from Nantucket aboard the *Pequod*, I have often lain awake of a moonless night seeing again the terrible surprise of answered destiny upon the face of Captain Ahab as the white whale bore him off into the unknown deep.

The concentric rings of the whirlpool that formed as the *Pequod* sunk pull at me still. Tashtego, Daggoo, and my man Queequeg, harpooners all, forever climb the masts and the water races upward. Ever practical, Tashtego strives to finish again his last earthly task, hammering home the nail to hold the flag which would determine the ship's setting of sails as it tattled on the wind. What strange twist of fate drew that sky-hawk to that particular dire, lonely spot upon the endless ocean in order to give the *Pequod* such a fitting tribute in celebration of her earthly demise?

In sooth, I watched in horror and longed for that bird to dive down and down and then flap free, lifting my tattooed savage above the waves as he climbed the sky like one of Helios' wild horses, even as I fought the pull of the ship and clung to the bit of board I had in hand to preserve myself. Queequeg's stout fingertips clinging to the mast were the last I ever saw of him. I stared at the tranquil wash of the waves over that mass grave for hours it seemed, but only minutes passed before his sealed and pitched coffin, which our carpenter had fashioned into a buoy, bobbed up beside me and a dark body rose from the depths to impel me aboard it before I should freeze to death there in the Pacific tropics on the Line.

But let me start at the beginning of this tale and relate to you, my faithful parchment, my loyal quill, both the things I knew then and the things I learned later. I'll speak as plainly as I can on the matter of Mr. Bulkington, he of the tall, fine form, the voice and rugged confidence of an Alleghany man, the deeply shadowed eyes and somber demeanor of a haunted man, for this is his story, not mine, not yet.


AS THE SAILORS lifted a cheer and broke once more into drunken song, Elias Bulkington's thoughts meandered again to the sea. Though not prone like some of his fellows to the sickness that caused the land to pitch and tilt for days after landing ashore, causing them to stagger bandy-legged about as if they were land-lubber greenhorns upon their first foray to the sea until they had quite expelled it with hard drink and the soft embrace of a woman or two, he did find it increasingly hard to tolerate the unmoving walls and still, trapped air of common rooms on land for any length of time. Although not born of the sea, his every cell longed to be sea-borne.

So it was not without some measure of relief that he felt that particular pull that had always seized him so inexplicably when his ownership changed hands, though he was faintly surprised by the speed of it. The investors had only split their company, the whalers paid shipboard and released, hours ago. Draining the remainder of the beer in his hand, Elias set the tankard aside, his gaze sweeping the room as he stood. Tucked in along the wall at the dining table across the room, a wiry, capable-looking man with thick blond hair slicked back behind his ears caught his eyes and held them. Elias recognized the look. It was one he saw often, though he couldn't know yet he would soon come to know this stranger so well and for so long.

Fastening his monkey jacket with sure fingers, he strode from the Sprouter-Inn into the frosted bite of a howling wind. Some good way along on his icy walk back toward the docks, he became aware of a cheery noise and laughing shouts behind him and turning, descried several of his recently decamped shipmates chasing after him, calling for him to turn back. With a sigh, for he had all his life drawn acquaintances about him like bees to some delectable long-throated flower, he slowed so that they might catch him up.

"Bulkington," the first of them huffed as he arrived in Elias's wake. "Don't tell us you are so soon quitting the night!"

Another, the ship's mincer, said between breaths, "Pray tell where you are rooming so that we may find you again on the morrow before we part ways to our wives and families."

"Sorry, brothers, I'm off tonight, Nantucket bound," he replied, although in truth, he knew not what yet lay in store for him come midnight. "Kiss your wives and children soundly and soon I'll see you on some gam along the Line."

"You're a tougher salt than I, Bulkington," said the mincer.

A multitude of hands patted his back and shoulders, various raised voices in the dark bidding him good voyages, though he did not stop, only continued plowing through the snow. Their merriment dropped off behind him, their calls fading into the night until he was alone in the winter's bluster, face to the wind as if already out at sea on watch.

On the docks, his feet carried him to the ship which had been home these four years past and up the thin ramp teetering in the teeth of the wind. He brushed the snow from his shoulders as he clattered through the cabin gangway and below decks, not caring that his master would hear him coming. A light burned yet beneath the cabin door. Elias knocked upon it without patience.

Captain Soring yanked it open. "You know already?"

"I do."

"Why, then, are you here?"

Elias drew back his right fist and let all his considerable strength uncoil from his shoulder and back, careful to follow through even as the backs of his fingers sung out upon landing on bone. The Captain staggered sideways, though being built stout, the man did not go all the way down. Blood sluiced down his face from the split skin of his cheek.

Elias shook out his fist, turning already on his heel.

The Captain did not follow him.

In the forecastle, he slung his sea chest atop his shoulder, then decamped to walk down the wharf, following his internal compass. The snow fell faster, the flakes larger. It began to cover the tramplings of the day. The wind rushed in his ears, hiding the sounds of any human life around him, but ropes and sails creaked and water slapped against the pilings.

A small packet rocked at the end of the last pier. A sailor shivered on watch along the rail. "You Bulkington?" the man shouted down above the growing gale.

"Yes."

"Pull up the plank behind you. We leave now."


"I WAS BORN IN A RIVER," Mr. Bulkington told me, once we had come to know one another.

"Beside a river, you mean," I said, because semantics matter, though he was not my student and I was not his teacher. Indeed, in our relationship, he taught me far more than he ever learned from me about the practicalities of a life without roots, though I returned the favor in the matter of history and the cultural references which so enriched our conversations regarding our shipmates and the many philosophical considerations that occupied our minds during the laborious daily toil a whaling ship requires.

"I was born in a river," he repeated, giving me that direct look of his meant to quell further interruption. "Beneath the water. My mother said that's why I seemed part-otter. She was indentured in childhood as an orphan and bonded yet again when she reached the age of majority. She spoke incessantly of the sea and we were on our way to see it when she fell ill. She made arrangements for my care and that was the last I saw of her."

"She died."

He shrugged. "It was the last I saw of her."


NANTUCKET SHONE under a layer of hard frost that crunched beneath Elias's boots. Every chimney sent tendrils of grey smoke spiraling into the moist still air. He stopped before the door that pulled upon his blood like the moon upon the tide. A young roman-nosed woman with large dark eyes answered his hard knock and led him into a shabby parlor where a man sat before a crackling fire in one of two chairs upholstered in a fancy floral print. Elias pulled his cap from his head, but the woman did not offer to take his coat.

His new owner gestured him around so that Elias's back was to the flames and eyed him with a glare from under his shaggy mane of grey. A massive scar bisected his cheek. He did not stand. His ivory leg tapped the floor as he gripped and released his thigh in a clasping grasp, worrying the fastening latched over his folded pants leg.

"Sir," Elias said.

"I've been guaranteed your helming skills. Told you have an unerring sense for direction and a nose for the Sperm."

"Yes, sir."

"Damn well better be worth your price. And I expect fresh provisioning. There will be no shoring."

"Yes, sir." He wondered if the man knew his true nature or thought him only a bonded servant with an unusual ransom.

"Report to the *Pequod*. Tell Captains Peleg and Bildad you are my shipkeeper."

Elias nodded, wondering if he'd be paid. He turned his cap within his hands.

"Go," the man said.

"May I say who sent me, sir?"

The man's eyes narrowed, glittering with the reflection of the flame. "I am Captain Ahab."

Elias nodded again and left, letting himself out into the bright, cold day. Two young maids bundled against the weather walked down the rutted street towards him. He took a deep breath and readjusted the duffle as he absorbed the fresh, salty air carrying the scent of fresh baked bread and wood smoke. The shingled houses lining the street, with their crooked garden walls and shutters closed against the cold seemed to him like grey ditty boxes meant to be lifted and set upon shelves. He couldn't imagine spending a night in one, let alone a lifetime.

The women passed him, both glancing his way, and then they dissolved into giggles, hiding their faces from him, although the older one looked back over her shoulder to see if he was watching. It was always so. If he wanted, he could catch up to them. Even the very best of good women would fold to him in a matter of days, if not hours. He turned instead in the other direction and headed back to where he had just come from, in search of the *Pequod* and a hot cup of coffee.

To his pleasant surprise, the *Pequod* was not only a sturdy, well-kept ship with a touch of barbaric, wild grace showing in her whale bone hardware, but, albeit with a side conversation between them as to the necessity of a shipkeeper given the quality of the positions already filled and a somewhat lengthy argument regarding his share, the Captains readily signed him on for pay before pointing him stern where he would bunk in steerage with the harpooners and craftsmen.

He worked alongside the seamen for several days, rigging and stowing extra sail and lumber and familiarizing himself with the stock and stores being brought aboard. He helped construct the live-stock pens and, on one blustery afternoon, hurried to help repair the odd baleen tent in which Captain Peleg sheltered from the cold as he surveyed the activity of the seaman and from which he bellowed directives to the mates as the mood struck him.

The evening Captain Ahab came aboard, the constant low tug deep in Elias's gut abated, an irritation he'd not been fully cognizant of until it released. When all but the two other mates staying aboard had trundled off to their hot suppers and shore beds, Elias presented himself at Ahab's service. The Captain waved him in. Without ceremony, he spread sea chart over sea chart upon the table in his cabin and so began their nightly ritual.


HERE, I, Ishmael, must inject and clarify, my loyal journal, that in striking my dear Mr. Bulkington from my record of the *Pequod*'s final journey, I endeavored to conceal him from the eyes of those readers in every way possible and so wrote at length of Ahab's solitary skills in navigating the hunt, of his knowledge in sighting the sun and stars and ability to re-magnetize our storm-lost compass, as I sought to explain the impulsive rashness which led him to destroy the quadrant by which he navigated.

While only flotsam to the waves of his condition and always at the mercy of the Anemoi, Bulkington could not be lost upon the seven seas any more than Moby Dick himself. This is the most abiding reason Ahab brought him aboard at great personal cost. In his monomaniacal passion for the white whale, Ahab could not leave anything to chance.

And just as Bulkington could not be lost, so, too, was he bodily aware of those toothed leviathans of the deep as they drew near, as surely as any of their normal oceanic prey might sense the great harm to befall them if they did not flee before the wide-open and ranging jaws, lest they join Jonah in his plight, yet fare not as well as he after they are devoured.

"I cannot be lost," he said one dark night as he passed Queequeg's pipe back to me. We had been most casually discussing our general direction of travel and whether it would soon bring us some place that whales might be when they are not on the Line in season.

I drew a long breath of the sweet smoke into my lungs and let it out slow. "How can that be," said I, at long last, and passed the pipe to Queequeg on my other side.

Bulkington did not reply.

We sat in a row on the quarterdeck, with our backs to the capstan.

Queequeg reached round past me to hand the pipe back to Bulkington.

The stars shone down upon us. Thousands and thousands of them. I had no more idea then of how to navigate by either the changing stars or the arc of the sun as Apollo commanded its constant presence each day than a babe in arms. Whole armies become lost on the march. How many of the ships that never return to safe harbor are simply navigated by error far from known shores until there is no hope they shall ever again come upon their own horizon? I said again, "How can that be?"

"He kekeno," Queequeg offered.

"No sabbee," said I.

"He swim-e sea doge-e."

"He swims like a sea dog?"

Queequeg nodded.

"And how would you know this?" I asked, since I had never seen Bulkington swim, even at the last brief port of call when a few of the crew took the opportunity to bathe in the warmer, though still frigid judging by their physical reactions, waters the *Pequod* now sailed.

"I see-e."

I took the pipe from a silent Bulkington. "That doesn't make him a sea doge-e," I said and took my puff.

"He sea doge-e," Queequeg pronounced with finality.

"He's late to bed," Bulkington said of himself and then took himself off below decks.


OUTSIDE THE WHALE'S Arm Inn, named after the one-armed proprietor's misfortune, a heavy fog rose in the pre-dawn hour, offering easy concealment as Elias waited for the men his master bade him meet and lead to the after-hold of the *Pequod*. There were already hammocks, new clothes, and pilot-cloth coats waiting for them. Ahab had stressed that Elias was not to say a word to anyone about them, seek them out after arrival, or in any way reveal their presence aboard the ship.

The street was still dark and empty, but the residents were beginning to stir. A cough, one lamp lit, then two, then more. The slam of a door, a rattle of cooking pots.

He kicked off the shingled wall when the door to the inn creaked open. An ancient Asian man slipped out. In a long caftan, with his white hair wrapped round and round his head like a living turban, he carried a ditty box under one arm and cradled three harpoons in the other. He was what Elias had heard called a Parsee aboard a ship on which he'd served. A Persian fire-worshipper. The Parsee's four slight cohorts did not seem quite the same as he, but were also, by their appearance, of some Eastern tribe. Elias well-knew, though, that appearances could be deceiving.

"*Pequod*," Elias said and held out his hands in offer.

The man nodded and handed Elias his wooden box.

They stole along the inner edges of the deepest shadows, sound-less on the churned ice, careful due to the same along the boards of the wharf, but the dark ships yet rolled upon the gentle swells in slumber. No ray of the sun penetrated the bitter cold gloom.

Aboard the *Pequod*, Elias saw them settled and was just accepting a cup of steaming coffee offered to him in the tiny galley by the steward, Dough-boy, when two sets of footfalls traversed the planks to the deck. He listened to them go forward of the mast and relaxed as the ship once again fell into a tranquil peace, though it did not last long.

Late that day, following the flurry of last minute double-checks; the seeking of storage for the final goods brought aboard; the excited distance-shredded last shouts of the Captains and final good-byes; once the pilot's boat began to drift away from the *Pequod*'s scrubbed, caulked, and voyage-readied hull, Elias shifted his hand on her jaw-bone tiller and surveyed the ship laid out before him. A seaman moving aft to a rigging order shouted by Chief-Mate Star-buck caught his eye. A wiry build, a bit taller than average, with greased blond hair tucked behind his ears. The seaman looked up and froze.

The man at the Sprouter Inn's table back in Bedford. He was the same. He felt the same and Elias knew this must be a manifesta-tion of his condition, but one he'd never experienced before. The man moved on and Elias scanned the rough seas before letting his attention settle on Ahab's stiff back as the *Pequod* drove forward into the salty, stinging wind.

Hours later, retiring for a few hours before the next watch, Elias made his way to steerage only to become more and more confused by the pull within him with every step closer. On the threshold, he came nose-to-nose with the blond man and those blue eyes that had burned like an afterimage in his mind since he'd seen them on deck. "Seaman aren't allowed behind the mast."

A sleepy voice rose from the furthest of the ten steerage bunks. "Mine."

"Excuse me?" Elias barked in the voice of command he'd learned from hearing it directed at him on innumerable occasions.

The blond said, "I'm his..."

"His what?"

"Second?" said the man like he was asking Elias himself if that was what he might be, although Elias, of a certain, wouldn't know since they had never met before this instance.

With surreal grace, a giant of an islander rolled out of the lower bunk from which the voice had issued, immediately gained his feet, and filled the narrow aisle. The dark crevices carved into his face under the dim light of the two lit lamps soon resolved themselves under Elias's focused gaze as tattooed cannibal marks.

A harpooner.

"Mine. You fight-ee. I kill-ee you."

Harpooners get what they want, if they're good at their jobs. Bulkington raised his hands, palms out. "Yours."

The blond stuck his hand out. "Call me Ishmael. That's Queequeg."

Bulkington's eyebrows rose of their own accord. What had Ishmael's mother called him?

"I'm due on watch," the blond continued after a long moment and it occurred to Bulkington that he'd stalled in the cabin door. Flustered, a rare and unusual condition for him, he stepped back so that Ishmael could come through into the passage.

As Ishmael ascended to the top deck, Bulkington called out, "Elias Bulkington. Pleased, I'm certain, to make your acquaintance."

Ishmael waved a hand back over his shoulder as he disappeared into the dark.

ONE BLUE, calm morning as we seaman worked the bailing line, Queequeg came striding along the deck railing, peering with no small intensity into the ocean below us. Recalling his heroic dive into the frigid waters of New Bedford from the little Moss to save a man overboard, I wondered if he was not contemplating a similar action. No lookout had fallen from the mast as yet, but men could go missing in other ways.

"Man overboard?" I asked as he brushed past me.

"Kekeno fish-ee."

"Bulkington?"

Ere the wind whipped his name away from my lips, the man to my right started and I descried a furrow of sea water aimed like the famed Samurai Minamoto no Tametoto's arrow and the *Pequod* a Taira ship. Shying away from the impact, we split ranks as a silvery mass tore through the current into the sky and fell among us to the deck. While we stared in cold shock at the great flopping fish, Queequeg fell upon it. Another came flashing through the air, a brilliant reflection of the blazing sun, to thump off Queequeg's back and fall thrashing to the deck even as blood flowed beneath him and he held the first fish's head up in triumph, which he had torn off by hand, while yelling some combination of gleeful exhortations in his own savage language.

Another seaman corralled and lifted the second fish with both hands. The great thick beast stretched from his neck to his ankles in length. Tearing my rapt gaze from these marvelous sights, I leaned over the rail, but Bulkington was nowhere to be seen. Shouts before the mast drew my curiosity and presently Second Mate Stubb began a kind of lively jig, singing out about a mermaid climbing the bow, which quick brought Third Mate King-post to his side to see it.

Bulkington, naked as the David and as fine a figure despite his greater years, climbed the railing and dropped with a light, near predatory, tread upon the boards, water streaming from him. His tawny skin was not bisected at the lines of his normal clothing, but covered his entire expanse in a most curious way that spoke of sun-baked sand on hidden isles, the kind where those delightful Polynesian girls have escaped the notice of the Quakers. Looking neither left nor right, he proceeded straight to Ahab, who stood unmoving in his usual spot before the mizzen shroud. Ahab nodded. His lips formed some sparse phrase I could not hear.

Bulkington lifted his head, turning his face to me as if sensing my gaze upon him.

And then he smiled, nay, grinned, which transformed his fierce visage in a most fascinating way.


IT TOOK some time for Elias to notice his raised heartbeat, the deeper rush of his breath, the uneasiness of his mind, so subtle were his unusual senses and so mild the threat that lay far beneath and leeward of the *Pequod*. The tiller lay shivering against his knee as the *Pequod* cleaved the heavy seas beneath an overcast sky. The water was yet blue. No portents loomed.

Biding his time, Elias split it between tracking Ahab's pacing strides in case the Captain should signal him for a change of direction, and idly exploring his curious inability to ignore Ishmael's presence wherever he might be aboard. Currently, Ishmael and Queequeg were weaving a sword mat, presumably for Starbuck's whale boat on which they crewed. Ishmael's gaze lay locked upon the work, but Queequeg's lingered on the far horizon, his arms and hands busy and competent without his heed.

When Tashtego eventually came through the stern gangway and onto the top deck for duty, Elias beckoned the native Gay Header to his side. "Keep a close eye on the seas, Tashtego, I've a feeling of whale today."

"Cap'n Ahab been say'n the same for weeks."

"Hast I?" asked Elias.

Tashtego frowned at him. "Why should ye?"

Laying a finger alongside his nose, Elias then flicked it forward toward the bow and the ocean beyond. "Watch leeward."

Pursing his lips, Tashtego watched him with regard for a long moment and then nodded. Elias watched him swagger to his duty and shout up at the lookout on the main mast. The man scrambled down, his feet barely touching the planks before Tashtego was clambering up to the cross-trees in his place.

Not long after, no more than another sultry hour, a long, undulating cry burst from Tashtego as he sighted a sperm whale's spout, the only kind he got paid to sing for on the *Pequod*. He sung out loud again, the sound dropping like a dream through the rigging to pool over the somnolent ship-hands below. All hands scrambled to hunting stations as Ahab bellowed, his voice cracking like a bull whip. Another shipkeeper ran to take Tashtego's place as the line tubs were snatched up and positioned.

In minutes, the boats swung out over the sea and the crews were mounting the railing and gunwale preparing to board them when Elias saw the white-hair-turbaned Parsee darken the hatchway from below. In a rumpled black Chinese jacket and black wide-legged pants, he made for a striking interloper as he stepped onto the *Pequod*'s deck for the first time since Nantucket. His dusky fellows in white formed a cloud around him that slunk starboard across the deck to Ahab's side where Ahab stood next to the Captain's whale-boat, a nominally designated spare that not even Elias, who had both brought the stowaways aboard and helped the carpenter customize for Ahab's unique needs, thought that the one-legged Captain would ever use.

The cessation of action at port drew his attention. He sought out Ishmael, who, like the others, was gaping at Ahab's secret crew. But the slither and clank of the spare boat's tackle and strapping had him whipping his head back to the only movement aboard as the *Pequod* climbed a soft swell and dropped into the gully left behind. Ahab's stealthy, swift crew expertly attacked the task of readying his boat. Elias held the tiller steady, glancing upward to check the mainsail was properly backed as Ahab spoke to the Parsee.

"Lower away!" Ahab bellowed and every man leapt back into action at the lash of his voice.

The boats splashed in on both sides. A seaman came running to take the helm, freeing Elias to take charge of the ship. The oarsmen began stroking as soon as they hit the seats, strong backs to the chase as Starbuck, Stubbs, and Flask implored them to ever greater effort. Once they were clear by several hundred yards, Elias took stock of the remaining shipkeepers and then set to work sending the *Pequod* leeward in the wake of her whale boats. Not too far back in case of trouble and to be immediately on hand in the event of capture, not too close so as not to spook the whales into outright flight or interfere with the maneuverability of the crews on the water should a whale take an unexpected turn.

Two sultry hours passed in this manner, the overcast skies giving way to a darker threat. The water churned green beneath the bows. Dead ahead, two of the four boats had whales harpooned, but not lanced. Heat lightning sheeted the horizon before the lowering clouds sunk upon the water.

"Back the main, trim all sail," Elias shouted at his skeletal crew. "Light lamps!"

They drifted into the mist. Stubb's voice was the first to reach their ears before the boat prodded the port side as if it were a whale calf bumping up to its mother to nurse. "Ha ha ha! Damn me," he said, laughing in the way he was wont to do. "Cutting that line was like cutting me own arm off, so reluctant was I!"

Ahab came next, and then Flask, but Starbuck's boat, and, by dint of being part of its crew, Queequeg and Ishmael, remained lost to the fog. Raindrops pattered against the rise and sickening drop of the tossing ship. Ahab took his position on the quarterdeck with a sharp nod to Elias, who strode back, handhold to handhold on the rigging and frame, to the helm, though he left the tiller in the seaman's hand.

The rain loosened its grip on the heavens and fell in pounding gales, bringing the blackest night down with it. The wind howled. Waves crested over the railing, sweeping the deck. Ahab ordered the ship kept on the current, drifting as the boat would, and the lamps kept lit. He retired to his cabin with a final admonishment. "Feather that tiller, Bulkington. I need Starbuck and that cannibal harpooner for Moby Dick."

Once the storm crested and waned, the *Pequod* dripped rain-water from her spars and booms and furled sails, her railings and spare boats and tryworks. The long hours of the morning watch dragged by as Elias waited to feel the tenuous connection that had sparked within him the first time he laid his gaze upon Ishmael in New Bedford. It had strengthened enough that he knew there was something about it he had never experienced before, but wasn't strong enough for him to trust he'd know if it were broken.

The forced link to Ahab remained stronger. He had but to close his eyes and concentrate to feel the man's heartbeat beneath his skin. He burrowed under it, seeking Ishmael's, finding only a flutter and a sensation of cold that fled along his limbs and then abandoned him. Maybe only his own nerves.

Dawn brought only a dense fog. They sailed silent, save for the creaking of their ropes and yards, now tacking across the current in a search pattern. Ahab came on deck. He didn't bother to ask about their bearings. There was no way to take them and after the many months together, Ahab had learned his money was well spent. Elias knew exactly where they were and had kept them close enough.

"They are gone," said Ahab in a hushed tone, as all men speak on such a morning. "But there'll be no sighting whales in this soup. Mayhap we'll come across an oar or a lance to carry home."

No sooner had the words left his mouth than a grinding bump and crack split the descending return to silence. Perth, the blacksmith, and Dough-boy, the steward, slippery-slid along the wet planks to either side of the bow. "Can't see anything, sir," Perth yelled over his shoulder.

A terrible thumping issued from beneath the boat. "Hold the tiller!" Ahab shouted back to the helm.

The sturdy keel would be unlikely to suffer damage and they could do without it, but Elias's belly still rolled at the awful noise. He lifted his head at Dough-boy's two-armed wave, feeling a sudden yank at his core at the same time. Dough-boy cupped his hands to his mouth and yelled, "Men overboard!" from starboard just as cabin boy Pip sung out the same, pointing from his perch aboard the capstan to port. Perth ran down the railing, shouting to the men in the water. He grabbed and threw a buoy. Ahab added his voice, shouting at the shipkeepers on the masts. Elias bolted to the stern, grabbing seamen and rope as he went. The mangled whale boat finally cleared the *Pequod*'s beam, bouncing into her wake.

Nothing builds a salt's trust in his fellows or his ability to lean into a common cause quite like a whaler and the unique dangers it presents. Whether in empathy or just because there was work to be done, the soaked and shivering boat crew was soon dragged aboard.

Queequeg shook like an overly exuberant hound, but appeared none the worse for wear. He lifted Elias from his feet in a cold bear hug before twisting his head to look all around. "Ishmael?" he grunted, releasing Elias of a sudden, so that he overbalanced and only a firm hold on his arm from the savage kept Elias from falling. "Ishmael," Queequeg shouted.

"Here," Perth answered from further astern. Peering over the railing and sighting along the side of the ship, Elias descried Ishmael being dragged upward. Ishmael glanced up and over, locking his eyes with Elias. That odd connection surged.

"Bulkington!" Ahab called.

Tightening his lips against the oath that sprang to them, he tore his gaze from Ishmael and spun away towards his master, noting as he did that Queequeg broke into a trot in the opposite direction to help bring Ishmael aboard.


FAITHFUL PAPER, committed quill, you are the keepers of my most secret words. I think here is when we both knew that if life so fated, as I cleaved to my bosom-friend Queequeg, closer still would I hold to Elias Bulkington, even though our intersecting lives might last but one day or one hundred years longer. I knew not then anything of him beyond the wish to be near him when he was near. Only later would I wish to be near him when he was far from me, a function, I believe, of our metaphysical bond. I often wonder now if the Parsee, who so accurately foretold the future, ever whispered our secret into Ahab's ear.

That our bond nearly killed all of us upon that storm lost whale-boat as Elias followed it like a shark tracking blood scent, holding the *Pequod* steady on its line beneath his feet, is certain. That our connection, more intimate, as it often is, between men who have served a higher purpose together, who can understand one another's motivations and deepest philosophies in ways that a wife, being female, cannot, was strengthened and sealed by that event is also certain.

To be on the *Pequod* under Captain Ahab, with his iron will and monomaniacal obsession for the white whale, might be construed as a hardship, but there were also compensations. While most of the ship's company was not allowed shore leave, he allowed services and goods to come to us in port. We never suffered scurvy under Ahab, nor starvation. When hard tack and salt horse seemed to overcome our energies, we shared the fresh fish the officers alternated with their chicken and pork culled from the pens. In point of fact, due to Ahab's generosity and Bulkington's skills, we never lacked for fish, even when they ignored our hooks and lures.

We were allowed music and books. We sewed and carved scrimshaw. Most importantly, we formed our own associations. Never once did I see a man lashed aboard the *Pequod*. After coercing our agreement to his mad scheme, Ahab, for the most part, ignored us as long as we jumped to when he spoke. In turn, as long as he ignored us, we jumped to when he spoke.

Of Bulkington alone was Ahab impossibly both more dismissive and more demanding. But if he knew of the deep well of emotion that bound us one to the other, he did not care enough to deny us each other's company.

"I thought you drowned," Bulkington whispered in the dark, after Ahab had finally released him from his duties late on the night I was returned whole from the sea. We were what passes for alone. Perth, Dough-boy, King-Post, Daggo, and the carpenter slept hard at the front of the cabin. The cooper, Queequeg, Tashtego, Stubb, and Starbuck roamed above deck.

"What is it, between us?" I asked, even then aware of the inescapable pull between us.

"I cannot explain it," said he.

I did not believe him then, but he told the truth.


OTHERWORLDLY WAILS ROSE from the lulling sea near the Line. The *Pequod* rocked under a full moon. Recovered from the ordeal of the Typhoon and unable to sleep for the cries echoing around them, most of the crew ranged themselves along the railings or bulkheads

or sat along the crosstrees of the three masts, watching the silvery
slip of the whitewater pass below.

Elias, pressed thigh to thigh with Ishmael at the stern, watched
the dark slide of the seals as they surrounded the ship, calling and
crying out in the voices of long drowned sailors, calling out to him
in warning of what lay ahead. A shudder stole long his back.
Ishmael laid an arm around his shoulder. Queequeg crowded their
backs, his tomahawk pipe lit. He drew long draughts into his deep
lungs and released it slowly, spilling sweetly scented smoke over
them.

At last, just as the first rays of sun brought a weak grey light with
them, the seals fell away in small groups and the crew began to stir.
Ahab came up from whence he'd been sequestered with poor, addle-
brained Pip. On hearing his distinctive tread in the gangway, every
seaman scattered to his duty or his bunk. Ishmael's callused hand
warmed the back of Elias's neck before he was away with Queequeg
in tow.

Minutes later, a sleepy mast man dropped from the foremast
with a plunging cry. Elias leapt to his feet in time to see the man hit
the heaving swell. Near the life buoy per chance, Elias yanked it
from its spring and as the *Pequod* sailed by, flung it into the very spot
where the man had sunk, but no hand reached for it. Turning, he
met Ahab's stern frown, his fingers already at the hem of his shirt,
but Ahab gave a faint shake of his head.

The sun-dried buoy filled and sank along with Elias's spirits.

Ahab's message was clear.

There is danger afoot and all men shall heed it and respond with
their best effort or perish.

As if in illustration and punctuation of this message, though not
by Ahab's order, by day's end, Queequeg's coffin, built by the ship's
carpenter weeks before when it seemed Queegqueg would succumb
to a fevered illness, and which, by his best effort, Queequeg had put
aside once he decided to live, had been caulked and sealed and in
complete reverse of its previous intended purpose, dangled from the
stern hook as the new last line of defense in support of life.

Elias spent the next two days in a furtive hunt for that which would sustain him in light of the dire dread slithering heavy through his gut. Already he could feel the chill of the deep seeping into his vulnerable flesh and he wanted it, welcomed it, wished more than anything to be gliding the cold darkness of the water below, following the mast man's bubbles down to where he rested now.

But his hands did not find the silky comfort he sought and his aching heart only led him back to Ishmael.

AND ERE I, Ishmael, have recorded in my previous writings the events that followed, our meeting with the Rachel, the tragic physical revelations of the Parsee's prophesies once we chanced upon that white monster of a whale who probably yet plies the seasonal grounds of his tribe, I will not dredge them up yet again.

After my beloved Queequeg, outlasting my very heart, the graceful Mr. Bulkington, disappeared beneath the cascade of swirling sea that spun the *Pequod* down into Poseidon's mighty arms along with the sailors who have cleaved to my soul in such ways that I had never known ere I stepped into Peter Coffin's inn in New Bedford, I contemplated the weltering sea left behind, keeping my chin just above it as I treaded the deep, cold water far from any ship or shore.

Sperm oil spread along the surface from broken casks, soon to reach me if I did not swim further away. Sharks circled, their fins cresting as they rose to snap at the floating debris—bits of the harpoon boats and shattered wood from the ships, shirts, the red cap of the mizzen mast lookout, a bit of spare sail, lengths of hemp rope and line—and then disappeared as they dove after the fleshy morsels of the dead or dying below.

A colder pool of water rushed up my legs and torso. On instinct, I kicked away, expecting jaws to close around me, mayhap even Moby Dick rising to take his final revenge, but instead, Queequeg's coffin cum life buoy bobbed up immediately beside me. Disbelieving my good fortune even as I reached for it, I cried out when a firm bump from a solid body propelled me halfway aboard the unexpected gift.

Scrambling all the way on top, which lifted me above the water by a full hands-breadth, I waited, breathless, for the shark to make a more direct attack. Instead, a large grey seal, quite out of its range, lifted its silvery head to consider me from its great round dark eyes. Ducking its head, it turned flippers and dove below to circle my new circumstance. Expecting it to overturn me and claim my perch at any moment, I kept a wary eye upon its repeated circumnavigations about myself and the wider area around and through the drifting wreckage of the *Pequod* until the horizon doused the waning sun.

Sometime in the night, I dozed. I do not to this day know if it were real or only my fevered imaginings that included the odor of my savage's pipe drifting on the ocean breeze and Bulkington's breath upon my neck, but I do remember lifting a hand to stroke the head of the seal as it rested its chin upon my coffin and the soft splash as it withdrew into the Line's inky depths once more.

SEVEN YEARS PASSED as if in a dream after I departed the Rachel and her bereaved Captain at Honolulu. I spent it island hopping, then on cargo ships. I saw Peru and Greece and the west coast of Africa from shore. I worked as a bargeman on the Thames, which seemed but a canal to me. Remembering the Manxman aboard the *Pequod*, I took passage to Ireland and from thence to the Isle of Man where I found my wife and home.

My thoughts were ever on Bulkington, Queequeg, and my time aboard the *Pequod*.

One dark afternoon, as I walked on the north shore watching a storm come in, I descried a tall, lean man with dark hair lifting in the breeze waiting for me at the head of the path on which I would return home. His form appeared familiar to me and yet I could not place him until I was nearly upon him.

My vital essence fled with recognition. I fell to my knees before my dear Bulkington, scarce conscious as he sunk and embraced me. "But, how," I cried. "How is it that you should be here with me now?"

"You called me and I came. I would have come, anyway."

I still did not understand. "But how did you find me?"

"I am never lost and you are here, inside me," said he.

"But where have you been these past seven years?"


ELIAS LET GO of the *Pequod*'s tiller as Tashtego's hammer fell silent, Starbuck ran forward, and the crew at the bow froze, all eyes upon the white whale spying them above a semi-crescent of broad spray as he made his run upon the ship. Reading the whale's intent, Elias made a mighty leap from the quarterdeck to the planks below, the ship shifting further beneath him when Moby Dick's head met the starboard bow. Seamen fell and slid across the wet wood, the great thud and crack of splintering wood echoing across the deck. Water rushed in, a roaring Niagara that flooded the forecastle below.

A hardy whistle caught his ears. Wavering off-balance, Elias stretched his hand up without thought to catch the spotted coat Pip flung at him from the cabin gangway. Understanding in an instant, he clutched it to him. Heavy and slick, the weight bore him down and seconds later, he was spinning, legs underwater, caught up in the sucking swirl of the sinking ship.

A heavy body blundered into him and grabbed a hold of the coat. For a moment, he and Queequeg spun as one, staring into one another's startled faces. Elias saw the knowing there, deep in Queequeg's eyes. The savage bastard grinned and let go. The vicious whirlpool took Queequeg under and whipped the coat around Elias, entangling him before the water closed over his head.

He had longed to wear it, it seemed, from the day of his birth. Now he fought to free himself from its silky confines before it drowned him. He stretched for the pinpoint of surface he yet could see above him beyond the writhing seamen fighting for their lives. His jaw exploded in agony from a wayward booted kick and darkness descended as the *Pequod*'s hull lolled over and rolled and then all was lost.

Still sinking and disoriented, Elias kicked and stretched and kicked again, his feet together, in the instinctual way he always swam, his mother's voice bright in his head, "Little seal, little otter, little fish, swim, swim away, as fast as you can. Now come, little seal, little otter, little fish, come to me, to the sea, as fast as you can!"

When he broke to the surface, his nostrils flared, absorbing the salt of the sea spray, heavy and fresh, the tang of blood, the musk of whale oil, the layers of scent he recognized as the men he served with, tar, and brick and wood and hemp and canvas and the wet, lost ash of the try works, all tangled and smashed. Ishmael's pull and scent lay hard to port.

Elias swam close to him, following in slow circles as Ishmael orbited the weakening vortex of the *Pequod*'s death spiral. But Ishmael did not notice him. When at last a great bubble of black air rose upward and burst above the gentle billowing swells, Elias dove down and down past the corpses and wreckage to Queequeg's coffin wagging above the point of the stern where it stuck up at an angle in the dark as it continued to sink. He nosed at the spring-loaded hook until it gave way and released.

UNBOUND EXCEPT IN the matter of his soul, the Isle of Man did not scorch Bulkington's feet. We passed many a happy year and long hours of contemplation in the sun and under the stars together as my children grew to adulthood. And while he remained a somber fellow, who sometimes sat for hours on the sand, his gaze on the sea, so, too, did our antics bring that brilliant smile from his uncharted depths to transform him and send him laughing in chase of the children or myself, his longing left far behind.

But the day came too soon when I awoke with the knowledge that he had already left me. The damp, cool air made gooseflesh of my arms and back as I walked barefoot through the house to check the empty hook by the door. My wife sat just outside on the stoop, a basket of warm eggs beside her. "Go," she said.

On the beach, the curling surf lapping at his feet, he stood naked, his face to the sun, his prior ransom—his spotted, silver coat, his true skin—over his arm as he waited for me. I took it from him, and he let me, before I leaned in to embrace him and memorize the heat of his skin, the shift of his muscles beneath his bronzed skin, the strength of the connection never lost between us from the first day to this one, that I hope might last beyond my dying breath that I might find him again.

"I have to go," he said.

"Will you be back?" said I.

Unwilling to lie to me, he only kissed each of my cheeks and then bowed his head and knelt before me. I spread his seal skin wide, draped it over his shoulders, and kissed his head. He rose and turned to the surf. Already, the skin was closing around him, becoming his once more. He stretched his arms one last time and leapt, diving into the next wave, and then he was gone.

My mute witnesses. Here is where I leave my tale and lay you aside forevermore. I have told all I might. With November mired in my soul, I came to the *Pequod* seeking Spring and found it.

ISHMAEL'S BODY *lies still abed, his two daughters attending it. A small puddle mars the worn wooden floorboards beside them. Wet footprints trail across the small room to the open window, where flower-splashed curtains flutter in the brisk breeze that brings the sharp bite of ocean salt from the storm-heavy surf rolling ceaselessly upon the golden sand of the nearby beach. The journal upon Ishmael's desk lies open and damp. The pen, freshly inked.*

I am Elias.

He called and I came.

Publish this record.

And un-mute the voices of our kind.

## AUTHOR'S NOTES- ELLE ANDREWS PATT

NO ONE KNOWS the actual reason why Herman Melville decided to have Ishmael take such notice of the sailor Bulkington, but many theories have been advanced. Some think Bulkington may have been the prototype companion supplanted by the subsequent appearance of Queegqueg, but Melville could not bear to strike him altogether. Or perhaps he was simply the "other", representing the multitude of unknown sailors who live upon the sea and die there with no one to tell their individual stories. To Q.D. Leavis, he represented Melville's quintessential American folk-hero. Jonathon Cook proposes him as Melville's nod to Hercules. Just this year, Brian R. Pellar has presented Bulkington, a Southerner, as one of the many devices Melville used to advance Moby Dick as an anti-slavery allegory.

For me, as a writer of speculative fiction, Bulkington represented a wonderful opportunity to exploit the opening Melville left in his Moby Dick canon by dropping helmsman Bulkington from the narrative just after the *Pequod* sets sail. Ishmael has waxed poetic over Bulkington, we know Bulkington is aboard the *Pequod*, and Ishmael is the only survivor. Why does he not share Bulkington with us as he does all the other named characters aboard the *Pequod?* Why, instead, does he imply Bulkington is an unmentionable "wonderfullest thing" of whom he has deep memories, that Bulkington is trapped between the sea and land like humanity between heaven and earth, is, in Ishmael's memories, nothing short of a demigod, yearning to be free of his mortal boundaries? Ishmael must be hiding something, right?

**The Legend of the Selkie:** While the origin of the legend is almost definitely rooted in a combined Celtic-Norse tradition, selkie/silkie/selchie lore has spread and other versions have taken root. There are many different versions of the selkie legend. In the most well-known the written Irish folklore, the selkie is a female seal who sheds her skin to reveal her human form. She is usually beautiful and attracts the notice of a young, male fisherman as she suns herself or dances in the moonlight upon the shore. Knowing he can bind the selkie to him by doing so, the young man sneaks up upon the selkie, steals her sealskin, and hides it.

The young man takes the selkie as his wife and a happy marriage is formed, although occasionally the selkie wife sits upon the beach to longingly watch the sea. On one such day, her children run up to her to ask what it is they've found hidden in the attic. Although she loves her children, she takes her sealskin from them and unable to resist the temptation, returns to the sea, leaving her husband bereft. Unable to return to her human form for years to come, she still occasionally returns to swim with her children as a seal.

In the Scottish version, the selkies are male and female. Both easily attract amorous human attention. A woman can perform a rite which includes shedding seven tears into the ocean to call a male selkie to her. The selkie often forms a lifelong bond to a human, sometimes to the person who first steals their skin, sometimes to the person who sheds seven tears into the ocean. Often, once the selkie slides back into their sealskin, they can not transform back for a set amount of time. Many writers and artists have created their own unique takes on the selkie legend.

You can find a FREE download of *Moby-Dick* at Project Gutenberg.

*—EAP*

# ABOUT THE AUTHORS

JADE KERRION
E.J. WENSTROM
T.L. WOOLSLEY
KEN PELHAM
KRISTIN DURFEE
JOHN HOPE
BRIA BURTON
VERONICA H. HART
SCOTT MICHAEL POWERS
ELLE ANDREWS PATT

# JADE KERRION

*"...This is the kind of series you'd expect to see with a movie deal"*
—Full Time Reader, *Amazon Reviewer*

USA Today bestselling author Jade Kerrion defied (or leveraged, depending on your point of view) her undergraduate degrees in Biology and Philosophy, as well as her MBA, to embark on her second (and concurrent) career as an award-winning science fiction, fantasy, and contemporary romance author.

Her debut novel, *Perfection Unleashed*, published in 2012, won six literary awards and launched her best-selling futuristic thriller series, *Double Helix*, which blends cutting-edge genetic engineering and high-octane action with an unforgettable romance between an alpha empath and an assassin.

*Earth-Sim* and *Eternal Night* won first place Royal Palm Literary Awards in the Young Adult and Fantasy categories respectively. *Life Shocks Romances*, Jade's sweet and sexy contemporary romance series, features unlikely romances you will root for and happy endings you can believe in. They prove that, at the very least, she knows how to alphabetize books.

If she sounds busy, it's because she is. Jade writes at 3:00 am when her husband and three sons are asleep, and aspires to make her readers as sleep-deprived as she is.

**www.jadekerrion.com**

# E.J. WENSTROM

E. J. Wenstrom is a fantasy and science fiction author, lover of monsters and consumer of stories from Washington, D. C. She is the creator of the *Chronicles of the Third Realm War* series starting with Florida Writers Association's 2016 Book of the Year *Mud*.

"Twisting and Turning, Mud won't let itself be defined or outsmarted…I'm hopelessly addicted."

—*Readers Lane*

The *Chronicles of the Third Realm War* prequel, **Rain**, is a stormy and seductive romance that will introduce you to the series' rich fantasy world.

*Tides, Chronicles of the Third Realm War* #3, releases in Fall 2017.

**www.ejwenstrom.com**

# T.L.WOOLSLEY

T. L. Woolsley is the pen name of writer Kim Campbell, who lives and works in the Fort Lauderdale area. She has been interested in science fiction since junior high, when she discovered that those fascinating creatures, boys, read SF, too. Then it was re-runs of "Star Trek" after school and "Dr. Who" (the fourth Doctor) on Friday nights…

Freelance nonfiction writing honed much of her writing skills while college, a career in public relations, and life experience rounded out the skills she brings to the page.

She is managing editor at a book publishing firm in Fort Lauderdale. At night and on weekends she writes short stories and works on *Whisper Sister*, a novel about a woman running a speakeasy in 1929 New Orleans.

Visit T. L. at **www.tlwoolsley.com** for updates on her work, and ramblings on writing, life, and the writing life.

# KEN PELHAM

Ken Pelham's debut novel, *Brigands Key*, winner of the 2009 Royal Palm Literary Award, was published in hardcover in 2012, in softcover in 2014, and in audiobook in 2015. The prequel, *Place of Fear*, a 2012 first-place winner of the Royal Palm, was released in 2013. A short story, "The Wreck of the Edinburgh Kate," garnered a second-place award in 2014.

His book on the craft of writing, *Out of Sight, Out of Mind: A Writer's Guide to Mastering Viewpoint*, won the Florida Writers Association's highest award—2015 Published Book of the Year—and has been translated into Italian, Spanish, and Portuguese.

Ken grew up in the small South Florida town of Immokalee, and lives with his wife, Laura, in Maitland, Florida. A member of International Thriller Writers and the Florida Writers Association, he's sometimes spotted cycling, fishing, or scuba diving, seldom simultaneously.

NOVELS
*Brigands Key*
*Place of Fear*

NONFICTION BOOKS
*Out of Sight, Out of Mind: A Writer's Guide to Mastering Viewpoint*
(2015 Florida Writers Association Published Book of the Year)
*Great Danger: A Writer's Guide to Building Suspense*

SHORT STORY COLLECTIONS
*Treacherous Bastards: Stories of Suspense, Deceit, and Skullduggery*
*A Double Shot of Fright: Two Tales of Terror*
*Tales of Old Brigands Key*

**www.kenpelham.com**

# KRISTIN DURFEE

Kristin Durfee grew up outside of Philadelphia where an initial struggle with reading blossomed into a love and passion for the written word.

She is currently working on several projects, including the next book in the Four Corners Trilogy, a new novel for Young Adults, and her first full-length suspense novel for Adults.

Kristin currently resides outside of Orlando, FL, and when not enjoying the theme parks or Florida sun, she spends most of her time with her husband and their quirky dogs.

She is a member of the Florida Writers Association.

PUBLISHED NOVELLAS
*Revenge From Within*
(*The Hunt 2* Suspense Anthology)
"Project Bright Star"
(*Return to Earth* Anthology)

PUBLISHED NOVELS
*Four Corners*
(Four Corners Trilogy Book 1)
*Two Worlds*
(Four Corners Trilogy Book 2)

UPCOMING NOVELS
*One Earth*
(*Four Corners Trilogy* Book 3)

**www.kristindurfee.com**

# JOHN HOPE

John Hope is an award-winning short story, children's book, middle grade, young adult, and nonfiction writer. His work appears in paperback, hardback, audiobook, and multiple short story collections. He gives informational and inspirational presentations to schools, conferences, and is a board member of the Florida Writers Association. John loves to travel and play games with his wife, Jaime, and two rambunctious kids.

## CHILDREN'S PICTURE BOOKS
*Frozen Floppies**— Story of Unlikely Friendships
*Floppyopolis*—Story of Taking Pride in the Community
*Watch the Butterfly*—Story of Learning Patience
*The Band Aid*—Story of Understanding/Dealing with Grief

## MIDDLE GRADE / YOUNG ADULT
Silencing Sharks*—*Fantasy/Adventure Story of Heroism*
No Good*—*Historical Fiction Story of Acceptance*
Pankyland*—*Adventure Story of Friendship*
Pankyland 2: The Movie—*Adventure Story of Sibling Rivalry*

## BOOKS FOR ADULTS
Colby in the Crosshairs*—*Poignant Story of Child Abuse*
John's Shorts Vol 1* & 2*—*Collections of Short Stories*
Lake Mary, Images of America—*History of a Small Town*
* Indicates winner of one or more awards

**www.johnhopewriting.com**

# BRIA BURTON

Bria Burton is a blogger and customer service manager at St. Pete Running Company. Her short fiction has appeared in over a twenty anthologies and magazines. *The Running Girls*, a novelette, is a 2017 Royal Palm Literary Award Finalist. Her novella, *Little Angel Helper*, won a 2016 Royal Palm Literary Award. Two unpublished manuscripts have won First Place in the RPLA. As a member of the FWA, she has led the St. Pete chapter and served on the statewide FWA Board.

### NOVELS
*The Running Girls*
*Little Angel Helper*
*Lance & Ringo Tails*

### SHORT STORY PUBLICATIONS
"A Dream Within A Dream" – *Journey Into…podcast, In Shadows Written* anthology
"The Mute Girl" – *Youth Imagination, eFantasy*
"Tight Pants" – *Page & Spine*
"Ticket to Heaven" – *Faith, Hope, & Fiction*
"The Wheels Must Turn" – *Broken Worlds anthology*
"On Both Sides" – *The Prometheus Saga*
"In Line at the DMYV" – *Welcome to the Future anthology*
"Switching" – *The Dunesteef Audio Fiction Magazine*
"Ligeia" – *Journey Into…podcast*
"This is Hollywood" – *FICTION on the WEB*

**www.briaburton.com**

# VERONICA HELEN HART

Veronica lives with her retired veterinarian/author husband, Robert, in Ormond Beach, Florida. They settled there after spending the major part of their lives traveling, living, and working in various areas of the world. Between them, they have six daughters and eleven grandchildren who keep their minds active trying to remember birthdays and anniversaries.

PUBLISHED NOVELS

*The Prince of Keegan Bay* \*– Blenders Book I
*The Swimming Corpse* – Blenders Book II
*Safari Stew* – Blenders Book III
*Midnight in Mongolia* – Blenders Book IV
*Silent Autumn* \*
*Escape from Iran* \*
*Elena – the Girl with the Piano* \*
*The Reluctant Daughters*

SHORT STORY PUBLICATIONS

All of the following are in the Florida Writers Association Collections:

Larry and the Cat - #1 – *From Our Family to Yours,* 2009
Standoff in the Alborz Mountains – #2 - Slices of Life, 2010
The Anniversary Dinner #5 – *It's a Crime ,* 2013
The Suitcase - #6 – *The First Step,* 2014
Poisonberry Wine– #7 – *Revisions,* 2015
Margaret Barnes - #8 – *Hide and Seek,* 2016
\* Winner of one or more awards

**www.veronicahhart.com**

# SCOTT MICHAEL POWERS

Scott is a national award-winning journalist based in Orlando, Florida, who, in the demise of the newspaper industry, has turned to his first dream, writing fiction. His first novel, *The Roswell Swatch*, was published in late 2016, receiving rave reader reviews. His second, *The Murder Plague*, is undergoing pre-publication editing. His third, under the working title *The Space Coast Out-Of-This-World News & Herald Tribune*, is nearly completed.

Scott's work uses minor elements of science fiction and speculative fiction to power contemporary action-adventure dramas. One review called *The Roswell Swatch* a "white-knuckle thriller with a splash of science fiction," while another observed, "Sometimes sci-fi books can get way out there...this book kept everything within the realm of believability," and another touted its "very creative plot with characters that jumped off the page."

Scott and his wife Connie happily live in a quiet Orlando neighborhood that has lots of big trees, and cops for neighbors. His midlife crisis didn't result in a muscle car (though he's still keeping a delusional eye out for a '71 Plymouth Roadrunner to show up in the driveway). Yet it did cause him to go back to his rock 'n' roll roots and start wearing hats again, as he did back when Billy Jack was as cool a look as it got.

He can be reached at scottmichaelpowers@yahoo.com, or on Facebook, at **www.facebook.com/ScottMichaelPowers/**

# ELLE ANDREWS PATT

Elle Andrews Patt writes speculative and literary short fiction. She received an Honorable Mention from Writers of The Future in 2013. She won the First Place Royal Palm Literary Award for Published Short Fiction from the Florida Writers Association in both 2013 and 2014.

When not writing, she can be found mucking stalls or photographing found things. She'd love to hear from you!

PUBLISHED NOVELLAS
*Manteo\**
*Someday Loyal*
*Regarding Mr. Bulkington*

SHORT STORY PUBLICATIONS
Karl's Last Night* – The Rag Literary Magazine
Becky's Story* – Saw Palm: Florida Literature
The Legend of Johnny Bell* – *Solarcide Anthology*
Prelude To A Murder Conviction* – Dark Fuse Magazine
Coming of Age – FWA Collection #6- *First Steps*

FORTHCOMING NOVELS (Working Titles)
*Billie Mae\** – Paranormal Murder Mystery
*Blind Mice Bite*- Paranormal Murder Mystery
*The Year of the Bear* – Mainstream Literature
*Anunnaki*- Science Fiction/Fantasy

* Winner of one or more awards

**www.elleandrewspatt.com**